LOVE TO HATE HER

J. SAMAN

Edited by: Gina Johnson

Cover Design: Shanoff Designs

Photography: Wander Aguiar

Cover Model: Lucas Loyola

PREFACE

Dear readers this book was originally two books. It was Love to Hate Her and Hate to Love Him. I have combined both books into this one for your ultimate reading pleasure.

Dedication

This is not a book about autism. This is a book about love. Adalyn is a fictional depiction of a real person. Her character is in no way meant to represent all children on the spectrum.

To E who fills my heart with her radiantly beautiful light. To D, H, R & E - you're the beat of my heart.

PART ONE

PROLOGUE

Viola

THE AIR IS HAZY, thick with the cloying scent of weed as I meander my way through the throngs of people laughing, smoking, and generally having a great time. I don't belong here. At least that's how it feels. Especially since I have a sneaking suspicion what I'm about to discover.

"Hey, Vi," Henry, the bassist for the band, calls out to me with shock etched across his face as he grabs my arm and tugs me in for a bear hug. His tone is an infuriating concoction of surprise, delight, and panic. "What brings you out here?"

I'm tempted to laugh at that question, though it's far from funny. As such, it forces a frown instead of a smile. It really should be obvious. But maybe it's not anymore, and that only solidifies my resolve that I'm doing the right thing tonight.

Even if it sucks.

"I'm looking for Gus," I reply smoothly without even a hint of emotion, and his grin drops a notch.

Knowing that my boyfriend of four years is cheating on me should resemble something along the lines of being repeatedly stabbed in the back. Or heart. It should feel like death is imminent as the truth skewers my faith in men, my sense of self-worth, and my overall confidence into tiny bite-sized pieces of flesh. I should be a sniveling, slobbering mess of heartbreak. I should be nuclear-level pissed while simultaneously seeking and plotting a dramatic scene and meaningless revenge.

That's how it always goes for girls like me versus guys like Gus. And maybe I am just a touch of all those things. But right now, I just want to get this over with and go home.

"He's umm...," Henry's voice trails off as he makes a show of scanning the room as if he's genuinely trying to locate Gus amongst the revelry. My bet? He knows exactly where Gus is and is attempting to buy him and his current lady of the minute some time.

"It's cool," I say, plastering on a bright smile that I do not feel. "I'll find him."

Because when you've been friends with someone your entire life, in a relationship with them for the last four years, you don't expect them to betray you. You expect loyalty and honesty and respect. *You expect fucking respect, Gus!* Gus cheating and lying about it is none of those things.

"I can find him!" Henry jumps in quickly. "I'd probably have a better shot of locating him in here than you will. Ya know, cuz I'm taller so I can see around the crowds better. Do you want a drink or something? Why don't you go make yourself a drink while I look for him?"

I shake my head and step back when he moves to grasp my shoulder. "Don't cover for him, Henry. It just makes you a dick and him more of an ass."

Henry pivots to face me fully, a half-empty bottle of Cuervo in his hand, his eyes red-rimmed and glassy. He crumples, his shoulders sagging forward.

"I know. I'm sorry. But it's not what you think, Vi. It's not. It's just..." He waves his free hand around the room as if this should explain everything. Sex, drugs, and rock 'n' roll. This room is the horror show definition of that cliché.

I don't begrudge Gus or his bandmates success. I'm sublimely thrilled for them that their first album is taking off the way it is. It's been their dream–*our dream*–for as long as I've known them, and that's forever.

Which is why I should have ended it when Gus left for L.A., and I left for college.

I knew the temptations that were headed his way. I knew women would be throwing themselves at him and that I was going to be thousands of miles away living a different life.

Does it excuse Gus's actions? Hell no. Have I cheated on Gus once while in college? Absolutely not, and it isn't like I haven't had my own opportunities to do so.

But do I understand how this happened? Yeah. I do. I just held on too long.

"It was coming anyway," I tell Henry. "But it's nice to know he won't be lonely."

Yeah. That's sarcasm. And I can't help it, so I might as well allow the bitterness to make an entrance and take over the sadness that's been sitting in my stomach like a bad burger you can't digest. Especially as Gus has been adamantly denying his trysts, and Henry pretty much just confirmed them.

Henry's like a fish out of water, and I lean in and give him a hug. I always liked Henry.

"He's going to be so broken up about this, Vi. He loves you like crazy. Talks about you all the time."

I pull back, tilting my head and shrugging a shoulder. "That doesn't matter so much, though, does it? I'm at school, and he's out here with..." Now it's my turn to gaze about the room, my hand panning out to the side, reiterating my point. "Good luck with everything, Henry. I wish you all the success in the world. You guys deserve every good thing that's headed your way."

Henry scowls like I just ran over his dog as he shakes his head no at me. "You can't end it with him. You're a part of this. We wouldn't be here without you. We wouldn't be anything without you. You're like...," he scrunches up his nose as he thinks, "our fifth member. Our cheerleader."

"Maybe once," I concede, swallowing down the pain-laced nostalgia his words dredge up. The backs of my eyes burn, but I refuse to let any more tears fall over this. I cried myself out on the flight here, and now I'm done. "You guys don't need me anymore. You have plenty of other cheerleaders."

He opens his mouth to argue more before just as quickly closing it. "I'm sorry, Vi."

"I can't change it. It's done. Stay safe, okay? And be smart," I add.

"You too, babe. I'm gonna miss you."

This is the moment it hits me.

I'm not just saying goodbye to my relationship with Gus, but to my friendships with these guys. To late-night band practices and weekends spent down by the lake just hanging out. I'm saying goodbye to my entire childhood, knowing that we're all headed in different directions, and there is no middle ground with this. My throat constricts as I try to swallow, my insides twisting into knots.

Bolstering myself back up, I hold my head high.

I need to find Gus, and then I need to get out of here.

Wild Minds, the band that Gus is the second guitarist and backup singer for, opened for Cyber's Law tonight. *The* Cyber's Law. One of the hottest bands in the world. They're also on the same label that just signed Wild Minds. This show is a big deal. This contract an even bigger one.

This is their start.

They had given themselves two years to make it big. They needed less than one.

Heading toward the back of the room, I skirt around half-naked women dancing and people blowing lines of coke. It's dark in here. Most of the overhead lights are out, but the few that are on mix with the film of smoke, casting enough of a glow to see by way of shadows.

I bang into a table, apologizing to someone whose beer I spill when I catch movement out of the corner of my eye. Jasper, Gus's fraternal twin brother and the lead singer of the band, is tucked into an alcove, a redhead plastered against him as she sucks on his neck.

Where Gus is handsome, charming, and completely endearing, Jasper is the opposite.

He is sinfully gorgeous, no doubt about that, but he's distant, broody, artistic, and eternally happy to pass the limelight to an overeager Gus. Jasper was actually my first crush. Even my first kiss when we were fourteen. But that's where it ended. Since that day, and without explanation, I've hardly existed to him.

Sensing someone's watching, he pulls away from the girl on his neck, and our eyes meet in the miasma. His penetrating stare holds me annoyingly captive for a moment before he does a slow perusal of me. Unlike Henry, Jasper is not surprised to see me. In fact, his expression hardly registers any emotion at all. But the fire burning in his eyes tells a different story, and for reasons beyond my comprehension, I cannot tear myself away.

He tilts his head, a smirk curling up the corner of his lips, and I realize I've been standing here, staring at him with voyeuristic-quality engrossment for far too long.

But I don't know how to break this spell.

The smoldering blaze in his eyes is likely related to what the girl who was attached to his neck was doing to him. Yet somehow, it doesn't feel like that.

No, his focus is entirely on me.

And he's making sure I know it.

A rush of heat swirls across my skin, crawling up my face. I shake my head ever so slightly, stumbling back a step.

Noticing my inner turmoil, Jasper rights his body, forcing the girl away. She says something to him that he doesn't acknowledge or respond to. He runs a hand through his messy reddish-brown hair as he shifts, ready to come and speak to me when my field of vision is obscured.

Gus. I'd know him in my sleep.

My gaze drops, catching and sticking on his unzipped fly.

"You're here," he exclaims reverently, the thrill in his voice at seeing me unmistakable. I peek up and latch onto the fresh hickey on his neck. A hickey? Seriously? I didn't even know people still gave those. When I find his lazy gray eyes, I want to cry. Especially with the purple welt giving me the finger.

"I'm here."

He wraps me up in his arms, and I smell the woman who gave him that hickey. Her perfume possessively clings to his shirt, and I draw back, crinkling my nose in disgust.

"What's wrong, babe?" His thumb strokes my cheek. "Long flight?"

I step back, out of his grasp.

"Your fly is unzipped, and you have a hickey on your neck."

He blanches, his eyes dropping down to his groin while immediately zipping his family jewels back up. "I just took a leak."

I nod, but mostly because I'm not sure how much fight I have left in me. It *was* a long flight. And a long eight months before that. But still, it's one thing to know your boyfriend is cheating on you; it's another to see it in the flesh, literally.

"And the hickey?" I snap.

"Not what it looks like, Vi. I swear."

I reach up and cup his dark-blond stubbled jawline. My chest clenches. "Don't lie, Gus. It just ruins everything. I don't want to hate you, and if you lie to me now, I will."

He shakes his head violently against my hand, his expression pleading. "You're here, Vi. You're finally here. Nothing else matters."

"But it does. It all matters. The distance. The way our lives are diverging. I love you, Gus, but it's not like it used to be with us. None of it is." I swallow, my throat so tight it's hard to push the words out. "Let's end this now before it turns into bitterness and resentment."

"I could never resent you."

I inwardly sigh. He really doesn't get it. "But your penis might. You're fucking any woman who looks at you," I bite out. "Where does that leave me? How could you do that to me, Gus? To us? Do you have any idea how awful that feels?"

"I don't know. I didn't mean... You weren't here and I fucking missed you and I... I'm sorry. I'm so, so sorry."

"It doesn't matter anymore. It's over."

"You seriously flew out here to end it?" He's incredulous. And hurt. And I hate a hurt Gus. Even if we're not the stuff of happily ever afters, I do love this man. I'm just not so sure how in love with him I am anymore. He broke my heart. He broke my trust. And absence hasn't made my heart grow fonder. It's made it grow harder.

"Would you rather I ended it on the phone?" His face meets my neck, and my eyes fling open wide, only to find Jasper watching us from over Gus's shoulder. A curious observer, and my insides hurt all over again. His expression is a mask of apathy lined loosely with disdain. The way it's always been with me. All that earlier heat a thing of the past. I don't care either way.

"I don't want you to do it at all," Gus's voice is thick with regret as he holds me. "I love you, Vi. I love you so goddamn much. I just..."

"I know. I really do." I squeeze him back, feeling like I'm losing the only good part of my childhood in saying goodbye. "We're just in different spaces now, with different lives, and that's the way it's supposed to be."

He shakes his head against me, holding me so close and so tight, it's hard to breathe. He smells like that girl. But he smells like him underneath, and I cling to that last part because the scent of some unknown meaningless girl hurts too much. It rips me apart, knowing he did that to me.

To us.

I close my eyes for a moment and push that away. It's useless at this point, and I don't want to leave here more upset than I already am.

"Don't end it," he pleads, cupping my face and holding me the way he always has. "I can't lose you."

I lean up on my tiptoes and kiss his cheek. Tall bastard. "And I can't come in third. I handled second well enough, but not third."

"Third?"

"Music first. Other women second. Me third. It's done, Gus. No more lies or I'll hate you, and I'll hate myself."

"No," he forces out, but it's half-hearted. We're nineteen, and just too young. There isn't enough of the right type of love between us to fight harder for something we both know will never work. He doesn't want to be the bad guy. The cheating guy who pushes his long-time sweetheart-best-friend away. "You're breaking my heart." A tear leaks from my eye as I battle to stifle my sob. "I'm in love with you, and you're ending it." I blink back more tears, watching as he accepts what's happening. "I'm going to regret this," he states matter-of-factly. "Letting you go is going to be the regret of my life. Years from now, I'm going to hate myself for not making you stay."

But you're not fighting for me now.

"And that's why I have to go." I lean in and kiss him goodbye and then run like hell.

I make it outside, the heavy door slamming behind me. Warm, stale air brushes across my tacky skin, doing nothing to comfort or bring me clarity. I'm a mess of a woman as useless tears cling to my lashes.

"You're leaving already?" Jasper's voice catches me off guard, and I start. Why did he bother following me? "You just got here."

"Yes," I reply, twisting around to face the green eyes that have been fucking with my head since I caught them ten minutes ago. "You can't be surprised."

"He loves you. He's just lost in this life, ya know?" I shake my head at him. Jasper takes a long step in my direction, wanting to get closer and yet hesitant to. "So that's it? You just walk away from him?"

"I can't ignore the fact that he's been cheating on me."

"No. You can't. And I can't make excuses for it either."

"What do you want, Jasper? You can't honestly tell me you're disappointed to be rid of me."

"I see we're at the zero-fucks-left-to-give portion of the evening."

I continue to stare because that just about sums it up.

His eyes, filled with anger, indecision, and frustration, bounce all around, the street, the lights of the neighboring storefronts, the crowd still dispersing from the show, everywhere but at me. I can't stand this any longer, so I turn away and start to walk out into the Los Angeles night, away from the arena where Wild Minds—the band and the boys I've loved my whole life—just performed.

"It's yours," Jasper calls out, and I'm so confused by his hasty words that I freeze, turning back to him. His expression is completely exposed. Utterly vulnerable. And he's staring straight at me. Directly into my eyes in a way he hasn't dared since we were fourteen. My heart picks up a few extra beats, my breath held firmly in my chest. God, this man is so intense, I feel him in my fingernails.

"What is?" I finally ask when he doesn't follow that up.

"The album," he answers slowly, reluctantly, like it pains him to confess this, his darkest secret. "Every song on it is yours. All of them, I wrote about you."

I stand here, lost in space as I grasp just what he's saying. What it means, as random lyrics from random songs on their album flitter through my head. Song after song filled with the most achingly beautiful poetry.

"Jasper?" I whisper, my hand over my chest because I'm positive my heart never beat like this before.

But he is already at the door, having confessed his sins without waiting for absolution.

"Why did you tell me?" I yell after him, praying he'll stop. Needing him to explain this to me. *Why did you tell me, Jasper? Why did you pick this moment to ruin me?*

His hand rests on the frame of the now open door, his head bowed, his back to me. "Because I didn't think I'd ever get another chance, knowing I'll probably never see you again." He blows out a harsh breath. "But it doesn't change anything, Vi. Absolutely nothing. So you can move on without us and pretend like I never said a word."

And then the door slams shut behind him.

Jesus.

It takes me forever to move. To force myself to try and do just that. To try and forget his words and ignore the havoc they just created.

Knowing it's futile. Knowing those words will reside in me forever.

ONE

Jasper
Seven Years Later

"NOT HER." I say the words slowly. Purposefully as I stare directly into my personal assistant Sophia's hard-line gaze. Her posture is casual and yet unrelenting at the same time. A look only she can pull off as she sits directly across from me, her legs crossed at the knee, her manicured hand resting on the arm of the sofa. She's a no-nonsense woman, and typically, I respect her for it. But in this moment, I resent it and the power it wields over my life.

This is something I cannot give in to.

"There are billions of people in this world. Thousands of other people who could do this."

"Viola Starr." She repeats her name as if the words 'not her' didn't just fall from my lips. Sophia needs to wipe that self-satisfied grin off her face. "If you're still unwilling to hire me for the position, then it has to be her. She is absolutely perfect. We just hired her. It's done."

I stare at her, equally pissed off and dumbstruck. The pissed off comes from the fact that I'm rarely dumbstruck. In fact, it's happened twice in my life, and neither time worked out so well for me. I run a frustrated hand through my hair, wishing I had something very large and heavy near me that I could throw. She's got to be kidding me with this. Did she put the Hogwarts Sorting Hat of specialists on Viola's head? *Jasper Diamond, I should think.* Or maybe she played the hometown card when conducting her search.

Either way, this isn't happening.

Wait... "What do you mean we just hired her? It's not done. There is no goddamn way this is done."

She smiles. Motherfucking smiles at me. I'm about two seconds from firing her, and I don't even care if that makes me a world-class dick. "You could still hire me instead."

It's so ridiculous a concept I never believed it required an explanation. "You're not a nanny, Sophia, nor are you equipped or trained to care for someone with Adalyn's needs. We've been over this. You don't even like kids." She frowns. Too bad. It's the truth. I lean forward, narrowing my eyes and staring my soon-to-be-unemployed assistant down. "I did not agree to you hiring anyone. You told me you were vetting qualified nannies and I was to interview them today and make the final decision tomorrow. What exactly changed with that plan?"

I'm losing the cool I'm famous for, but right now, I don't care enough to compose myself. Certainly not for Sophia's sake and most definitely not on this subject.

Her eyes twitch for a flicker of a second before she relaxes her features into something resembling confidence. "She's the only one, Jasper. I was not pleased with any of the other candidates' references, credentials, or resumes, and now we're out of time. Regardless of that, this girl is absolutely perfect for us. Her name was given to us by your brother."

I shake my head at that, essentially cutting her off.

Fucking Gus.

"Gus has always loved her. Always regretted the way things ended between them. I'm not letting him use my daughter as a vehicle to win back his ex-girlfriend. Whoever we hire has to know their shit and be responsible for Adalyn." Sophia smirks, practically rolling her eyes at me, and I'm about a half-beat from losing my shit completely. "I'm not sure you're appreciating the gravity of this," I snarl at her. "Viola Starr and I have never seen eye to eye, and just because *Gus* says she's perfect does not make her so. I'm done talking about this. Find me someone else."

The simple truth is, I cannot interact with Viola day in and day out while she nannies Ady and Gus works his magic on her again. I don't care how long it's been.

A man can only live through certain things once.

"I've already told you, there is no one else. You trust Gus, and Gus would lie down in traffic for you."

I scoff at that. Seriously? *That's* her argument? "That's what brothers do."

"Not mine. He'd kill me in my sleep given the chance." I sigh heavily. Her brother works for the record label I'm signed with and is not nearly as cutthroat as she makes him out to be. "But Gus also loves Adalyn and would never do anything to hurt her. He gave me Viola's name and resume, which is exceptional," she quirks a challenging eyebrow, "and when I spoke with her, I knew she was the one. She's educated to our particular needs with solid experience. She's smart, discrete, cares nothing about fame, has zero social media accounts, and is financially destitute." That last one catches me off guard, and I do my best not to wince or shift my position. I don't like thinking of Viola in that way. I don't even know how it's possible. She was fine the last time I checked.

That was what...six months ago?

"She agreed to this?" I'm incredulous, regardless of the fact that I don't want to reopen the Viola Starr box, I cannot imagine after the way we parted that she'd want anything to do with me ever again. Or Gus, for that matter.

Sophia glances off in the direction of the kitchen as she simultaneously folds her hands in her lap.

Something isn't right with this.

"What?" I bark, growing impatient with all this waiting bullshit.

Sophia sighs, blinks slowly, and finds me once more. "She doesn't know it's for you."

I can feel the color draining from my face. "What does that mean? How can she not know?"

"Because I didn't tell her who I work for. I wanted to feel her out first, to see if she met our specific requirements, before I explained who her actual employer would be."

I shoot out of my chair, spinning around and storming toward the back wall of windows, staring out at the pool and the grounds beyond without seeing any of it. My hands go to my hips, but all I can think about is slamming my fist through the glass.

Viola Starr.

"She's going to say no when she finds out it's me. Then she'll know my situation with Karina and all about Adalyn."

"I'm not so worried about any of that."

"Well, I am," I yell, losing my last shred of composure with this. My fist does meet the glass now, but all it does is rattle. It doesn't even crack. How unsatisfying is that? "I don't want the world to know about Adalyn. They'll look at her differently. They'll treat her differently. She'll be followed." I puff out a crazed, exasperated breath. "She's too young to face the circus. We all agreed we wouldn't go public with her diagnosis until after the tour. This tour is about our band and our music. Not my child."

"Eventually, it's going to come out, Jasper. You cannot keep it a secret forever, and I'm not sure how practical it is to wait until after the tour."

"She's a little girl." *And I have to protect her.* It's my job, and I won't let the ugly world I live in, work in, hurt her any more than it already has.

"Sooner or later, people will find out anyway."

"I know that," I growl, my ire is slipping as I think about my daughter, who is upstairs napping at this very moment.

Dropping my forehead to the glass, I close my eyes.

"I'm not hiding who she is. It's part of what makes her so incredible. But she just turned three with a professional musician for a father who is about to go out on a world tour for five months and a mother who ran off and then died on her. Not to mention, the press already have a bizarre hard-on for her. She's vulnerable because of my job, and she's already vulnerable to start with. She doesn't like crowds. She doesn't like strangers speaking to her. She doesn't like people touching her or coming too close. How do you think she'll fare if this comes out at a time when the press are already around us? That is not in her best interests, and you know it. I just want to keep her safe. It's all I care about."

"Which is why you need Viola," Sophia interjects firmly, and my eyes cinch even tighter. I don't know how to see Viola again, let alone have her working for me and watching my daughter as we travel the world together. "I explained the situation to her, and she's on board with the travel, the long hours, Adalyn's diagnosis. Everything."

Just not me. Or Gus, I want to say, but keep my mouth shut.

Mostly because I know Sophia is trying to help. I haven't been on tour since before Adalyn was born. We've mostly been in L.A., where I wrote, and we recorded our last two albums. Adalyn's mother split about six months after she was born. Just about the time she accepted that I wasn't going to marry her and that she preferred a life of sex and drugs over raising a baby.

Incidentally, she overdosed about five months after that. I hired a nanny instantly, but she was in her sixties, and when her daughter had a daughter, she decided she needed to move closer to them. So for the last three months, I've been on my own.

And it's been fine.

Ady and I have been learning together. Getting through with the help of her multiple therapists.

But this tour? It has to happen.

The record company is breathing down my neck about it. My bandmates are breathing down my neck about it. Even fucking Sophia and Gus.

So that means Adalyn travels the world with me.

But I can't be on my own anymore without help during this tour, and we need this tour, so rock meet hard spot. Ady needs someone with her, someone who is educated in autism spectrum disorder. Someone who can continue the work we've started. None of her current therapists could manage it, and evidently, all the other applicants Sophia researched weren't right. I have to wonder at that, but unfortunately, it's too late to begin the process of trying to find someone new. We leave in a few days.

So, Viola Starr is evidently the one.

Gus's ex-girlfriend.

The only woman I've ever loved.

My first...well, kiss, I guess. Even though I know she's so much more than that. She's the reason I don't get involved. Even Karina was never a girlfriend. She was just the woman I got pregnant one stupid drunken night.

Our first album is entirely comprised of songs I wrote for Viola. Years of poetry put to music for her. Just thinking about this woman makes me hurt in long forgotten places. I haven't seen her or spoken to her since that night she broke up with Gus seven years ago.

And the way I left her standing out there? She has to hate me for it. *I* hate me for it.

"She's going to say no."

"She won't," Sophia presses back with way too much authority. It makes me wonder...

"Elaborate." I bang my forehead against the glass again, closing my eyes, and bracing myself for it. I don't want to know, but I do at the same time. It can't be good.

"The town she was teaching in ran out of money for special education and laid her off." *Fuck.* "Her mother stole all her savings and ran off." *Double fuck.* "She hasn't been able to find another full-time teaching position because the majority of those aren't posted until the end of the school year at the very earliest, though most become available mid-summer–"

"It's March," I interrupt.

"Yes," Sophia agrees like I'm starting to get it now. "It's March. Which means she has a little money coming in from substituting when there are jobs available and working nights at a bar. But that's it since her bitch of a mother stole everything she had saved in her bank account."

"She's destitute." Her mother has always been trouble. A junkie who was never much of a mother to Viola while we were growing up. The theft has to be new. Viola was rolling along like a steamboat on the Mississippi not even six months ago.

"You got it. But she's a special education teacher with a specialty in autism. She's trained in Applied Behavioral Analysis therapy. She knows you. Grew up with you. Doesn't give a shit about money other than needing it to get by and doesn't live in the demented orb of social media like the rest of the world. She also loved Gus and was friends with the other bandmates for years, which makes her loyal." She pauses, and I can't bring myself to say anything. "Do you hear what I'm saying? She's it."

I bang my forehead again and bring my clenched fist up to my chest. I can't help but feel responsible. Even if I'm not. But if I, or Gus for that matter, had still been in her life, well, these hardships wouldn't have been so hard. I can't say yes to this, but now there is no way I can say no.

Christ, this is a mistake. "Tell her whatever she needs to hear to get her to do it."

"I offered her twenty-five grand a month."

I grin at that. No way she can say no to that amount. "What else?"

Sophia is silent, and I don't like that. I pry myself away from the glass of my window and face her, ready to do battle.

"That's it." She stares at me baffled, as if the money should be sufficient to close the deal. And it probably is. But I want Viola to have more. "Isn't that enough? A hundred and twenty-five thousand for five months of work?"

I shake my head no. "Pay whatever debts she's accrued since her mother took her savings. I want a zero debt balance on everything for her by the end of today. You don't even have to tell her. But I want it done whether she accepts the position or not."

Sophia's about to object but realizes I'm not to be bargained with at the moment and nods. "Done. Anything else?"

I start to walk off, so very done with this conversation. I can't think straight when it comes to Viola. I cannot handle the notion of her becoming a part of my life again, even temporarily. Just her name bouncing around my brain is making my body hum. I don't have time for it. For her.

Viola Starr. Fuck. I seriously cannot–

"If she agrees, I'll have her here tomorrow to meet Adalyn."

Nervous anticipation slams into my chest at those words. *Tomorrow.* I'm going to see Viola tomorrow? I need to get out of here. Away from Sophia. But no matter how fast I walk or how far I go or where I lock myself away, there is no escaping this demon from my past.

We leave in four days. I haven't packed. I haven't finished setting up Ady with the things she's going to require. I won't sleep on an uncomfortable bus with her every night. We'll have to stay in hotels sometimes, large suites so she can be close to me. There will be no familiarity for her other than me and Gus. And Viola, I guess, now that she's become a part of this.

Jesus.

I run a hand through my hair and tug on the ends. It doesn't help, but then again, I don't think anything will. This is a monster I'm going to have to face head-on.

"An apartment for her close to whatever new teaching position she's hired for," I tack on as I hit the first step. "And if you have any strings, it would be great if you could find her a job for when this madness is done. Preferably, one on the opposite side of the country from here. But that I definitely don't want her to know about." I grip the wood banister, white-knuckling it. "I take it she doesn't have any money left?"

"You're correct," Sophia answers mildly, and I hate everything. Just everything. This world. The unfairness of it. The way people like me have enough to fill five lifetimes and people like her can barely scrape by.

"Then I want her to have a nice apartment filled with furniture. She likes contemporary blended with antiques. At least she used to." I sigh out at that last part. I don't really know her anymore. Seven years and three albums later, right?

"You don't have to do all of this."

I pause, one foot on the bottom step, the other on the floor, my head bowed. I don't have to do this, and yet, it doesn't feel like nearly enough. "I know."

"I'll get it done," she replies, and then I hear her heels clickety-clacking against my dark wood floors as she walks toward the front door, seeing herself out.

Viola Starr. How on earth will I make it through five months with you?

TWO

Viola

LYING on my bed with my arms butterflied up on my pillow, my hands behind my head, I stare up at the water-stained ceiling. I hate this place. This apartment. But it's been my home for the last three years. It's small. Cheap. Old. And awful.

Awful as in, it rains in the house every time it rains outside. Awful as in, I hear mice and other critters I don't care to name scurrying about at night through the walls. Awful as in, the shower never runs hot, and the water is tinted yellow.

But it's got nothing on my new gig.

On the new gig I need so badly I cannot come up with a reason to say no other than one.

Jasper Diamond.

I should have known there was a catch. That too good to be true always is. They didn't just pick my name from a list of specialists. And that last part makes me want to throw something hard and breakable, because how stupid can I be? How easily duped?

I know the answer to that. I don't even need to ask the question.

But why now?

Why would he want me to nanny his daughter? To work with her? Me, of all people?

I haven't seen him since he followed me out of the smoky, whiskey-tinted back room seven years ago. For seven years, I haven't existed to him. And now, suddenly, he needs me? I don't like it. And I'm desperate to say no.

I can't, and he must realize this if he knows anything about my current situation. And that leads me to another thought. Guilt. Is his reaching out to me forged in guilt?

Or is Gus driving this train?

Because I do not want their charity. I want nothing to do with their pity. They moved up while I moved down, and that's just life. I accepted it a long time ago. Some people are born under a golden umbrella while others are permanently out in the storm. I'm the latter, and they're the former, and that's how we've always been.

They left Podunk Alabama behind and became rock gods, adored by the masses worldwide. I came back after finishing college and managed to get my master's degree online while working in a school with no money and taking care of my hateful mother, who turned around and stole everything I had when she left without a backward glance.

Then there's Jasper. And Gus.

We ended ugly.

But over time, resentments fade, even when the memories don't. Then again, when you have nothing else beautiful to fill the passage of time, and you're stuck in purgatory, remembering that beauty is all you have. Memories warp, like waterlogged wood, and before you know it, you're doing stupid things like listening to the album he wrote for you.

That's what I'm doing now, the album playing through the speaker on my phone. My knees bent, my shoed feet unable to resist tapping along with the beat. This is my favorite song on the album.

The lyrics sound almost like this was once a dream he had. The melody is hypnotic. The words pulverizing. But if you didn't know, didn't listen all that closely, you'd just get lost in the addictive tempo of the electric guitar paired with the heavy drums.

I shouldn't be listening to this.

It's mostly to torture myself. Or maybe it's a reminder of what my singular focus is for the next five months: his daughter. His *daughter*. I shake my head at that. I have no idea who the mother is. I just know she's no longer part of the picture.

Jasper Diamond is a single father.

And in three hours, I'm to fly out, first-class mind you, to Los Angeles to meet her. I should have already left. Everything is by the door.

But I'm so freaking nervous about seeing them that I haven't been able to pry myself up and off my lumpy mattress.

That entire flight home after I ended things with Gus, and Jasper left me alone outside after ruining everything, I listened to this album. I had heard it dozens of times before, but never like that. Never in a place where I analyzed every word. Every verse. Every goddamn note. They were all for me, he said, and as I absorbed them, the heartache, the torment, the angst of something so desired and yet so forbidden, I started to hate him.

And fall for him.

An angry, frustrated growl rips from the back of my throat as my feet drum faster, attempting to rut out those useless thoughts.

Adalyn. Focus, girl!

I don't know Adalyn, but I do know children with ASD or autism spectrum disorder. Sophia didn't discuss how severe her deficits are, but it doesn't exactly matter. Taking care of an Autistic child on a five-month road trip around the world will be the equivalent of running a gauntlet blind, and I am not talking about her father. Autistic children like routine. They like consistency and familiarity, and she will have none of that.

But I guess that's where I come in.

That's if she takes to me. Autistic children aren't the most adaptive to new people.

I'll try, though. How miserable for her to be put in this position. I'll be her familiarity, and I'll do my best to give her consistency and routine. I'll work with her, and I'll help her. And I'll ignore her father to the best of my ability with the exception of Adalyn–related matters. If this nanny arrangement is going to work, then that's the way it has to be.

A knock at my door startles me out of my reverie, and I slowly peel myself up and off my bed. It's probably my landlord, wanting the keys back from me, but when I swing the door open, I'm greeted with a tall, slender man in a black livery uniform, and a smile etched on his hollow face. "Miss Starr?"

"Yes?" *Why did that sound like a question?*

"I'm Jonathan Young, your driver to the airport."

"Oh," my voice rises an octave as my eyes widen in surprise.

"Yes, ma'am." His gaze wanders past me to the two large suitcases I have set on the floor, tucked next to the door, patiently waiting on me as I work up a nerve that continues to elude me. "Is this all of your luggage?" I nod, still too surprised to speak proper sentences. "Excellent," he grins. "May I?" He gestures toward my bags, and I step back, allowing him to enter. "I take it you weren't expecting me?"

"No. Miss Bloom didn't mention you to me."

Jonathan shrugs a shoulder. "Happens. If you're ready, I am."

My head swivels around the small studio apartment, and I realize that everything I own is in those two suitcases, with the exception of my phone and purse. "I guess I'm ready," I say as a wave of reality hits me square in the chest. This is happening. I'm leaving, and I'm never coming back.

I'm about to face my ex and his twin, who has managed a way to occupy more of my thoughts than I'd like.

Grabbing my purse and phone, I leave, locking the door behind me and slipping the key under the mat. I should feel something leaving this apartment and this town that I've spent nearly my entire life in, behind. But I don't. I'm numb, and I'm hoping the sensation lingers like Novocain in my blood until this job is done, and I'm settled...somewhere.

Jonathan drives me the forty minutes to the airport in near silence. I might be the one directing that more than him, though. I'm regretting this. To the point where the anxiety is starting to eat at me, turning into full-blown panic. I want to call that Sophia Bloom woman and tell her I cannot do this. That I do not want to see Jasper or Gus Diamond. That I left them behind years ago and I'm afraid of what will happen, what I'll *feel*, when I see both of them again. The sick knot of dread that's become a resident in my stomach since I found out who my employer is, swells.

I don't have a choice. Apartments and moving and starting over is expensive. Life is motherfucking expensive, and these five months will give me a huge cushion. The debt I've accrued from my mother's theft is strangling me month by month. I need this. I can do this. I can—

"We're here," Jonathan hesitantly calls out from the front, like he's afraid of speaking too loudly and startling me. I might just look that unstable right now. I pivot to the window, but instead of finding the departures terminal for American Airlines, I discover a private terminal with a sleek black jet waiting. I inch closer to the window and then turn to catch Jonathan's eyes in the rearview mirror. "Change of plans," is all he offers before climbing out of the car and heading toward the trunk to retrieve my luggage.

I stare at the jet for another minute, unable or unwilling to follow. I can't decide which it is. "Goddamn you, Jas," I murmur to the quiet cab of the luxury car. "Goddamn you for making me an offer I can't refuse. For reaching out to me now after all these years. For telling me about the album in the first place. Just goddamn you. And I'm going to hold onto this crap anger with both hands. It's going to be my go-to. The thing that keeps me separated from you for the next five months. Because I don't think I'll survive this any other way."

Right. Now that I've got that cleared up, I suck in a deep breath, open the car door, and step outside into the mild spring day. The jet's engines are already roaring impatiently as if I'm the one who is late and holding everything up. Maybe I am, because Jonathan is handing my luggage off to a man who is loading it onto the plane. He didn't even open my door for me. Aren't chauffeurs supposed to do that? Or maybe they don't for the hired help, which is what I am.

Slipping my purse strap up my shoulder, I walk with my head held high, and a confidence I do not feel, toward the jet. The stairs that lead up into the plane are down, and that's where I go. I cannot imagine that they sent a private plane just for me, and as I glance at the tinted windows, I realize I'm walking into this blind.

I soldier on because that's the sort of girl I try to be. And even though I want to run away and hide from the perpetual sucker punch that is my life, I won't.

I won't allow Jasper to think he's got me.

That he won and I lost, even though I pretty much did. I'm not too proud that I won't accept his money. I assume he's got plenty of it. I'm not too proud to work for my ex-boyfriend's brother and help his daughter get through a daunting five months.

And when this is all said and done, I'll walk away from them again.

Hopefully, with fewer tears and less heartache than I did the last time.

My hand glides along the metal railing, my heart thumping like a jackrabbit, as I take the steps up and then enter the main cabin of the plane, which is the epitome of luxury. Butter-colored leather chairs and couches and dark wood grain accents make up the front end. Toward the back are two giant flat screen televisions encompassing nearly an entire wall with a large sofa facing it. Abutting it is a long bar in the same wood accent, topped with every kind of alcohol one could ever need. There's an office on the opposite side of the televisions as well as an eating area. Behind all that are a series of doors that are all closed.

My inspection doesn't last long. Because sitting on one of the loveseats facing forward, is a woman with a black bob and inquisitive dark brown eyes, wearing a cream blouse, black pants, and a no-bull-shit expression.

It holds me uncomfortably captive. "Come sit down, Viola." I blink at her and then silently do as I'm told.

I can tell by her voice that this is Sophia Bloom, though I've only spoken with her on the phone twice. It's the natural high-pitch cadence mixed with an unmistakable authority. The leather is as soft as it appears, and I sink in, trying to come off as casual and unaffected. Crossing my legs, I give her a slim grin.

"I have Jana Lancaster and Robert Snow on the phone." I have no idea who either of these people are, so I stay quiet. Sophia must realize this because she immediately starts in with the introductions. "Jana is the band's press agent, and Robert is the CEO of Turn Records."

Fantastic. "Hello," I greet them.

"We're going to cut to the chase, Viola," Sophia jumps right in. "This tour is going to be bigger than anticipated. The demand for tickets is far exceeding availability. Venues are selling out in a matter of minutes, and as a result, we've added on additional dates. It's the band's first world tour in four years, and it's going to be epic." I nod, but honestly, I don't know what I'm agreeing to with this nod. "You've signed the NDA, so we're going to speak candidly here. Jasper will not travel without Adalyn. She is coming along for the full extent of the tour. We have arranged hotel suites and buses that will allow Jasper and Adalyn to stay together, and your room will be next to theirs."

"I don't have to share a room with them?"

"No," Sophia replies, grinning when she notices how I practically sag with relief. "You will always have your own bedroom. At no time will you be sharing a room with Jasper or Adalyn." There is definitely a hint of something behind the way she says that.

"Yes. Your space at night is your own, but you are to keep Adalyn protected at all times during the day," a female voice, who I assume is Jana, barks through the cell phone resting on the narrow wood table that separates me from Sophia. "Our goal is to keep her out of all pictures and published press. We do not want the paparazzi to have access to her. Anything you do with her outside the hotel or bus must be done cautiously and with the utmost care for her well-being."

"Of course," I bristle automatically, because really? What did they think I was going to do with her, flaunt her to the press?

"Sophia, Gus, and Jasper believe you would never exploit Adalyn or her situation for your own personal gain, but I'm here to tell you if I have any doubts or her story *miraculously*," she emphasizes sarcastically, "ends up on TMZ or pictures of her somehow make it to the internet, I will haul your ass into court. Same goes if you try to sell anything from your previous relationship with Gus Diamond."

"Jesus," I whisper, running a hand through my long hair, my ire climbing steadily by the second. "You've got to be kidding me."

"Ah, but I'm not. You see, we're paying you a handsome fee for your services in addition to paying off the debts you've piled up thanks to your degenerate mother who stole from you." *What?!* "So, if you fuck with us, that all disappears."

I stand up abruptly. Because screw these people. All of them. And that most definitely includes Gus and Jasper.

"Very smooth, Jana." Sophia rolls her eyes dramatically, trying for a reassuring grin and failing miserably. She silently points to the seat, but I don't comply so quickly this time. In fact, I think I'd rather stand. "Remind me how you became a press agent again?" Sophia sighs out.

"I don't know who you people think you are—"

"What Jana is inarticulately expressing, Viola," a male voice interrupts, blasting through the speaker with a force not to be ignored, "is that Jasper and Gus and the entire band are very protective of Adalyn. This tour is crucial for their new album and the band, and we'd like it to go off without a hitch. If you do not feel you're capable of protecting this little girl from the world that is anxious to gain access to her, then we'd like you to step down now, before you fly out to California and begin this tour."

I lock eyes with Sophia as I speak to all three of them. "I would never exploit any child. I do not care what their physical or intellectual situation is. I do not care about their parentage or circumstance. My priority is Adalyn, and I will protect her, care for her, and help her in any way I can. That said, I cannot control or stop people from taking pictures if they recognize her somehow. But I will never be the one to sell her out, and I will always do my best to prevent her exposure." Sophia gives a relieved, closed mouth smile, but I'm not done yet. "As for my previous relationship with Gus Diamond? That is the business of no one, and that is how it will remain. I don't know what this is about paying off my debts; you can tell Jasper I do not want his guilt or pity money. I do not want him paying for my mother's theft. That is my responsibility. Not his. I will take my agreed-upon salary, and that's where it ends."

"So, we're all in agreement then?" Jana clips out, and I do not like this woman. Not even a little.

"Yes," I reply coolly.

"Yes," Sophia repeats, her eyes still on mine. Her collagen-infused lips pull up at the corners into a half-smile that might resemble something close to pride and respect and then points once again to the seat for me to sit back down. I do, but I take my time, reinforcing that even though I may work for them, they do not own me. "We're good. I'll call you both when everything is settled." They say their goodbyes, and the call is disconnected, and then I'm left alone with Sophia. "We're good to go," she calls out to the pilots, I assume, because then the door of the plane closes and we're locked in, and the engines roar to a whole new decibel. "We'll be in California in a little more than five hours. I hope you're ready."

Not even close.

THREE

Viola

SHORTLY AFTER TAKEOFF, Sophia went over to the built-in office and was busy the entire flight. It was a relief. The last thing I wanted to do with her was make small talk. I feign sleep with earbuds in my ears, listening to anything other than Wild Minds. But the moment I feel the plane beginning to descend, my eyes pop open, and I find Sophia right there, staring at me as if she knew I was faking all along.

"What was he like back then?" she asks softly, like we have a shared secret. It makes my stomach churn. "I've always wanted to know."

"Which one?" My voice is equally soft, surprised by her personal question.

"I can imagine what Gus was like," she half-snickers. "Probably the same as he is now. I meant Jasper."

"Why don't you ask him?"

She grins at me. It's the same grin she had when I told Jana and

Robert that I wasn't out to destroy their golden band. "He doesn't talk about his past much."

The way she says that, like she already has intimate and personal knowledge of him in the present, makes me believe that she and Jasper are something more than business associates. And for the life of me, I cannot figure out why it makes me hate her just a little. Maybe because this woman does not seem like his type. Or maybe for other reasons I refuse to acknowledge. I've avoided tabloid magazines whenever his or Gus's faces were on the cover. I never gave in to the pull of looking them up online, especially not Jasper. Not once. And hell, there were some dark moments when I thought that urge would take over everything.

"I wouldn't know."

"I'm glad to hear that," she says sardonically with that smirk still on her lips. She bends forward, her arms folded in her lap as she leans across them. "Here is how this will go, Viola. We're driving directly to Jasper's home. He wants to see how Adalyn responds to meeting you. If he feels comfortable with it, you'll stay the night in the room next to her nursery. Tomorrow, he wants you to spend the entire day with them, so Adalyn is familiar with you. At that time, he'll go over her routine and particular needs. You can ask him questions pertaining to her care, but I believe we should leave it at that, regardless of your history with the band. They play a show in L.A. tomorrow night and the night after that, and then we move on to Las Vegas."

Any goodwill I was accruing toward this woman evaporates into a cloud of aggravation. In this moment, I realize I'm stranded. I have no one and nothing as my ally.

Oddly enough, it feels like I need one.

Like my history with the band, as she put it, is well and truly over. My former friendships inconsequential. It's unsettling to say the least.

I mimic her position and reply with, "You may recall you hired me for this position prior to my having any knowledge of my actual employer. I have no interest in speaking to Jasper about anything other than his daughter. But one thing I don't need is a babysitter or a jail warden, so if that's your gig with me, you can put me on the next plane home. I'm here for one reason and one reason only and that's Adalyn. Everything else is above my pay grade."

"Then I think we understand each other."

I shake my head slowly, but contradict myself when I say, "I guess we do." These people, I swear. The Gus and Jasper, and even Henry and Keith, I once knew would never have surrounded themselves with people like these. They only care about the tour. Adalyn and her safety and her comfort are only a concern because Jasper Diamond is their front man, and obviously, the welfare of his daughter is paramount to him. I haven't seen the Diamond brothers in almost a decade, but I like to imagine I still know them to some degree. Know their core. But I'll admit, I'm having a difficult time imagining them with this as their world.

The wheels of the plane hit the tarmac, and as we slow our momentum, heading toward the hangar, Sophia leans back in her seat, satisfied that she put me in my place. For about the hundredth time today, I regret saying yes to this job.

Five months feels like an eternity.

Pulling out my cell phone, I find a text from my best friend, Jules. Jules and I have known each other longer than I've known the boys, and for a hot second, she dated Keith.

Jules: *Call me when you can. I'm dying for details. And remember, you can always come home. They need you more than you need them.*

The tiniest of grins quirks up my lips, but it doesn't last long. I don't feel like they need me as much as I need them. I don't feel like I'm on anything remotely resembling an even playing field. I'm outnumbered and outgunned, and I'm about to come face-to-face with a man who somehow managed to break my heart when I never knew he possessed it in the first place.

But that album. And his words that night...

Is it possible to fall in love with a man's secret? With his private poetry? Even when he spent years ignoring, avoiding, and generally acting as if he hated you? Every time I listen to that album, it feels like I'm slipping into a secret world only he and I exist in. I love that secret world as much as I resent it. Resent him for it. Part of me wishes he had never told me. The other part...

Sophia is quietly staring at her phone, doing who the hell knows what, and after texting Jules back with the promise of a call later, I gaze out the window. Bright sun and palm trees. Could be worse.

The plane comes to a screeching halt, and we're immediately ushered into another waiting car, just as luxurious as the one that delivered me to the airport. It's difficult to imagine Jasper like this now. Swimming in money to the point where he can send cars and waste first-class tickets while dispatching his assistant to fetch me in a private jet. *His* private jet, I assume. Or maybe it's the band's? I'm not sure how much it matters.

When I knew him, he was wearing Wranglers and old black t-shirts with worn Chucks. He drove his grandfather's pickup that had seen many a better day and could be heard from a mile down the road. He was never without his guitar, a notebook, or a pen. He was perpetually scratching a line or two down when he thought no one was watching.

But I was always watching, even when I wasn't supposed to.

Jasper Diamond was nothing if not intriguing. An unsolvable puzzle.

Sophia said that Gus hasn't changed. Or at least, she assumes he's always been the same. I can believe that. Gus was larger than life, and now he has the fan base to support his claim of being master of the universe. Even if becoming a rock star turned him into the worst version of himself. The man who cheated on the woman he promised to love forever. But Jasper was always something different.

The car weaves us into the Hollywood Hills, up steep roads with magnificent mansions tucked away behind heavy, impenetrable gates. The air is warm, hazy; the sky bright blue. It's everything I expected of California.

We continue to climb, all the way up until we reach one particular gate that parts with a simple code and swipe of a badge. The house is Spanish-style with a cream sandstone exterior and burnt-orange terracotta tiled roof. There's a balcony that takes up the majority of the second floor, long and sweeping with an ornate wrought-iron railing. Even the windows are impressive, tall with detailed moldings. There's a five-car garage off to one side, and in the center of the circular stone driveway is a water fountain.

The home is massive and beautiful and appears more like what I imagine a five-star hotel to be like rather than a place where anyone actually lives.

The car door opens on Sophia's side, and I follow after her like Dorothy in the Land of Oz. I never imagined Jasper lived in a place like this. When I came to grips with who had actually hired me, and I envisioned coming out here, never in my wildest dreams did I conjure up something like this. I assumed he was more of a beachfront condo guy. Or living in a cool loft somewhere closer to the action of the city.

Just goes to show you how little I know of this man now, and in a way, it's a relief as much as it's a disappointment.

A flash of something catches my eye from the second floor, but when I glance up, I find nothing other than glass reflecting the sun's rays. I stand here a moment longer than I should evidently because Sophia glances over her shoulder and asks, "Change your mind already?" I stare at the window another second, wondering if my mind is already playing tricks on me and then shake my head no. I'm not changing my mind. I'm here, and I won't run now. "Then come on."

Reluctantly I pull myself away from the window and follow Sophia through the tall glass and iron doors into a breathtaking open space. The rubber soles of my Docs squeak against the dark wood floors as I furtively peek around without daring to be obvious about it. It's like a game. One I know I lose instantly as my head swivels and pivots in every direction. Straight in front of me, through a few rooms, I can see an outdoor living area, complete with couches, chairs, televisions, a bar, and a pool table. Beyond that is an infinity pool that appears to drop off over a cliff. I realize it's an optical illusion, but wow, and the view beyond it of Los Angeles is stunning.

"Nice, isn't it?"

"Yes," I answer quietly, though nice seems like a wholly inadequate description. This place is a palace. I slowly take in the rest of the great room. White. This man has a lot of white furniture with a toddler running around? I wonder if poor Adalyn is allowed to touch anything because every inch is pristine. Walking in a little further, I spot the kitchen all the way off to the right, but I don't get to admire the marble or the high-end finishes because off to my left...footsteps. Heavy footsteps at that.

My heart thunders in my chest, my stomach roiling, filling me with woozy butterflies that quicken the urge to jump out of my skin and throw up at the same time. I turn around, doing my best not to fidget or knot my fingers; my breath paused in my lungs as I find the nerve to face the man I knew once upon a time, in a land far, far away. This is no fairytale, I remind myself. He's no Prince Charming, and I'm no Cinderella, and this palace is the ultimate misconception.

My eyes slink along the floor until they reach the curved staircase where they bounce up, step by step until they discover bare feet. *Bare feet!* Dark wash jeans over long, strong legs. Black t-shirt that clings to a rippled abdomen and chest. Tattoos. The man has colorful, indeterminable tattoos on his corded, tanned arms, the fabric of his shirt suffering heavily against his muscular biceps as he adjusts the girl in his arms.

The girl...

She is small and beautiful, and if I had encountered her at random, I'd have known she was Jasper's within seconds. She's his clone in female child form. Her long ribbon-like, reddish-brown hair and sparkling green eyes are exact replicas of their maker's. Her round, pink-tinted cheeks make her appear cherubic and so very sweet that my fingers itch with the desire to touch them just to see if they're as soft as they appear.

She's so absolutely, perfectly lovely.

My god, Jasper Diamond is a father.

I don't think I fully appreciated that until seeing her.

The side of her face tucks securely into the man's chest, holding onto him as well as Mickey and Minnie Mouse stuffed animals. And now that I look, I notice her leggings are Mickey Mouse, and her black t-shirt has Minnie ears and a bow on them. I smile at that before I can stop myself. I love that she's in leggings and a t-shirt and not some frilly pink dress with a large bow on it. I love that he dresses her in a way that makes her feel comfortable and secure.

Finally, when I cannot avoid it any further, and long-suffering curiosity gets the better of me, I finish the journey up and find the man I never thought I'd see again. Jasper Diamond. It's like I'm having an out-of-body experience. Like my brain and my body are disconnected. Was he always this *hot?* I mean, he was always gorgeous and mysteriously sexy, but wow. Just...*wow.*

If beautiful and gorgeous got together and created a love child, it would be Jasper. Unruly reddish-brown hair. Piercing green eyes. Jawline chiseled from stone. Muscular body that makes every hormone in my body stand at attention and zap with electricity.

He's staring at me, his expression indecipherable, his eyes everywhere all at once like he too can't help his morbid curiosity. Like the pull to discover what seven years have done to me is too alluring to play it cool. He takes me in feature by feature, and I watch with a barely contained smirk as he does.

He's completely unrepentant about his perusal, and despite the apathy of his expression, I catch the hint of appreciation in his eyes. I'm tempted to ask, 'Like what you see?' but I haven't managed to reach the forming words part of my mini freak-out.

"Hi," he finally says, breaking the tension as a slow, easy smile blossoms across his face. *That smile.* I want to die in it. I assumed it would be awkward. I assumed it might even sting a little. But this? I have no words for what this sensation is. For the way emotion after emotion slams into me with the force of a Mack truck hitting a bunny.

And in case you missed it, he's the truck, and I'm the bunny.

"Hi," I manage, my voice low and cool. Does he have to look so good? Does my stupid, traitorous body have to react to him like this? I take a step, my feet inadvertently guiding my way. I want to hug him and slap him. Kiss his full soft lips and punch him in the face. It's the oddest thing in the world, and yet, they don't feel like nearly enough.

This is a straight current. A rush of static. A tingle up my spine.

I take another step, noting how Adalyn secures herself further into him with every inch closer I get. That lures me too, if only out of inquisitiveness for the small, pretty creature. Another step and the rubber tip of my boot somehow manages to catch on the floor–on namely nothing–and I fall forward before I can stop myself, my knees hitting first, followed by my hands as they slap against the wood. The sound reverberates, not only through my body, but off every hard surface.

I freeze, praying that this did not just happen. *Why, oh why, can I not be smooth, just once?* Especially when I'm desperate to look formidable and together.

A giggle. I hear the giggle of a little girl, and I instantly glance up, brushing the strands of my hair out of my face. Adalyn's beautiful green eyes are on mine, filled with sparkling mirth as she laughs lightly at my blunder.

Jasper's lips twitch while trying to suppress his own amusement and failing.

I shrug a shoulder, laughing too, because what the hell else can I do.

Pulling myself up, I flatten out my tee, tuck my wild hair behind my ear, and sigh. "That wasn't supposed to be how I met you, Adalyn." She doesn't respond, but I didn't expect her to.

"I see your coordination hasn't improved since I saw you last," Jasper teases, his voice deeper, richer, warmer than I remember it being. Adalyn giggles some more as if she understands the zing he just sent flying my way. I don't know if his words are for her benefit or my embarrassment or both.

"I see your manners haven't either."

He grins at me, and I force myself to look away from him, back to Adalyn.

"Are you hurt?" Sophia asks without an ounce of genuine concern in her voice.

I shake my head, my eyes still on Adalyn, who is no longer looking at me. She's locked herself back into her father. "As Mr. Diamond so kindly pointed out, I can occasionally be trouble on my feet."

I catch him cringing out of the corner of my eye. "Mister Diamond?"

"Manners," I remind him, when I'm really using the word as a euphemism for boundaries. At least with myself. "You're my boss now, right?"

He shakes his head lightly, like I'm already trying his patience. I suppose I am. My hackles are up, shooting out poorly disguised venom, and I've barely made it past the foyer.

"Do I have to call you Miss Starr?"

"If it makes you more comfortable."

He grumbles something under his breath that I don't fully catch, but I think it's something along the lines of, nothing with you makes me comfortable.

I don't know why I'm being so hard on him. Maybe it's because he started this and hating him feels a hell of a lot safer than anything else. A hell of a lot safer than wondering, *what if*. And *why*. That's mostly what plagued me, at least immediately after I left Los Angeles.

All the what-ifs and whys.

What if he hadn't stepped away after that first kiss when we were fourteen? What if it had been him who pursued me instead of Gus? What if I had dated him for those years? Would we have ended the same way Gus and I did?

And why didn't he try?

What happened to make him pull back and let Gus take the lead? I don't know. But those questions burned me. I told myself that him writing an album for me didn't mean anything. He told me as much. *'But it doesn't change anything, Vi. Absolutely nothing. So you can move on without us and pretend like I never said a word.'* Words not actions, right? I was the only girl around them–the only girl they really spent time with at least.

I blame that album on that.

And now, seeing him in all his rare, rock star daddy, untouchable glory, I realize he's a stranger to me. The boy I knew, grew up with, is gone, and in his place is this man. This man with a daughter. This man who is known, loved by the entire world. That boy from my memories, the one I spent entirely too much time thinking about, is merely reflected in his general appearance, the hair, the eyes, but everything else?

No. I don't know him. Not anymore.

"You've always had a penchant for bringing out the worst in me, haven't you?"

"I didn't realize I had any sort of effect on you at all."

He chuckles lightly before it transforms into a smirk that has my blood racing. "Now you know. In the past, ignoring you just seemed easier. And more polite. I suppose I won't have that luxury anymore."

I shake my head, making a tsking sound at him. "Still a jerk, I see. Nice to know some things haven't changed."

"Yeah. Like your mouth."

I narrow my eyes, wondering how we've jumped so far so fast into adversarial. If we continue at this rate, neither one of us will survive the next five months without killing the other. "Like your attitude."

"Like the way you look."

A smile unwittingly springs from my lips. "I can't say the same about you."

The simple truth is, money and fame have turned Jasper Diamond into a God amongst mortals. His dark auburn hair is wavy, messy, and sexy in that artfully crafted I-don't-do-anything-to-it-and-yet-it's-still-perfect way. His jaw is more angled, sharper with two days' worth of stubble. If he were clean-shaven, I'd find an irresistible dimple in his chin. He's taller, more built without being overly bulky. He's covered in tattoos. And fuck all to hell, he's holding a little girl in his arms, which naturally makes my ovaries scream in beleaguered anarchy.

Stupid, overly attractive bastard.

"It's nice to see you too, Vi. Though, I can't say I've missed you."

Such an asshole.

"Luckily for me, I'm not here for you. I'm here for Adalyn." At the mention of her name, she peeks out at me, and I smile, giving her a small wave.

"No," I hear her mumble into Jasper, and I cock an eyebrow at him. She's going to pick up on his cues, and then we'll be nowhere.

He nods in understanding.

From somewhere behind me, Sophia clears her throat, the sound startling me as I almost forgot she was here.

"Clearly, introductions are necessary for the two of you." Her tone is different now. Sharper. Crueler. "You shouldn't fret, Viola, Adalyn takes a while to warm up to everyone."

I glare over at her as she hands me a condescending smile that makes me dislike her more than I already do. Oddly enough, I think Jasper agrees with me as his expression grows acerbic. I wouldn't like someone else speaking of my daughter that way either. Especially, with said daughter in the room able to hear her.

I swallow down my biting remark when she follows up with, "I think it's best if I go. Let the three of you become...acquainted. I'll see you tomorrow before the show, Jasper. You and I can have a few minutes together in private. I think we'll need it." His eyebrows furrow before smoothing out just as quickly. "Best of luck, Viola. It was a pleasure to finally meet you." Sophia's heels click loudly along the floor, the door slamming shut behind her.

Suddenly the three of us are alone together.

FOUR

Jasper

WHEN I WAS A KID, my life wasn't all that great. I mean, it wasn't bad either. Let's not whip out the violins and start serenading me. I had all the essentials and a lot more. But I was also missing one key ingredient. A key ingredient that was gone entirely because I was careless. Irrevocably imprudent. With that heartache, a piece of my soul slipped away, becoming one with the ocean who stole it from me.

Then one day, I met this girl.

And this girl smiled at me.

And I managed to smile back for what felt like the first time in forever.

Unbeknownst to her, she sewed my tattered heart back together. She was bright sunshine and enthusiasm and enjoyed holding the world in her palm when all I could do was glare at it from a distance. I envied this girl, though admittedly, in retrospect, she had far less than I did—no father and a junkie, degenerate mother who was never very good to her.

If you didn't know that about her, you'd never for a second believe her world was anything other than perfect. Being around her was the equivalent of setting off fireworks. Burning hot, exhilarating, and gloriously brilliant with color.

I fell in love under an Alabama sky, in the heat and humidity of summer, watching a pretty towheaded girl with long, long hair and bright hazel eyes make me the ultimate fool. I was hers instantly. She was like coming up for air. A sacred breath after suffocating for years.

I would know. I had mastered the art.

And then, one day, I worked up all my nerve and kissed her.

And she kissed me back.

It was glorious. A reality that even the most creative imagination could never conjure up. It was the permanent smile of an adolescent boy who found heaven in a set of pretty pink lips. It was the pinnacle of my life–something I knew would be nearly impossible to eclipse even at the tender age of fourteen. Life hadn't been all that favorable for me.

Until I met Viola Starr.

The girl of my dreams.

The one who breathed life into spaces where it had already been snuffed out.

Then I went home. That unstoppable smile still affixed to my lips. I didn't think it could ever wane. I certainly hoped it wouldn't.

Then my brother shattered it without trying.

Then I stepped back, giving Gus everything I knew I'd never get over.

He took it all too willingly. Kept her, holding on tight, until he threw her away.

Now she's back, more beautiful than ever, already pushing me, but instead of infusing me with air and life, she's killing anything I had left.

I watch Viola, and she watches me, but she really doesn't. I mean, we did the whole back and forth. We did the whole initial takedown. But now, we're stuck in this mess, and this mess is consuming us both. Because this mess is not about me. It's not even about my brother.

It's about my daughter, and that's the only reason she's here.

I could have gone forever without seeing her again. Now I can't stop looking.

I saw this moment going very differently in my head. I wonder if things would be this tense if I hadn't been stupid enough to open my mouth that last night. *You wanted a reaction from her, and you got one.* I did, and I don't even know why. Maybe it was the way she first looked at me, emotionless. Aggravatingly blank with a touch of politeness. Like I was just any new boss she was coming to meet, instead of seeing a man who bared his darkest, best-kept secret to her.

I want her eyes on mine. I want her to see me.

I'm standing here, staring at her...my goddamn heart feeling like it is going to explode, and I need her to be feeling the same. Dizzy. Off-balance. Angry. Fucking turned-on when I should be anything but with my daughter in my arms.

Seven years. It's almost a decade. Yet, it doesn't quite feel like that. It feels like a minute. Like a half-beat ago, she was walking out into the night, and I followed her.

Now she's a mirage. An illusion. A nightmare and a dream combined into one.

Viola Starr walked into my home, and I forgot how to breathe.

And in truth, I don't know what to do about it.

It's like the atmosphere inside the house has altered, filled with static and sound. A pulse. A beat. A rhythm. What is it about this girl that drives me to write music?

Shifting Adalyn in my arms, she snuggles further into me. I tilt my head, trying to catch her eye. "Ady, you want to meet daddy's friend?"

"No," she whispers back, shaking her head.

My gaze darts back to Viola, who is still near the foot of the stairs, watching us with blatant curiosity.

My lips set into a thin line. I don't know what to say to her anymore, and I'm not sure she does either.

I meant what I said though. She does look the same. Well, for the most part. Viola's light wavy hair is shorter, just to her mid-back. It was nearly to her waist the last time I saw her. But everything else is exactly the same.

The brightness of her big, hazel, almond-shaped eyes. The long fan of her dark lashes that frame them. Her high, pink-tinted cheeks and full bow-shaped lips that are permanently stained a deep rose color even though I've never seen her in lipstick.

She's thin. A little thinner than I remember. Her long, smooth, tanned legs are leaner, and judging by the way her purple t-shirt hangs just the smallest bit from her narrow shoulders, I wonder if this weight loss is new. Viola always liked her clothes tight. This shirt is not.

Purple. Adalyn's favorite color.

It feels intentional. Everything about Viola is.

That woman sees everything. But I have no idea how she could have known. The coincidence of it takes the burn that's been sitting at the back of my neck since she walked in and swarms it around my body until it settles in my chest.

Shit. It's a brush fire. Wild and unwelcome.

I cannot give her life or room to breathe inside me.

If ever I was good at something with this woman, it was being cold and indifferent while blatantly ignoring her. Shouldn't be a hard habit to pick back up.

Silence descends upon us, thick and heavy like a weight that's anchoring me to the floor and sealing my mouth shut. Slowly. So goddamn slowly, Viola slides toward the stairs again, and I just now realize I'm still standing on the top one with Ady in my arms.

Ady hears the movement and adjusts herself to watch Viola glide up the stairs toward us.

Viola is in my house. And she's meeting my daughter.

Jesus Christ. My heart starts to batter mercilessly in my chest.

But it's for more than just about Viola. I need her and Ady to like each other. I'm officially out of time and out of options. Ady needs a nanny to take care of her for the times during the tour when I cannot.

It seems that nanny has to be Viola.

Adalyn senses what's happening because she sinks further into me. "Hello, Adalyn," Viola speaks softly, and my chest tightens once more at the sound of her voice talking to my daughter. "My name is Viola, but my friends call me Vi." I can't speak. I can only stare. Watch. Barely breathe. "I see you like Mickey Mouse," she continues, and I catch Adalyn peeking at Viola, her eyes growing with interest at the mention of the love of her life. And in case you missed it, it's not me. "I have something for you if that's okay." Viola glances up at me for a flash of a second. Just long enough for me to nod my head in assent to the gift before she returns her focus fully on my daughter, who is starting to squirm in my arms. "I've always been a big fan of Rapunzel personally. It's the hair and eyes, plus the love of adventure, but I'm cool with Mickey and Minnie if you are."

My lips quirk up at that, and I watch in stunned amazement as Viola unzips her threadbare purse and slips out a small Mickey Mouse figurine followed by a Minnie Mouse one. They're simple. The kind you pick up at the Disney store for a few bucks, but we don't have any of these, shockingly enough. Adalyn's face leaves my chest, and her arms untuck themselves as she reaches out for the toys as if Viola just offered her the last golden ticket to Willy Wonka's chocolate factory.

"Mickey. Minnie," Adalyn exalts, her sweet smile lighting up her face. Ady quickly grasps them from Viola's outstretched hand, shifting her stuffed Mickey and Minnie into her other hand to accommodate her new plastic friends.

"Can you say thank you?" I speak low in Adalyn's ear. She doesn't, of course. That would be pushing it with someone new. "Thank you," I manage on her behalf, but Viola doesn't even hear me. It's like I'm not here.

"Adalyn, can you show me where you like to play? Where your

toys are?" Adalyn stares at Viola who smiles endlessly at her. "Do you want to go play with me?"

"Play?" Adalyn parrots.

"Yes," Viola practically cheers. "Let's go play together. I really want to see your toys. I *love* toys," she hums with exuberance. "We can bring Mickey and Minnie with us. Daddy can come too if he wants." It takes a few beats. A lot of Adalyn quietly analyzing Viola. And then Ady squirms in my arms until she forces me to release her onto the landing at the top of the stairs behind me, where she waits for Viola.

She. Waits. For. Viola.

My daughter does not like strangers. My daughter does not like anyone she is not completely, one hundred percent comfortable with, who is no one other than myself and my brother. She's okay with Henry and Keith. Same goes for my dad, stepmother, and our manager, Marco. But she's waiting for Viola to follow her, and instinctively, I know it's more than just the present or the purple blouse or the falling to the floor.

It's Viola.

She renders all who encounter her defenseless and utterly captivated.

Viola breezes past me to join her new friend, the smallest brush of her vanilla fragrance wafts up, hitting my nose and I breathe in, wanting to close my eyes and savor everything about the memory as it assaults my senses. But then they're gone. Walking down the hall toward Adalyn's playroom, leaving me standing here like the asshole I am.

That didn't go as expected.

It was both better and worse.

This is the only way it can be with you and her, I remind myself.

"Shit and fuck," I mutter under my breath, scrubbing my hands up and down my face and back through my hair, staring miserably around my house. A sardonic chuckle finds its way past my lips. Christ, I'm already so screwed.

The past doesn't matter.

The things I told her that night don't matter.

She's the nanny. Nothing else.

Right? Right.

Hell, I survived four years of that woman with my brother, five months will be the easiest time I've ever served. I shake my head to myself. God has a real sense of irony, and I just got bitch slapped with it.

FIVE

Jasper

I FEEL like I've been standing on these steps forever. Locked in place, because even though I want to go watch the nanny with my daughter, I'm already dreading being around Viola again. Then I hear it. The electronic sound of something saying, "Stop," followed by Viola repeating the word in a short, succinct clap of sound. But it's what comes after that has me straining to hear better.

Giggling.

Adalyn's giggling. And it's not just at Vi falling to the floor. It's at whatever game they're playing. *How on earth?*

Briskly walking down the hall, I slow my pace as I approach the playroom door, not wanting even the sound of my bare feet slapping against the floor to get in the way.

"More," Adalyn half-squeals in anticipation.

"More...what? More stop? More game?" Adalyn doesn't reply. Viola waits.

"More."

"Okay. More. Great asking," Viola praises before I hear that electronic, "Stop," again followed by Viola repeating the word and Adalyn's happy laughter. With each pass, that laughter grows until Adalyn is practically in a full-on belly laugh. It has me smiling so goddamn big as I listen. "I love your playroom, Ady," Viola comments appreciatively, using the pet name version of her name like they're already the best of friends. "That slide is epic. You're a lucky girl. So tell me, kiddo, do you want me to do it again? More game?"

"More," Ady replies enthusiastically.

"Can you say more game?"

"More...game," Ady parrots, the second word slower, with more care, but she did it.

"How did you do it, Vi?" I whisper to myself, mentally shaking my head. *How could I have underestimated you so quickly? Been so fast to dismiss the idea of you and Adalyn?* I should have known. You ensnared me and Gus in a matter of seconds, and we were eight. Adalyn at three took you mere minutes.

Hovering against the doorframe, I try to remain hidden as I watch her with my daughter. Adalyn is tucked into the small blue Calico Critters car she likes to squeeze her butt into, rolling back and forth. Back and forth. Viola is on the floor, lying flat on her belly and propped up by her elbows, so her position is lower than Ady's, but is still able to maintain eye contact. Her combat-boot-clad feet–I see that hasn't changed either–are in the air, scissoring slowly, tantalizingly. The backs of her tanned thighs on display below the hem of her black skirt are just enough of a tease to make me pause and take notice.

"More? More what?"

"More game." Ady gets up and presses the button on her pretend remote control, before returning to her car.

"Great, Ady. Really nice job using your words, kiddo. You're such a smart cookie, aren't you?" The whole process begins again, but Ady is looking at Viola. Directly into her eyes. While my daughter makes exceptional eye contact for someone with autism, it's rarely her go-to and only with me and Gus. "Does she typically make such excellent eye contact?" It takes me a beat to realize Viola is asking me a direct question.

Clearly, I'm not as stealthy as I wanted to be.

"Did you just read my mind?"

"Pardon?" Viola's eyebrows crinkle together.

"Never mind," I chuckle. "Yes," I answer, edging ever so softly into the room, afraid to disrupt their playtime. "It's actually one of her strengths."

"And her speech?" Viola tacks on. "She has a lot of words and learns how to use them quickly to get what she wants. She anticipates me. She asks me to do something and waits for it. She makes that eye contact with me and tries so hard to get those extra words that aren't a natural part of her speech yet. It's fantastic." Fuck. I cannot hold back my prideful smile at that. No one, not any of the specialists, has said anything Adalyn does is fantastic. She just turned three but has the verbal acuity of a child at least a year younger.

"It's something her therapists and I have been working on a lot."

"Does she mostly speak in one or two-word sentences?"

"Yes. But she does have a few rote sentences that are three or four words. Like 'what's that noise?' or 'what is that?' or 'who's that?' We have some breakthroughs occasionally. Like the other day, she came up to me with a bag of crackers and asked, 'Daddy, can you open?' I nearly fell off my chair. She also likes to say, 'I can't reach it.'"

Viola grins softly, staring at Adalyn, who is now expectantly staring back at her as she rolls the car back and forth. "What happens when she cannot verbally express her wants?"

"Depends," I answer automatically. "She'll physically show me what she wants or needs. Get it herself. Or...," I trail off for a beat, swallowing hard as I think about the last time this happened, "she tantrums," I finish.

Viola rolls over onto her side to face me, digging her elbow into the floor and propping her face up with her hand, pinning me with a gaze I'm not quite ready for. She slides the remote across the floor to

Ady, who eagerly picks it up, playing with it as she continues to glide in the car.

"And what are those like?"

I sigh and turn away from her, choosing to watch Adalyn instead. I can't look at Viola like this. It's messing with my head in far too many ways.

"She bangs the back of her head on the floor after throwing herself onto it. She kicks and pushes and screams. She hits at me. Slaps her hands against whatever hard surface is near her. Whimpers. Cries. She yells, 'Stop!' or 'No!' at the top of her lungs," I laugh mirthlessly. "It all depends on the situation and where we are. But it can be any or all of those things. Stop and no are the worst possible thing for a toddler to scream, especially if you're in public with her when she does." Out of the corner of my eye, I catch Viola nodding in understanding as I watch my daughter play.

"Does she cry?"

"Sometimes. Not often."

"Does she bang the back of her head a lot or more as a way to get your attention?"

"To get my attention, I think. Same with the hitting and slapping her hands on the floor." I shrug. I honestly don't know.

I know my daughter in so many ways, and yet, I feel as though I'm missing so many vital pieces. She's three, and I cannot have a conversation with her. She doesn't answer when I ask her if she slept well or had good dreams. She's never walked up to me and said, 'Daddy, I'm hungry.' Hell, she only has a few sentences, and most of those are rote.

I know how lucky I am to have that. To have her speaking to me at all. And that's what I cling to. How goddamn lucky I am to have this beautiful, happy, sweet, smart girl as mine. Everything else is gravy.

But at the same time, it's not what you expect when you become a parent, and I break for how hard Adalyn's world is for her sometimes. How the smallest of things, like taking a pair of shoes from her hands and handing them to the cashier to ring up, can set her off. I've wondered if things would be easier for her if she had a mother. If I'm doing the right things.

I do my best. Hell, I give her everything, but I've made so many mistakes where Adalyn is concerned. Done things that can no longer be fixed or changed.

"How do you get her to stop them?" she asks, dragging me out of my dark thoughts.

"I hold her. Sometimes apply gentle pressure to her chest, and that helps. The therapists told me to ignore her tantrums, and I try. I really do. But that's not always so easy. She's my little girl." Viola taps her fingers along the floor, her teeth sawing into her bottom lip as she thinks. "She tries so hard," I say, almost to myself, feeling Viola's eyes on mine, though I can't quite meet them. "She really does. She learns incredibly quick. Parrots words and short phrases that she inserts at times she feels they fit the situation." My hands meet my hips, my eyes drop to the floor, a small smile tugging up the corner of my lips. "It's all in there. I've seen it. Heard it. She knows some numbers and shapes and colors and a few letters even. She just has trouble expressing them sometimes. Particularly on demand."

"Does she sign?"

"Sign?"

Viola rolls her eyes at me, turning back over and playing the game with Adalyn two more times before daring to answer me. But I don't care because Adalyn still thinks this is the best game in the world, especially now that she has the remote, so I'll gladly stand here and watch my daughter giggle.

"Sign language," Viola finally supplies.

"A little."

Viola hums. "There are two schools of thought on that. Some of the old school speech therapists, who are obviously trained to get kids to speak, feel it's a hindrance. But I believe it can be an adjunct therapy. Something that will help her communicate with you in a non-frustrated way. I'm big into saying the word along with the sign so she gets both. If you're cool with it, I'd like to teach her some sign language. Obviously, I will push hard for her to use verbal communication as her first-line, and yes, getting her to speak more is our ultimate goal." I nod my head, because I'm willing to try anything. "She has words, Jas, which is awesome. A lot of children on the spectrum don't speak at all, or they have a tremendous amount of difficulty communicating their wants and needs. Adalyn speaks, and can probably get a few of her basic needs across, but she doesn't have enough words. Not yet. Signing would help that. And you need to work with her on catching your eye when she's trying to ask for something. She does it, but it takes some prompting, and it's not consistent. Eye contact is the foundation of communication, and as you said, it's one of her strengths."

Jas. Viola just called me Jas, not Mr. Diamond. Progress.

But instead of acknowledging it, because we're finally having a productive and civil conversation, I say, "Sign language and eye contact."

She hums out softly, and I study her profile, reining in my emotions as she plays the game with Adalyn again, the two of them giggling like girls do. "I have videos with singing. She'll love them."

"Okay," I say, because I think she might know more than all the specialists in fucking Los Angeles who have been ineffective at reaching my daughter.

Maybe they were too old or just not the right fit, but Ady is already taking to Viola. And I don't think I can say no to her.

She's here.

That seems to be all I can focus on. Viola Starr is here.

Any ground I ever put between myself and my past seems to be crumbling beneath my feet. But parents don't typically have the luxury of putting themselves first, and right now, I'm out of options where a nanny is concerned.

"Whatever you think is best for Ady, I'm on board with it. I'll do anything, whatever it takes. I just have one non-negotiable stipulation."

The corner of Viola's mouth quirks up, and it's the first smile–well, real smile–she's directed at me since she arrived. "What's that?" Her eyes dart in my direction.

"You keep her safe at all costs. She's your number one priority. No one and nothing come before her when you're on duty."

Her gaze never wavers from mine. "Without question, Jasper," she promises, no doubt noting my troubled expression. "You have my word on that."

I give her a slim nod, my heart in my throat.

She turns away from me, and I take in a silent breath. "How did her autism evaluation come about?"

"Slide," Adalyn announces, running over into her built-in tree-house. Climbing up the stairs that are partially hidden inside the 'tree,' she then slides down the metal slide back to the floor. "Weee."

"Slide. Down," Viola says, enunciating each word.

"More slide," Adalyn responds, going around and doing it again.

Viola beams. "Yes. More slide."

"Her speech, actually. I have a buddy who has a daughter the same age, and I noticed how Adalyn wasn't speaking as much as she was. And what she was saying was just one or two words. No sentences. Adalyn also wasn't particularly interested in playing with her. In fact, she really doesn't enjoy spending time with other children. I mentioned it to her pediatrician at her two-year physical, and she suggested I have her evaluated by Early Start–that's the California early intervention program. After they worked with Ady for a few weeks for her speech, they recommended the autism screening."

Viola nods her head. Swinging her legs around, she shifts to a sitting position with her legs folded. I watch the two of them play for a few minutes, lost in my own reverie. Adalyn crashes into her beanbag in the corner, tossing herself upside down so her feet are in the air. She squeals in delight.

"Okay," Viola finally says, slapping her hands down on her thighs. "She's a total vestibular bug, isn't she? Really sensory-based."

"What?" I laugh the word.

"She rocks back and forth. She flips herself upside down. She slides down the slide repeatedly. She crashes into things. She likes to hold things in her hands. You just told me she likes it when you squeeze her. I bet there's more."

"Yes. She does all that."

"That's good to know. We can help her with that, Jas." Viola smiles like the thought makes her just as happy as it makes me. "She obviously needs that input. We can work on a sensory diet with her. I mean, I'm not an occupational therapist, but I've worked with them enough and seen enough that with a little research, I can come up with something."

I'm blown away right now. The urge to hug this woman is real. Intense. I have so much I want to say to her. So much to apologize for, and yet she's here, talking about all these things she's going to do to help my daughter. Not just as a nanny. Even if that's exactly what she is.

"Vi, I–"

"Don't," she cuts me off quickly, her eyes flashing over to mine. "Whatever you're going to say, don't. We don't have to talk this out or rehash things that don't need rehashing."

"You have no idea what I was going to say."

"Maybe not, but you had a tone."

"A tone?" I echo, trying not to grin. But I quickly lose it when I think of all the unsaid things I should say. Like, I'm sorry I told you about writing the album about you. Like, there are reasons I've always been a cold, indifferent prick to you. Like, I'm sorry your mother is the ultimate bitch, and you deserve better. Like, I'm glad you're here. But really, I'm not sure how much any of that matters. She works for me. I'm her boss, and she will forever belong to my brother, and this is just the way it is for us. But still... "Vi, don't you think we should–"

"No," she interrupts again. "I seriously do not think we should do anything. There is nothing to say at this point, Jas. The past is where we left it. I just want to focus on the job I'm here to do."

I shake my head at her. I forgot how infuriatingly stubborn the woman can be. "So, you're just going to spend the next five months hating me?"

She gives me a fisheye and then returns to Adalyn. "I don't hate you. But I don't like you all that much, and as I recall, once we hit high school, you weren't all that fond of me either."

Her cheeks color a bit at that, and I wonder if she's thinking about what I told her that last night. About the album I wrote for her. Does she honestly not know how hot I've been for her all these years?

"I'm your temporary employee. That's it. This is an arrangement. That's the extent of things and all we should ever discuss. I don't know what you and Gus are—"

"Gus?" I snap out quickly.

She pins me with a look that questions my basic sanity. "Yes. Gus. I assume he's the one who put me up for this?"

"Why...how would he...," I trail off because just what the fuck? Then I remember what Sophia said. That Gus had given her Viola's name and resume. I didn't think to question it because I was too out of sorts at the mention of Viola to think straight. Of course, Gus put her up for the position. I'm an idiot for not seeing it sooner. "How did he know what you do for a living?"

Viola rolls her eyes, tucking a piece of long blonde hair behind her ear and refusing to make eye contact with me like it physically pains her to do so.

"He checks up on me. Asks around about me. Spencer Johnson, you remember him," she smirks knowingly, glancing in my direction quickly, "let it slip out one night at the bar he owns."

Crafty bastard. Then again, I haven't exactly told Gus that I check up on Viola as well. She must have known. That's what that look says. But I haven't done it in about six months or so, which is how I missed all that stuff with her mother. But my checking up was general. I never got in deep. I knew she was a teacher by day and a bartender by night. I had no idea what her specialty was.

"You mean Spencer from high school?"

"Yep. One in the same. He and I dated for a bit. Or didn't you know that?"

I didn't actually know that.

Folding my arms across my chest, I move further into the room before I sit down and face her. I'm close to her. Closer than she likes judging by the way her posture grows stiff.

It's funny; I used to avoid this woman by any means necessary. I couldn't stand to be in the same room as her. Hated looking at her. Every single goddamn time I did, it was like a jagged knife twisting in my gut.

But now, I want to look. I want to see everything these years apart have done. And part of me, the ugly dark masochistic part of me, wants her to see how affected I am by her. Still.

"If you're so against being near me, then why did you take the job?"

Her head drops, her finger running along the grain in the wood floor. "I didn't know it was for you until yesterday."

"How is that even possible?"

"I didn't know you had a daughter, Jasper. When I got the call, and the position was described to me, I assumed Gus gave my name to someone he knew out here. It wasn't until your bitchy errand lady, Sophia, called yesterday that I knew the job was for you."

"Fucking Gus," I mutter under my breath, so my Ady doesn't hear, and Viola nods, fighting a small grin, her face still downcast.

I blow out a breath, drumming my fingers along the floor to an unknown beat as I look over at Ady. She's running around and around, climbing up and sliding down. I'm surprised she hasn't asked for her swing yet. I glance over at Viola again and watch as she follows my daughter around her playroom.

So this is how it has to be. And there really isn't much else to say on that. She didn't know the job was for me, and she clearly needs the money. Gus, her ex-boyfriend, my brother, essentially brought her here.

She admittedly doesn't like me. Wants to keep her distance and refuses to allow me to explain or apologize. She's probably right in that. What the hell would I say to her?

"Okay then. Five months. Adalyn seems to like you and is already comfortable enough that I feel it will continue to grow as you two spend more time together. You seem to know your stuff when it comes to children with autism, and I've reviewed your resume." *Obsessed over it for most of last night like it was going to tell me everything I've missed over seven years.* "If you agree to everything that comes with this job. To keeping her from the press, as best you can. Keeping her safe when you're out. Helping her with her speech and behaviors and giving her a sense of routine and consistency. If you're on board for the travel and the hours and everything else," I glance over at her, "then I think we can sign the contract and move forward."

She gnaws on her bottom lip, and finally nods her head. "Yes," she says softly, reluctantly. "I'm on board. As long as this is entirely professional. All of it."

"Absolutely."

"Good."

"I'll let you two continue to get to know each other." I stand up, drop a small kiss on Ady's head now that she's sitting in the corner playing with her dolls. I leave Viola alone with my daughter because I need a minute.

I was much better at this before. And once my body remembers how it's supposed to behave around her, everything will be fine. It has to be.

SIX

Viola

THE MOMENT JASPER leaves the room, I feel like I can breathe again, the knot in my stomach slowly unfurling. Christ, that man is intense. I can't remember the last time I was this nervous, and it's a wonder I was able to speak to him with a steady voice and coherent thoughts.

I'm stubborn. And prideful. And both of those combined can be lethal.

But maybe it's all for the best. Maybe my crap anger and his hurt over me brushing him off will help us maintain our distance. Our professional boundaries.

Adalyn has been quietly playing with her dolls, and in addition to feeling like shit for snapping at Jasper, I've been ignoring my charge.

I like her already. She has so much life and personality. So much character and untapped wealth. Like oil in the ground, and once you hit into that right spot, it all comes shooting out. That's this girl. I can feel it.

She reminds me so much of her father in that way.

That's how he was. Quiet, reserved, but once you gave him a sheet of paper and a pen, or a guitar, he came to life. He opened his soul up in ways he was otherwise unable to.

I watch as Ady moves from toy to toy. She's not much of a sit-in-place-and-play kid. She likes to move, and her gross motor skills are likely above her age level. I'd love to see what she could do in a gymnastics class, but we won't exactly have that opportunity with all the travel we're going to be doing. Still, I'll have to come up with something for us; otherwise, we'll both go nuts.

"What do you like to do, Ady?" I ask, but she does not look up when I speak. "Do you like to run and jump?" I scoot closer to her, and she stills ever so slightly. "I've seen you climb and slide. Do you like coloring?" She peeks up, but doesn't answer and isn't looking at me directly. I need to find out more about her strengths and limitations. That Sophia woman didn't tell me all that much, and I wonder if it's because she was intentionally vague given the people involved or if she doesn't know.

Adalyn stands up, glancing around before running across the room and jumping onto the couch against the far wall, flipping upside down again and squealing with delight.

"Upside down," I say, and then she flips back, hops off the couch, runs a circle around me, and then does it again. She likes to repeat her motions. Perseveration is what it's called, but so far, I haven't seen her do that with much other than movement. "Ady, can you say upside down?" She just blinks at me from that position, and I wonder if she's uncomfortable now that Jasper is gone. "Should we go find Daddy?" She stares at me, the two small Minnie and Mickey figurines I gave her now clenched in her tiny fists. "Do you want to—"

"Is she here?" a loud, booming voice that I'd know anywhere rips through the air. "Is my girl here?"

"Gus," Adalyn says softly, a smile in her voice and features. I love seeing that. It means Gus is close with her. She twists her body so that she's sitting on the couch, and I'm tempted to get up and join her.

Nervous anticipation slams through me for the second time today. The last time I saw Gus, I was ending things between us. His girl. That's what he just called me, and it's a title I lived by for four years of my life.

It simultaneously makes me smile and cringe.

"Vi," Gus bellows. "Where are you, girl? I've been counting the goddamn seconds."

"Gus," Jasper calls out, with a slight edge to his tone, from somewhere down the hall. I'm still sitting cross-legged on the floor, and I can't seem to pry myself off it. I'd be lying if I said I wasn't at least a little excited to see Gus. "We need to–"

"Later, dude. We'll do this shit later. But first...," and then he rounds the corner into the playroom, Jasper hot on his heels. Gus's gray eyes take me in, every single inch, and with each inch, his broad smile grows.

He's the same. Everything about him is. His voice. His shaggy light hair, his large frame, and big muscles. Everything.

It makes me smile in a way I couldn't force with Jasper. Because Jasper was right. Fucking Gus. You can't be mad at him. You can't hate him.

It's impossible.

I mean, the asshole freaking cheated on me, and I still didn't yell at him. I still hugged him goodbye. *Bastard.*

"There's my girl," he whispers reverently, his tone softer, gentler. "God, Vi, how is it possible you're even prettier than I remember?"

I open my mouth to say something, but he launches himself at me, tackling me back to the floor and covering my small body with his large one. I laugh out in surprise, my hands landing on his back to return the hug.

But then it's like déjà vu.

Jasper is standing by the doorway, his fists balled up, and jaw clenched. He looks so...I don't know. Angry? Resentful? It doesn't last

long before whatever that is slips back into the cool mask of indifference. It happens so quickly I wonder if I even saw it or if I made it up
in my head.

"Get off her, Gus," Jasper drawls, his voice now completely void
of emotion. And even though his features follow his tone, our eyes are
still locked on each other's. He frowns as he observes me, appearing
utterly unimpressed. "You're going to crush her."

"Nah," Gus says playfully, propping himself up on his elbows so
he can gaze into my eyes from just a few inches away. "We've done
this move a million times over. Am I crushing you, babe?"

"Yes," I laugh.

"Shit," he laughs too. "I don't want to move. You're all warm and
soft. And you smell good. I forgot how good you always smell." He
leans in and rubs my nose with his. "I've missed you," he whispers.
"So much."

"Me too." Because it's the truth. But that doesn't stop me from
shifting my hands to his hard chest, trying–and failing, I might add–
to push him back. "Gus, oxygen is essential. I'm about two seconds
from blacking out." I'm all smiles, so I doubt I'm fooling him. He sighs
out dramatically, glances at Ady, and winks.

"Fine. I'll move. But let it be known, I don't want to."

Sitting back on his haunches, he extends his hand to help me up.
My skirt is bunched, practically to my panties, and I hastily tug it
down. I peek up to see if they saw it, and I can tell by the direction of
both of their gazes that they did.

Gus is smiling like this is all so much fun. Jasper is the complete
opposite, looking pained and tense.

"My beautiful, Vi, you are a sight for sore eyes." Gus takes me in
once more, but for some reason, I don't get the same type of butterflies as I did when Jasper pulled the same move. "I've missed the hell
out of you, girl. Did I tell you that already?" I roll my eyes, and he
laughs before turning back to Adalyn, who has been quietly
observing this interaction. It makes me blush for some reason.
"There's my other favorite girl. Come here, darlin'." Adalyn doesn't

move. "Oh, come on." Gus pats his thigh. "You know you love my hugs. I give the best hugs, remember?" Adalyn looks to Jasper like she's asking permission, but instead of going over to Gus, she scoots off the couch and runs over to Jasper. He bends down and picks her up, squeezing her a little and kissing her forehead. The two of them stare into each other's eyes with matching smiles, and my heart lets out an extra beat. "Ouch, Ady. I'm hurt. Really hurt."

"What can I say? The girl has perfect taste."

Gus shrugs and blows Ady a kiss, and I realize I've missed him. So much more than I thought. "We going to the beach or what?"

"Beach?" Jasper echoes.

"You said that's what you wanted to do today. You said it might be the last time Ady will have a chance to go before the tour."

Jasper flickers his gaze over to mine for a beat before turning back to Gus. "That was before Vi got here. I have a lot to go over with her."

Gus growls something under his breath. "Do you have a bathing suit, Vi?" I nod. "Then you can discuss all that stuff with her there. Let's *go*. It's getting late. I packed a picnic of adult and Adalyn-approved goodies, and we can use Lyric Rose's house in Malibu. I already spoke to her. She's in New York and said it's ours for however long we want it."

Wow. Lyric Rose. They know Lyric Rose? She's the daughter of rock legend, Gabriel Rose, but she's very much a celebrity in her own right. A very cool one at that. At least to me, she is.

Jasper hesitates, his gaze darting back and forth between Gus and me. I wouldn't mind going to the beach. I have a feeling it's going to be non-stop go, go, go for the next five months. It's also a good opportunity to see how Ady does when she's out of her home, her comfort zone.

Oh, and I've never actually seen the Pacific, so there's that.

Finally, he asks Adalyn, "Do you want to go play in the sand?"

"Sand," she says simply, in a low sweet voice.

"Do you want to splash in the ocean? It might be cold."

She doesn't respond this time, but she's still looking at him. "Is that a yes, bug?" No response, she just drops her head, nuzzling into his neck.

"I guess we're going, then. Give me five minutes to get her stuff together and get changed."

And then Jasper walks out. Just like that. Adalyn still in his arms. Wow, that man really doesn't like me. *Can you blame him?*

"Is it weird that my first inclination is to kiss you crazy?" Gus asks, and I laugh.

"It is weird, right? This whole thing?"

"A bit." I perk up an eyebrow. "Yeah, it's a lot weird. But in a good way. In a great way." He tucks a lock of hair behind my ear and stares deeply into my eyes. "I'm so glad it's you who's going to be taking care of Ady. For the longest time, I've been thinking of calling you or just showing up at your door. But this is so much better. It's us again for five solid months. He'll warm up, so don't be so hard on him. I know Jasper can be a tightfisted cunt, but it comes from a place of love. At least where Adalyn is concerned."

"It's fine. We're fine." We're not fine. My fault. His fault. But not fine. "But, I should totally kick your ass for all your scheming shenanigans."

He grins. "Babe, you have no idea how deep my scheming shenanigans go when it comes to you. But for real, give Jasper a break. I can already see how tense this is."

I shrug. Jasper and I will eventually find some sort of middle ground. There isn't much of a choice if this is going to work. But with Gus, it feels like we're picking up where we left off. Like all we did was hit the pause button.

I tilt my head, dragging myself up and off the floor. I have to get myself together too, and change into my suit. "What makes you think I was being hard on Jasper?" I ask over my shoulder as Gus follows me out of the playroom and back toward the stairs. I have no idea where my suitcases are, but I'm assuming they're downstairs where I came in. "Maybe he was the one who was hard on me."

He shakes his head. "Only you can rile him up like that."

"I don't think I have that sort of power over him, Gus. Ninety-six percent of the time, he ignores me completely. He left because he was giving me alone time with Ady so we could get to know each other better. His attitude is nothing new."

Gus cocks his head to the side. "You'd be surprised," he says as we reach the first floor, but before I can ask him just what that means, he heads out the front door.

I stare after him for a moment. This day has been so very different from what I expected. Weird might just be the understatement of the century.

I locate my suitcases in the foyer. I guess they weren't sure if I was going to make the cut. Digging through one quickly, I pull out the first bikini I find, followed by a pair of flip-flops, a tee, and linen shorts. Finding the bathroom, which luckily for me, isn't too far away, I shut and lock the door behind me.

Christ, the bathroom that doesn't even have a shower or a tub, is twice the size of my only bathroom at home. "You're not in Alabama anymore," I say with a snicker, shaking my head.

"Move your ass, Vi," Gus yells at me from outside the bathroom.

God, could those twins be any different? Fraternal in more than just looks? They're freaking polar opposites.

And yet, you've been hot for both of them. Fantastic, even my subconscious is being snarky.

"I'll be out in a minute, Gus. You can't rush a lady."

I get undressed, folding my clothes that I came in with and setting them on the marble counter. I change into my black and red rockabilly-style bikini, cover it up with the shorts and tee, and slip into my flip-flops. Piling my hair on top of my head in a messy bun, I grab the clothes I changed out of and exit the bathroom.

I'm ready, I decide. I don't even throw myself a cursory glance.

Because I've got this.

I can handle Jasper Diamond. I can ignore the way my body reacts to him. The way he makes my traitorous heart sprint with a simple glance. It's only five months. Piece of cake.

SEVEN

Jasper

BEACHES IN SOUTHERN CALIFORNIA are misleading. At least at this time of year they are. When you think of Los Angeles, you think eternal sunshine, perfect sandy beaches, and endless waves to be ridden. Most of that is true, but no one talks about how mother-fucking cold the Pacific Ocean can be in early spring. Adalyn doesn't care. She sees water, and she sees waves and fish, and she's sold.

Me? Not so much.

Good thing her new nanny is in the water with her. Wearing a bikini that is designed in form to be the death of every man who looks upon it. Her tits. Christ almighty, I'm doing my best not to look, but they're there, and they're beautiful, especially in the way they curve and overflow out of the top of her red and black bra-like thing. And her legs. I was struggling before with her in that damn skirt, but now?

"At least you don't have to be in the water with Ady," Gus remarks, his voice distant as he too watches Vi. And Ady, I suppose, but I know his eyes are on Viola in her bikini. I wonder if he regrets letting her go all those years back. We never talked about it after she left. Gus isn't a big one to talk about his feelings, and I certainly wasn't going to bring it up. But looking at her now, I have to imagine he's kicking himself. "It's nice having her back. It feels... I don't know. Complete or something."

Gus and I are sipping on expensive beers as we lounge in beach chairs directly behind Lyric Rose's Malibu beach house. This is an exclusive, private beach, but we're both still wearing large sunglasses and baseball hats. Mine is New Orleans Saints; his is Crimson Tide.

I love my brother, but I sort of hate him in this moment.

"How did you know about her, Gus? How often have you been checking up on her?"

"Every couple of months. Spencer Johnson and I stayed close after we left, and he's always had a big mouth. Did you honestly think I'd let a woman like Viola walk away from me without keeping tabs?"

"No," I answer easily, because Gus has always considered Viola to be his. It's why he won, and I lost all those years ago. "You just never mentioned it."

He shrugs a shoulder but otherwise seems unaffected. He takes his time, sipping his beer. "I've loved her forever."

I close my eyes behind my sunglasses before reopening them, blowing out a silent breath. I hate that response. It's the eternal sucker punch he doesn't even realize he's delivering.

"Besides, who else would you trust with Ady for five months on the road? She's perfect for this, Jas. In every goddamn way imaginable."

"Are you using my daughter and her unique situation to win your ex-girlfriend back?"

Gus smirks, the corner of it catching my eye and making my jaw tic. I'm like Pavlov's freaking dog. That's how predictable I already am. "Like I said, she's perfect for this. For Ady. For us. For me."

I rub absently over the tight spot in my chest.

"Just try not to fuck my daughter's nanny. That's not part of the arrangement. We're going on tour, and we all know how you get when we go on tour. I don't want her quitting on me halfway through when you break her heart again."

Gus snickers, taking a sip of his beer. "We haven't been on tour in four years, brother. A lot has changed since then."

"So, you're not planning on sticking your dick into every groupie who looks your way?"

"Maybe," he says slowly, lifting his shades and taking in the girls in the water. *My* girls. "Maybe not." I finish off my beer, chuck the empty into the cooler with a little more force than needed, and pull out another one. He smirks knowingly at me. "She driving you to drink already?" I don't reply. "Ady likes her." I already knew that. She liked her instantly. "And you're sure you don't want to do this all by bus? It's not too late. There's more privacy for us that way."

I know, and I've thought about it. Gone back and forth between that and hotels more times than I can count.

I can't determine if my reasons for not wanting to do this entirely by bus are selfish or not. If we're on a bus, our band would be divided in two because of Adalyn. It would be me, Ady, and now Viola in one bus, and Gus, Keith, and Henry in the other.

Or fuck my life, me, Ady, Viola, and *Gus* all in one bus. Can I survive five solid months sleeping on a tiny bus with that woman right next to me? With my brother and her sleeping right next to me?

The hotel suites feel...larger. Like I'll have more space to breathe air that won't be saturated in Viola Starr. And Gus won't have the option of automatically sleeping so close to her.

However, that's all just reinforcement. No one likes sleeping on a bus longer than they have to, and I'm no exception. But like I said, maybe I'm being selfish.

"Do you think Ady would do better that way?"

Gus leans forward, propping his elbows on his thighs as he watches them, his reflective shades back over his eyes so I can't read him.

"It's a lot of hours on the road. A lot of time where she'll be confined to the bus. If we fly, it's short bursts of travel, and I'd assume more free time between gigs where she can hit up a park or run around and be a kid." He twists his head to find me. "But she thrives on consistency. I don't know. I honestly don't."

I run a hand through my hair, resting my beer on my thigh. "Buses are mad uncomfortable. That said, I don't want my lack of wanting to be close to Viola to impact what's best for Ady."

Gus lets out a loud, exasperated sigh. "When will you stop hating that girl?"

I shrug because I don't have a real answer for that. Let Gus think what he wants. It's easier that way.

I don't keep things from my brother. There are no secrets between us.

Except for this one.

This woman.

She's the dividing force between us, and as a result, part of me does actually resent her for it. Even if it's not her fault. I fell in love with her, and he got her, and that's just how it all went for us. But if you've ever tried to force yourself to stop loving someone, you know how impossible that daunting task is.

Especially, when everything about them draws you in deeper.

"I think hotel rooms are better as often as we can do them. Sometimes the bus is unavoidable. But sleeping on those buses sucks and who knows how Ady will handle that. She's used to sleeping in a real bed, and last time we went to Palm Springs to visit Sally and dad, she was fine with staying in the hotel. She's also familiar with the plane. It'll be fine."

"If it's not, I'm calling it short. Adalyn is a motherless child. One who has been followed by the paparazzi since she was born like there are no other children in fucking Hollywood. If things don't work out with Viola for whatever reason, I won't risk her well-being for a tour. Even if our fans and label want one."

"It'll work out with Viola. She's part of our blood." Gus stands up, tossing his empty into the cooler and taking off his shirt. "Now get your ass up and play with your daughter in the freezing cold water. It's our last day of freedom. The shows begin tomorrow."

Pulling myself up and away from the pleasant comfort of the chair, I slide my shirt off and follow my brother down toward the surf. Viola is discovering something beneath the waterline, both she and Adalyn are bent over, their eyes searching the wilds of the California coast. And for a moment, I find myself pausing to watch them from afar. Differently than I was just moments ago.

I just said this, didn't I? My child is a motherless child.

But I'm watching Adalyn grasp Viola's hand.

I'm watching as the woman I've obsessed over, in one way or another for most of my life, plays with my child.

I'm watching them, and I hurt for my daughter, who has never known that sort of love. The love of a mother. I hurt for a life I was never able to give her. One that will never be possible with the woman holding her hand.

When did it become so hard to breathe?

"You coming?" Gus calls out, and I blink, forcing myself away from emotions I need to get control over. Viola glances up, her eyes locking with mine. I try for a half-grin, knowing anything else will betray me, and I head for the frigid water.

Viola straightens, her hand still holding Adalyn's, but the way her eyes feast on me, devour my chest and abs like I'm a meal she's dying to taste, makes my cock spring to life. She blushes and quickly looks away when she catches my eye again, and fuck, that makes it even better. Maybe this cold water isn't such a bad thing.

"Fish," Ady announces as I approach, her right hand—the one not being held by the nanny, as I shall now refer to her—moves on its side like a wave. I'm assuming that's the sign for fish.

I step into the water and flinch. "Holy fu-udge," I correct, "that's cold."

"You get used to it," Viola offers. "Ady, tell daddy how the waves feel on our feet." Ady looks up at Viola and then me. She blinks. And stays silent. "Do they tickle your toes when you're in the sand?" Ady smiles, giggles lightly, but doesn't verbally reply. Viola smiles, running her fingers through my daughter's long hair and then glances up at me with a what can you do shrug. "She said yes to me before. Even repeated the word tickle."

"Come here, Ady," Gus says, scooping her up into his large arms. "Let's go find some sea glass."

I watch the two of them jaunt off into the surf, and suddenly, I am completely alone with Viola.

She looks uncomfortable, her weight shifting before she splashes out of the water toward the sand, her feet squishing into the golden powder as she stalks toward the chairs Gus and I recently vacated.

"She's incredible, Jas. Like wow. You must be so proud of her."

I glow like a torch on the darkest of nights. "I am. She's the thing I'm most proud of. I can't even find it in me to regret her mother. Without her, I wouldn't have Ady."

"Can I ask?"

She peers over her shoulder, and a second earlier, she might have caught me staring at her ass. "She was a drunk night. A girl I met at an after-party. The condom broke, or so she said. I honestly don't know. That's how wasted I was. Six weeks later, I got a call that she was pregnant." Viola wipes her lower body of the excess saltwater and then slips back into her shorts before taking a seat. I follow, sitting directly beside her. "Do you want a beer?" Viola nods her head, and I open one and pass it to her. Our fingers brush, a jolt of something intoxicatingly forbidden and exciting zaps through me at the contact. Gooseflesh skates up her skin, and I smirk despite myself.

She clears her throat. "Then what happened?" she continues when I don't finish my story.

"Do you honestly not know? It was everywhere for a while."

Viola shifts away from me, staring out at the waves as the late afternoon sun sits heavy in the sky. "No. I honestly don't. After that night, that last one I mean, I stopped...," she swallows. Laughs lightly. "I stopped paying attention. It just hurt too much to keep track." I nod my head, a bit broken by that, but I don't know if she catches the movement. She takes a slow sip of her beer, licking her lips. "So, if you don't mind telling me, I'd like to know."

"I had only met her that one night. And yet, she was telling me I had to marry her. That it was the right thing to do. I told her I wasn't going to do that without, first, confirming the baby was mine, and second, getting to know her better. I promised her I'd take care of her and the baby, but I wasn't just going to marry her outright. But in truth, I was excited over the idea of being a dad. It didn't bother me the way it bothered Gus. He believed I had been taken for a ride by an opportunistic woman, and though he was right, I didn't care so much."

Viola smiles gently at that, turning her attention back to me.

I return her smile before I can help it. "So, you had a baby with her."

I laugh, though there is no humor in the sound. "Sort of. She had the baby, and the paternity test showed Ady was mine. Six months later, Karina was gone. She had been staying with me since she was about five months along, sleeping in the guest bedroom. We hardly spoke. Barely interacted. Then I woke up one morning to feed Ady and found a note, and Karina's room cleaned out. Five months after that, she was dead. Overdosed."

Viola's eyes glass over, her expression stricken. "I'm sorry for Adalyn. And for you."

"Mothers aren't always the best."

Viola takes a large swig of her beer, wiping her mouth with the back of her hand and leaning back in her seat, crossing her long, long legs at the knee.

"No. They're not. But still." She lets out a long, weighty sigh, and I don't push it. If she wanted to talk about her mother, she would. Besides, heart-to-hearts aren't exactly my thing, especially with women named Viola Starr. "Tell me about tomorrow. About what the days are going to be like."

"We're flying or driving from location to location. Staying in some longer than others. Ady and I have a two-bedroom suite, and your room is always next to ours. The shows are usually late, starting around nine for us since we're the main act, but we have to be there for sound checks in the afternoon and then whatever other bullshit we have to do like radio or television or online appearances. You'll need to give Ady dinner. A bath. Get her ready for bed and then put her down. You'll have to stay in my suite or on the bus until I return after the show. Mornings are usually low-key, and you can have some of that time for yourself. You'll need it since this gig is pretty much seven days a week."

She takes another sip. "I don't want you paying off my mother's debt. You're already paying me enough. More than I would earn in two years of teaching."

"It's already done, Vi. Just consider it part of your salary."

She blows out a breath, slinking down further, her crossed leg dropping back down, her toes wiggling through the sand.

"Thank you," she whispers, the sound carrying away in the breeze. "You've saved me in a way. Life sorta sideswiped me, and you pulled me out of the wreckage."

Wow. That's just... Shit. What would her world have been like if I had stayed outside the arena that night? If I hadn't walked away in the first place?

"That was Gus. Not me."

She shakes her head no. "Maybe initially, but it's you, Jasper. You claim to hate me, and I get it. Partially. But you've always been there. Watching from the wings. Letting Gus take all the glory when you're the front man." She stands up, looming heavily over me. I stare up at her, too afraid of what I'll do if I stand and stare directly into those eyes of hers. My green to her hazel. "Spencer Johnson has a big mouth when he drinks. You boys will need to find a new guy to keep tabs on me when this is all over. I don't plan on going back."

Viola walks off, back toward the surf.

I let her go. Because that's what I do where she's concerned.

There is no following her. At least not for me. It's an act I'm going to have to learn to remaster. Because the urge to change everything up isn't so easy to kill this time.

EIGHT

Viola

THE TOUR BEGAN in Los Angeles. The morning after the beach, Jasper and I went over everything I'd ever need to know about Adalyn. What her sleep habits are like. What foods she likes and dislikes. What her eating schedule is. She's on a special gluten and dairy-free diet, so we had to go over that. He explained how long she's allowed to watch either her tablet or television. How well potty-trained she is. The list went on and on.

And it just goes to show the staggering difference between being a teacher and a nanny. One is not easier than the other, and I can't decide which I prefer yet.

Jasper doesn't complain. Not even a little. Complaining is all my mother ever did as a single parent.

Jasper left around three in the afternoon the first two days. I think it was harder on him than it was on Adalyn. That girl is a trooper. Yes, she cried when he first walked out the door, but it only lasted a few minutes, and she let me pick her up and comfort her. Then we played. Had dinner, watched Frozen, and went to bed—me too since I still haven't acclimated to west coast time.

Today everything is different.

There is a buzz in the air. People scurry around Jasper's mansion, gathering suitcases and supplies. That Sophia woman is back, barking orders at everyone she comes upon.

I've stayed out of her way as best I can, having packed up all of my stuff and set it in the front hall first thing. Our flight for Las Vegas leaves in a few hours, and a car is coming to pick us up soon.

It's the beginning of something that makes my insides squirm with turmoil.

Some of that has to do with Jasper.

Whatever air was cleared at the beach between him and I stayed there.

I'd love to say we found a commonality in caring for Adalyn. That we're on friendlier terms. That it's less strained or awkward or that the ceaseless tension between us evaporated.

It hasn't.

If anything, I'm more aware of it now that he's slithered back into the frigidly distant Jasper Diamond I spent my high school years with.

He's always been a kingdom unto himself. Elusive with a confidence and enigmatic sex appeal that renders him untouchable and unattainable.

But he's emotionally removed. Cold and isolated—all part of his charm if you buy into that sort of thing.

And yet, when he's with Adalyn, all that ice melts.

His perfectly crafted barrier that separates him from the rest of the world crumbles, and he smiles with warmth and feeling. She humanizes him. Adalyn is his life force, and it's absolutely breathtaking to watch.

I never believed it was possible for Jasper to be more handsome than he already is, but when he's with his daughter, there has never been a more beautiful man in existence.

Like right now.

Jasper is sitting at the kitchen table, and Adalyn is wrapped up in his arms, simply sitting in his lap. Her head resting on his chest as she listens to the steady rhythm of his heart that beats only for her. They're even wearing matching expressions of quiet apprehension.

He's applying gentle pressure to her back, and that seems to be exactly what she needs to help get through the chaos surrounding her. It's their calm moment before the storm, and though I feel like an interloper, I can't walk away to give them their privacy. I've never had what they have, and it's an odd thing to feel jealous over a small girl, but there you have it.

I never had a father. My mother was too into her drugs and random men to be bothered with loving me.

Maybe that's why I clung to Gus the way I did. He gave me so much love, and I absorbed it like the needy sponge I was. It's not always easy to find the light through the darkness of life. Especially when you don't have a choice but to persevere and move on when that light temporarily dims.

"The car should be here any minute," Jasper speaks softly, afraid to disrupt Adalyn's peace. I can't tell if he's talking to me or her until he tilts his head in my direction. "Are you ready?"

"As I'll ever be." And it's the truth, because saying yes would be a lie.

Like I said, I didn't have a choice but to persevere and move on with my life after it all fell apart. And that's what I'm trying to do here, with this tour, with this girl.

I just wish it had been a different boss driving my path forward.

I don't mind being alone. I don't mind being a loner, and I make it through with that as my reality more days than not. But being here, seeing Jasper and Gus again? I'm afraid of succumbing to something I have no business entertaining simply because I'm lonely and lost, and old habits are hard to break.

And it's only been two days.

The doorbell rings, and I hear Sophia clickety-clacking across the foyer to open it, her dark bob as pristine as the rest of her. Jasper stands up, his baby girl still in his arms.

"How about you, bug? Are you ready to go on a big trip?" Adalyn pulls back to stare into her father's eyes from inches away. Their noses brush, and a smile spreads across my face. "We're going to get into the car and then go to the airport. Then, we're getting on the plane that has the bed you like to jump on. And tonight, we're sleeping in a hotel instead of your bed. Do you remember talking about this trip?"

She stares at him, blinking rapidly.

"You can do this. We can do this together." He kisses her nose and lets out a deep, mournful sigh. "Las Vegas is going to be impossible for her." He adjusts Adalyn, so she's now on his hip, and turns to face me full-on. "It's bright and disorienting, and there are huge crowds of people. She hates all of those things. I don't want her to stay in the hotel the whole two days we're there, but I don't know what there is to do for her."

I take a step forward and run my fingers down the back of her silky hair. She doesn't push me away, but she does shrug a bit, and I know it's because she's still growing accustomed to my touch, my presence.

"There is an aquarium at Mandalay Bay I'd like to take her to tomorrow." He gives me an approving grin as I stare down at Adalyn and ask, "Do you want to go see fish with me tomorrow?"

"Fish," she says softly, and I lean in and kiss her cherubic cheek, running my hand down her hair again.

When I pull back, Jasper is staring at me, and maybe it's just because he feels vulnerable and conflicted about taking Adalyn on this tour or the fact that his most precious possession is still in his arms, but I see everything in his eyes.

It's as if the earth beneath me slips away. Like I'm freefalling, and I don't care where or how I land.

Because God. The way he's looking at me.

So open. So vulnerable.

In those emerald-green depths, I see a million unanswered questions. A world of history between us. A frenetic energy we both seem to want to play off as if it's not there. He stares at me, into me, and I stare right back. I don't flinch or blink or dare look away.

He steps forward, his fingertips brushing mine in the gentlest of ways that slams through me with the force of a tornado. Violent and destructive.

My breath catches, and he whispers, "Viola." But the edge to his tone is sharp. An angry expletive. An unmistakable warning.

I don't know what this is between us. What my name on his lips represents to him.

My throat constricts as his lyrics float unbidden through my mind. *All my dreams die at your feet. My heart spilled, broken and incomplete. No way to stop it or control this angry beat.*

Is that what we are, an angry beat? Something broken and incomplete?

All I know is that its power is intoxicating. Its magnetism wild and uncontainable.

That is until Sophia loudly clears her throat, and his shutters crash back down. He steps away from me, and instinctively, I know I'll never see something that real from him again. More importantly, I shouldn't search for it.

"Everything is loaded into the cars, and we're set to go. The buses with all the equipment left an hour ago and will be in Las Vegas by the time you reach The Colosseum at Caesars. Sound check is scheduled for four, followed by an early dinner. Marco is already there, ensuring everything is set up for your suites and the venue."

Jasper blows out a silent breath and turns back to Adalyn. "Time to go, bug."

His gaze skirts mine as he blows past me toward the front door. I follow after him and climb up into the large SUV on the other side of Adalyn's car seat, which is located in the middle of the backseat. It's a silent drive to the airport; all three of us lost in our thoughts. Sophia did not join us, and I haven't asked if she's tagging along on this tour as well.

I'm hoping not.

We reach the private terminal of the airport and Jasper groans. "Here we go." I lean across Adalyn and him and spot Keith and Henry standing outside the plane, staring straight at the car. "You might as well go and say hi, Vi. They're waiting for you. I'll get Adalyn settled."

"Should I be afraid?" I muse, laughter dancing in my tone.

"Let's just say it's going to be a very long five months."

Jasper gets going on Adalyn's car seat, and I slide out, shutting the door behind me and walking around until I'm a solid fifty feet away. Both boys break out into huge, breathtaking smiles.

"Get your scrawny ass over here. You're only making it worse on yourself by standing there," Keith calls out, and I giggle, throwing my head back for a second before I take off into a sprint and launch myself into his waiting arms. He catches me—this bear of a man could catch a mountain lion—before he spins me around, laughing just as hard as I am.

When he stops, we're both breathless, his arms tucked against my lower back, holding me in mid-air. "I'm so glad it's you. This wouldn't have worked any other way."

"It feels complete now," Henry agrees, smacking Keith on the arm like it's his turn. Keith sets me down, and then Henry wraps me up in his arms, holding me so close. "We've missed you so damn much. I'm sorry I didn't keep in touch. It was shitty," he whispers into my ear. "But now you're back."

I step out of his embrace and cup his bristly face with my hand, staring up into his dark eyes. "For a while. But I've missed you boys. It feels like coming home seeing y'all." I release Henry and look over my boys. "Damn," I hiss through my teeth, shaking my head. "Five months and I'm stuck traveling around the world with you gorgeous assholes. How will I ever keep my hands to myself?" I jest.

"You'll have to," Gus growls behind me, and I roll my eyes

dramatically, making Henry and Keith chuckle. "At least where they're concerned." He snakes his arm around my waist and yanks me into his side, planting a kiss on my temple. "But you can put your hands all over me any time you want, babe. Your sexy donations are always welcome."

I elbow Gus in the flank, and he puffs out a satisfying oomph, rubbing his side and feigning injury.

"I don't think I can handle the two of them for five months," Henry groans. "It was barely survivable the first time. Do you remember all their PDA? It was like watching softcore porn."

I blush furiously at that, but Gus just laughs it off, squeezing me tighter against him and kissing me once more. "Next time, don't watch if you don't like it."

I glare up at Gus, but he's undeterred as he smiles playfully at me. "There is nothing to survive, and there will be no next time or PDA of any kind." I point my finger at him, and he leans in, kissing the tip.

"We'll see about that, babe. I'm even more irresistible now, and we all know you couldn't resist me back then."

"Obviously, it was your modesty that drew me to you," I snark, elbowing at him again. I narrow my eyes at the other two who are just standing there, amusement glittering across their faces. "Besides, I'm not here for you, *babe*. I'm going to be busy working while you all play."

"This is going to be so good," Keith says, his eyebrows bouncing suggestively. "And speaking of porn, I'm thinking we can turn this whole you working and us four dudes playing situation, into something even hotter."

"And this is where I get on the plane and proceed to ignore all of you." I shake my head. "Four boys," I grumble to myself. "What the hell was I thinking?"

"That there is only so long you can stay away?" Keith calls out to me.

"It was rhetorical," I snap back.

"But true all the same." Gus reaches out and snags a quick kiss on my cheek. He dodges back, my hand whiffing past him as I try to slap him away once more. I make a run for the steps of the plane, squealing as Gus chases me.

But the moment I enter the plane, breathless and laughing, I find Jasper sitting in one of the forward-facing seats staring coldly at me.

I practically swallow my tongue and my laughter simultaneously.

This guy seriously only has one gear: Intense. He makes me feel like an errant child caught raiding the cookie jar. And I'm guessing Gus is the cookie in this scenario.

Adalyn is nowhere to be found. I search all around the plane but come up empty. "Did we decide to leave Adalyn home alone after all?" Gus deadpans, clearly wondering the same thing I am.

Jasper ignores the question. "Are you done with your mini high school reunion? We're running behind now."

"Sorry, Your Majesty. Yes. The troops have been assembled and are ready for battle." Jasper's gaze grows acerbic. "Quit being so serious, man. We'll land in Vegas in one hour. That still gives us three before sound check."

Gus wraps his arm around my waist once again, and Jasper's eyes laser in on it before they slowly slide back up to Gus.

"What did I tell you about fucking this nanny, Gus?"

I gasp, my eyes widening in shock. Taking a step back, I trip over my own feet, bumping into Keith, who has to reach out and steady me before I fall on my ass.

"Steady there, girl," he says as he rights me.

Embarrassment skirts up my face.

I can't believe Jasper just said that in front of everyone. Like I'm not even here. Like I'm really and truly nothing to him other than his employee. I resent the hell out of that like it's no one's business.

I'm not some groupie here to fuck Gus. I'm not just the help. Not *just* the nanny. I won't be a throwaway girl. Not anymore. Never again. That's all I've ever been to everyone, and the reminder of it steals my breath and hardens my insides.

"You're a bastard." I don't even care if he's technically my boss and can fire me any second he wants.

He nods his head sharply. "Never said otherwise."

Taking a step in his direction, I loom tall over him. I'm fuming with barely contained rage while he sits there as casually indifferent as ever.

I hate him for that. I wish he were as discomposed as I am.

He stands up slowly, getting right up in my face, our noses inches apart. His gaze is volcanic as it drops to my lips for a half-beat and then back up to lock with mine. My heart rate jacks up, blood thrumming through my veins, making me jumpy, feral. I know there are at least three pairs of eyes on us, but I'm not about to let Jasper get away with speaking to me like I'm the shit he just stepped in.

"Here's the thing, Jasper," I purr, my voice wrapping around him like smooth velvet. "You need me just as much as I need you. Let's not forget that not-so-insignificant piece of this arrangement. You want to go on tour, and you want your daughter to be taken care of. And I need your stupid, hateful money. But not enough to be treated like I'm nothing. I am not *this nanny*. I am *not* nothing. You talk about me that way again, and I walk."

"I don't want him touching you," he seethes.

"That's not your call to make."

The cocky bastard smirks, and I think I'm going to strangle him. "That's where you're wrong, sweetheart. You don't want me to talk to you like you're just the nanny. Fine." He straightens his spine, squaring his shoulders and, if possible, steps in even closer. "But I own your pretty ass for the next five months. And I won't have every-thing with Adalyn or this tour getting fucked up because my brother has a perpetual hard-on for you and every other skirt he likes to chase." He licks his lips, his hand skirting against mine, similar to the way it did this morning.

Only, everything about this moment is different.

Hate ripples from us, covering the tense air like a poisoned cloak as we continue to stand off against each other, neither willing to be the one to back down first.

I lick my dry lips, and his gaze falls instantly to them, black pupils eclipsing green irises. Taking a deep breath, I inhale the scent of his masculine cologne, making me dizzy, and my nipples tighten.

What the hell is going on? My skin buzzes with adrenaline that I grasp onto like it's the only thing keeping me upright and sane.

"I think I hate you."

He grins. "That's what I was hoping you'd say. Makes all this easier."

I have no idea what that means, but I catch the sound of Adalyn in the back room, the door to what I assume is the bedroom, open. I take a step back, my mind clearing, and I storm past him, marching away with heavy steps in that direction.

I may hate her father, but I'm really starting to love this little girl. How can he be so warm and sweet with her and so cruel with me?

The boys all start talking in low, measured tones. Henry's strumming "Dust in the Wind" on a guitar as if that will drown out the sound of their voices. Honestly, I don't want to hear what they're saying behind my back.

I promised myself I'd keep my distance from Jasper.

That I'd keep this professional, and thus far, I'm not sure I've accomplished much of that. I don't have to like him, but I do have to tolerate him, and I think the only way I'll manage that is by staying away from him as much as possible.

I enter the bedroom to find Adalyn upside down by the soft fabric headboard. She smiles at me, and my heart melts a little. *You are the only good thing about that man.*

I climb onto the bed beside her, and she flips her body back over, lying down beside me. "Are you hungry?" She doesn't reply. "Do you want a snack? Some popcorn or granola or grapes?" Silence. "I could really use a good cuddle before we have to go out and take our seats."

The sound of the plane's engines roar to life, and Adalyn crawls up next to me, sinking down and settling in. I breathe out a heavy sigh, my body melting into the firm mattress and soft linens. I give her a hug, a calm I've never felt before cascades over me as her sugary sweet fragrance hits me. This little girl might just be the best thing ever.

"Are you ready to go find daddy? I think we have to sit while the plane takes off." I scoot off the bed and lift Adalyn into my arms.

"Where's daddy?"

"We're going to find him now." Adalyn starts to brokenly sing the theme song to Mickey Mouse Club House, and I hum it along with her, saying a few of the words when she loses momentum.

The last thing I want to do is go back out there and face him. Unfortunately for me, with this gig, I have no choices when it comes to Jasper Diamond.

And I'm starting to think he likes it that way.

NINE

Jasper

"YOU TRULY ARE THE ULTIMATE FUCKSTICK," my brother snaps at me, attempting to get right in my face the way Viola just was. Only, he's far less appealing this close up.

That woman will be the death of me.

That makes twice today I lost myself with her, and it's not even noon. I blame my temporary insanity on the skirt she's wearing. Who travels in a miniskirt? Does all the shit she owns have to show so much skin? Would it be wrong of me to explain how wearing short skirts around a young child is impractical? Demand she wear something else like baggy jeans and heavy sweatshirts? Inform her that her legs are distracting, and I can't focus on anything else when she walks in the room because my eyes have a mind of their own and my dick follows suit?

If it's not the skirt that's killing me, it's the goddamn bikini she wore in the ocean.

It's been three days since she arrived, and I cannot get that image out of my head. Or maybe it's my brother's hands all over her that's driving me up the proverbial wall.

I sit back down, effectively dismissing Gus. I won't get into this with him. I always lose, and right now, I'm not in the mood. Not after that little showdown where Viola told me she hates me.

I deserve it, and I seek it, but it still stings to hear.

Evidently, Gus didn't get the message because he drops into the seat directly across from me, legs spread, elbows pressed into his thighs, fuck you finger aimed in my direction. Freaking Henry is strumming away like he's playing the theme song to our Lifetime movie.

"She was my girlfriend for four years, Jasper. Four. Years. She was my best friend before that. You know how I feel about her. So get over your shit with her and me. I'm not doing anything wrong, and she's a big girl. I won't hurt her again. Some lessons only need to be learned once." And yet, I never seem to with her. "I'm not going to screw her over or this tour up." I knew that's what this was for him. A way back. My heart plummets into the pit of my stomach where the churning acid begins to feast on it. "If I want to try and win her back, that's between me and her."

I want to clench my jaw until all my teeth crack under the pressure. I want to reach across the meager divide between us and strangle him.

I'm so stupid for saying yes to this. So stupid for not planning ahead and thinking all this through. When Sophia told me she was going to find me the perfect nanny, I let her have at it, but with the caveat of having the final say.

So much for that.

Instead, I force myself to remain placid.

Because that's all I ever am. Emotionally detached. Cold. Distant.

The world has no idea how far from the truth that is.

"Your love life, or should I call it fuck life, is your own. But when it starts interfering with my little girl, we have problems. When it starts impacting our work, we have problems. How is that woman going to handle it when you screw around on her again?"

His eyes blaze. "That *woman* is Viola, not some whore you picked up at a party and fucked."

Now I'm seeing red. Because whatever the hell Karina was, she was also the woman who gave me Adalyn. And Karina is dead. Meaning, my daughter is down a mother. Something I'm all too familiar with. So yeah, sore subject.

"Don't," I warn, my tone menacing. No matter how pissed off my brother may rightfully be at me, he knows better than to push that subject.

Gus blows out a heavy breath, losing most of his edge. Sinking back into the soft leather of the seat, he runs his hand through his short light-brown hair. Behind me, the televisions switch on—now that Henry is done with his serenade—and I hear Keith and him starting to do battle in Fortnite as the plane revs up, heading for the runway.

They're no doubt pissed at me too, but they won't get in the middle of me and Gus. In a minute, I'm going to have to go back to that bedroom to find Adalyn. It's not like she'll let me buckle her in, but she'll sit on my lap and let me hold her tight during takeoff.

I brought her on a commercial flight once, and they forced me to hold her down in her own seat and buckle her in. You'd think I was pouring battery acid on her, that's how strongly she reacted.

That was the moment I accepted my daughter is different.

That it was more than just a diagnosis, a speech delay, or not being all that social. It was more than just quirks or idiosyncrasies. Her brain works differently with some things, sensory and tactile things in particular, and bullshit like a seat belt that doesn't bother other children, physically pains mine.

It's another reason I only fly us on this jet. Seat belts are more of an option here, and the one stewardess we have could care less if I hold her. Adalyn's far safer in my arms than she is thrashing around with a seat belt half-across her.

Gus leans forward again, and I cut him off quickly. "I don't want to talk about it anymore. You've made your point about her, and I've made mine. Where it goes from here is up to you."

Gus shakes his head at me like he's done. Like he's so very tired of dealing with my moody ass. Once upon a time, I was a different person. But that was so long ago, there are barely any remnants of him left in me now.

"You don't have to like her. But you do have to respect her. Respect her as the girl we grew up with. The girl who was once your best friend too." I blink at him, wondering if he knows the how or why that all changed. "The woman who is going to keep your little girl safe from the madness we're about to thrust her into."

"Are you done?" He rolls his eyes at me but nods his head yes all the same.

Behind me, I hear the soft sound of Ady's voice. She's singing or humming something, and I drag my head over my shoulder to find Viola carrying Adalyn in my direction. Viola won't meet my eyes, and I don't blame her. I don't deserve anything special from her, like her pretty hazels on mine.

"I figured we'd need to sit and buckle up for takeoff," she says softly, as if she has to explain why she's coming out here.

Her gentle tone is a peace offering, and I hate myself just a little bit more.

Gus is right. Viola's right.

I don't have to engage with her in any way other than as her boss, but I do have to show her the respect she deserves.

I never want to hurt her. The thought makes me sick, but sometimes, I can't seem to rein in the storm of chaotic thoughts and turbulent emotions she swirls up inside of me.

Eventually, I'll remember how to shut these feelings off. How to shut her out again.

"I'll take her," I offer, my tone equally as soft. My own version of an apology. "She won't buckle up. I usually hold her."

Viola nods her head once, staring down at Adalyn, the floor, Gus. Even the door to the cockpit. I stand up and gather Adalyn from her, my hands brushing against her bare arms, and I catch the creep of gooseflesh as it crawls up her skin.

That reaction doesn't help my battle.

Ady buries her head into me as I sit down. She knows the drill. We've flown enough to know what's coming. I sing softly in her ear. It's her favorite song, and she becomes one with me. I hold her tight and kiss her sweet chubby cheeks that still have that touch of baby softness to them.

"Come here, babe," Gus says to Viola, patting the seat beside him and treating me to a sly grin. Now who's the fuckstick? "Sit next to me. It's a quick flight, and this is the best seat in the house. Don't worry about the bloody vagina over there," Gus juts his chin toward me, still grinning like an asshole. "I shoved a tampon in his mouth, and he took his Midol. Shouldn't bother you again."

Viola shakes her head, her nose scrunching up. "Thanks for the mental image. I might have just puked a little in my mouth," she quips.

Slinking down in the seat, she crosses her legs at the knee. The hem of that goddamn skirt rides up when she shifts her position, and I have to force my eyes away.

Gus tosses his arm over her shoulder, tugging her body into his. She goes, but it's reluctant, her gaze that had been dodging mine, finally drifts to me, and I hold it, curious if she's aware of the turmoil she elicits in me.

She swallows, and I watch the roll of her throat, taking in the jump of her pulse at the base of her neck. I bet the skin over it is warm, smells like vanilla–which is probably one of the most basic fragrances out there, but mixed with the scent of her skin is like nothing else.

Is that racing pulse residual uneasiness from our fight or something else?

Viola shifts more in her seat, and Gus's hand drops from her shoulder to her lower thigh, directly above her knee. My jaw clenches before I can stop it, and I hold my daughter tighter as the plane picks up speed, lifting us off the ground and into the air. My stomach drops, and my ears pop, but I can't look away from this woman. Gus is yelling over to Henry and Keith, commenting on their game. Ady is half-asleep in my arms if her heavy breathing is any indication.

It's just me and Viola, locked in some sort of perpetual war.

A dare passing between us. A challenge that attemps to shred what little composure I have. Gus's hand slides up ever so slightly, I'm not even sure if he's aware of it, but Viola is, and she knows that I am, and she smirks. *Tease.*

"She's asleep," Viola comments, breaking the silence. I wonder if it was grating on her.

"It's the white noise of the plane. Puts her out."

"She likes to sing."

My lips hitch up at that. "Wait till you see her at sound check."

Viola's eyes widen. "We get to go to that?"

I lean back in my seat, adjusting Adalyn's small body, so it's more comfortable in my arms, without waking her. "Haven't heard us play in a while, have you?"

She shakes her head no, glancing over at Gus, who is still very preoccupied with Keith and Henry, and then back to me, her cheeks pinking up ever so slightly. "I haven't heard any of your albums since your first one."

Now my eyes widen because that takes me by surprise. I always, foolishly it seems, believed she was following our career. Our music. She was such a large part of it. Always there for practices and gigs.

But when she walked away that night outside the arena, she walked away from us completely. It hurts, though maybe it shouldn't.

"We have three albums since that one, four in total."

"I know," she replies, her cheeks growing warmer by the minute, and Viola is not a big blusher. "I just haven't listened to them."

I wrote the entire first album about her.

It was a product of years of poetry. Our kiss under the giant oak tree in the back of the trailer park she lived in. Walking away from her because I knew the way my brother felt—it was painfully obvious, and he did little to hide it—and I kissed her anyway. Years spent on the sidelines, pining away after the one girl I always felt could see through my facade into the real me. Years of watching her with my brother.

The one person I was dying to have, but never could.

It was an album of love and heartache and the types of fantasies only adolescent boys are capable of.

Even if my obsession with her never felt adolescent.

I wrote the second album after I let her walk away. After I revealed what still feels like my darkest secret—one only she knows. After she broke up with Gus and the rest of us.

Gus was a mess for a very long time. I think we all were in a way.

Viola Starr has a life force unlike any I've ever encountered. She's the brightest star in the night sky—no pun intended. It's impossible not to be drawn to her. Not to want to seek out every mystery and hidden thought behind her warm, sweet smile. After she left, nothing felt right between the four of us for a very long time. Our second album reflects that in my lyrics and Gus's haunting arrangements.

Not every song on that second album is about her. But there are enough that are, and part of me wishes she had heard them, and part of me is relieved she hasn't.

Bearing your soul to the woman who will never be yours is the equivalent of cutting open your chest just to watch it bleed.

My wants versus reality are chronically disharmonized. My desire for her to know everything versus self-preservation is in continuous discord. My thoughts are forever disjointed, which is why I write. It's the only way I make sense.

"We'll have to play something you've never heard during the sound check."

She nods. Swallows. Glances at Gus and then pointedly says, "I already know your first album by heart."

The breath leaves my body in a whoosh. And when I manage to drag some air back into my ravaged lungs, my heart picks up the beats it had missed. A warmth spreads through my blood. A carnal desire.

It's not surprising that she does. She certainly heard us play it a bazillion times over.

But that's not what she's telling me, and both she and I know it.

I want to ask her what she thinks about it. What her favorite song on the album is. Hell, I want her to sing it to me, so I can hear my words flowing out of her sweet mouth.

Gus takes this brilliant moment to prove he was listening to us all along. "I think our latest album is our best. I feel like we really came together as a band with it." Viola blinks away from me, angling her head over to him. "I wish you could come to the show. See more than just the sound check. Watch me play in front of a live audience."

She beams up at him like he's the sun, and I turn away.

"I don't see how that's possible."

"We could figure something out." Gus eyes me quickly, like he's begging me to say yes to that, before turning back to her. "Maybe there is someone else who could watch Ady. Just for a few hours. Marco, our manager, could do it."

Viola shakes her head before I can even respond. "Not to start the tour. All this is going to be so new and unsettling, and I'd like to get her as used to me and comfortable as possible."

Gus sighs but gives in. He knows that's true.

I shift my focus to the small oval window as we fly high in the pale blue sky. No clouds today. I don't listen as the two of them talk. I don't care about anything they have to say to each other, and when the plane begins to descend, I tighten my hold on a still sleeping Ady. Her warm body keeping me grounded, reminding me what's important in my world.

We land with a skip and a hop and the Strip just beyond. Viola's eyes were glued to the window as we were landing, and she still can't seem to pry them away.

"Never seen the Strip, huh?" Gus asks, and Viola shakes her head.

"Nope. Alabama and California are the only two places I've ever been." She glances over her shoulder at him with an unstoppable smile. "Until now."

"Babe, we're about to show you the world. The real one. Not the copy of it." Gus juts his chin toward the window and the Las Vegas Strip. "The real New York. The real Paris. The real Venice. All of it. Vegas is fun, but it's not the same as the real thing."

Viola laughs, giddy and excited by the prospect. "You always did promise me that, didn't you?"

"I made you a lot of promises. Haven't kept most of them yet, but I'm working on fixing that." He winks at her, and I close my eyes, leaning my head back, wishing it were five months from now, and all of this was over, instead of being painfully aware that this is only the beginning.

TEN

Viola

I FEEL LIKE SUCH AN IMPOSTER. I don't belong here, and I'm not sure how I'm going to fake it like I do. It's unlike anything I have ever seen before. The scale of the casinos and billboards are so much grander than I had imagined. I'm like a child glued to the glass of a toy store window. My eyes can't keep up as we drive from the airport to the Strip. But the moment we step foot into the suite at Caesars Palace, my eyes bulge out of my head.

Never in my life have I encountered such over-the-top opulence.

The view of the Strip is all you can see out of the floor-to-ceiling windows that take up the entire wall. There are sitting rooms and dining rooms and a pool table, and wow, just wow. It's incredible.

"Gus, Henry, and Keith are sharing a bigger suite," Jasper announces from behind me, his voice tickling up the hairs on the back of my neck. "Theirs has a staircase and a private Jacuzzi. I didn't think that was the safest thing for Ady."

I snicker, shaking my head incredulously at just how far my friends have come since I knew them seven years ago.

"The life of a rock star," I muse, walking back toward one of the bedrooms since this suite has two. "Must be a drag to have a child holding you back from the parties and the women and the Jacuzzis."

I'm only half-serious, but I'd be lying if I said it wasn't something I was curious about. I overheard Keith and Henry discussing which clubs they wanted to hit up after the show tonight. Talking about the VIP area and the women they were likely to meet, fuck.

Jasper has to come home to his three-year-old.

"Are we being honest right now?"

I spin around to face him, something I've been trying to avoid since our little standoff on the plane.

Jasper is staring at Adalyn, who is running around like a madwoman in what I assume is her bedroom. It's as if all that energy she was bottling up on the plane and the car ride here just exploded out of her.

She's climbing onto one queen bed, jumping down, and then doing the same on the other one since this bedroom has two queens in it. Every time she jumps up on the bed, she screams, "Weee," in pure delight. Every time she jumps off the bed, she yells, "Big jumps." She's also trying to sing five little monkeys, and it's the cutest goddamn thing I've ever heard in my life.

"Yes. We're being honest. I don't think I can handle less between us if this arrangement is going to work."

He nods his head slowly, still watching Ady run and jump and sing before he takes a few small steps toward the entrance of the bedroom and then walks out into one of the sitting rooms. I follow him because now I'm intrigued as hell. He leans his hip into the bar, folding his arms and crossing one leg over the other.

It's funny, sometimes Jasper comes off as so stiff and formal. So rigid and unforgiving. And then I catch him in moments like these where he's just a guy. I never saw much of him like this in high school. He was always so detached with me. So every time I find

Jasper like this, I can't help but take him in, lock it down in my memory for moments he's nothing but austere.

"I miss going out with Gus and the guys. I miss spending time being young without the weight and responsibility of a child. I miss going out for a few beers and watching the ball game on television. I miss losing myself in moments I know better than to lose myself in. But some of that is related to the life of a rock star as you put it. I lost the option of going out for a beer and a game a long time ago. Even before Adalyn. Once Rolling Stone put us on their cover and we had a second number one album, everything changed for us. But the truth is, even though I do miss some of those moments, they're fleeting. I get more pleasure out of watching my daughter than I do in losing myself to a night of partying and women."

Jasper is known for being an asshole. At least he is with me. Rough and unpolished like a hidden gem. But I'm attracted to him in this moment in a way I've never been with anyone before.

It's his crooked grin, maybe. Or the way the green in his eyes is almost lighter now that we're in the confines of a hotel room and Adalyn is happily playing. Or the way he looks so boyishly hot in his black button-up shirt with the sleeves rolled up, dark jeans, and bare feet.

Or maybe it's just the way he loves his daughter.

"What about you, Viola?"

I swallow down everything and ask, "What about me?"

"What's missing from your life?"

That question would almost be laughable if the answer wasn't so goddamn pathetic.

And since we're being honest...

"Life is missing from my life, Jasper. I've been surviving on stagnant air and stale dreams. I think that's why I was so excited about this job. Well," I laugh lightly, biting down into my bottom lip. "Before I knew who I was working for." He smiles back, a warm, genuine one that seeps into my pores like a hot shower on a cold day. "I wanted a way out. A way forward. A change. Something so drastically different, that when it was done, I wouldn't recognize myself anymore."

"That would be a shame," he replies, and I shake my head, not understanding his meaning. "You're the antidote to this life. The sober honesty in my drunk lie. No up or down. Only heaven in hell. Your name on my lips. Your face on my mind. The sober honesty in my drunk lie."

"You wrote that for me." He stares at me, and I can feel my face flush. Neither of us has mentioned this. Not directly anyway, and the words just sort of slipped out now. But still... "That was the bridge for 'Sober Honesty.'"

Pushing off the bar, he breezes past me into the room where Adalyn is still jumping like she's on a never-ending sugar high. "The other bedroom in this suite is yours. It's Ady's first night in a hotel in a while, so I'll sleep in here with her. Sound check is in an hour."

With that he shuts the door behind him, essentially locking me out.

One step forward, six steps back. We're chronically on a seesaw. Up and down–isn't that sort of what he wrote? Always at odds. I wonder if Jasper and I will ever find our balance.

I shrug. I shouldn't have brought up the album he supposedly wrote for me. I should have known better.

Shaking it off, I walk across the suite that is a solid ten times bigger than my ugly leaky studio back in Alabama. It takes longer than it should, but I manage to find what is to be my room for the next two nights. That bed is calling me, and I collapse onto it, pulling out my phone and calling Jules.

She picks up on the second ring, and I don't think I've ever been so grateful for her in my life. I need a girl I can talk to. Bitch with. A friend who will always have my back, even when I'm wrong. That's Jules.

"Why aren't you FaceTiming me?" she asks instead of a greeting, and I roll my eyes, pressing the button to connect us. When her face pops up on the other side of the screen, I flip my phone around and show off my temporary digs. She lets out a low whistle. "Ho-lee-shit. That's some serious cheese those boys are spreading around. Is this room just for you?"

I flip the phone back around to see her. "Yep. It's a two-bedroom suite. Jasper and Adalyn have the other bedroom tonight, but I think in most hotels I'll have my own room. At least that's what they told me initially."

"And how is all that going? Jasper. Adalyn. Gus," she tacks on, quirking an eyebrow with a smirk.

"Fucked. Amazing. Intense. In that order."

She shrugs, tucking a piece of her ash-brown hair behind her ear. "Then it sounds like it's all the way it's supposed to be. Those boys have always been fucked and intense. But as long as the girl is amazing, the rest can be ignored or pushed aside."

I hum out something resembling agreement.

"Or, if it's too much already, being back around Gus, you could come home." She throws her hands up in surrender when I narrow my eyes at her. "Fine, I'll stop. I just miss you, is all, and you already look like they're putting you through hell." I shrug, glancing away, out toward the window. "Can I ask the hard question since you never told me?" I turn back to Jules. "You're the best with kids, especially kids on the spectrum, but you've never worked as a nanny before. You'd think there would be thousands of other possible nannies for this gig, right? Do you know what made them contact you now, after all this time apart?"

"Gus put me up for it. He's the reason I'm here," I admit.

She nods her head like it all makes sense now. "Do you think he's trying to get back together with you? Have you two even talked about what happened all those years back? Does Jasper know what Gus is trying to do with you?"

"Slow down, Rita Skeeter. Stop with the million questions. Gus and I have not talked about what happened, and I honestly don't know if he's trying to get back together. It doesn't matter, though. Nothing is happening there."

This is the part where I should tell my friend about what's been going on between me and Jasper. But I don't. I never told her about the album either. Certain secrets stay in your heart because vocalizing them, putting them out there, ruins every special thing about them.

"It's just crazy to me, is all. It's been seven years, Vi, and suddenly these bastards show back up? I just don't want you getting hurt again. Gus aside, Jasper was always so standoffish and never the nicest to you."

"Thanks for the reminder," I grumble.

"Sorry, but it's true. You know it's true. You're talented as hell, Vi, but you're not a random therapist or teacher. You're Gus's Viola, and that means something is definitely up with you being there. This could get super ugly, super quick, with *both* of those guys, if you're not careful. Jasper can be such a dick, and I'd hate for you to get fired if, *when*, things turn south."

As much as I hate to admit it, she does have a point with all of that. Which makes my interactions, what feels like hidden moments and private rendezvous, with Jasper even more difficult to swallow. Or maybe I'm delusional in all that. Jules is right. Jasper never liked me. I'm not sure anything is different now. I need to keep my distance from him, and yet every time I tell myself I'm going to, something else happens that sucks me right back into him.

I need to find a way to stop the pull he has over me.

"Whatever, stupid boys aside, I want to hear about Adalyn. And you're going to have to send me pictures, Viola. Lots and lots of pictures mixed with lots and lots of juicy details."

I roll my eyes at her once more, ignoring her last statement. "Adalyn is wonderful, but she's a lot of work. Good work, but very different than teaching was."

And then I pause, because I've signed an NDA, and I have no idea how much I can say to Jules without getting my ass sued or fired or whatever would happen for breach of contract. Then again, Jules is a fellow teacher. Just not a special education teacher, but it's not like she doesn't know or understand.

"It's too bad she doesn't have any older siblings. Older sisters. Young girls she could watch, emulate, and learn from."

"I agree. They've said she doesn't do well socially with other children, as you'd expect, but I have yet to witness it. She's also never had a woman in her life. Not really anyway."

"But that's you now, right? At least for the time being. Excluding those crazy assholes, you and this girl can have some fun. Can connect with each other. It sounds like she just needs someone to help unlock all that potential."

I smile as I consider that. I can just hang out with Ady. Help her along, help her learn, but also help her just be a regular little girl. I doubt she's ever had anyone play tea party or dress-up or take her to the playground. Jasper said so himself, he can't just go out anymore without being recognized. But no one knows me. I can do all of these things with Adalyn. For Adalyn.

"I can take her out. Go places with her. Let her experience life."

"That's what I'm saying."

"You're right. I think I will. I was going to take her to the aquarium here. But there are so many things in this world for her to see. It's good for her to push her boundaries."

A new sense of calm and purpose flows over me, and for the first time since I left home, I know I made the right call in coming.

Jules and I continue to talk for the next twenty minutes until I need to get ready for sound check. I'm actually majorly excited about that. I haven't heard the boys play together in such a long time. I hop into the mammoth shower quickly, run a brush through my hair, throw on a smattering of makeup, and then change into ripped skinny jeans, a tank top, and my Docs.

A knock on my door startles me, and when I open it, expecting to see Jasper, I find Adalyn standing there. She's changed too, wearing a Peppa Pig t-shirt where Peppa is covered in mud, jumping in puddles.

"Peppa Pig," she sings and then snorts loudly.

I laugh, crouching down onto one knee until I'm nearly eye level with her. "Jumping up and down in muddy puddles. Splish-splash-splosh," I sing in return. Adalyn erupts into a blissed-out smile, showing off her tiny perfect white teeth and a small dimple in her chin that matches her father's. This girl really is so adorable. "Can I braid your hair? Make it look like Anna's from Frozen?" I ask, staring at her reddish-brown locks. It's long with fantastic curls on the end, but God, how cute would she look in pigtail braids to match her pig shirt?

"She won't let me," Jasper answers for her, walking up behind her. "I tried once. Watched a YouTube video and everything. She squirmed a lot, and then once I finished, she ripped it right out."

"That's a shame. Something we might need to work on, Miss Adalyn." I stand up, touching the top of her head. "How does she do with sound checks?"

Jasper shrugs a shoulder, his eyes on my outfit as he slowly takes me in head to toe and back again. "She's never been to one, actually. But she loves it when we play so it shouldn't be a problem. I have headphones for her if it gets too loud. Sound checks are a bit different than us messing around in the studio or at home."

"You've thought of everything."

Jasper ignores me, bending down and scooping Adalyn up and into his arms. "Wanna go listen to daddy and Uncle Gus play? I'll sing your favorite song."

"Daddy play music."

"Yup," he beams, kissing her cheek. "That's what we're going to do. Will you sing with me?" She wraps her arms around his neck, hugging him instead of answering.

"What's her favorite song?" I ask, unable to resist. I wonder if it'll always be like this between us. Tense. Slightly awkward. Exhilarating.

"Pretty Little Thing." I shake my head because that's one I don't know. Jasper winks at me with a playful smirk etched on his too-handsome face. "I wrote it for her. Sat up all night watching her sleep one night shortly after she was born and wrote it out."

Palpitations. I'm having freaking palpitations. *Stop it heart. Stop it right now before I kick your ass.*

"Then I can't wait to hear it," I manage, suddenly feeling like the walls of this humongous suite are closing in on me. The place already smells of woodsy cologne and summer rain, and Jasper is wearing a black tee that hugs his arms and chest, practically like a second skin, his colorful tattoos mocking me because I cannot explore them. And he's wearing black high-top Chucks like he's still fucking sixteen.

This, right here, this is my problem.

There is nothing more maddening than being attracted to an asshole. To a man you categorically shouldn't want much to do with, because he's not nice or sweet or even good for you. He's cold. Moody. Utterly infuriating, and yet, the heat of his gaze on you becomes your ultimate fix, the hit you seek out like the junkie he's turning you into. I'm already having a bitch of a time shutting him out. Explain that one.

Thankfully, Jasper doesn't like spending any more time with me than I like spending with him, and we leave, silent as we ride down in the elevator because talking civilly to each other for an extended period of time is not only exhausting, it's an exercise in futility.

When we reach The Colosseum, Adalyn and I are directed over to a couple of floor seats by a guy who introduces himself to me as Marco, the manager extraordinaire—his name for himself, not mine.

"Sit here, beautiful ladies," he says with a big smile. "This is the best view of the stage." I sit down, and Marco takes the seat directly beside me. "It's great to finally put a face to the name, Viola. Gus doesn't shut up about you." Marco's eyes are large and so dark they're nearly as black as his hair. He's wearing white skinny jeans that no straight man would ever try to pull off, and a salmon-colored t-shirt that makes his dark skin look so beautiful I can't help but be envious.

"How long have you been their manager?" I ask, ignoring the Gus statement.

"Five years. I started before their last tour, but this one is going to be so much better. This last album of theirs hung in the top ten for twelve straight weeks. It's insane." He stands up, plants a gentle kiss on top of Adalyn's head, and then extends his hand to me. I place mine in his, and he kisses my knuckles. "We're going to be besties in no time, Vi. Trust me; we'll need each other with all this delectable, ego-filled man candy about." I laugh so loud I catch curious glances from the band. I shrug, and they go back to their banter. "Oops. Time to get back to work. I'll see you later, princess Adalyn. So nice to finally meet you, Vi."

"You too," I tell him genuinely. I think Marco is right. We'll be besties in no time.

Marco leaves us, and I'm instantly assaulted with a swarm of butterflies that take flight in my stomach, filling me with a giddy, nervous excitement. Gus, Keith, and Henry are already set up, shooting the shit with each other. Jasper joins in, and the four of them are talking shop, I assume. It's all a bunch of stuff I cannot hear. Adalyn climbs onto my lap, and my hand starts to rub her silky-soft tummy under her shirt.

"More belly," she says the second I stop, and I continue my ministrations that are lulling me into a dazed-like state.

That is until I hear the sounds of Gus's electric guitar.

Adalyn squeals, squirming a little in my lap before standing up on my thighs as I hold her steady. Gus plays a few chords, tuning his guitar as he goes, staring at Jasper, who is doing the same, the two of them having some sort of silent conversation. Henry isn't doing much with his bass, just sorta watching Gus and Jasper and nodding his head to the loose sound.

A woman wearing a microphone and something on her waist walks up to Jasper, handing him an earpiece that he immediately tucks into his right ear. She does the same with each of the guys, and then Keith drops a countdown, in time to a beat he drums out.

Then the boys start playing, and my smile is unrestrainable.

It's a song I've never heard before. Adalyn goes nuts, squealing and jumping up and down on my thighs–*ouch*–so I'm assuming this is her song.

I stand up with her, holding her steady and swaying with her in my arms as we watch the band.

And God, they're so freaking good.

It's really no wonder they've become as big as they are. That they managed to land a deal straight off the bat and continue to produce chart-topping albums. It's so much more than four guys playing music together well. It's the way they play. The sounds they produce. It's the type of music you feel throughout your whole body. The kind that when it comes on the radio, you scream 'hell yeah' before turning it up to full blast and rocking out, singing along at the top of your lungs.

Adalyn sings the words, and I've noticed that singing is one of the only times she'll string words together. I'm not a music therapist, but I'm guessing this girl is as affected by music as her father and uncle are.

Jasper catches Adalyn singing and moves over to the edge of the stage, dropping down to sit on it as he continues to play and sing. I head over to him, still holding Adalyn, and the two of them sing the song together, staring into each other's eyes as they do.

And fuck my life, I'm choked up.

Like seconds away from hiccupping sobs. I can't even blame my overemotional state on my period or anything useful. We'll call it lack of a father-figure and leave it at that.

The song ends, and Jasper's smile is dazzling. Bright and completely uninhibited. I can't help but match it, and when he finds me, breathing hard and slightly sweaty, I swallow my tongue and my breath and my freaking pounding heart.

"Come on stage with us," he offers with a wave of his hand. He gets up, rejoining the band to start another song. He presses his finger into his earpiece and then turns around, nodding to someone sitting with a laptop all the way across the arena.

I hoist Adalyn up onto the stage, which is set at the top of my chest, and watch as she runs off, dancing around in a circle on the other side of it, her hair twirling with her.

Then Gus is there, a hand outstretched to help pull me up. "What do you wanna hear, babe? I'll play you anything you want."

Gus tosses his arm over my shoulder, dropping a kiss on my cheek. He takes my hand and twirls me, matching Adalyn's moves until I giggle, before releasing me to play something on his guitar.

"I have no idea," I laugh. "I don't care. I just want to hear you guys play some more."

"Do you want it fast or slow, baby?" Keith calls out, a shit-eating grin spread across his face, his brown eyes alight with mischief. "Hard or gentle. I can give it to you any way you like."

"Watch it," Jasper growls out. "Ady is here."

"Yeah, but she thinks I'm talking about the music."

"You're not?" I jest. He gives me a head shake and a dirty wink. I laugh, rolling my eyes. "Shouldn't you be?"

"Where's the fun in that?" Keith asks, tapping one of the drums in front of him with his drumstick.

"The fun is me shoving that stick up your ass," Gus snaps, and Jasper throws him a death glare. Gus throws his hands up in the air. "Sorry. Up your butt."

"It's like you never left, huh, Vi?" Henry says, walking over to me, taking his bass off and tossing it over my head. The weight and size of it knock me back a small step because this one is much larger than any I've ever held. It's pretty, though, black and sleek with just the right amount of polish. "These boys are still fighting over the pretty girl, and Gus still has to have the last word." He pulls my arm through the loop of the strap and plants a big wet kiss on my cheek. "Play for us, honey. We all know you can."

I stare at him like he's crazy. "I haven't played for almost ten years, Henry."

"Sure, but I taught you how. It's like riding a bike." I position my fingers on the frets, bringing my other hand up, strumming the strings a few times. "Yeah, girl. Just like that."

"Yeah, Vi. Just like that," Keith echoes in a suggestive tone, and I flip him off in between chords. They all laugh, as Gus joins us, watching me play and matching his guitar to the sound I have coming out of the bass. It's very basic, because I'm not able to do anything more, but it's fun, and I'm hit with the most overwhelming sense of déjà vu and nostalgia all rolled up into one.

This is how I spent years of my life with these boys.

Playing music and teasing each other. It's in this moment that I realize just how much I've missed this. Missed them. I've been lying to myself for seven years, but the truth is here, and it's real, and it's so beautifully raw that I can't help but breathe it in, never wanting to let it go.

Gus and I are smiling stupidly at each other, lost in our shared past, but when I glance over at Jasper, my smile slips, my heart ricocheting around in my chest. He saunters over to us, his intensity making my fingers falter. It's the kind of look that makes lightning zap up your veins and sets the ends of your hairs on end.

"Pick a song, Vi," he offers when he reaches me. "Any song, and it's yours." His eyes sear into mine, making my skin hum, and my knees sway.

He smirks knowingly, a heat to his gaze that wasn't there before.

Fuck. I swallow and stop playing; taking off the bass, I hand it back to Henry. "I-I don't know," I stutter just above a whisper. "Pick a song for me. One I haven't heard before."

Jasper's smirk spreads into a grin as he slides his fingers along his electric. A few seconds later, Adalyn starts jumping up and down, excitedly screeching. Gus and Henry move closer to her as they quickly pick up the song and play, leaving me alone, standing here in this emotional abyss with Jasper.

"This is from our second album," he whispers to me just as Keith comes in with the drums. "I wrote it about seven years ago. After a particularly long night in Los Angeles." He winks at me. My eyes widen, my lips parting in a silent breath. My heart? Well, who the hell knows where that traitorous bitch went? "We never play this song live anymore. Only when goofing off and messing around. It reminds us of home." He locks eyes with me. "Of the people we let walk away."

We're toeing the line. Dancing along the edges.

He saunters off to join his band, and I'm forgotten once more.

But there's something brewing here.

Something wild and dangerous. Something with the power to destroy. Something neither of us seems particularly adept at ignoring.

ELEVEN

Jasper

THE SHOW WAS FUCKING AWESOME.

I enter the back room on a performance high unlike any I've had before. We're all feeling it. Our smiles uncontainable. We're covered in sweat and salt and fucking elation.

"Motherfucker," Gus bellows, chugging down an entire bottle of water and chasing it with a few hefty gulps of Patrón. Why they felt the need to set up an entire bar back here, I'll never understand. It's not like we asked for it. Feeding the cliché, I suppose. "That was the end-all. I mean, there is no up from there."

"You, asshole," Keith points at me, "were on *point*. I don't think you've ever hit those notes like that before. I mean, what the hell?" He shakes his head in bewildered awe. "And the crowd, man. They were eating us up. We killed it!"

"Did you hear my solo?" Henry asks, staring at his hands like they're works of art. His dark eyes wide in wonder. "That riff, broth-

LOVE TO HATE HER 111

er." He shakes his head, smiling like the devil. "Gus, you have to write more like it for me."

I stare at my brother and then my lifelong best friends, and I blow out a breath. I'm ready to jump out of my skin right now. I can't stop moving, and this buzz is taking over everything. I can't remember the last time I felt this...*good*. Like everything in my universe is balanced.

"Thank you," I say to them. "For pushing this tour on me. I forgot...," I shake my head, suddenly turning pussy and overcome. "I fucking forgot this." I splay my arms around the room. Around us. Between us.

"Epic," Henry agrees, taking a step toward me, slapping his hand on my shoulder. Then Gus and Keith do the same with each other until we're all linked together. Like one entity. One force. I don't even care if it's cheesy. This moment feels that big.

"Legendary."

"Incendiary."

"Prodigious."

The four of us stare at each other for a long moment and then burst into peals of laughter.

"I'm taking a shower and then going out to get laid. Big time. Like crazy Vegas-style sex. Who's with me?" Keith asks, and for a moment, that sounds so damn tempting. I cannot remember the last time I had sex. I mean, I know it was sometime back when my last nanny was still around, and she stayed late to watch Adalyn so Gus and I could go out. Translation, so I could go out and get laid. But that was at least six months ago.

So, sex? Yeah, that sounds pretty damn good.

But...

"Vi is with Adalyn in the suite, right?" Henry spits out, reading my thoughts. "You deserve a night out. A night off daddy duty. Seriously. When the hell was the last time you had a break?"

I shrug, because like I said, it was a while ago. I'm always on daddy duty. Especially since I've been nanny-less.

But here's the other side of this coin. The last meaningless sex I had was just that, meaningless. I cannot even remember what the girl looked like. How we did it.

It was just sex.

There was no connection. Nothing beyond the standard get in, get off, and be done. The woman signed an NDA–talk about hot–and then we got down to it. It was all so boring. Mechanical. Wholly unsatisfying.

And unfortunately, the thought of jerking off in the shower to images of Viola Starr on her knees sucking my dick is far more appealing.

Besides... "I don't want to be hungover, stinking like random pussy when I wake up tomorrow morning in the same room as my little girl."

"Thank God," Keith drawls with a loud chuckle, sipping from a bottle of Jack Daniels. "The girls never look twice in my direction when you're there."

"That happened one time," I grouse, some of my show buzz wearing down. I wish I could bottle up this high. Drugs have nothing on this. They don't enhance it either. Maybe that's why I never got the fact that rock 'n' roll was last in the whole sex, drugs, and rock 'n' roll thing.

Gus looks at me. Hard. And for the first time in my life, I cannot read the open book that is my brother. "Do you want me to stay with Ady tonight?" He's genuinely offering. It's not even a half-hearted, trying to be a good guy when he really wants to go out, thing.

My brother is an incredible man. A stand-up guy. He's offering to do me a solid, knowing just how long it's been since I acted like a guy in my twenties. But all I can think about is him being alone in that suite with Viola while Adalyn is sleeping.

It's fucked up.

It's completely wrong.

And yet...I can't stop it.

I don't want Gus to have Viola, but I want both of them to be happy. Gus loves Viola. And Viola likely still loves him back, if the way she looks at him is any indication. If he had never been a cheating swine, I'm sure they'd still be together. Probably in wedded bliss with multiple babies.

But I can't see it. I can't watch it. And I'm certainly not ready to face it.

"Another night, okay?" I say, which feels ridiculous. *Another night I'll let you be the stand-in dad, so I can go out and fuck someone.* That's essentially what I'm saying, right? But screw it, I'm so very done with random and meaningless. Especially when I can't get one particular woman out of my head.

And it's only been a few days. Right. Awesome.

"You sure?"

"Yeah. I'm sure. I'll go raid my mini bar, watch some crappy television, and go to sleep. But hey," I smack Gus's chest, clasping Henry's shoulder. "We rocked it."

The four of us gather our shit, Keith and Henry heading for the door when Keith, the asshole, turns back over his shoulder and says, "Let me know what Viola wears to bed." He grins devilishly, "Better yet, take a picture and send it to me."

Keith is a ballbuster if ever there was one. He's been saying crap like that about Viola, to Viola, since we were teenagers. I also know he loves her and isn't really serious. At least I don't think he is. I shouldn't care that he just said that.

But I do.

Because I haven't yet found the magic pill to lock her back out of my thoughts. It's like I can't find the off switch I once possessed.

I don't even get the chance to respond. Gus smacks Keith upside the head. And not gently. "Watch what you say about my future wife."

My steps falter. If I had any illusions about Gus going after Viola, they're now gone. *Future wife.* Christ, that's a jagged knife to the gut, twisting back and forth. And it *hurts.*

Five months.

But even I know that's a lie.

Because if Gus plans to make Viola his again–and that's obviously what he was trying to do by offering to watch Ady for me tonight–then I'm stuck with them together for an eternity.

The acrid taste of jealousy and resentment burn my throat. I plow past the guys, thrashing my way down the long corridor, before I'm stopped by a large black man who introduces himself to me as Marsellus Wallace, only to follow that up with, "And if you mention Pulp Fiction to me, I'll let the fans have at you."

I grin wryly, shaking the large man's hand as I say, "I wouldn't dare. But can I ask?"

He shrugs. "My parents had a thing for the movie, and our last name is Wallace."

"Okay, then." Not much else to say about that. "Are you my guy here in Vegas, or are you joining the tour?"

"Joining the tour."

"Awesome. Then you know my situation?" He nods his head in the affirmative. "Are you assigned to my daughter as well?"

"No, sir. I'm assigned to you. Your assistant, Sophia, assigned someone else to look after your daughter and her nanny."

"Perfect. But never call me sir again."

Marsellus grins at me, a big white toothy grin, and I decide I like this guy. Pulp Fiction reference and all.

"I must tell you that we've had a lot of women attempt to sneak backstage. We've also had a lot of them try and discover which suite you're staying in so they can find you and your bandmates." Fantastic. Who needs a club when the harem comes to us? But again, random and meaningless... "None of them had passes and were not permitted access. Is this how you guys do things, or should we let some of them back?" He shrugs a large shoulder. "Every band I've worked with is different."

I shake my head. "No. I don't like a lot of groupies backstage, and the other guys don't either. Especially before a show. If the opening acts have a few, that's on them, but I don't want them in our area."

"Got it. I should also tell you that there have been a lot of press around. I was told this is not standard for a show around here."

My eyebrows knit together. "How so?"

Marsellus shifts, facing me head-on. "Hanging around after the show was over. Same as the girls, but even pushier. Marco said it's just because this is your first stop and that it will likely die down soon. But he wanted me to make you aware of it."

"Thank you. They haven't accessed any of the suites, right?" He shakes his head, and I practically sag in relief. "Good. But going forward, I'd like to make sure the hotels are aware that this could potentially be a problem. I don't want my daughter or her nanny at risk."

"Of course. I'm on it."

We make it back to my suite, up the private elevator, and no one so much as stops us. Marsellus leaves me at the door, and the second I slip the keycard against the lock, my heart begins to hammer.

Because, what *does* Viola wear to bed?

And why on earth did I agree to let her stay in the same goddamn suite as me tonight?

The door lock disengages, and I reluctantly open it, shutting it behind me as quietly as a person can shut a hotel room door, which let me tell you, isn't all that quiet. The curtains in the main living space are still spread open wide, the bright lights of the Strip filtering into the dark room, providing me with plenty of street light pollution to see by.

I glance to my left and notice Viola's door is shut, and then to my right to find my bedroom door is also closed. I blow out a silent breath, somewhat relieved to be alone.

Locating the bar, I pour myself three fingers of something with an amber tint to it, crack open a thing of mini bar peanuts and walk over to the chaise that rests in front of the windows and the Strip beyond.

Only, before I can get halfway across the room over to that chaise, a head pops up from it. A sleepy Viola blinks at me, her wild light hair in disarray. She catches sight of me and waves. Fucking adorably waves at me.

Standing up, she stretches out her long limbs, and I now have the answer to that question.

Viola sleeps in a tiny, cut-off, see-through, white tank top and smaller than small cotton shorts. Her long, satiny legs flex as her hands stretch up above her head, raising the hem of that too-tight, too-small, and too see-through tank even higher. The outline of her full, perfect tits is staring me in the face.

That might be my own fault since I can't seem to force my gaze away.

"Hey," she says, her voice rough and irresistibly sexy, thick with sleep. Her cheeks are flushed, and her eyes are heavy and *fuck...* "How was the show?"

It's moments like this that I hate having a dick. At least an interested, single-minded one because if it weren't dark in here, she'd see the tent I'm pitching, even through my snug-fitting jeans.

"It was incredible," I admit, my smile coming back to me as I think about the show. "Shit, Vi. It was the best we've ever done, and this is only what? The third night of the tour? Our first real stop?"

Viola smiles so brightly, and once again, I forget how to breathe.

"Pour me one of those, would ya?"

I head back to the bar, grabbing another crystal tumbler and pouring her a few fingers. I take a steadying breath. Then another. Willing my heart and body to remember who this woman is and the danger she poses for them.

"Why didn't you go out with the guys? I figured you would. It's why I was camped-out here, so I could hear Adalyn if she needed me."

Christ. What do I say to that?

I may have a million issues with this woman, but she really is as sweet, considerate, and caring as they get. You'd think she'd be hardened or bitter by all she's dealt with in her life. No father. A mother who barely took care of her before she stole from her. A cheating boyfriend. A best friend who turned his back on her after kissing her. Losing her job. It feels like it never stops with her. I mean hell, I'm as bitter as they come, and though I've been through more than my share of misery, I feel like it's nothing compared to hers.

But Viola is always smiling. Eternally optimistic with a heart so big it can hold the world.

She asks for nothing.

Gives easily.

Maybe that's why she's taken advantage of so readily.

For me, it only makes me want to protect her more. Give her everything.

"Thank you," I start with. "That was amazingly generous of you, but I didn't want to be a mess in the morning when she wakes up." That's not exactly a lie. "Did she go down okay?"

"Yes. I read her two stories, sang the song you wrote for her, and then she passed out. All that jumping around and that dairy-free, gluten-free pizza. Oh, and we can't forget the dairy-free, gluten-free ice cream." Now she's just messing with me. "Can I ask if that diet helps?" I return to her, handing her the glass of bourbon. Simultaneously we lift our glasses, clinking them against each other. "Congratulations on a fantastic start to your tour."

"Thank you. Cheers."

We each take a sip, our eyes locked as we do. I sit down on the chaise, staring out the window at the glowing lights. At the faint hint of the mountains beyond. Anything but her.

"I don't know if the diet helps," I concede. "When she was first diagnosed, I did a shit-ton of research and found blogs and parents' testimony that described how their child did this diet, and suddenly, it was like they weren't autistic anymore. Most of their reports seemed to be behaviorally linked, but I feel like Adalyn isn't so bad with some of that. No more than what I expect any three-year-old to be. Yes, her tantrums can be extreme. Yes, her reactions to random things I would consider innocuous aren't always typical. Yes, she makes random facial movements and verbally perseverates. I don't know. I don't see those as things to change–they're part of who she is. In any event, I haven't seen much improvement with the diet change, but I keep it going all the same."

"You know I'm just teasing you about the diet, right?" Her elbow juts out, running up my arm once before it's just as quickly gone. "I would do the same thing if she were mine. You're an incredible father, Jasper." My head whips over in her direction, a little stunned by the compliment. She smirks at me, like she can read my thoughts. "Don't let that go to your head. I still think you're an asshole, and I still don't particularly like you all that much." I chuckle, taking another sip of the smooth, buttery bourbon, enjoying the rush of warmth as it flows through my veins. "But you are an incredible father. Adalyn is a very lucky girl to have you as hers."

"Thank you. And because I don't particularly like you either, I can tell you that means a lot."

She giggles, sinking back down on the chaise and crossing those long, long legs of hers. "All of this is so different, so far removed from how we grew up." Her arms pan around the room and toward the Strip beyond. "I assume I'll adjust to it like it's anything else, but how do you get used to this? To fans and stardom?"

"Can you keep a secret?"

Her gaze zeroes in on mine, her lips flattening out into something so very serious. "Anything you ever tell me will always remain between the two of us."

I believe her, and it's a brutal honesty I need and respect like nothing else.

"It's an adjustment. I fly in private jets, live in a mansion, and if I want to go to the grocery store, I have five different cars to choose from to take me there. I like that Adalyn never has to worry about money. My current circumstances aside, I've ensured that for her. I like that I'm able to donate to charities and live in a nice place and drive nice cars. Other than that? Well," I chuckle, "it makes me feel like a pretentious dick."

She smiles conspiratorially. "You handle it well. All this fame and money. Nothing pretentious about you. I admire you for the way you take care of Adalyn. For the way you put her first. Even above your tour. This must be such a change for you."

"You being here somehow doesn't make it feel so."

"It's weird, right? This situation."

"It is. But I guess I shouldn't be surprised. It was only a matter of time before Gus came back for you." I do my best to hide every single bitter note from my tone. I'm not sure I fully accomplish it.

Viola blows out a breath. It's weighty. Laced with questions she doesn't seem to have the courage or desire to ask. "Seven years is a long time," is all she finally says, sipping her drink as I sip mine. "I'm not the same girl, Jasper. A lot of things in my life have changed since Gus and I broke up."

"I know that. You're not the same, and yet you are. We rocked that show tonight because of you. Because our fifth member is back, and now it all just feels complete." *And I don't know how to process any of that.* "You're our missing piece."

The words slip out, and I regret them instantly. All of them. My tone is a combination of reverence, resentment, and jealousy, and I don't want her to know the power she has over me. Over us.

She glances over at me, our eyes meeting in the darkness. And instantly, I feel stripped bare. The way her bright eyes take me in, make me feel seen in a way I don't think I ever have. How did she do this to me so quickly? Or had I never truly pushed her out, and this is just reawakening a slumbering beast?

"You've been doing just fine on your own without me."

Have I?

Suddenly, I'm not so sure.

Maybe it's the performance high that's making me hyper. Maybe it's her or what she's wearing or the way I cannot unsee her now that I've seen her again. I don't know. But right now, here in this moment, I wish I could turn back time and find someone else to nanny Adalyn. I wish I had never seen her again, because now that I have, she's the only woman I ever want to look at.

Here's the thing with obsession. It's engrossing.

That's what Viola is, has always been for me, engrossing. I used to think about her constantly. Fantasize about her every which way to Sunday. Ignore her like the petty, jealous asshole I was.

But I was goddamn consumed.

Everything in my life revolved around her. Our music. My poetry. Our band. My brother. My lust. My heart. Even my avoidance, jealousy, and anger. She owned all of it.

This woman unwittingly ate me alive from the inside out for years, and I don't want to let her do that to me again. I've had enough for one lifetime.

I can handle jerking myself off to images of her. I can handle her taking care of my daughter. But this drink after the high of the show? This knowing she's meant for Gus and not me? They might just be my tipping point.

"I'm going to bed," I finally manage to say. She frowns, and I can't tell if she's disappointed or just able to read me better than I'd like.

"Probably a good idea."

Neither of us moves. We just continue to watch each other like there is nothing more fascinating in the world.

I glance down, catching her swallow, only to continue the journey and discover her nipples are hard, poking through the thin fabric of her shirt. My cock jerks back to life, begging me to take action. I'd kill to know what they taste like. To lay her flat on her back on this chaise, remove these bullshit excuses for clothes, and devour every inch of her. To make her wild, crazy with my touch and my tongue until she's begging me to fuck her.

To make her fucking *mine*.

I want...*her*. I've always wanted her.

Time and distance have changed nothing with that.

"Good night, Viola."

"Good night, Jasper."

We still don't move. *Move, dammit. Walk away,* I silently plead.

But then I remember that's my part in all this.

So I slam down the rest of my drink and force myself up and off this goddamn chaise and away from her. She watches me go. I feel it. And I vow to avoid her from here on out. To treat her like a nanny. A caretaker for my daughter. No more playing songs written about her. No more innuendos or late-night drinks.

No more.

I survived you once, Viola Starr. I'm determined to do it again.

TWELVE

Viola

"YOU LOOK TIRED," Jules says to me.

I roll my eyes at her. "That's because I *am* tired."

"Where are you exactly?"

"Trying to sleep in the bed on the plane. We're delayed, just sitting here on the tarmac."

"Then why are you talking to me if you're trying to sleep?"

"Because you FaceTimed me. And I can't sleep; it's like two in the afternoon. And Adalyn is running around. And Keith and Henry are doing battle on Fortnite right outside the door."

"Oh," her eyes widen. "Are they any good at that? I totally suck, but the guy I'm fooling around with fancies himself a gamer."

"I honestly have no idea. And what guy you're fooling around with?"

She grins wickedly at me, her eyebrows bouncing up and down. "He's new."

"Must be. I've only been gone a couple of weeks."

"Time flies when you're busy jet-setting," she says with a tone I can't quite decipher. "How are things going with the man meat? Have you two fucked each other out of your systems yet? Is Jasper Diamond officially dead at your hands, and you need me to help you cover it up? And where are my pictures? I want pictures."

"I'm going to ignore those non-questions. And I'll send you pictures soon."

"Is now a bad time to tell you that your mother came to the bar the other night?"

"What!" I screech, bolting upright. My long hair covers my face, and I have to brush it away quickly so I can catch Jules's expression and decide if she's just messing with me or not. Nope. She's telling the truth. "Seriously? For what? I thought she had skipped town."

"I don't know," Jules sighs, shaking her head and biting into her bottom lip, sympathy etched in her features. "She was there looking for you. Spencer was stupid and told her about your new gig, and then she left. That was it. I didn't serve her, and she barely spoke to me. But the devil was in her eye, Vi. Especially after she heard what your new gig is."

"Fantastic. Just brilliant. Because only good things come when my mother is trying to find me. She's already bled me dry financially. What the hell could she be after now? And seriously, why the hell did Spencer have to open his big mouth with her?"

"No idea, pumpkin. But if I were you, I'd be careful. That woman has a way of getting access to things she shouldn't and exploiting them."

Ain't that the truth.

A swell of uneasiness creeps up my spine. What if she tries something? Tries to hunt me down? Tries to come after Jasper and Gus? After Adalyn? I put nothing past that woman. She's a liar and a cheat. A thief.

"I didn't mean to freak you out, Vi. It'll be alright. Like I said, she left, and really, it's not like you're in one place. You guys are everywhere, staying in nice hotels with great security all around you."

I nod numbly, my insides still unsettled. I do my best to shake it off, scrubbing my hands down my face, and yawning into them.

I really am tired.

Adalyn did very well the first couple of nights going down, but for the last week or so, she's been having a lot of trouble getting to sleep when Jasper is not around. And a lot of nights, his show doesn't end until after midnight. To say the poor thing is sort of a hot mess is an understatement. All the confusion and on-the-go and new places to stay are throwing her through a loop.

And me along with her.

"I know," I mumble. "I'll never get the cash back that she took. And the bank is still holding firm on not calling it theft since her name was still on the account. But I positively never want to see that woman again. I don't even care if she apologizes. Her taking that money was the final straw."

"I'll let you know if I hear anything else."

A knock sounds on the door. "Vi?" Gus asks gently. "You okay? We heard you scream."

Jules's eyes widen, a knowing grin crawling up her lips. "You can come in, Gus," I call out. "I'm talking to Jules."

The door to the bedroom opens, and Gus enters, jumping up onto the bed beside me. He leans in, staring down at my phone, and then smiles brightly. "Hey, Jules. You still taking a sad song and making it better?"

"God," Jules snickers. "That's so lame. You look good, Gus. A little fat, maybe, but good."

Gus fumes. "Fat? You think I'm fat? Check this action out." He climbs up onto his knees, lifting his shirt and flexing his abs, revealing his hard six-pack that dips into his low-slung jeans.

Yeah. Definitely not fat.

"Oh, nice," Jules hums appreciatively. "Vi, touch those for me. Let me know how they feel. Wait, I can't see from this angle. Does he have that V thing? I'm taking screenshots as we speak. Vi, run your hands down those bad boys."

"I'll pass."

"For the record, I'm calling supreme bitch that he's your guy, and I'm left with pudding abs."

"I have no idea what that even means, and he's not my guy."

"Pudding abs?" Gus howls with laughter, smacking the thin mattress a few times for good measure. Very helpful. "That's a tragedy, Jules. You should have stuck with Keith. That dude lives in the gym." Jules's gaze narrows before it turns into a bloodthirsty glare. Keith dumped her a decade ago. Gus is oblivious. "And don't lie, Vi. I'm always your guy. Now come on," Gus encourages. "You can touch. We all know you want to. I didn't look like this the last time we were naked together, did I, babe?"

I open my mouth to say something snarky, when he grabs my hand, forcing it up and down his washboard abs. And yup, they're as impressive as they appear. Very sexy, if we're speaking truths. And he most certainly has that V thing. Not an ounce of pudding to be found.

I yank my hand back, giggling and shoving him away. "Pull your shirt back down, Superman. We all know what you look like without your clothes on. Hell, you've got a ten-story billboard of you in your underwear in the middle of L.A."

He does. I saw it when we drove to the beach that day, and he was sure to point it out in case I missed it. I didn't. I stupidly stared at it because I'm still a dick-loving female, and no, Gus most certainly did not look like that the last time we were naked together. I can only imagine the number of accidents and traffic jams that billboard has caused.

"That reminds me," Jules says as Gus slinks back down next to me, kissing the side of my face and nuzzling his nose into my cheek. I push him away again, and he grins, loving the hell out of bothering me like this. "Did they stuff your junk for that picture? I mean, you're selling underwear, but I don't remember Vi ever mentioning your dick was that big." She holds up her pinky finger, wiggling it back and forth.

I burst out laughing, but Gus is most definitely not laughing.

"Bye, Jules," he growls, hitting the red button on the screen of my phone and tossing it to the edge of the bed. "You told her I have a small dick?" He's back up on his knees, staring down at me. I can't tell if he's serious about this or not. I gnaw my teeth into my bottom lip.

He's unbelievably sexy like this, and it's throwing me off.

"Well...it's wrong to lie to your friends."

"Maybe you just need a reminder of how big I really am."

He grabs me by the legs, swinging me around to face him and then yanking them until I'm on my back, his body large and looming. I scream out, laughing so hard I'm practically crying as he climbs on top of me, straddling my thighs. His knees dip into the firm mattress as he crawls up my body.

"Gus–" I warn as he starts to unbutton his jeans, his eyebrow cocked up in challenge, an impish grin spreading across his handsome face.

"I used to rock your world." He leans in a little. "Remember?" his tone turns husky. Heated. His eyes dark charcoal. "You'd scream from the orgasms I gave you. It'd be my pleasure–and yours–to do it again."

"No," I squeal, laughing as he jostles me between his muscular thighs. I try to smack his hands away from his button and zipper. "I don't want to see it, Gus. I still have nightmares over that thing. When they interview me for 60 Minutes, asking me how large your dick is, I'll tell them it's huge. I'll lie. I promise."

"You fucking brat," he hisses, grasping my hand and shoving it against the bulge in his pants. My eyes widen, and my mouth pops open. Holy crap, he's *hard*. Like full-on boner hard. "You so sure that would be a lie, darlin'? Does this feel small to you?" He grinds himself against my hand, and his eyes darken further. "How big do you think it would feel inside of you? How good?"

Oh, Lord. My body bristles like an overused scrub brush. "Gus Daniel Diamond," I half-squawk, trying for stern and foreboding while smiling like the Cheshire Cat. I shouldn't be smiling while a man presses my hand against his dick, but something about Gus makes this playful and me unafraid.

Or stupid. I can't determine which.

His hand squeezes against mine, which in turn presses against his dick, and he emits an exaggerated groan. Maybe I was wrong about playful.

"This is not friends behavior." I try to slide my hand out from under his, but it's not going anywhere. I can't believe how turned on he is.

"Oh, I disagree. This feels *very* friendly."

I tilt my head against the bed, surveying him harshly. "Release my hand before I scream creepy pervert. Or punch your balls and watch while you cry out like a little bitch."

He laughs, finally allowing my hand to slip away, falling back down to the bed. He stares at me, deep and hard and filled with wonder.

"Do you have to be so pretty?" His fingers caress my cheek. "You make it damn hard to be friends when all I wanna be is more. Do you remember being more with me? We were really good at it."

We were until we weren't.

"Is that what you were with the girl I saw you with the other night? The one you brought into your hotel room after the show?"

The truth is, it didn't bother me.

I don't know what I was expecting, but I didn't even get a flicker of jealousy. Which is why this moment is more fun and amusing than erotic. I'm not all that turned on by touching his cock–I mean, maybe I am a teeny-tiny bit. Gus is supremely hot. But I'm still not all that turned on. Not enough to want to do anything about it, and I feel like this is the sort of thing that should turn me on more than it is.

Because yeah, Gus isn't small. He's quite big actually. And yeah, he used to rock my world.

But now? Now I don't see this man through lust-tinted glasses. I see him more as a best friend. The way I see the other guys.

Well...with the exception of their asshole front man.

Maybe it's because Gus cheated, and once that happened, I was emotionally done.

Cheating is my hard limit. My ultimate trust breach. One of them at least. He knew it, and blew right past it. So, I don't think I could ever look at him the way I once did.

He shrugs, not even bothering to hide it or deny it or look broken-up that I saw him. "She was just a girl, Vi."

"That's all they ever are, Gus."

"Not you. You were never just a girl. You're *my* girl. I'd give them up for you, you know. This second."

I shake my head, smiling up at him. My lost boy. Will he ever find contentment in the long-term? Will he ever find the girl he stops sleeping around for without her having to ask? I hope so.

"No, you wouldn't. And I'd never ask you to. That time is behind us."

"One day I'm gonna get serious, and you'll already be gone."

"If you're not serious about me now, you never will be."

And that's the truth.

If he loved me more than he loved the random girls, we wouldn't be having this conversation. Hell, our entire relationship all those years ago would have been different. But Gus and I aren't it. We're not the couple we were when we were seventeen, and all we could think about was each other. People change. Relationships evolve. Sometimes you grow together, and sometimes you grow apart. Gus and I are the latter.

Gus smiles gently, a sparkle in his eyes. His face shifts closer until we're inches apart. His nose glides against mine, our lips brushing. He pulls back the smallest of inches, staring deeply into me.

"I couldn't love you more, Vi. It's the only reason I can do this with you."

I furrow my eyebrows, utterly baffled by his meaning. I open my mouth to ask him what he's saying when someone clears their throat so aggressively it causes me to start. Jasper is standing on the threshold, his hands holding the thin frame of the walls like they personally offended him.

"Don't you knock?" Gus calls out without turning away or moving an inch from me to acknowledge his brother.

"No. Get off her," Jasper bites out, his gaze dark and cool. "The plane's ready to go."

"We'll be out in a minute," Gus smirks, winking at me, knowing Jasper can't see. Fucking Gus. Will he ever tire of pushing his brother's buttons?

Jasper takes a small, measured step into the room. "Now, Gus. We've already been delayed, and they won't take off with you two in here."

"I said we need another minute."

Jasper growls out, scrubbing his hands up and down his face, his movements flustered and slightly uncoordinated. He curses under his breath and spins around, pressing his hands back onto the frame of the door.

"Adalyn was asking for you, Viola. And since you're clearly not sleeping like you said you were, maybe you could do us all a favor and act like the fucking nanny I pay you to be and come be with my daughter."

Gus's eyes widen, his smile spreading into an 'oh shit, he's really pissed now' expression.

"You're no fun anymore, Jas," Gus declares, maneuvering off my thighs and standing before his brother. He makes a show of adjusting his hard package. "You used to be a lot more fun." He turns back to me. "Don't you remember, Vi. Jasper was fun."

I peel myself up and off the bed, running my hands down my Gus-wrinkled tee that says, *Hogwarts wasn't hiring so I teach Muggles instead.* It was my departure from employment gift, and if it weren't so perfectly me, I'd hate them for it. I stare Jasper down, his angry sea-glass-green eyes slaying me with an anger I hardly deserve. Maybe it's the fact that he's been callously ignoring me for the last week.

We had that afternoon, that night, in Vegas, and since then, I don't exist to him.

No more secret moments. No private glances. Nothing.

Adalyn is the only thing left between us, and though I know it's the way it should be and is for the best, I can't help but feel the residual burn. It's like history repeating itself. Because when we were fourteen, Jasper Diamond gave me my first kiss. And then immediately after, he stopped speaking to me. Imagine what that sort of thing does to an adolescent girl. Especially when she really, really likes the boy.

Jasper may not have kissed me that night in Vegas, but I wanted him to. I seriously, desperately did. I fell asleep that night touching myself to visions of him, and when I woke up the next morning, he had morphed back into this version of himself with me. Asshole Jasper is what I've silently referred to him as. It's like I'm a teenager all over again with these men, and it sucks.

And because he makes me feel like that teenage girl, I say, "Jasper stopped speaking to me when we were fourteen. I believe it was shortly after our afternoon under the oak tree." I charge past him, raising an eyebrow to him as I go, daring him to contradict me. He doesn't, of course. "You remember, right?"

I've officially hit juvenile. And my wanting him to acknowledge me as something more is asinine.

"He's like the opposite of a fine wine, Vi," Gus asserts as he takes his seat next to Adalyn, who is wearing headphones and watching Frozen—of course, it's Frozen—on her tablet. Clearly, she wasn't asking for me. "He gets worse with age."

I shrug, settling across from them, and then Jasper sits beside me. Close enough that I can feel his heat and smell his cologne. Far enough away that I wear his chill around my body like a cold winter day.

We're a game of chess.

Every move we make is calculated against the other. We're watching, desperate to outmaneuver and always be three steps ahead.

But I'm so tired of losing where he's concerned. I feel as though the moment I get ahead, grapple for some breathing room, he sucks all the available oxygen from my lungs, and then I'm suffocating.

I just want to breathe without drama or boys stealing my air.

The plane gets ready for departure to Dallas, the engines roaring to life. Keith and Henry are already doing battle, trying to kill each other with various weapons on the large screens. Gus pops on his noise-canceling headphones, closing his eyes and sinking his body back, snuggling next to Adalyn, who hardly notices he's there.

"I see you and Gus are picking up right where you left off all those years ago."

It's the venom in his voice that's poisoning me against him, and yet, I'm still hypnotized by this dance. Forever at odds. Eternally outmatched.

I shouldn't care, but I do. I should hate him back, but I don't. Not fully anyway.

His malice shouldn't upset me, but it does.

The ugly part of me wonders if I didn't need the money so badly, would I walk away? If I didn't adore his daughter, would I abandon them and save myself? I guess I'll never know since I'm still here, and everyone knows I'm stubborn enough to see this through.

"Love me or hate me. Both are in my favor... If you love me, I'll always be in your heart. If you hate me, I'll always be in your mind." The quote escapes my lips before I can stop it. But it's been resonating within me, sticking to my soul like gum on the bottom of an old shoe since I arrived in California. I have no idea who said that, but somehow, it puts all of this into place.

"I'm sure Gus would appreciate the sentiment."

I roll my eyes. He knows that's not for Gus.

I pull my earbuds and my old as hell paperback of Persuasion out of my purse. Plugging the buds into my phone, I set my book down on my lap.

"That wasn't meant for Gus," I hiss under my breath, hitting play and smiling almost gleefully when Taking Back Sunday blasts angrily into my ears.

I want to read, but with a broken e-reader and the man sitting beside me, I decide to close my eyes instead, allowing myself to drift. I'm so tired. Acting like a teenager and trying to avoid the bad boy is exhausting.

THIRTEEN

Jasper

SHUTTING the door to Adalyn's bedroom softly behind me, I let out a heavy sigh. Sometimes she goes down so easily for a nap, practically falls asleep before her head hits the pillow, and other times, like today, she fights it tooth and nail. Or maybe it's me. Maybe I'm the one who is exhausted and in need of a nap.

When was the last time I had a decent night's sleep? One where I didn't go to bed at one in the morning only to wake up at six? Ambling across the hotel suite, I don't even throw the windows or the view of the Dallas skyline a cursory glance. No, my sights are single-minded: bed. But when I reach my room, my bed, I find it already occupied.

Shit, I forgot Viola's room isn't ready yet.

She's sitting up, her long legs crossed at the knee, that stupid skirt I hate so much is riding high up her creamy thighs, and her face is buried in her new e-reader.

Good. I'm glad she's using it.

I'm too tired to avoid her, and she looks too content to push her out and make her go to the living room, so instead, I crawl onto the bed, sliding over and flopping down beside her, but with enough room between us that I can barely feel her there.

"Do you want me to move?" she asks, just a touch above a whisper, like she knows how close to sleep I already am. It's the first cordial thing spoken between us in what feels like forever. Maybe that's why I'm so exhausted.

"No," I manage, my eyes already closed and my back to her as I rest on my side.

"I should yell at you again, Jasper, but I can't seem to find my anger."

"What did I do now?"

I hear her soft laughter, and it has me inadvertently grinning like the stupid fool I am.

"You bought me this e-reader." She pauses, waiting to see if I'll deny it, and when I don't, she continues, "I found it here in your suite, in the living room with my name on it. I realize you were just trying to do a nice thing, and those for you are few and far between, but this truly is too much."

I chuckle, the bed shaking with it. "Thanks. I think."

The bed shifts, and even though my eyes are still closed, I know she's moved closer to me. I know she's staring at the back of my head because I can feel her eyes boring into me.

"You didn't have to do that. And you really didn't need to get me the most expensive one. But...," she puffs out a breath, like what she's about to say is impossibly difficult. "Thank you."

"You're welcome. And I did have to do that. Yours broke, and I couldn't stand watching you read that same old tattered paperback anymore. It was grating on me."

The bed shifts again, and now I feel her body heat against my back. Can smell her unique scent. She's on my bed, and I'm lying down, and how easy would it be to just roll over, grab her, and kiss her?

Her fingers find their way into my hair, running down the length of it before diving in and massaging my scalp. Christ, that's so fucking good I have to press my lips together to hold in my groan. Viola has never touched me like this before.

"Can I pay you back for it?" Her voice is so light. So sweet and achingly soft. It floats over me like a dream, and I wonder if that's what this is. A dream.

"No."

"But you filled the e-reader with books and a huge credit for more. Jasper, it's too much. I really cannot accept it."

"Keep doing that until I fall asleep, and we'll consider it even."

We fall silent, her fingers continuing to rub and scratch at my scalp, but even though I'm so tired and what she's doing to me is pure euphoric magic, I can't succumb to sleep. It's her. Her body so close to mine. The thick sexual tension in the air. The energy bouncing back and forth between us. I'm so acutely aware of her, so attuned to every breath, every movement she makes. I'd tell her to leave if I didn't love having her here, touching me, so much.

"You need a haircut," she muses, almost as if she's talking to herself. Like she's not sure if I'm awake or asleep.

"I know," I reply. "I forgot to get one before we left, and now we're on the road."

She laughs, sinking further into my back, her nails gliding down my neck and back up, and this time I do groan, unable to stop the bastard before it slips out. "You like that?"

"Mmm," is all I can manage.

The beautiful witch does it again, and my eyes roll helplessly into the back of my head. "I'm sure there are places you could go to get your hair cut. I don't get this 'we're on the road' excuse. Henry gave me the same bullshit."

I smile wide at that. "He just wanted you to cut his hair."

"Probably," she laughs the word.

"You did a good job, though. I'd let you cut mine."

Her hand freezes in my hair, and the more I let that settle into my brain, the more I'm loving the hell out of that idea. I mean, it's the devil dressed up in nun's clothing, but I'm too tired and horny and wired and screwed to care.

"You want me to cut your hair?"

I shrug up a shoulder, pressing back into her hand, hoping she'll take the hint and keep rubbing my head. "Sure. Why not? I doubt you could mess it up too bad, and I could always buzz it off if you did. Look more like Gus for once," I laugh. "But I'm telling you, this is why musicians grow their hair out. It's not because we like the way it looks, it's because we're lazy and the road makes us even lazier."

She's gone completely mute, and though I should probably pull back and hit the retreat button, I let it ride. Probably because I was insanely jealous of Henry when she cut his hair, and I'm hoping she's considering this instead of trying to find a way out.

Finally...fucking *finally*, she says, "Okay."

"Okay."

"Now?"

I open my eyes and stare straight ahead. Now? Do I want to do this now? *You started this, asshole.* Right. I did that. "Sure. Now's good."

"Okay."

"Okay."

"I'll uh..." I hear her swallow. "I'll go get my scissors and meet you in the bathroom."

"Great."

"Bring a chair in from the dining room."

"Okay."

"Okay."

She slides off the bed, and now my heart starts to pick up a beat. Shit. She's really going to cut my hair. And I don't even care if my hair is long or short or buzzed off, so I have no reason for doing this other than to torture myself.

I pry myself up and off the bed, carry a dining room chair into the bathroom, covering it with a towel, so we don't get my hair all over it, and by the time that's done, Viola enters the bathroom.

Her eyes meet mine, and I swallow my tongue. "We need to wet your hair."

I walk over to the sink like I'm on autopilot, turning on the faucet, so the water is warm, and then pull my shirt over my head. Just as I'm tossing it on the counter beside me, I catch Viola's reflection in the mirror. She's staring at my back, her eyes touching each muscle before they slide to the mirror to take in my chest and abs. I can't stop my smirk when her eyes finally meet mine. She blushes, turning away quickly.

I would say something, call her out on the fact that she was just blatantly checking me out, but this woman has a pair of sharp scissors in her hand, and she's about to take them to my head.

Bending forward, I dip under the water, allowing it to cascade over my hair. My hands run along the strands, trying to get my entire head, which is not an easy feat in a bathroom sink. Water is gliding over my face and the back of my neck, dripping down my shoulders.

"You're making a mess," Viola chastises behind me, and I splash some water in her direction. "Hey," she laughs, smacking my shoulder. "I was coming to help, but now you're on your own."

"I think I got all of my hair wet and then some."

"Then some is for sure." A towel drops onto my shoulders, and I right myself, rubbing the white cloth over my head and back. "I think you're wet enough. Come sit down."

"Yes, ma'am." I take my seat, sitting back only to have Viola push me upright until I'm ramrod straight.

"This chair really isn't the best," she asserts, tapping her bottom lip with her finger as she takes me in. "I'm too tall and you're too short in this, but I guess we'll have to make do."

"Whatever you say. I'm at your mercy," I tease. She cocks an eyebrow, opening and closing the long sharp blades of the scissors, smiling evilly at me. "Shit. I'm starting to regret this. I forgot how much you hate me."

"Don't worry, you'll still be pretty when I'm done with you."

"Men aren't pretty, baby. Sexy. Hot. Fuckable. I'll even take gorgeous, but not pretty."

Her hand reaches out, cupping my chin and drawing my face up to hers. Her gaze glides along my face as smooth as silk, lingering on my lips before returning to my eyes. "You're very pretty, Jasper. I don't know about those other adjectives you just mentioned, though." She shrugs a shoulder, and I bat her hand away, making her laugh. "Are you ready?"

"Do your worst. Or should I say best?"

Her fingers rake across the top of my head, her nails scratching along my scalp. My head rolls, sways with the movement of her hand as I instantly give in. She yanks sharply on the strands, and I jerk back upright.

"Keep your head straight."

Easier said than done.

She walks around to the back of me, combing through my hair with a brush and then *snip, snip.* The sound of the scissors slicing through my hair practically echoes off the marble walls. Cold water slides down my chest in thin tendrils, and I suddenly realize just how hot my skin is in comparison.

And when it hits my nipple...shit. I'm fucking turned on.

With that unfortunate realization heavy in my mind, with the sensation of Viola strumming her fingers repeatedly through my hair, touching me, her scent surrounding me, my cock catches up and thickens in my jeans. Perfect. I can't even adjust myself without her noticing. If she glances down between my legs, she'll see everything.

Even through the fabric of my jeans.

But right now, she's oblivious. At least I assume she is because she's snipping away at the back of my head, humming one of my songs, and Christ, that makes me smile so goddamn big. It's not even one I wrote for her. It's the one I always sing to Ady. Thank God. If she were humming a song I wrote for her, I'd probably lose my mind completely.

I have no idea how many seconds or minutes tick by. She's lulled me into some sort of hypnotic wet dream. I'm having the best visions of her sitting on the bench in the shower, hot water and steam everywhere, my face pressed between her thighs. I kiss her, touch her, toy with her sweet pussy as her back arches, her lips parting as she whimpers from the pleasure I'm giving her. Her legs wrap around my head, and I lick her out so good she comes on a loud cry, pulling my hair until it hurts. Then I pick her up, carrying her out of the shower and bending her over the counter. Our eyes lock in the mirror as I slide into her, taking her slowly at first, building her up until she's moaning, gasping my name and begging me to take her harder.

And I do. I fuck her until she screams, my legs trembling, our bodies breathless.

I fuck her until she knows she's *mine*.

Jesus, I think that's my new favorite.

Get a grip!

Except, I can't.

It continues to get worse as she reaches the front of me, standing between my parted thighs, bending forward so she can reach the top of my head and torturing me with the most insane view of her lacy bra and full tits that are spilling out of the top.

She's still humming, and now I am too because if I don't find something to distract me from this woman and the dirty, dirty things I'm dying to do to her, I'm going to do something I shouldn't.

I'm sitting here, half-naked with her between my legs, and she's touching my head, and I'm not touching her, and I think this is one of the most absurdly erotic moments of my life.

She takes a step back, and I'm so relieved not to breathe her in that I automatically suck in a huge rush of air. "Something wrong?" I ask, glancing up. She's gnawing on her bottom lip, troubled with what she's seeing, and my hand reflexively leaps up to the top of my head, patting around to see if I can determine just how bad off I am. "Did you mangle me?"

"No," she replies, tilting her head to the side. "I'm liking it a lot, actually." I blow out a breath I didn't realize I was holding. "But I can't get the front of your head. Your hair is super long in the front, and I want to trim it up to match the rest, but I can't get a good angle."

And because I'm a total masochist, I slide my feet and knees together and pat my lower thighs. "Come sit on me then."

"What?" She lets out a startled laugh.

"It's either that or I stand, and then I'm a lot taller than you."

She shakes her head, those teeth distractedly going to work on her bottom lip, and I'd give anything to do that to her. "Why do they have to make dining room chairs so low to the ground?"

"No clue. Should we leave it?"

She shakes her head. "No. It's always falling in your face, and I like it short, Jasper. It looks...," she smirks. "Pretty." I roll my eyes at her.

"Then I guess you have no choice."

Our eyes lock.

"I guess I have no choice."

She swallows. Takes a small step in my direction, watching me as she does. What the hell was I thinking? I can't have her sit on me. I'm hard as a fucking steel pipe, and she's going to be straddling me. In a skirt! Face-to-face and chest-to-chest, and her legs will be spread, and oh fuck.

What the hell was I thinking!

"I can just go and get it done professionally," I push out, except it's too late. Her legs are on either side of mine, and she's lowering herself down. Mercifully, she's on my lower thighs, just above my knees, but my cock is pointing at her through my jeans like it's the needle on a compass, and she's its true north.

"This shouldn't take long," she whispers, her sweet breath floating across my face.

I swallow past the thickness in my throat, my voice still coming out raspy. "Okay."

Her eyes focus on my hair, and I don't so much as move a muscle.

My eyes train themselves to the base of her neck, not too high and not too low.

Except... I can see her pulse thrumming there. Fast.

Her heartbeat is going so fast, and mine is too, and she's right here. Her skirt is fanned across my thighs, covering her, but I can feel the heat of her pussy through my jeans, and I can't stop picturing what type of panties she's wearing.

God, let it be a thong. Something thin and lacy.

"How's it going?" I bite out through gritted teeth, because if I don't speak, something utterly mindless, I'm going to reach under that skirt and discover for myself.

"Good. Hold still."

I haven't moved. My hands are gripping the hell out of the bottom of the chair, my knuckles tingling from lack of blood.

"Almost there."

Except then she slides forward. The top of her inner thigh drifting along the head of my cock, and I grunt, unable to hold it back. Her hands pause, her eyes widen, and now she knows just how turned on I am by this. By her. I don't know what to do or say. There is no apology. There is no brushing it off.

"You're hard."

My eyes meet hers.

"You're straddling my thighs in a skirt, Viola. What did you think would happen?"

"You told me to."

Viola goes back to my hair. *Snip. Snip. Snip.* I'm dying here. "Are you finished?"

"No. Hold still."

She's trembling. I'm throbbing.

I don't know how much longer I can take this. "Viola, I think we're–" She rolls her hips forward, sliding her pussy along my aching dick, and I groan, my head falling back against the cushion of the chair.

"I told you not to move," she berates, but her voice is breathy. Needy.

The sound shoots straight to my balls.

My head snaps up, my hands flying to her hips as she does it again. Her cheeks are tinted the most perfect shade of rose, and her lips are parted, and her pupils are dilated, and holy motherfucking shit, Viola is just as turned on as I am. Hell, I can smell her arousal. Practically taste it. And it's so goddamn good I can't help but lick my lips.

With her eyes on mine, I maneuver her hips against me again. She moans as my cock rubs her heat; the friction of my jeans against her panties hitting her perfectly. Viola lifts and scoots her body up until she's directly over my lap, her tits in my face. Her mouth right there. Lowering herself back down, she grinds on me, and I lean back, watching her in awe as she dry-fucks me.

Her eyes close as another moan slips out, and I cannot believe this is happening. I cannot believe I'm sitting on a dining room chair in the bathroom, with Viola Starr in my lap getting herself off.

It's the sexiest fucking thing I've ever seen in my life.

This feels insanely good, but I don't dare shut my eyes, afraid to miss even one second of it. Of her.

"Does that feel good?"

She whimpers.

"Open your eyes and tell me, Viola. Do you like grinding on my hard cock? Getting yourself off on me?"

Her eyes open, her pretty hazel nearly all black. "Yes," she pants.

This girl... She's a goddess, and I'm doomed.

With a soft gasp, she quickens her pace. I can't believe how she's responding to me. As if she wants nothing and no one else. Her tight little body instinctively arching to meet mine. Desperately. As if she can't get close enough. Needs so much more.

It's blowing my mind.

"Then do it, baby. Rub that sweet pussy all over me. I want to feel you come, Viola. I want to see how beautiful you are when you let go."

"Oh God," she moans.

The scissors and comb slip from her fingers, clattering to the floor as her hands grip my shoulders. I'm desperate to kiss her. To snake my fingers under her skirt and drive them into her. But I can't do it. It will ruin this, and she'll stop. I know it. I see it. This is on her terms, and I'm just here for the ride. Literally.

But I don't care.

Nothing has ever felt this amazing in my life. I'm like a teenager all over again, about to come in my pants.

Her hips undulate, up and down and side to side until she finds her rhythm. Discovers where it feels the best. Her pussy is so hot, directly over my dick as she jerks me off through my jeans. Harder. Faster. It's killing me not to touch her. Not to take over and throw her against that sink, fucking her from behind exactly the way I envisioned.

"Jasper," she cries my name in a slow, sexy purr, pleading. Her body building up as she clutches my shoulders, digging her nails into my flesh.

"That's it, baby," I growl hoarsely. "You're so fucking hot. You feel so good. Harder. Grind on me harder."

"Yes," she hisses, her body trembling. "I'm so close."

"I know. You're so beautiful, Viola. Come for me. I'm going to come, too. I'm right there with you. You feel it?" She nods her head, her teeth biting into her lip so hard I'm surprised she's not drawing blood. "You make me so hard. Yes. Like that. So good." *I'm so crazy about you,* I don't say. *I'd give you everything. My world. My heart. My soul.*

"Jasper," she screams, her eyes cinching tight as she comes. I come too, grunting and groaning, shooting hot cum down my thigh and all over the inside of my jeans, but I don't care. I can't remember a time I came so hard. Her forehead drops to mine as she continues to ride out the last of her orgasm, our skin sweaty as it presses together, trying to steady our ragged breathing.

Her eyes flick open, and when she finds me right there, they widen.

"Oh my God," she whispers, stunned, and maybe even a little embarrassed that she, we, just did that. "I...," she trails off, and I can't say anything. I'm paralyzed. *Don't regret this, Viola. Don't say we shouldn't have done it.* "We shouldn't have done that."

Everything hurts.

She climbs off my lap, hastily picks up the scissors and comb from the floor, and flees, taking my heart with her.

FOURTEEN

Jasper

MY PEN FLIES FURIOUSLY across the paper, scribbling line by line like I've taken enough speed to kill a horse. I haven't taken any. I'm just in the zone. Right now, we're on a bus, traveling down from Dallas to Houston. Why a bus and not our plane, you might ask? Because the freaking plane shit the bed in Dallas and is apparently going to need some parts. Which means it won't be ready for a bit, which means we travel by bus for the foreseeable future.

Luckily, my girl, Lyric Rose from Turn Records, came through for us big-time, and as fate and the stars would have it, there were a few tour buses not too far away that don't need to be anywhere special for the next few weeks. And these buses are super nice. Big bedroom in the back. Four sleeping cabins that are a little bigger than a traditional twin. Two full bathrooms, a small kitchen, televisions, a dining area, and a huge sprawling couch thing.

The other buses are identical, and right now, all of the security guys, Marco, and other personnel are on the other two, and all of us, Keith, Henry, Gus, Viola, Ady and I are on this one.

Adalyn and Viola have been engrossed in activities all morning. Good thing because driving is slow going as it's pouring freaking rain. They've been coloring and singing songs and playing pretend with Adalyn's dolls. They even watched a signing video Adalyn really seems to like.

I try not to watch them.

Try not to watch Viola with my daughter.

Like right now, Adalyn is in Viola's lap, straddling her thighs, laughing uncontrollably as Viola pretends to eat her neck, cheeks, and belly. Then Viola hums, "Mmmm. Delicious."

"More. Delicious," Ady begs immediately after Viola stops, still giggling. And the whole process begins again.

But it's this moment that's silently killing me. Chipping chunks out of the wall I'm perpetually rebuilding around myself to keep this woman out. I can't stop replaying our encounter in the bathroom. I can't stop thinking about the way she looked when she came. The sounds she made. The way she called out my fucking name.

That kills me.

But after she ran out of the bathroom two days ago, she's barely spoken to me. And because I'm goddamn childish where she's concerned, I'm avoiding her too, because what can I say? Hey, what we did in the bathroom was the hottest moment of my life, and I want to do it again with you times infinity?

No. I can't do that.

She's not mine. She's my brother's, which raises me to a whole new level of dirtbag asshole.

So we haven't spoken about what happened. Haven't acknowledged it either.

It's for the best, I tell myself.

I know it is.

But she won't look at me, and I can barely handle that. I'd much rather have her yelling at me than completely ignoring me. It's not like we can be friends, not with the amount of fire blazing between us. That's never been our thing.

Love her or hate her. Still, it's a fucked-up thing when you're jealous of your daughter and the attention her nanny is giving her.

Viola finishes eating Adalyn's neck and then stares directly into her eyes, smiling adoringly at my little girl. She closes her eyes, leans in, and rubs her nose against Ady's, whispering, "Nosie, nosie, nosie." Opening those almond-shaped eyes, she kisses the tip of Ady's nose, saying, "I love you, sweet girl."

"Love you too," Addy replies instantly in her broken way that sounds more like, lobe you do.

I thought I knew what heartbreak felt like. I thought I understood what heartbreak at the hands of Viola Starr felt like.

But this?

It's excruciating, hitting me on a guttural, visceral level. My chest actually, literally hurts to the point where I can't take a deep breath, and I wonder if I'm having a heart attack. Isn't that what they tell you it feels like? Like an elephant sitting on your chest?

I've never felt anything like this before. The longer I watch them, the warmer, hotter, more beautifully terrifying this feeling intensifies and grows. *Jesus Christ, make it stop.*

Viola loves my little girl, and my little girl loves Viola.

And Viola is the only woman in her life.

And in a few months, she'll be gone. What will Ady be left with then?

Maybe it is better if I don't stand in Gus's way as I have been. Maybe if he does win Viola back, she'll stay and still spend time with Ady? Maybe some of Viola, even like that, is better than no Viola at all.

I could endure that for Ady.

I haven't allowed myself to dwell on Karina, on how selfish she was. I've always stood up for her. Always played the 'mother of my child' card, because I don't want her bad-mouthed in front of Ady. I never allowed myself to care how she only went after me because she was looking to fuck a rock star, possibly even get knocked-up by one.

I never could prove that either way.

But when she found out I wasn't going to make her mine in more ways than just the mother of my daughter, she grew bored, restless, and resentful.

I know I should have done right by her, for Ady's sake. Married her with the biggest prenup the world has ever seen. It's a regret I don't know how to compensate for. Because now she's dead, and how can I not take most of that responsibility on myself? If I had married her, she would have stayed. She would have been a mother to Adalyn. She would not have run off and died.

At least, I like to think so.

But I didn't love her.

I didn't even like her all that much, and I knew any marriage between us would end in divorce. I didn't see how that would benefit Adalyn in any way, especially in the long run. My parents were very much in love before my mother died. Another guilt I can't un-live or let go of.

I saw that love growing up. Gus did too. But after she was gone, it was not a happy home until my father remarried.

And I always knew, instinctively, there was no one I was going to fall in love with, marry, who would be right for me, or Adalyn, when the only one I ever dreamed of, was spoken for.

I wanted only happiness for Adalyn and watching her parents argue about anything and everything didn't seem like the best world to raise her in. And argue is all Karina and I ever did.

I just never expected Karina would leave.

I never understood how a parent could abandon their child. Could betray them like that. And then she died. Leaving us for good. No reconciliation. No do-over. No, I'm sorry.

Viola understands betrayal at the hand of a parent better than anyone. Her mother is still trying to pull shit, coming to Spencer's bar, looking for her. Who knows what that woman is after or what she's up to.

I guess there are some people out there who don't want to be parents but become them anyway and never manage to rise to the challenge.

But Adalyn deserves everything, and I'm not sure I'm giving it to her.

Viola catches me watching them, and I blink, clearing my thoughts, and hastily return to my pen and paper.

"Is any of that any good?" Gus asks, coming to sit beside me in the U-shaped booth at the dining table. I shrug. I think it could be, but until Gus and I work out the music to accompany it, it's just poetry. He starts reading over my shoulder as I continue my thoughts before I lose them. He whistles low between his teeth. "Keith," Gus calls out. Keith's head pops up from his iPad, sliding his headphones back so he can hear. Henry is asleep in one of the bunks, I think. "Do me a favor, brother, and grab my guitar and your sticks."

"Sure thing."

Keith gets up to do as he's asked, and Gus steals one of the blank pieces of paper from my pad, sliding a worn pen from his pocket. Some people work on a computer when they write. They have all kinds of apps and software you can use to create your songs or work out the notes.

We don't do that.

I like my pen and my paper because that's how I've always done it. Because they're always with me, and if inspiration strikes me, then I need to be able to write it down immediately.

Gus is similar like that. We feed off each other. I don't know if it's a twin thing or a brother thing, or if we just understand the way each other's mind works, but I don't think I could write music without my brother. He's the other half of this coin.

Gus starts to scratch out some notes as he reads over my shoulder, and I love that he's already hearing sounds to this. That he's garnering notes from my words.

"Here, man." Keith hands Gus his acoustic, and Gus instantly starts to strum away. It's an intro, I realize, since it doesn't quite meet my words. An intricate arrangement that has his fingers flying up and down the frets of the guitar while his other hand strums. "Yeah." Keith nods his head, finding a rhythm in Gus's notes. "Here. How's this?"

Keith starts to tap out a beat against the table since he doesn't exactly have his drums here, and I pause my writing to listen to it.

And then it hits me.

What Viola said to me the other day on the plane.

I inwardly smile as I think about it. How she said it. My beautifully defiant girl. I finish the song with: *Love me or hate me. Fuck me and break me. Rob me blind, you're stealin' my time. Thieving my dream, it ain't a new theme. This time I'm ready. Love me or hate me. Fuck me and break me.*

"Shit," Gus whispers, snatching my pad of paper from beneath my hand and showing it to Keith. The two of them practically press their heads together as they read over the song I just finished in no time. And when they're done, they glance at each other and then simultaneously over to me. "This is the best thing you've written in years." Keith nods in agreement.

I blink at them, a little stunned, my gaze automatically casting over to Viola before I can stop it. She's watching us, the corner of her mouth turned up in the smallest of perceptible smiles. Our eyes lock, and it's the first time in days that I've actually allowed myself to look at her.

Really look *into* her.

To indulge in her long, glossy honeycomb-colored hair. Her big, beautiful eyes that are a symphony of green and brown. Love me or hate me. Fuck me and break me. Yes, Viola. That's all for you. No one else has that power.

"Are Keith and I laying this down, or is this something you

already have in your head?" Gus asks, pulling me away from Viola and back to my job.

"Let's play it out." I get up and locate my guitar in the back bedroom, walking it back over to the table as I strum something similar to what Gus had going, only a full octave above, but in the same measure. "I like this as a solo to open it. I'm not sure how well it works with anything else," I say, letting my fingers take over.

"Agreed," Gus maintains, matching me, our eyes meeting as we discover this sound together.

"Yo," Henry bursts out, rubbing his bleary eyes as he joins us. "What the hell is that?"

"Listen and shut up," Keith demands.

Gus stands up too, confronting me from mere feet away, and the two of us go head-to-head, adjusting and altering as we go.

"I'm recording," Henry whispers, typing away on his Mac. "It's all there. Just play." So we do. Gus and I play, and I end up singing the lyrics I just wrote down, and by the end, we have a new song. It's rough, sure, but that's how it's meant to be at this stage. That's why we need Lyric Rose. The woman who makes rough, polished.

"It's too bad we can't call the album fuck me and break me," Henry muses, reading over the words. "Thieving Dream works, though."

"It's one song. Let's get some others going before we name it."

Henry shakes his head, smiling to himself. "They're coming. When you start out like this, the rest are already there. And it's going to kill everything else you've ever written."

"Shots?" Keith calls out, because that's what Keith does. "This demands shots. And we don't have a show tonight, so I'm calling getting shitty to the shittiest degree." I narrow my eyes, pointing to my daughter. "Sorry," he shrugs helplessly. "I didn't mean it. I'm just...feeling it, ya know? I want to jam. Without pressure or fans watching. I want to play for the love of playing. The way we used to." He slaps my back hard, an unstoppable smile spread across his face. "This is why we fucking tour, bro. This is why we do this. For moments like these. Don't balk. Don't skip out. Ady is straight." I glance over at Adalyn, who is now playing piano on the piano app on her iPad and singing along without real words to whatever she's playing. She's not listening to us at all, and I pause. Stunned stupid. "She's yours, dude. Don't look so shocked. She jams out all the time when we play. Have some shots and let the bus drive us."

Viola stands up, glowing, and that goddamn pain in my chest is back.

She swallows hard and clears her throat. Her hand reaches out like she wants to touch me before it drops just as quickly down to her side.

"She heard you playing. Singing." She lets out a small, incredulous giggle, like even she's overwhelmed by the moment. "She found her tablet and pulled up her piano app. She did that all by herself, even unlocked it by herself. She learns so quickly." She reaches out for me again, even though I'm a solid five feet away. "She heard you make music and started to make some of her own. She's singing a song she's making up. I've never seen her do this before. Have you?"

I nod numbly, because even though I have heard her do that, I've never seen her do all that by herself and start to play and sing because that's what I was doing. My little girl is so much like me, not just in appearance, and I wish there were a more powerful word than love to describe this feeling.

The way I love my daughter is so much more than love.

I listen to her and start to sing along too. I have no idea what words are coming next, but who cares? She's making a song the way I just was, and I don't think I've ever been prouder of my little girl in my life.

"I'm recording this too," Henry jumps in, slowly sliding in beside Ady as she continues to play and sing.

Viola is bursting with exuberance and joy, and I'm right there with her. *You're killing my resolve.* I stare into Viola, and I think those words. I don't even bother to hide them. It's the music. It's lighting my soul on fire. It's Adalyn making music because I was making music. I'm insane over this woman and this girl, and I accept every-thing that's hitting me square in the chest. That elephant can jump all he wants. Let this bleed me dry. Let everyone here see. I cannot shut this off. They're part of my soul. The ones who give inspiration a voice.

My muses.

My art.

My life's blood.

Gus stalks over to Viola, throwing his arms around her body and kissing her face, her cheeks, the corner of her lips, like he's just as high on her as I am. She glows up at him, *still goddamn glowing*, staring deeply into his eyes as something so intimate and raw passes between them.

That pressure in my chest alters.

That pain takes on a different life force.

I can't watch them.

So instead, I shut down. I disconnect. I let go of everything I was just allowing to consume me.

I blow out this awful noxious bitter breath and compose myself. The way I always have. I'm untouchable. An island. The way I've always been.

It was stupid to think anything else. To risk so much, knowing I'd never get anything in return.

I won't slip up like that again.

I was ready to give her everything, consequences be damned, only to be reminded of who she is. Gus's.

I need to keep Viola, and yet, I can't. I cannot keep her. Not for myself anyway. But it's like I thought before... I'm writing like this. And she loves my girl. And she's fucking crying over her making music.

I can't lose this woman again.

I hate her, and I love her, and I'll do anything to keep her for my little girl who might actually need her more than I do. It's time I call a truce. It's time I extend an olive branch. Ignoring her isn't helping anything or anyone. Now I just have to figure out how to do that without giving her more of me than she already owns.

I need to keep her for Adalyn. Even if it kills me not to have her too.

Even if it means I have to watch her love my brother and not me.

FIFTEEN

Viola

FLICKING off the light of the bathroom, I pad barefoot and blind in the direction of the large bed that occupies the center of the room. It takes my eyes a few minutes to adjust, and I just narrowly miss clipping the corner of the wall. Pulling back the sheets, I climb in, blowing out an exhausted sigh, and I slink around in the cool silky sheets of the hotel bed.

My eyes close just as my phone vibrates from the bedside table.

A growl gnashes past my lips as I begrudgingly scoot over to pick it up.

Jasper.

He rarely texts me, and never at night, so I unlock it quickly, staring at his words for a moment and ignoring the way him texting me feels. I shouldn't have a flutter low in my belly from such a simple question. I shouldn't feel any of the millions of things I'm feeling for the asshole otherwise known as my boss.

But I do.

Are you asleep yet?

I quickly type out a reply. **No. Just got into bed. Every-thing okay?**

I want to take Ady to the zoo tomorrow.

I grin stupidly at my phone.

So take her to the zoo.

I want you to come with us.

Oh. Unplugging my phone, I roll onto my back, the bright screen that begins to darken hovering over my face. I tap the screen and read his words a second time. Then a third. Maybe he's drunk? He didn't seem it when he came in tonight, but maybe he is, and I missed it? Why else would he willingly want to spend time with me when ignoring me has become his favorite hobby once more.

Bad idea? He types when I don't reply.

Yes. It's an insanely bad idea.

I'd love to go. Will it be everyone or just us? I ask because I have to know. I have to prepare myself for spending a day with Jasper. Even if Adalyn will be there as a buffer. He came in from the show tonight and quietly thanked me for staying late before I ran out with a simple goodnight.

That's how it's been with us since the bathroom.

Those couple of days in Dallas and then the bus ride down here where I lost my shit over a little girl playing a piano app. The truth is, I was already losing my shit over the song he wrote. Love me or hate me. Isn't that what I said to him on the plane? He wrote it into his song, which meant I was on his mind.

He didn't notice, but I was already choked up before she even started to play, and then that threw me over into some kind of psychotic, emotional state I have no business entering.

Especially when I caught his eyes, only to discover he was staring at me like I was something toxic to him. It was the same way he looked at me in the bathroom. I know it's my fault. I lost control with him. I gave in, succumbed to a desire I had no right to, and then when I opened my eyes, he looked...sick.

I had gotten myself off on a man who admittedly does not like me. Who refers to me, still, as the nanny. He didn't even kiss or touch me anywhere other than my hips.

I practically threw myself at him, and he looked sick for it even if in the heat of the moment, he was into it. I know he was. And occasionally...well...maybe sometimes I feel like I see something in his eyes. But the moment I start to believe it's there, that he could possibly be feeling this too, it's gone.

So, I'm claiming temporary insanity for both of us. Sleep deprivation and too much hostility and too little sex—at least for me—in forever, and I lost my mind on the guy I think about way too much.

So, I ran from the bathroom. Embarrassed and hurt.

And since then, I don't exist to him. We don't exist to each other. And damn, that's like... So, yeah. Awkward. Strained. Exhausting.

Though that only seems to be between the two of us, because no one else notices or cares. I think by now, they just accept our mess for what it is.

I was thinking just us. Go early, before the zoo even opens. Marco said he'll take care of it.

I pause, my breath in my chest. My fingers tremble slightly as I type out, **Okay.**

Can you be ready at 8?

Sure.

I swipe away from our conversation and set my alarm only to realize that I'm smiling. *It's not a date; he just wants you to come to the zoo with him and his kid.*

Right. It's an olive branch.

I'll take anything other than his ignoring me. Pathetic? Maybe just a bit. Wanting someone you shouldn't, who doesn't even treat you well, is the self-esteem equivalent of biting your lip until you make it bleed. You're literally hurting yourself, but the pleasure-pain of it makes it impossible to stop, driving you to question your basic sanity.

Can I ask you something else?

Shoot.

Did the crowd swarming the hotel and bus bother you?

Is he kidding me? Of course, it bothered me.

Women—and I'm talking hundreds of them—mobbed the front and back entrance of the hotel, clamoring not just for their favorite band, but for the elusive Jasper Diamond himself.

They were crazed. They overran the bus. It was like those videos you see of when The Beatles first came to America. Girls were screaming and crying and thrusting not only band t-shirts out, but their tits too.

It was so insane that eventually the guys did step off the bus just so Adalyn and I could safely get into the hotel without being mobbed.

I knew they were famous. We wouldn't be here if they weren't. But I hadn't witnessed much of it until now. I've mostly been hidden away from it, off with Adalyn doing our own thing. This was eye-opening in the worst and best possible way.

Why do you ask?

You made a face, and it was the first time on the tour it's happened like that. Where fans swarmed us like that, I mean.

Are you referring to your harem of obsessed women? Why on earth would that bother me?

The message bubble appears almost instantly, and I roll to my side, my phone clutched in both hands, an unstoppable smile still clinging dumbly to my face.

I like this way too much to stop.

Even stupid banter and easy back and forth is better than evil eyes and long, lingering stares that make me simultaneously want to throw up and crawl out of my skin.

And because it's late, and I'm so f-ing tired, and he texted first, and I feel like being snarky, and it's taking him forever to reply, and I

LOVE TO HATE HER   159

obviously need a million excuses, I write, **In fact, why aren't you out with any of them? I'm sure they'd love another chance at The Jasper Diamond. Sexy man and supreme rock god.**

The dots dance before they disappear only to start again and disappear once more before they do their thing one final time and then his words appear on my screen. **Not interested in any of them. And I'd prefer it if you'd call me sexy god and supreme rock man. Has a more realistic touch to it, don't you think?**

I snort out a laugh, rolling my eyes.

Seems a bit arrogant and inaccurate to me. I'm not sure I'd call you sexy god. Sexy man was already pushing it, but maybe you should run that one by some of those girls who were screaming for you earlier. They might have a different opinion than mine.

Don't want their opinion. Yours is the only one I want, and the only one that matters.

I stare at his words for longer than I should, doing everything I can not to read into them. Rolling onto my stomach, I prop myself up with my elbows, clutching my phone just a little too tightly. I don't know what to say to that. What to write back.

He is a sexy god. Insanely so. Everything about him sets my blood on fire.

Those girls will be devastated to hear that.

He replies instantly, and that flutter in my belly spreads, shooting sparks across my skin. **If I didn't know you better, I'd think you were jealous.**

Maddeningly.

Why would I be?

You have no reason to be. They're just girls.

And I'm just the nanny.

You're not just the nanny. You're my nanny, Viola.

Christ. This has to stop.

Right. The one you fight with. The one who drives you crazy.

You have no idea how true that is. You do drive me crazy. Always have.

I can't tell if he's actually saying something beneath all this. If his words are coded. I know what my heart hopes–it's already sprinting about my chest like a methed-up bunny.

But the smarter, more practical side of me appreciates how Jasper Diamond really operates, and if I allow myself to tilt in his direction, even just a little, I'm liable to fall right over, and there are only so many times a girl can pick herself back up again.

I should tell him goodnight.

You drive me crazy too.

I shut my eyes and blow out a breath. I can do coded too. I can do it with the best of 'em. Only...he doesn't reply for what feels like forever, and now I'm wondering if I was misreading everything. I really need to learn when to quit.

Until he finally replies with: **You think that could work for you again? Me driving you crazy some more?**

Shit.

Work for me how?

The way it did in Dallas, lights up my screen, and even though I'm alone in my room, in my bed, and he's in an entirely different suite, my cheeks flame, and my cleavage sweats, and my panties? *Oh no.* **Especially now that I know you think I'm sexy.**

Jesus shit, is he attempting to sext me?

And Jesus shit, am I really giving in to this?

YES! NO! Don't text him back. Don't give in. Say goodnight and turn your phone off and throw it out the window for good measure. My forehead pounds against my pillow as I scream into it.

Brushing my hair out of my face, I type, **You know you're**

insanely sexy. You're all shiny hair, piercing green eyes, tatted muscular arms, and devastating smirk. You make girls across the planet wet. Myself included.

I jump up, literally, out of my bed, half-squealing and biting down on my lip.

OMG. I just wrote that to him.

I toss my phone on the bed and spin away from it, staring out the window. *So stupid, Vi. So freaking stupid. What fire are you tempting?*

The deadliest, most seductive kind.

My phone vibrates against the expensive linens, and I grin and frown and cover my face with my hands as I laugh-shriek into them.

Twirling around, I grapple for my phone, fumble it twice, and catch it.

I'm extremely happy to hear you're one of them since there has only ever been one girl I'm interested in making wet. In fact, I think her bedroom is directly beside mine since I'm nearly positive I just heard her squeal. Again.

Oh my god. He heard me?!

More importantly, is his bedroom actually directly beside mine? I think about the configuration of this floor and face-plant into the plush mattress in defeat. Yes. Yes, it is. And he just heard me freak-out over his texts. Awesomeness.

It's, without a doubt, one of my favorite sounds. I'd love to make you do it again.

Popping my head up, I read his text before dropping my face back down and scream—more quietly this time—into the sheets. Once that's done, I grab my phone, biting my lip so severely I'm shocked I'm not drawing blood.

And how would you do that?

The dots jump, and I watch them like a woman on the edge of her sanity, bouncing on the balls of my feet and tugging on my hair. I have zero cool with this. Probably because I'm inviting the devil, the one who ignores me and treats me like I'm invisible most of the time, to sext me. It's like I'm always playing a game with him. Broke-ass nanny versus rock god. I'm at...o. He's at...oh, about a billion.

Obviously, I'm killing it with this whole life/man thing.

But that afternoon in the bathroom? And his texts tonight? *There has only ever been one girl I'm interested in making wet.* He doesn't even have to try with me.

But does he mean it?

In my dreams, she enters the room with a seductive grin just for me before she walks over, crawls up my body until she's straddling my chest, her eyes on mine from above. I glide my hands up the backs of her thighs, under her skirt, watching her face the entire time. She shivers beneath my touch, especially as I guide her up my chest until her pussy is right below my mouth. This girl. God, she's so beautiful. So sexy. I can barely think straight when she's near me. She moans as I reach out and touch her over her damp panties. So wet. So soft. So mine. Then I lock eyes with her right before my face dives in and I smell her. So. Fucking. Sweet.

I drop my phone on the bed and literally fan myself. These hotel rooms. There is no air in here. I march over to the thermostat and crank it down to sixty-four degrees. Then I strip out of my tee and shorts, the cold blast from the vents doing nothing to stop the inferno raging within.

Then what? I question, my body somehow supine on the bed, my head slightly propped up against the headboard. My hand... trailing slowly down my body? How I got here is really not much of a mystery. I'm a spring, tightly coiled around this man's finger. He looks at me, licks his lips, smirks in my direction, and I release.

Why? Well, that's anyone's guess.

Maybe it's because I know there is so much hidden beneath his layers. So much he holds at bay, from me, his brother, his band, everyone. His daughter is his secret, hidden world. The one he hands over the keys to the castle to. That I'm one of the lucky few to catch a glimpse of the private man within feels like a prize to tuck away in my pocket, hiding it there as something special I can hold onto. The universe he opens up just for her is sacred.

And occasionally, when he feels the need to torture, he reveals some of that magic to me too.

But it's those layers. That secret. The torture.

They keep me pinned to the edge of my seat. Wanting, *craving*, for more. I'm a junkie for those lost moments. They're the sustenance that keeps me going. The butterflies in my tummy cling to them as if they know they're the only thing to give them flight.

Then I slide her panties to the side and lick her pussy. I watch as her head falls back and she moans.

I pant, my hand sliding further south, toying, teasing.

Does she like you watching her?

She loves it. Her beautiful hazel eyes dip down to mine as my tongue swipes out, licking at her sweetness over and over and over again. She rocks against me, fucking my face. It drives me *crazy*. Giving this girl pleasure is like nothing else.

How we got so far so fast is anyone's guess. I honestly cannot say. But he's taking more risks with me. Showing me his vulnerable underbelly. Letting me know that I'm the one in his mind and no one else. The same way he is for me. Making each other crazy as he put it.

Are you picturing me while you touch yourself, Viola?

Yes. Do you need to hear how good it feels, Jasper?

Yes.

Oh God.

My cheeks flame up as my fingers rub my clit, slick and ready as my body hums, already about to detonate. He didn't even say much.

It's more the power behind his suggestion. The way he wants me but refuses to take me. The dance we do–forward, backward, and all over again.

I don't hold back as my body takes over, my fingers bringing me closer and closer to the precipice as I picture everything he just imagined for me. My pussy over his face. My body riding him. His tongue and fingers inside me.

Him watching me the entire time.

My back arches, and my eyes pinch shut, and I cry out *his* name.

The wall bangs behind my headboard, and in the next second, I hear his muffled moan. *My* name.

A moment of silence passes between us before my phone, almost forgotten and slightly discarded, vibrates and lights up against the white duvet. **You have no idea how many times I've done that with you.**

About as many times as I've done that with him.

Don't get shy on me, dream girl.

I'm still here.

My teeth sink into my lower lip, my hand reaching up and pressing against the wall, knowing he's on the other side of it.

Does that mean you'll still come to the zoo with me and Adalyn?

My eyes close as a stuttered breath evacuates my lungs. What am I doing with him? We're stolen moments of lost lust. Misshapen desire trying to remold itself into something tangible.

He hates me, and I hate him. He wants me, and I want him more. And somewhere, in between all that madness, is Adalyn.

Our connecting force.

I'll be ready at 8.

It's impossible to sleep knowing you're right on the other side of this wall.

It's impossible to dream knowing you're all I'll see once I close my eyes.

You'll manage. Adalyn deserves the full zoo experience.

Goodnight, dream girl.

I grin, my heart still thundering in my chest and it has absolutely nothing to do with my recent orgasm.

Goodnight, Jasper Diamond. Sexy God. Rock man.

He doesn't reply, and I'm grateful for it.

My hand slips from the wall, and I slide my pajamas back on. My body slinks fully under the covers, and my eyes close once again, even heavier than before.

Only this time, there is a smile curving my lips.

I've never done that sort of thing with anyone. I'm not even sure what you'd call it. All I know is that tomorrow morning at eight am is going to be one of the most awkward greetings I've had in a very long time. And I can't help but look forward to it.

SIXTEEN

Jasper

I WASN'T LYING when I texted Viola that I wouldn't be able to sleep knowing she was on the other side of the wall.

I couldn't.

Her sounds, muffled by the wall, echoed in my head. The knowledge that I got her off once again, clawed at my skin. Me. I got her off. The understanding that I said a lot of things I likely shouldn't have, churned in my stomach.

I tossed and turned and walked around the room until, finally, the only way to shut off my overworking brain was to either storm into her room or climb in bed with Adalyn who likes to sleep in the center of the bed like a starfish, affording me only a small space on the edge.

It still felt like more than I deserved.

I don't know what came over me. Why I texted Viola in the first place.

But I walked out of that show with her crawling through my

mind. The songs I sang. The words dripping from my tongue. The new songs I've been writing like I haven't in years.

She was in all of that.

And then, as I was finding my way through the arena, I stumbled upon Gus feeling up some chick in the dark. He was laughing, and she was giggling, and I could smell her floral perfume, and I was sick. Angry and sick.

Why the fuck should he get to continue screwing every girl who glances in his direction while I'm stranded alone, pining after the girl he claims to love?

Sure, I could go after the screaming girls as Viola called them. I could score a chick in the back room too. Easy. I'd hardly have to blink. In fact, I bet I could point my finger at any of the girls in the crowd, and they'd come running. That's not even arrogance. It's a simple fact. I'm a rock star. I make music for a living, and because of that, women fall at my feet.

Do they give a shit that I have a daughter? That my days with her are what my world revolves around? That she's not just any neurologically typical kid, but a kid with challenges that I face day in and day out? Do they give a motherfuck about me other than my profession and the fact that I'm rich?

The answer is no.

And that's why, when I entered my suite and looked at Viola, her hair plaited in two long ropes, her hazel eyes smiling, even when her lips barely were, another piece of me cracked open. Gus was off fucking some girl, and I was there, staring at the girl I am in love with who loves my little girl and doesn't care a lick about my money or fame.

In fact, I don't think she likes any of that stuff.

Talk about a turn-on.

So I texted her about the zoo–something I was already thinking of doing with Ady–as I texted Marco, asking him to make it happen. Then things got out of hand from there, but I'd be lying if I said images of her riding my cock in the bathroom weren't spurring me on.

What I never expected was to hear her.

Now I'm sipping coffee while trying to get Ady to go potty before I get her dressed to meet Viola. "No potty."

"Ady, you need to go potty before we leave for the zoo." I set my mug down on the counter and crouch down, smiling at my naked little bug. "Don't you want to go see the animals today?"

She stares at me as if she's mulling this over when really, she's stalling. She's insanely clever and stubborn, two attributes I love and admire, but I have a strong feeling I'll like them less when she's fifteen and more when she's twenty-five.

Finally, her eyes widen, and I know she has to go, and without a word, she climbs on and does her thing. "You want to wear your new Minnie dress?"

"Minnie dress," she agrees after washing her hands, and by the time I'm finished putting on her shoes, there's a knock at the door. Anticipation slams into me, and I suck in a deep breath, wondering just what this will be like.

There was no need for Viola to run from me last night.

This morning, anything with her is possible.

With Adalyn's hand tucked in mine, I open the door.

Viola is standing there, wearing one of her stupid-short skirts–this one black and red–a matching red shirt and black Chucks. Her long blonde hair is braided, hanging heavily over one shoulder.

I stare at her.

Fuck, I can't help myself.

Her eyes rove around, but the moment they latch onto mine, a blush rises on her cheeks. Is she thinking about our sext conversation last night? She has to be. I sure as hell am.

But is she thinking about more than that?

About the bathroom when her body was straddling mine? The way she was grinding on me, losing herself in pleasure. The way we made each other come like two teenagers dry-humping.

Does she want to do that again with me?

Does she want me to take her into my room and do everything to her that I described last night? My dick starts to swell in my jeans, and for the very first time in my life, I wish Ady wasn't standing here with me.

What would happen if she wasn't?

The three of us are silent, not even a good morning or a hi between us to break the tension.

Luckily, Marco comes rushing over, half-dressed and slightly out of breath, and any awkwardness that was sitting between Viola and me becomes his. "OMG. I'm so sorry if I'm late. But I've got everything you need right here."

Marco thrusts tickets into my hand that I take reflexively. "You're fine," I say, clearing my voice once while dragging my gaze reluctantly away from Viola over to him. "Vi just got here."

"Great," Marco sags with relief, dropping his head onto Vi's shoulder.

She scrunches up her nose. "OMG is right. Ugh. Marco, I can smell strange man all over you."

"I know. He's still in my bed." Marco grins, closing his eyes before twisting his head and finding Viola. "I wish I could show you this one because he's insanely hot, but I don't think hookup show-and-tell is a good idea with the boss and his kid." Marco juts his thumb in our direction as if Adalyn and I aren't standing here. I narrow my eyes, shaking my head, but he disregards me completely.

"Probably not," Vi laughs. "Maybe next time you have a hot stranger in your bed, I'll meet him."

"Mmmkay. It's a date." Marco leans further into her. "I'm going back to bed while you responsible people get to go play. I'm flipping exhausted. You wouldn't believe what time we rolled in last night. Your brothers in blood and arms have some serious stamina." He yawns loudly, and Adalyn giggles.

"Big yawn," she says, mocking the sound of his yawn.

Marco smiles brightly, righting his body and staring down at Adalyn. "Can I pick you up? Carry you down to the car?" he asks her.

"Shirtless and stinking like strange man? I don't think so."

Marco shifts to me and nods. "Right. Good call on that one." He drops into a squat, dotting Adalyn's nose with the tip of his finger. "Take a picture of a giraffe for me. They're my favorite." Adalyn doesn't reply, but she doesn't shirk away from him either. "Have fun at the zoo, princess Adalyn. I can't wait to hear all about it." He leans in, kissing the top of her head. Marco stands and begins to walk back down the hall, the three of us following after him but stopping at the private elevator Marsellus is waiting patiently at. But before Marco enters his room, he twists his head over his shoulder and calls out, "Oh, and Vi?"

"Yeah?" she replies with a bemused tone to her voice.

"Thought you should know that you look out of this world gorgeous this morning." He throws me a conspiratorial wink and then enters his hotel room, laughing lightly to himself as he goes.

Bastard. Was I that obvious?

"He's right. You do," I tell her and then feel like a fool. Jesus. I did not just say that to her after Marco did. Fuck.

"Thanks," she mumbles, and I want to smack the butt of my hand against my forehead. Fourteen all over again. This girl takes any cool I've ever had and smashes it beneath her feet.

We step onto the elevator, Marsellus silently flanking me.

Viola takes Adalyn's other hand and whispers to her, "Men are trouble, Ady. The sooner you learn that life lesson, the better equipped you'll be."

Can't argue that.

HALF AN HOUR LATER, we're walking through the mostly empty grounds of the zoo. There are zoo employees about, feeding the animals and making sure they have enough water and whatever else they need. It's hot out. Not terrible at this moment, but you can feel the heat coming as the sun blazes high overhead without the added benefit of clouds or even a gentle breeze.

Adalyn, for her love of the water and fish, isn't so into the land animals.

The director of the zoo greeted us at the gate and asked if we'd like a private tour and an opportunity to feed some of the animals. Viola seemed into the idea, but Adalyn screamed as we approached the petting area, scaring a baby goat. After that, we decided it was best to go off on our own, though Adalyn hasn't quite rebounded.

Even with keeping our distance behind all the safety fences and barriers.

Viola and I are holding Adalyn's hands, swinging her small body between us while we walk along, chatting about...well, nothing. And everything.

We're just talking, and I don't think she and I have ever done this.

At least not since we were very young. By the time puberty hit, my interactions with her consisted of me staring from a distance and writing everything I ever wanted to tell her down in my note-book–all nerdy awkwardness. By the time we reached high school, she was dating my brother; I was ignoring her and generally hating life.

But today...

Today shouldn't feel like this with her.

Like a beginning. Like potential.

We approach the lion area, leaning along the railing and watching as the female lions lick and clean the two baby lions they have. The male lions are off on the side, sunbathing on two huge boulders.

"See this, Ady?" Viola asks, picking Ady up so she has a better view. "This is what the real world is actually like. Women do all the work, hunt, tend to the babies, while the lazy men sunbathe and relax."

"Hey," I grumble, leaning in just a little–or a lot–closer and nudging my elbow into her arm. Her skin erupts in goosebumps at the contact, and I can't stop my smile. "Not all of us are lazy." Ady peeks over at me and giggles as I make a silly face at her.

Viola bobs her head, winking at me. "True. Ady, your dad is the exception. Otherwise, that my dear, is the law of the jungle."

"Or maybe you just haven't been with any real men yet," I quip, unable to hold back my smirk. I tug on her braid, twirling the thick plait around my hand and pulling it enough to make her face me.

I need her eyes on me.

"Considering they're as easy to come by as that cheetah in the wild, I'll let you know when I find one."

Her brow arches, and my body shifts, desperate to be just a little closer. Our gazes tangle, her lips parting. So full. So lush. The bottom just a little fuller than the top. I lick mine.

Leaning into her, I whisper against her ear, my breath fanning along her skin, "I'd be happy to prove you wrong. To be your sexy god again, dream girl. Or do you like it better when I call you my nanny?"

Her breath hitches, and I don't know what's happening between us. A shift? A truce? The build-up to some mind-blowing, incredible sex? Whatever the hell it is, I can't get enough, and I don't want it to stop. Even if it feels like the ultimate cheat.

I watch the erratic pulse at the base of her neck, wanting to put my lips there, to taste it with my tongue and teeth. Scrolling back up to her eyes, everything in my mind clears but her. My brother. My band. This tour. The fact that I cannot take what I've always wanted.

Gone.

It's just us in this moment—the way maybe it has been with us all along. She looks as though she's going to say something else—something that will no doubt cut me off at the knees—when Adalyn squirms in her arms.

I step back, and Viola clears her throat, her eyes blinking rapidly. "What do you think of the lions, Adalyn?" She doesn't answer. Just watches them, her expression pinched and intense. "What does the lion say?" Viola tries again.

"Rarrr." Ady glances over at the lions and then trembles exaggeratedly, her eyes widening until they look like they're about to pop out of her head. "Eeek. Scary lions."

"Those fat things?" I point, chuckling lightly.

"Okay. All done lions. Say no thank you lions."

"Good words, Ady," Viola praises. "Nice job telling us, kiddo. Okay. All done lions."

Ady shakes her head violently. Reaching out for me, her fingers crawl up my chest, and I lift her into my arms, holding her snugly against me. "I feel so bad," I murmur, kissing her crown. "This was supposed to be fun for her. An escape. And I think she hates it."

Viola stares at me helplessly. "What should we do? Do you want to leave and try and find a park or something? It's such a beautiful day." She runs her fingers down the back of Ady's hair, feeling just as bad as I do.

I bluster out a loud breath. "Let's sit down. At least enjoy the sun and outdoors before we have to go back. I brought her a snack, maybe that will help with things."

"Certainly can't hurt." Viola searches around before quickly whipping back to me, her eyes bright and a smile on her lips. "There was that long rectangular water feature we passed earlier. The one with the fountains. There were a bunch of benches around it. I bet Ady would like it there."

Perfect. I carry her back through the zoo until we reach the area Viola spoke of. Sitting down on one of the benches, I rest Adalyn's head against me.

"What's that?" Ady asks, shooting up straight while twisting her back and neck to find the four small fountains spraying water in the long pond-like structure. The sound of water slapping against water fills the air, stealing Adalyn's full attention.

"That's water. Wanna go see it?"

"What's that? What's that? What's that?"

"That's the fountains spraying water, bug. Are you hungry? I have your crackers and almond butter."

"What's that? What's—"

"What do you see, sweet girl?" Vi interrupts her repetition. Adalyn jumps out of my lap. I stand up, following her. "Do you want to go look at the water? I bet we can touch it with our fingers if we're really careful and daddy says it's okay."

"No touch water, Vi." Except Ady starts to run for the pond, full steam.

"Shit," I hiss under my breath. "Stop, Ady!" I yell, bolting toward her as fast as my legs can carry me. Reaching her just as she bends over like she's about to dive right in, my arm flies out, wrapping around her waist and yanking her back, so she doesn't fall in.

Viola is right beside me, one hand touching my back, the other on her chest over her heart, just as alarmed as I am.

"Sit down, Adalyn," I bark sternly, not loving how she just sprinted for the water. My heart hikes up in my chest just at the thought. She loves water like nothing else, and I swear, it's the universe fucking with me after what happened to my mother. I turn her to face me. "When daddy tells you to stop, you stop. You hear me? We do not go near water unless daddy or Vi are with you and holding your hand. Ever." Her green eyes meet mine, but she's not really listening, the distraction of the water is too much for her to care about what I have to say. I puff out an exasperated breath. "Here. Sit on the stone, and you can touch the water with your hand if you want. But that's it. Keep your bottom right here and no closer."

I drop to the ground, helping her sit beside me while still holding onto her as if my life—and hers—depends on it.

"You okay?" Vi asks, sitting with us and watching me with wary eyes.

"Yeah. I just...," I bluster out a sigh. "I wish she didn't like water as much as she does. It scares the hell out of me." Vi hums something out, observing Adalyn as her palm, fingers splayed, smacks at the murky pond, kicking up water and splashing it everywhere.

Silence stretches between us, my mind going in a hundred different directions. My mom. Viola. Adalyn. Viola.

I watch her intently, dragging my gaze down her shoulders, over her full tits to her narrow waist, all the way to her feet. I have so many things I want to tell her, and yet, the right words elude me as they always do where she's concerned.

I inhale sharply, thinking about the things I wrote to her last night, desire licking up my spine.

I'm staring at her, grappling with the need to kiss her. To take her. To make her mine. To get up and walk away. To stop this fucking insanity once and for all and shut her out completely.

Eventually, she'll find a new teaching job—I know she's been applying. Eventually, this tour will be over, and she'll leave. Or worse, Gus will pull his head out of his ass and stop fucking around and reclaim what has always been his.

Never mine.

What the fuck was I thinking texting her last night, bringing her here today?

I clear my throat, standing up and dragging an unhappy Adalyn away from the water. I've already lost so much. I can't lose any more.

SEVENTEEN

Viola

"I HATE THIS STATE," I mumble, staring around the hotel suite. "Have I mentioned that?"

"Only once or fifty times," Jules jests with a dramatic eyeroll as she munches down on some gluten-free, vegan macaroni and cheese, only to pull her fork back and stare at the pasta like it just personally offended her. "This shit is awful." She scrunches up her nose in distaste. "Jesus. How does this kid eat this garbage? Jasper should be brought up on charges for feeding inedible crap to his daughter."

I scowl at her, glancing quickly toward the bedroom Adalyn is fast asleep in. "It's not so bad once you get used to it. And Jasper is a fantastic father. He's just trying to do what he thinks is best for her."

"Oh," Jules exclaims with a knowing gleam to her eyes. She drops her fork back in her bowl with a small clang. Swiveling around on the couch, she crisscrosses her legs until she's facing me head-on. "Now we're defensive over Jasper, are we? A man you claim to hate...," she trails off, an uptick of an eyebrow to punctuate her point. I can feel my stupid cheeks warming.

"I'm not defensive over Jasper," I squeak out.

I might be a touch.

Especially when it comes to the way he parents that little girl in there. I may hate on him, and I may want to jump him the other half of the time, but all that drama aside, he's everything I would ever want for the father of my children and more.

That thought alone makes my stupid ovaries jump up and holler, yes girl, us too!

"You're totally screwing his brains out. You're blushing like a virgin in a sex shop."

I roll my eyes back at her, getting up off the couch and grabbing our bowls. Anything to get away from my nosy friend. "I'm not screwing anyone." I put the bowls back on the tray from room service. "And I'm not blushing." I might be a bit.

"Oh my God. This is the best thing ever. Wait!" She holds her hand up in the air. "Does Gus know you want his evil twin?"

I throw her a narrow-eyed, hands-on-my-hips, all-attitude glare. "I don't want Jasper." I totally do, despite the truth behind the evil twin stuff. "That's coco-loco crazy talk, and I don't want Gus either. I'm the nanny, and this is a temporary arrangement, and that's all there is to it. So, stop. Please."

I simply do not have it in me to tell Jules, my very best friend, what's been happening between Jasper and me.

The bathroom in Dallas or the sext conversation in Houston. Probably because I've never told Jules anything about the dark chemistry and twisted world that is me and Jasper.

"That line between love and hate?" Jules continues because she can be a bitch like that. She clicks her tongue, still smiling like the cat who ate something delicious and fattening and wholly satisfying.

"No love here. Just hate."

"Not even for Gus?" she frowns.

I sigh. A rush of air collapses my lungs. "Jules, please. Nothing is happening or is going to happen with any of the Diamond boys."

"You're such a liar. Not even a good one. He's your dream guy."

Dream guy. *Dream girl.* I bite down on my lip to hide my smile.

I don't even bother asking her to clarify which one she's referring to. "Dream guys don't exist, and any girl who foolishly allows herself to hang on to that notion will only get burned."

Hashtag truth.

"Wow. Bitter much?"

Maybe. Yeah. Because I seriously thought Jasper and I had something going in Houston, and now? Now I don't know. I feel like he's put a wall back up between us, and all I want to do is smash it down. I feel this thing between us, and I know he does too. I know it.

But is it just physical for him?

Is that why it's so easy for him to get lost in me one minute and brush me off the next? Is this building up to yet another epic heartbreak for me?

I once played this game in college: Tell us how you meet your dream guy in terms of your ultimate fantasy. Most girls laughed. Some blushed. Many were too drunk to have fucks to give. So, it's safe to say, the answers were all over the place.

One girl said at a sex club. One said at the library. Another said in the middle of a rainstorm while he was saving a cat from up a tree. The list went on.

The entire stupid time this game was going on, I was drinking.

Because Gus and I had just broken up a few weeks before.

And I had been incessantly listening to their album and Jasper's words that were written for me.

To say I had a conflicted heart was an understatement. To say I was a bit torn-up would have been putting it mildly. So, when it got to me, I swallowed whatever concoction I was consuming and said, "There is no such thing as a dream guy. Only our dream we allow imperfect men to be a part of."

You can imagine how popular that response was.

But all these years later, I'm not sure how untrue it is. I mean, what the hell is a dream guy? Does he wait at our feet? Praise us continually? Fuck us senseless?

Or is he just some guy that we can't get out of our heads?

Is he the guy who consumes our every waking hour? Drives us up a proverbial wall while setting our souls—and our bodies—on fire? Is he the guy who challenges absolutely everything about you, and still you cannot get enough of him?

"Nothing to be bitter about. Nothing is going on with either of them, and I'm happy for that."

"Vi, not every guy will burn you. What happened between you and Gus was so long ago. You can't live your life like this. Especially not when they all want you." Her eyebrows bounce up and down suggestively, but her eyes hold sympathy, her lips flattening as she tucks her ash-brown hair behind her ears. "They've always wanted you. All those boys. Every goddamn boy." She throws her arms around the empty suite. "They orbit around you like planets to the sun. Hell, even fucking Spencer wouldn't shut up on the ride up here about how excited he was to see you again. Not the guys. Not the band play live. But *you*." She points at me, enunciating the word you. "It's always been like that. If they're not the ones for you, then fine. But eventually you have to give someone a real try. Allow yourself to be happy again. You deserve it."

I shake my head, because she's got it all wrong.

"I am happy."

She cocks a dubious eyebrow that I turn away from. No one likes their miserable reflected back at them.

The truth is, prior to this tour, I didn't have a whole lot to be happy about. My world vacillated between stagnant and awful. So, it's not really my fault if I haven't been happy for so long that I hardly understand what the word means. But I try. I do. I go into every day with a smile because every day is filled with limitless potential. I know better than anyone how quickly life and luck can change.

Besides, men aren't the antidote to unhappiness.

If anything, they're partners in crime with it.

"Gus screws every woman with a pulse, a heartbeat, and a pretty smile. Jasper treats me like I'm a plague he's forced to endure. Keith and Henry view me as a little sister, and as for Spencer?" I shrug my shoulders helplessly. "I don't know what to tell you on that. That's just Spencer. He and I dated for like a hot second and ended ages ago. We've stayed friends, as you know. So enough about men, Jules. It's not what you're making it out to be."

She throws her hands up in surrender, forcing a smile. "Fine. I'll shut up. You're a big girl and more than know how to handle yourself. I just think you're ignoring something very obvious and potentially hot. Think of all the reverse harem situations you could get yourself into."

I roll my eyes at her again, and she laughs. "I can't even manage one dick."

"But, God," she sighs, fanning herself dramatically. "Could you imagine what a night that would be with all those dicks? I'd give my right tit to have those men in one sitting."

That's when the door to the hotel suite opens. That's when Gus comes sauntering in, sweat coating his large, muscular form, making his white tee like a second skin. Keith, Henry, Spencer, and Jasper follow, all with dopey smiles on their faces, laughs lingering on their lips.

Jules smirks at me, arching a brow and tilting her head to the side. "See what I mean? Gives hot as fuck a new meaning."

A laugh bursts from my chest.

"What?" Gus asks. "What did we miss?" He wraps his arms around me, pulling me snugly against him and nuzzling his face in my neck. I swat him away, and he chuckles when he sees me crinkling my nose. "You used to like me sweaty."

"Only when you made her sweaty, which you don't anymore because your dick is too interested in other pussy," Jules snaps, and Gus steps back from me like she just zapped him with a cattle prod.

"Jesus, Jules. Way to make a guy feel like shit."

Jules glowers. "It's not my job to make you feel good. You hurt my friend. You cheated. And though it's been seven years, I never got the chance to kick your ass for it."

He stares at me as something sorrowful and despairing crosses his features. I frown in return because I get Jules on this, but it's also been so long, and as I told her, nothing is going on between me and Gus. So, intentionally hurting him for past transgressions, really isn't my game.

Even if he does deserve a little bit of a beating for it.

"Okay. That's it." Gus grabs me, picking me up and hauling me over his shoulder. He starts to march me toward the door of the suite as I squeal as quietly as I can so I don't wake up Ady.

"Put me down." I pinch his shoulder and back, and his only response is to spank my ass that's hiked up high in the air.

I'm wearing a skirt. Marvelous. I can only imagine the view I'm giving everyone. I can't even tell if it's still covering my ass.

"No. You and I need to talk in private."

"Gus," Jasper barks in that way of his. "Put the nanny down."

I raise my head from Gus's back and flip off Jasper. He slays me with a cocky grin, a self-satisfied gleam to his eyes. He knows he's pushing my buttons and loves the reaction it produces.

Unfortunately for me, it also makes him look sexy because his wavy reddish-brown hair is even darker and brushed off his face, slightly damp from his sweat. He's wearing a different shirt than the one he left in. One that's not covered in sweat like Gus's but still sticking to his muscular arms and cut abs and fuck.

I hate how attracted to the devil I am.

He stares at me, and I stare back at him. He mouths the words 'my nanny' to me, that grin still doing wild things to my insides.

I mouth 'sexy god' back at him, and now that cocky grin is a full smile. He nods, his green eyes turning heated as he raises a challenging brow at me. One that says, wouldn't you like to find out just how much?

Why can't he be like this all the time with me? Why does he have to be so damn mercurial? So hot and cold? He's giving me whiplash.

"She's off duty, man. And mine. So fuck off."

Jasper's smile falls instantly.

I smack Gus repeatedly in the back. Hard. So hard my hands sting. "Knock it off, Gus."

But of course, he doesn't.

He's Gus.

Gus has no concept of limits. Jasper glares at me, his gaze searching mine before it drags endlessly over Gus and how he's holding me. All the delicious heat in his eyes is gone, replaced with pure, unfiltered enmity. He shakes his head, his jaw clenching as he lets out some kind of sardonic growl.

"Whatever. I'm taking a shower." Jasper storms off in the direction of his bedroom, closing the door with a firm click behind him.

"Sorry, Vi. Looks like I started something here," Jules winks at me, not sorry at all. "Maybe once you and Gus become Facebook official again, the entertainment shows will stop referring to you as the unknown woman touring with Wild Minds."

"Huh?" I raise my head again to find Jules.

She shrugs. "That's what I saw the other night." She holds her fist up under her chin as if it's a microphone. "There have been a lot of speculations as to the identity of the mysterious woman traveling with the band. Unfortunately, Wild Minds was not available for comment," she says in a tone mocking a news reporter before she rolls her eyes.

"The hell? What do they care about who the nanny is?"

"Because you're more than that, aren't you?"

"Stop it, Jules," Keith warns. "And shut up about it, okay? Jasper hates any and all press. Especially when it comes to Adalyn and the people around her. The press have been giving us a wide berth so far, and we'd like to keep it that way."

I shake my head, dropping back down against Gus. "Can you put me down already?"

"No. Not until we've talked."

"Gus. I don't want to have a talk with you. At least not until you've showered." I swat at him again, but he doesn't put me down. He's a man on a mission.

"Then come shower with me. We can talk in there."

"My Viola, does it drive you crazy?" Jules asks. I groan, letting my head drop completely against Gus because I have a really good idea where this is going. "I mean, the girl walks into a room, and all men turn stupid and desperate. It's pathetic, gentlemen. Vi, I'm like in awe of you and would love your secret, but these men are beneath you. You deserve better."

"Sounds like jealousy to me," Spencer drawls, dropping onto the seat beside Jules on the couch and tossing his arm over her shoulder.

She casts an annoyed scowl at him. "More like curiosity. I mean, yeah, she's my girl, and she's awesome, but you men drool in a puddle at her feet. She's ten thousand miles above you. Get a life already."

Gus spins around, nearly knocking my head into Keith, who is standing by the door, sipping from his bottle of Jack and grinning stupidly as he enjoys the show we're all providing him.

"You wanna know why we fall to her feet?" Gus asks as Jules's eyes tilt toward his. "Because she's more than just beautiful or smart or sweet or fun or funny. She's the package. The whole show. The one you're dumb to let go of."

I swallow down a lump in my throat. Jesus. I had no idea Gus actually thought that way about me. All this time, I assumed his comments were playful and far from serious. Especially since he regularly has a revolving door of women.

With that, Gus spins back around, pushes Keith out of the way, opens the door to the suite, and starts to march me down the long hallway. Marsellus and Thomas, the other security guy, are still there, hanging out in the hall and shooting the shit. They throw us a questioning brow, and I shrug at them helplessly, reaching out for them to help a girl out. They chuckle and go back to their conversation, no help at all.

"Gus, if you want to talk, we'll talk, but put me down. You're killing my stomach like this."

Gus lets me slide down his chest, but I don't get far as his arms encircle my waist. He stares down into me. "I fucked up, Vi. I fucked up so bad with you."

"Aww, Gus. Stop it." I cup his face in my hands. "That was a long time ago."

He shakes his head, pulling out his keycard and leading me into his room.

Dropping down to the edge of the bed, I'm left standing before him with only the glow of the lamp on the bedside table to see by. Gus stares up at me, his expression conflicted and pained. I hate seeing Gus this way.

Maybe if I still loved him in that way, I'd be angry with him. More resentful of the way we ended and the distance that spawned between us. I know he checked up on me. Spencer was joking around about it all night when he and Jules first arrived, but it's not the first time I've heard about it.

Even Jasper did a few times, though not as often as Gus did.

Gus caring about me was never the problem between us. I always knew how he felt. He never tried to hide it.

It was everything else that got in our way.

"The first time Jasper and I met you, we were eight. Just little kids, right?" I watch him rub his jaw with his fingers as he works this through. "Jasper met you first, and he came home and told me had met an angel. I thought he was kidding. I mean, Jasper was always a bit on the deeper, more dramatic side than I was. Way more poetic with his thoughts and words. But then, when I met you, I knew precisely what he was talking about."

"Gus—"

He shakes his head, stopping me. "Just let me finish, okay?"

I reach out, running my fingers through his short sandy-brown hair. He leans into my touch, blowing out a heavy penetrating sigh.

"In my head, in that moment, I knew you were the girl for me. It was just a feeling I had, and even though I was only eight, it never dissipated. You were going to be mine, and I was going to be yours, and that was the end of it. Hell, I made sure that was the way it was going to go." I furrow my brows at the way he says that, because it sounds like there's something behind it. "I was a selfish bastard. I never let anyone get in my way when it came to you. *No one.* Until I got in my own way."

I kneel down before him, setting my hands on his parted thighs. I hate seeing him hurting this way, but I think I also have to hear it from him. I feel like part of me still needs this closure on such a big chapter of my life. The Gus chapter. The one that consumed so many years of my life. That brought me so much joy.

The one that ended abruptly with tears and heartache.

"I never considered what the other girls would do to us. To you. In my head, they were just there. Meaningless. Stupid fun I wasn't serious about, or even gave a second thought to, after it was over. I couldn't tell you any of their names or what they looked like. I was drinking and smoking a ton and doing blow, and they were throwing themselves at me. In my head, you were so very separate from that life. From those women and the drugs and alcohol. You were my Vi. The one I held high on the pedestal while all that other bullshit was so far beneath you, I never considered it'd reach you."

His fingers glide up my arms until they reach my face, his gaze tracking the movement as our eyes meet.

"God, Vi. You have no idea how brokenhearted I was when you ended things. Losing you," he shakes his head, "especially like that, was never a factor in my head. I always assumed you'd go to college, and I'd do the rock star thing, and eventually, when that ride was done, we'd come back together. Get married and make babies. But we got famous so quickly, and you weren't there, and then we were over, and I was a fucking wreck."

A tear slides down my face, followed quickly by another. He

wipes them away, leaning in and kissing my cheeks, erasing the moisture on my face along with the ache in my heart.

"I am so sorry I hurt you." His thumbs glide up and down my face. "That I betrayed you like that. That I ruined us in that way."

I raise myself up, my knees pressing into the stiff carpet as I wrap my arms around his neck, cradling him so close to me. God. Gus. This man.

"Thank you," I whisper in his ear, sniffling lightly. "I needed to hear that, I think."

"I love you, Vi." He holds me back with equal ardor. "And I've been trying to fix things. Fix all my mistakes for you. To give you everything I ever promised you." He chuckles humorlessly. "I've made you so many over the years. But no matter what I do or try, I feel like I'm making things a million times worse."

"No." I draw back and meet his eyes from inches away. "No, you're not. You and I have always been straight. Even after things ended, I had a miserable time being mad at you. I knew what you were in the middle of, and I was so damn happy and proud. I just...," I tilt my head back, staring up at the ceiling as I try to make sense of things before I find him again. "I just couldn't do it anymore. I didn't *want* to do it anymore. The cheating hurt, and ultimately, that's what ended us. But we were growing apart before that." He looks like he's about to argue, but I stop him. "You're in my heart, Gus. You're always going to be. It's just different now than it was when we were kids."

"I sometimes wish I could change that different."

I smile softly, running my hands up and down the back of his head. Our foreheads press together, and Gus smiles back at me, like the weight that had been resting heavily on his shoulders is lighter.

I don't know what to say to that.

Sometimes, our pasts have to be left where they are.

Sometimes, another's actions change everything inside you.

Sometimes, words hold on so strong you can't unhear them or pretend they didn't reshape your core.

Because, while I love Gus, he's not the one who owns my heart anymore. That's the first sign that we fall in love without reason. That our hearts are blind to all that surround them.

One brother already broke my heart. The other is gearing up to destroy it for good.

EIGHTEEN

Jasper

STEPPING OUT OF THE SHOWER, I towel myself off quickly, throw on some clean clothes and down another gulp of bourbon, finishing off my glass. It doesn't burn the way I wish it did. The expensive stuff never does, and that's all Marco gets me, unlike Keith's Jack Daniels. Maybe I should steal that from him because this doesn't hurt the way my insides do, and I seriously wish it did.

When will this stop?

How the fuck do I *make* it stop?

I pour myself another three fingers and then blow out a heavy breath before I twist the knob and exit my room. Keith and Spencer are sitting on either side of Jules, laughing and touching in what comes off as something intimate, all with half-empty drinks precariously held in their hands. Henry is in the chair, scrolling through his phone with singular focus.

Gus and Viola are nowhere to be seen.

I've tried to make the worst scenario better. Filled it up with every rationalization I could throw at it. But the simple truth is, she's not here because she's with him. And I can't do a damn thing about it other than watch her go.

"We're scouting clubs," Henry announces without even bothering to glance up at me. I stare down at myself, my tee, jeans, and bare feet, and then my drink. I'm not going anywhere tonight, so instead, I spill my latest refill down the back of my throat and wipe my mouth with the back of my wrist before I set my glass down.

"Around here?"

He shrugs a shoulder. "There are some. You in?" He smirks, already knowing my answer.

"Oh yeah. Dancing and easy pussy, here I come."

Jules snorts. "God, you're so grumpy. Were you always this grumpy, or is having Viola fucking around with your brother throwing you off?"

I twist to her, and she's smiling wickedly, a devil-may-care aura coupled with something else incredibly sinister.

I don't think I've ever realized it before, probably because I never exactly gave Viola's best friend, Jules, much consideration, but this girl has motives and plans, and right now, they all involve messing me up.

What the hell did Vi tell her about us?

Jules likes it. Whatever it is.

I narrow my eyes at her.

"What makes you think I give two flying shits where Gus or Viola are?"

That wicked smile grows an inch, like a lion toying with its prey.

"Because I saw the way you looked at her. *Especially* when Gus was all over her, staking his claim."

"Knock it off," Keith snaps, but Jules ignores him.

She rises off the couch, approaching me slowly, and thanks to the bourbon, my reflexes have slowed. Or maybe I'm just too caught off guard by this woman and her unexpectedness to react the way I likely should.

I didn't think Jules cared much about anything. At least she never seemed to before. Then again, like I said, I can't say I paid much attention to her.

"I know you and Vi haven't been getting along. She told me how much you guys fight. How much you two *hate* each other. I'm sorry, Jas," she purrs without an ounce of genuine remorse. Sidling up directly before me, she tilts her head coquettishly, slipping her hand up to my shoulder. "Must be aggravating to have your nanny, as you call her, be so in love with your brother. I thought you'd be more used to it by now."

"Jules–" Keith warns, but she waves him off.

My eyebrows knit together, my heart quickening in my chest. What the hell?

"I'm not saying anything y'all don't already know. I mean, you hired her for a job, and she sneaks off every chance she can get to be with him?" Jules shrugs, her smile morphing into something resembling sympathy without coming close to achieving it. "I just feel bad for you, is all. You can't blame her, though. I mean, those two, right?"

She giggles, smiling brightly and squeezing my shoulder. Her touch is like acid. I stare into her eyes, wanting to believe nothing she's saying is genuine.

"They've always been head over heels." She glances at the other guys to back her up, and I can't even register them right now. "Honestly, I think it's so great that you've given them this second chance. Viola has always wanted one. She was heartbroken when they ended the way they did. She was just telling me tonight how much she still loves him. How special this time with him has been."

Suddenly, it feels as if the room is spinning.

My axis altered just enough that I sway and step back.

Mercifully, her hand falls away from me.

I can't breathe, and I can't make sense of any of this. Viola was just telling Jules how much she still loves Gus? As in, telling her that tonight? They sneak off every chance they get? How did I miss this? Not even two nights ago, I made her come and–

"You're so full of shit, Jules," Spencer bites out, glowering at the back of her head.

But Jules is adamant. She shakes her head, staring into my eyes with pure fucking sincerity. "I'm sorry, cupcake. Your love of Viola will have to be put on hold. Were you here tonight while you boys were down at the show?" She rolls her head over her shoulder, raising an admonishing brow in his direction. "Oh, that's right, you weren't. You're just pissed because she broke up with you, and you're still crazy about her," Jules retorts, and Spencer grows pale.

I knew Viola dated Spencer briefly.

I thought I knew everything that was going on.

All the history. All the ins and outs of this tour and this trip and my brother and Viola.

How have I miscalculated this so poorly? Been so blind to what was happening beneath my nose? Jules is Viola's best friend, and frankly, I can't imagine why she'd lie to me about this, about her best friend.

Up until this moment, I dumbly assumed it was words. Gus posturing and puffing out his chest.

"You're drunk, Jules," Keith snaps. "Stop being a bitch."

"Whatever. Who gives a shit if she and Gus get back together anyway?" That's Spencer, and right now, I seriously wish he weren't here. I seriously wish none of them were here.

Especially Jules, who just annihilated my universe.

It's one thing to know my brother is after her, still loves her, it's another to find out she returns the feelings wholeheartedly. Especially when–

I shake my head.

They're together right now. He carried her off like a caveman to his lair. He's probably deep inside her at this very moment.

"You can talk all this shit, but I haven't seen them sneak off together," Keith interrupts my nightmare, and I can feel him staring into me, though I can't quite meet his gaze. "I haven't seen them together in private once. In fact, I can't even imagine when all that could have happened. She's always with Adalyn, and when we go out, Gus always has a woman with him. A woman who is not Viola."

"Still...," Henry muses. "Gus has been staking his claim again. I think we all know that's ultimately what he's after. It's probably just a matter of time." He lets out a loud chuckle. "Then again, they're in his room alone together now so...," he trails off, a wry grin etched on his face.

I swallow the lump in the back of my throat and push myself away from Jules and her omnipotent expression. She's staring at me like she can see through me, and it's setting my teeth on edge.

I already feel the buzz from the alcohol. I'm not a big drinker. One or two tops.

I should probably stop before I'm a hungover mess in the morning.

I find the bar and pour myself another half glass of whatever the hell we have out here. My hand plants onto the granite counter, my lungs ragged as I try to pull in air. I wish the truth didn't feel like this. Like a sucker punch to the gut and a bat to the head.

"Gus and Vi aside, I meant to tell her this earlier, but then she left with Gus, and I didn't have a chance." I take a long pull of my now tasteless drink and spin around to face Spencer. His expression is troubled, his brow furrowed, and lips pulled tight, and even though I have a storm going on inside my body right now, I focus on him. "Her mom came back to my bar again last week."

Jules blanches, flipping away from me back to Spencer. "I didn't know you saw her," she whispers.

"Yeah, Jules. I see everything. It's my bar," he points to his chest, widening his eyes. He takes a slow sip of his drink, resting the glass on his thigh. "I saw you arguing with her outside."

"Did you hear what we were saying?" Spencer shakes his head, and Jules lets out a loud sigh. "I was telling her to screw off. To leave Vi alone. She was asking how she could find her. Crazy, money-grubbing bitch wouldn't listen. I threatened to call the police on her, and she left."

"Does Vi know?" Keith asks, and Jules shakes her head miserably. "I mean, how long before her mother hears about those entertainment shows talking about the mystery woman and puts it together that it's Viola?"

"I didn't tell Vi," Jules admits. "I didn't want to upset her. Obviously, her mother is an extremely sore subject for her. I told her about the first time her mom came by the bar, and Viola looked like she was going to be sick. I don't really see the benefit in telling her her mother came back again, do you?" Jules raises an eyebrow at Spencer, folding her arms over her chest. "Besides," she scoffs, "I highly doubt her mother has a television or is watching those shows."

Spencer stands up, finishing off the rest of his drink and walking the glass over to the bar, resting it on the counter beside me. "Probably not. Just seemed odd that she'd come back, is all."

"You're the one who told her about this job," Jules snaps.

Spencer glares at her. "I figured she already knew and that's why she was there, trying to get more money out of her. Still doesn't explain why she came back."

Jules huffs out a breath, shaking her head incredulously. "I don't get it either. But Vi has always taken care of her, even when her mother was a total drugged-out, cunt witch. Maybe she figures she'll do it again even though she stole. Maybe she was just looking for some quick cash to score some drugs. Whatever. I told her off pretty good this last time. I don't think she's coming back again."

"And on this pleasant note, I'm going out." Henry stands up, slams down the last of his drink and heads for the door. "Who's coming with me?"

"Me," Spencer calls out, slapping me on the back. "It was good to see you, man. Thanks for having me up. It was an amazing show." I give him a quick hug and a handshake, and then he follows Henry out the door.

Keith throws me a wink and joins them, leaving me alone with Jules.

"Tell my girl whenever she pulls herself away from Gus that I'll call her tomorrow."

"Right. Have fun."

"I could always stay," she offers, her brown eyes meeting mine from beneath her lashes, a seductive smirk curling up her lips. It draws me up short. "We could have another drink together. Talk some more."

"No thanks."

Jules lets out a caustic laugh. "I was serious, you know. I saw the way you look at her."

I tilt my head, studying her. "What's your point, Jules? You think you saw something. Good for you."

She grins. "She loves him, is my point. Not you. I don't want to see either of you hurt. I know she's been putting all her efforts into him, neglecting her main job here." I open my mouth to challenge that, because whatever Viola has going on with Gus, she's been incredible with Ady, but Jules cuts me off before I can get the words out. "I wonder if maybe she's not the right nanny for you? I'd be better at it. I'm not saying to get rid of Vi. Let her stay with Gus, and you and I can take care of Ady. She really liked me tonight. We bonded quickly." Her hand reaches out, gliding up my chest, her lashes fluttering as she steps into me, trying to press her chest to mine.

Is she kidding me right now? How drunk can this girl be to even suggest that?

I hardly know Jules.

Only by extension, and in truth, I never liked her all that much.

This encounter certainly isn't changing my initial opinion of her.

I remove her hand from my chest, and she frowns. "Go out, Jules. I'll let Vi know you said bye."

With that, I turn away, dismissing her. I hear her indignant snort. "God, you boys are so dumb. You fall blindly and helplessly for her, and she's only ever loved Gus."

And with that, she's gone, slamming the damn door behind her like a goddamn child. Only I could give a fuck about her temper tantrum or if she's butt-hurt over the way I want Viola and not her.

Scowling at the door she just left through, I shift over to Adalyn's, listening against the wood. I don't hear her stirring, so I open it as gently as possible. Ady is in the center of the bed, with her stuffed Mickey and Minnie on either side of her, the plastic figurines Vi gave her clutched in her tiny fists.

I watch Ady sleep for a moment, smiling softly to myself. "I love you, bug," I whisper, shutting the door behind me.

I flick off most of the lights in the suite, pick up my drink, and carry it over to the sofa. My head falls back just as I hear the lock on the hotel door disengage.

And in walks Viola.

NINETEEN

Jasper

VIOLA GLANCES around the hotel room before her gaze catches mine. "Hey," she says, sounding surprised to find me here alone. "I'm sorry I took so long. Did you want to go out?" she questions, crossing the room until she's sitting on the couch beside me.

I don't want her sitting this close.

There's still a solid foot plus of room between us, but I can smell her and feel her, and I don't want to. They say there's a thin line between love and hate, but I think they've got it all wrong. It's not love that battles so closely with hate.

It's lust.

It's desire wrapped in poison.

Love is a casualty.

"Where's Gus?"

"Showering so he can go out with everyone else." She reaches out, touching my arm, trying to snag my attention, which I refuse to give her. "Seriously, Jas. You haven't been out at all this entire trip. You should go out with them."

"Would you rather go?" I ask, trying to hold in my bitter tone. "Be with Gus. Spend more time with Jules. I'm fine here."

Viola lets out a long-suffering sigh. Then a slight giggle. "Not really. As much as I do want to spend more time with Jules, I'm so freaking tired from all the travel and long nights. I don't know how the guys go out so much only to wake up and do it all again the next night."

I shrug up a shoulder, taking another sip of the drink I should have stopped drinking an hour ago. "It's the life they live for."

Viola sinks down into the sofa, inadvertently shifting closer to me as she does. "What about you, Jasper Diamond? What do you live for?"

I swallow my tongue before I say something stupid like *moments like these* or *you*. Instead, I give her something far simpler, but no less true. "Adalyn."

She smiles a hidden smile at that. Like it makes her heart flutter the way she makes mine.

"What about you, Viola Starr? What do you live for?"

Her head swivels toward mine. Our eyes lock, and she stays so still, just like that. Almost as if she's waiting on something. Something I cannot give her in return.

"Don't you enjoy going out. Being part of the insanity that is this tour?" I continue amidst her heavy silence.

She frowns. "Not sure that's really for me. It's certainly not what I live for. Ady had a good night," she offers, changing the subject. "I've been working with her on something, and so far, she seems to be doing pretty well with it."

"What?" I shift toward her, staring at her, a goddess before my eyes while she talks about my daughter. After she was just with my brother. I'm a real bastard.

"I've noticed she has trouble transitioning with things. Especially away from a favorable activity. Or even getting her to partake in a less favorable task. So, this evening for example, she didn't want to get ready for bed. Hates brushing her teeth. But loves her *Brown Bear, Brown Bear* book, right?" I nod. "So I said to her, first we brush teeth, then we read *Brown Bear, Brown Bear.*"

"And she did it?"

She hums out a yes. "I've done that a few times with her, and she's been very receptive. You know, first the less favorable task, then something she likes. It incentivizes her, and she understands that if she does what I want her to do, she'll get what she wants after. She even repeated it back to me, so she's verbalizing this as well. She's so goddamn smart, Jas. Like, insanely so."

I reach out and grab a lock of her long, golden hair, twirling the end around in my fingers.

It's so soft. So silky.

And I'm drunk. On bourbon. On her. Always on her. On the way she loves and cares for Adalyn. Yet another champion my baby didn't realize she needed.

Jules is certifiably crazy. *She loves him. Not you.* Maybe not fully crazy. Maybe just drunk and jealous? I get that inclination. That desire. I can't exactly fault her for it either.

Viola is everything Jules could never be.

"I'll have to try that with her. I'll watch you do it, and then I'll try." Viola observes my fingers in her hair, a thick silence growing between us. "Do you remember the first time I did this?"

I have no idea why I just asked her that.

"When you kissed me. That day under the tree."

I haven't kissed her since. My mind roves back to that day. To that afternoon that somehow changed the course of my entire life.

I watched her walk along the grass in my direction, all long legs and toned stomach peeking out from beneath her white billowy shirt. I had finally worked up the nerve and slipped her a note in Algebra. I asked her to meet me here, at the tree near her home. And she came.

"Hey," I said, my smile growing as my eyes danced along her feature by perfect feature. "You made it."

"I made it," she echoed and then winced slightly. She was as nervous as I was. Tucking her hands into the pockets of her cutoff jean shorts, she rocked back on her heels, taking a silent breath. "What were you writing as I was walking over here?"

I took a few steps in her direction, a color I rarely exhibited rising up my cheeks. I was writing about her. I always wrote about her. "Just some poetry. Nothing special."

"Can I read it?"

I never let anyone read it.

I shook my head, reaching out and grasping a lock of her waist-length blonde hair, twisting it around my fingers. I had hung out with her a hundred times. Maybe more. Alone. With Gus. But something about this moment felt different to me. There was a tension between us, something sweet and magical. Something that tasted like the early autumn air we were bathed in. Something that pulled me in closer to her like a moth to a flame.

I tugged gently on her hair, coaxing her forward until our bodies were practically aligned with only inches to spare between us. "I wanted to ask you something," I said, my voice slightly jumpy, my eyes dancing along the lines of her face. My heart was skipping out of my chest as I narrowed in on her lips. So full. So pink. So pretty. Hers did the same to mine, and my blood roared in my veins.

"What's that?" she asked when I didn't follow that up.

"This," I whispered, tugging again on her hair until she crashed into me. Her hands reflexively grasped my shoulders for support. One of mine landed on her hip, the other digging deeper into her hair.

I grinned like a fool seconds before my lips pressed to hers. For a long second, they held there, not moving, but breathing in and out. I was terrified. Waiting for her to push me away.

She smiled against me, and it was as if that was what I had been waiting on because the moment I felt it, my head tilted one way and

hers the other, and our lips began to move in sync. Like they were prac-
ticed when they were anything but.

She smelled like vanilla and sunshine and tasted like candy.

I pulled back an inch, stared into her eyes, and smiled the way she
was smiling. Then I kissed her again, feeling drugged and weightless.

I couldn't get enough of her.

Fleeting pecks and deeper dives that left me dizzy. I stepped back,
needing to take a breath, and watched as she licked her lips. My fore-
head dropped to hers.

"We're tied to each other forever now," I promised. "You know
that, right? A first kiss with you could never be enough."

I stare at her, reliving the taste of her on my lips. I went home and
wrote an entire fucking song all about it. A first kiss with you could
never be enough–I bet she knows I wrote her that line too.

Years later and look at me, still obsessed with the same girl.

She finally finds the nerve to glance up into my eyes. I wrap the
lock around my finger, tugging gently. The way I did that day. "Your
hair is shorter than it used to be."

"I go to a place every year and have them cut off a ten-inch pony-
tail so they can donate it."

"Donate it?"

She nods. "To be made into a wig for people who have cancer
and lose all their hair."

Her fingers find the back of my head, running through my hair
the way she did in Dallas on the bed. It feels so good, and she smells
so good, and I– "Gus is probably waiting on you."

She shakes her head. "No. He's not."

And then she climbs up and over, straddling my legs.

My hand drops to her bare thighs, my gaze follows. "Why do you
always wear skirts?"

"I like them. I feel pretty when I wear them."

"You are pretty when you wear them. You're always pretty." She
removes the glass from my other hand, taking a small sip before
setting it down on the side table.

"How drunk are you?"

"Pretty drunk," I admit, still staring down at her creamy thighs. How did she get on my lap? Why am I letting her do this to me? "What made you want to become a teacher?" I ask because if I don't ask her something ordinary, I'm going to kiss her.

I can practically hear her smile. "I've always wanted to be a teacher."

"Why special education? Why autism?"

Because... What are the goddamn odds that Viola–*my Viola*– would become a special education teacher with a specialty in autism when I just so happen to have an Autistic daughter. I know she didn't know. I realize she picked this before I had Adalyn. I know this is a coincidence. But, are there really such things?

Does this somehow mean that this woman is meant to be mine?

"I like helping kiddos who need a little extra help. When I was in college, I did a rotation in an elementary school. There was a little boy there who wasn't verbal and was reported to have a lot of behavioral problems, especially around other kids. Anyway, none of the other students in my group wanted to work with him, but I would catch him watching me, and one day, I sat down next to him. I didn't talk to him. We just colored together for a while, and then I had to go. The following week, I sat down beside him again, this time I tried signing a little with him while I talked and he listened. He didn't know much, which was surprising to me since he didn't speak at all. The main teacher informed me that his parents were in a bit of denial about his diagnosis. Felt he was just being stubborn by not speaking. It broke my heart, and I started teaching him to sign. By the end of my time there, he was signing fluently, and his behavioral outbursts were less. Obviously, he had other deficits, but I felt like I really made a difference in his life. I even sat down with his parents one time, and they agreed to learn to sign and work with him on it. After that, the decision to get my master's with that as my focus was easy."

What started out as a nothing of a question has totally and completely blindsided me.

I didn't realize I could fall in love with her again and again.

But that's exactly what just happened, right here, right now.

Every goddamn day she does something. Or says something. And I'm a fool all over again. "How do you do that?"

"Do what?"

"Smile through everything. Greet every goddamn day with optimism? Don't you ever feel the weight of it?"

Her hand comes up, running along my jaw, and I close my eyes, leaning into her touch.

"Of course, I do. Sometimes, all that weight sits so heavy on my chest I can hardly breathe through it. My life hasn't been all that great." My eyes eat up the lines of her face, so fucking beautiful, even when she frowns the way she is now. "Actually, it's been pretty shitty, if we're being honest. And yeah, I could sit around and indulge in that. I could become bitter and resentful. I could give up. It wouldn't even be that hard to do." She tilts her head, her hair spilling around her narrow shoulders. "But then where would I be?"

Her question hangs between us, and I have no answers for her. Giving up is not who she is, so I don't even bother entertaining her rhetorical question.

"I smile through it, Jasper, because it's so much better than the alternative. All I can do is keep marching forward, hoping the next step I take will be easier than the one before it."

"I want to make your next steps easier."

Her eyes glisten at me. "You already have."

I shake my head. Nothing I've done feels like enough for all that she's done for Adalyn.

For me.

"I'm so happy Adalyn has you," I tell her with so much sincerity, the truth behind it steals my breath. I am. I'd give anything for this to last beyond the five months. I could offer her a permanent job, but I'm not that brave. My heart wouldn't be able to take it.

Instead of saying the easy thing. The simple thing. Viola decides this is the moment to steamroll me.

Her fingers rake through my hair, tugging until my eyes drag up to hers.

"I have a million reasons to leave, Jasper. A million. You push me past my every limit day in and day out. You hate me. Ignore me. Fight with me. Tease me. Tempt me. Make me feel alive and forgotten in the same breath. I have a million reasons to leave. I need one reason to stay. One reason that isn't your little girl."

I stare into her, my fingers brushing back the long strands of her hair from her face. I hold that reason on my tongue, tasting its sweetness as it burns me like fire. It's a truth I can't let go. One I'm not ready for her to have.

I'll probably never be.

"He loves you. You love him. How's that for a reason?"

She shakes her head at me, her frustration palpable. "Is that what you're really thinking right now while I'm sitting on your lap in the dark? With all that we've done together this past week? That I love him?"

"It's the only thing that matters between us."

"You're a liar."

"Am I?" I question, tilting my head, Jules's words pounding through my skull so loud I can hardly see, let alone think, past them. *She loves him. Not you.* Again, what reason would Jules have to lie to me about that? They're best friends. Best friends who likely tell each other everything. Isn't that what girls do?

"I don't want to hurt like this when I look at you anymore. I'm tired of hating you while not being able to stop thinking about you."

My lips descend into the base of her neck, directly over her pulse that thrums beneath me. My eyes close, and I inhale a silent breath. *I'm tired of loving you while not being able to have you.*

"You don't hate me, Viola."

"You're right. I don't hate you, Jasper. You're the one who can't make up his mind."

"What is it you're looking for from me?" I speak against her skin. "What is it you think I have to give you when you belong to him? You want me to stop hating you? Done. You want me to be nice? I can fucking try. You want me to fuck this thing out of us? I will. Tell me what you want, and I'll give you anything. Because while you have a million reasons to go, and you're looking for one to stay other than my daughter, she's the only reason I can give you to stay when I also have a million for you to go."

Her breath hitches, her head falling back as my tongue swipes out, stealing a taste.

My hands drop from her hair, sliding along her narrow shoulders, over the top of her chest, down her ribs, my thumbs brushing the sides of her full tits through her shirt as I go. Her body trembles against mine as my hands grasp her waist, my nose gliding up the long column of her neck.

My body unable to hold back as I lick and suck and kiss her there. Only there.

If I kiss her mouth, there will be no going back.

"You need me more than I need you," she whispers, her voice saturated in desire as she tugs painfully on the ends of my hair, attempting to punish me for punishing her.

I grin against her, nipping her jaw.

"I've always needed you more than you need me." My fingers trail down to the hem of her skirt, toying with the edge. "But the question right now is, how badly do you need this?" I slip under her skirt, skimming up and down her silky panties. I bite back a groan when I feel how wet she is through the thin material. "Is this for me or from him?"

She rasps out something between a moan and a growl. "Nothing between us is about him. When will you finally accept that?"

Everything between us is about him. When will she finally understand that?

"Tell me what you want, and I'll give you anything," I murmur again, licking and nibbling along her skin.

I can't stop. I can't stop myself even though I know I should. I've never tasted her skin before, and now that I have, any willpower I was grasping to has vanished.

I'm an animal with her when all I've ever wanted to be is her everything. To own her. Possess her. Drive all else from her mind, but me. I may be drunk, but I'm so fucking high on her.

She yanks back from me, my head lazily falling against the sofa as I gaze up at her, my finger still brushing against her heat. She lets me do this for a moment; my desire reflected back at me in her eyes has my cock straining against my jeans.

I know she feels it.

Feels how hard she makes me.

How easy would it be to shove her panties to the side? To push inside her? To finally *feel* her?

"Will you?" she asks, and my hand freezes. "Will you really give me anything?"

She clutches my wrist, dragging my hand away from her panties and out from under her skirt. She adjusts her grip, forcing my fingers to my lips. I open automatically, and she slides them into my mouth. I suck her essence off, dying just a little at the way she tastes.

It's everything and more and not enough.

"Because something tells me that you will not, or cannot, give me the one thing I want." She leans in, capturing my bottom lip with her teeth and tugging on it, tasting herself. "I can't have anything less from you than this." She runs her fingers down my chest, pausing when they're poised directly over my heart. She pushes in on that spot hard enough that it's impossible to mistake her meaning. "Let me know if you're ever ready to put yourself on the line, Jasper. I'll be waiting."

And with that, Viola Starr climbs off my lap and walks out my door.

She walks away from me, taking the biggest piece of me with her.

She's right. I haven't been willing to put myself on the line. I haven't been willing to fight. To challenge everything for her. Maybe Jules was lying. Maybe Viola doesn't love Gus.

Maybe, just maybe, she does want me instead.

If putting myself on the line is the only way I can win her, then I guess I have nothing left to lose.

Except my heart.

Except my brother.

Except my entire goddamn world.

PART TWO

TWENTY

Viola

"NICELY DONE, MISS ADALYN," I praise, giving her hand that I'm holding a squeeze. "You're absolutely right. That penguin is eating fish." Adalyn glances up at me, tearing her gaze away from the penguins she's fully obsessed with, and treats me to a pleased smile.

This girl really loves her aquariums.

Almost as much as she loves going to the playground. Or playing music. But it's raining today in Atlanta, so we went with the aquarium.

The boys are busy all day, doing radio interviews and some kind of photoshoot for a magazine and then another interview with a YouTube blogger and then sound check and then the show tonight.

We've been at this for a month now.

I'd be lying if I said the schedule, the constant packing up and unpacking, the moving from one hotel and city to another, sleeping on uncomfortable buses, wasn't grueling. It's taxing as hell, and we're only a fifth of the way through.

The perpetual buzz of tension between Jasper and me isn't helping either.

After I walked out of his hotel room, after he let me walk out, we've returned to...us.

To how we were before I put myself out there.

I told him I wanted his heart and nothing less, and he let me go.

Maybe I've been selfish with him. Gus is his brother. Gus is my ex. I know, I *think*, Jasper wants me as much as I want him. But obviously, our story is too complicated and convoluted to overcome.

Or maybe he's just not as interested as I thought. Maybe it was all just physical for him, and he decided I'm not worth the effort.

The drive from Birmingham to Atlanta on the tour bus that should only have taken like two and a half hours took closer to four because it's spring in the south, and that means crazy storms. I think I was just anxious to get the hell out of Alabama. The guys were all excited to play to a 'hometown' crowd, but I wasn't so jazzed.

I left the state in a bit of a mess. Jobless. Penniless. Swindled by my mother.

A mother who came looking for me after she swindled me.

I half expected her to show up at the concert, pull some sort of stunt, but she wasn't there. At least not that I know of. Doesn't exactly make me rest easy where she's concerned, though.

I try to push her out of my mind as best as possible.

Jules was...I don't know. She was different, distant, back to her old baseless jealousies. Keith told me he didn't hook up with her, despite her attempts, when they went out to the club. He said she drove him up a wall, and he couldn't stand the way she was acting and the things she was saying, but he wouldn't elaborate further on that.

Overall, Adalyn has been doing extremely well, given all the transitions and moving around. She's only had a few major meltdowns, and I think those were mostly related to being hungry or tired.

I'm also getting better at determining when she's hit her wall, as I call it. She gets to a limit, and you can just sense that she's done and needs a break from whatever she's doing. Typically, that entails her mentally shutting down for a bit, going inside herself, and regrouping.

A lot of times, I'll sit with her in my lap, my arms squeezing her tight–she loves pressure–or rubbing her back gently. Sometimes she slips to the floor into a cocoon shape, her head and arms tucked under her body, and that means do not speak to me or bother me until I come out on my own.

When we're in the hotel or even on the bus, she'll run and jump, crash her body, and flip upside down–the sensory and vestibular change resets her.

All of these techniques are her coping mechanisms, and they tend to work well. Every day with her is a new learning experience, and it thrills me like nothing else that I can be part of this with her.

It's when she's overloaded with too much external stimuli and no way to process it or release it that she has trouble adapting.

But mostly, it just makes her very clingy. And it's that clinginess that I can't get enough of. For better or worse, this girl is an absolute love bug. She's also silly and has a fantastic sense of humor. She giggles all the time. Loves to play games–especially tickle games. Her energy is infectious.

We've been working on her speech, and with that, some signing, and I've found that when she signs something, most times she'll say the words with it. Like she just did now. She signed eat fish and said, "eat fish," while watching the penguins. Her primary form of language is parroting, but that's how she seems to learn best.

Is it obvious yet?

I can't get enough of this little girl.

Watching her is like discovering that true magic exists.

"Are you getting hungry, sweet girl? Do you want some crackers and almond butter?"

The word cracker is a loose term. They're made out of lentils, brown rice, and flax. Honestly, they taste like salted cardboard, but she loves them. Especially with almond butter. I could probably lather a shoe in almond butter, and she'd eat it. Adalyn doesn't reply, and she's starting to get that glazed over look to her, where she zones out, goes into her own world.

"Come on. Let's go sit down somewhere and have a snack." If only it weren't raining, I'd try for a picnic.

I tug gently on her hand to get her moving. We've already been here about an hour and a half, and that's typically her maximum for being places. She follows along, but our progress is quickly halted by a man standing in front of us.

"Sorry," he exclaims, as if he didn't mean to get in our way. His eyes drop down to Adalyn, and he smiles indulgently. "She's beautiful. How old?"

"Three," I reply, also peeking down at her to see how she'll react to the stranger near her space. She's not paying him much attention, still staring off in the direction of the penguins, so that's a good thing.

"That's a fun age. I remember when mine were that young." He looks off to his left, I assume in the direction of his children, and then back to us. "I saw you signing with her. Is she deaf?"

Wow. That's just...I don't know, very personal maybe? "No," I reply and leave it at that.

"Doesn't talk much then, huh?"

What the hell? I don't reply this time. I offer him a slim smile. "We need to get going. Have a nice day."

I shift to step around him, but he quickly cuts me off, sliding a little closer to Adalyn, and now I'm growing uneasy. Bending down, I pick her up, holding her close to me as I try again to maneuver around the guy. Adalyn is either picking up on my worry or is uncomfortable with this guy's proximity.

She reaches her hand out like she's trying to push him away, groaning as she does. "No. Say no thank you," she asserts, her mouth set in a thin line. I've worked with her on saying no thank you to someone instead of no or stop, and of course, because she parrots, she repeats it exactly the way I say it to her.

"What's wrong with her?" the guy continues with a barely

contained, knowing smirk. "I mean, she doesn't act like a three-year-old. I've been watching you with her."

"Who the hell are you?"

"That's probably not the best language to use in front of a little girl, Viola. I would expect the nanny working for Jasper Diamond to display better decorum when dealing with a child who is...what is she?" He glances at Adalyn again, his expression growing with intrigue and excitement. "It's something, right? I can tell. Her language and behavior aren't that of a normal three-year-old."

The fuck?

In the next second, the guy shoves his phone in my face. A phone he had in his hand. A phone that appears to be recording and is now raised up to Adalyn's face.

Oh. My. God.

I squeeze Adalyn closer to me, tucking her face in my chest and plowing past him.

I run. I run as I've never run before.

Where the hell is our security guy? Isn't he supposed to stop things like this from happening? Dread, thick and heavy, pools in my stomach.

And poor Adalyn is now starting to lose it.

She's squirming in my arms and fussing, loudly. "Stop!" she screams at the top of her tiny lungs. Her small body twists around, kicking and thrashing, and let me tell you, this kid is freaking *strong*. It's growing more and more difficult to maintain my hold, and I'm terrified she'll squirm her way out of my arms and fall. "No! Stop! *Stop!*"

All eyes are on us. All. Eyes.

I see them. Hear them whispering. Likely wondering if I'm kidnapping this girl. *Jesus Christ.* Someone is going to call the cops on me.

She's about two seconds from a total meltdown in Atlanta's Georgia Aquarium in front of everyone, including someone who I assume is press. Or a crazy stalker. Shit. There's that possibility too.

And they're filming this.

"Shhhh," I whisper into her hair, kissing the side of her face as I try to apply some pressure to her chest. "It's okay, sweet girl. It's okay. Just calm down. Listen to my voice, Ady. It's okay. I've got you. Just calm down."

She doesn't. The doors have come off the hinges.

Just as I reach the exit, doing everything in my power to hold onto Adalyn, our security guy, Thomas, catches up with us.

"Where were you?" I cry, losing control of myself completely.

Tears sting the backs of my eyes. This poor little girl. Who knows where whatever that guy recorded is going to end up. *What's wrong with her*, he asked. What an asshole. And really, what the fuck does he know about what's neurotypical behavior and language and what isn't? Is he a child psychologist? Give me a goddamn break!

"There is nothing wrong with you, Adalyn," I whisper into her ear, kissing the side of her round cheek. Holding the overwrought child closer to my body, I squeeze her tighter, hoping it helps to calm her down. "Don't ever let anyone tell you otherwise. You're absolutely perfect. So sweet and smart and silly and fun. I'm sorry, sweet girl. So very sorry I let him get to you."

"I–I'm sorry," Thomas stutters, clearly flustered. "I just went to the restroom, and when I came back, I saw you running for the exit. What happened?"

I want to pummel this guy, but I can't exactly do that. I mean, he was using the bathroom. It happens, right? Just bad fucking timing.

Or maybe that's what that guy with the camera was waiting on, and we were optimal prey.

"We need to get back to the hotel," I tell him. "Now."

Adalyn is starting to scream louder, garnering further attention. I glance around quickly, and sure enough, that guy is there. And he's recording us. I want to flip him off so bad, but that would end up on the news or something.

Instead, I flee the building.

Thomas is on the phone, calling the driver who works for the security team the band uses. "He's two minutes out."

Perfect. In two minutes, we could have a real storm on our hands. And not the kind we're standing in now.

But somehow, the rain is distracting Adalyn.

She pauses her tirade and stares up at the sky as cool drops of rain pelt us, wetting our hair and running down our faces. I start to sing rain, rain, go away, and she's calming down, listening to me. Adalyn clings to me like a little monkey, holding on so tight, her arms and legs wrapped around me. I clutch her closer, kissing her face and singing into her hair. Rain, rain is no longer doing it, so I go with the song her father wrote for her. She falls silent, becomes withdrawn, and I don't think I've ever felt so awful in my life.

This is my fault.

I had one job to do. One they specifically stipulated time and time again. But more than that, I hate that Ady got so upset. That her world is forever changed because I wasn't more aware of our surroundings.

Jasper. I have no idea how he's going to react to this, but I imagine it's not going to be pretty.

The car pulls up along the curb, and seconds later, I'm strapping Adalyn into her car seat.

She doesn't fight me.

She just blankly stares at nothing, lost in her head.

We speed off, and as I turn to peek back toward the aquarium, I find the guy with the phone camera, smiling gleefully and waving at us.

This is bad.

Really bad.

Sliding my phone out of my bag, I dial up Jasper. I rarely call him. In fact, we communicate mostly via text if I'm out with Adalyn or he's out somewhere.

"What's up?" he barks. "I have two minutes." I blow out a breath, glancing over at Adalyn, who is now pretty calm, focused beyond the tinted windows of the car. *This would be easier if your father didn't hate me so much most of the time.*

"We had a situation at the aquarium," I start, nervously chewing on my bottom lip. "A guy came up to us and started talking. At first, I thought he was just being friendly. Making small talk. But then he asked if Adalyn was deaf because I was signing with her. And then he called me by name and mentioned your name and asked what was wrong with her. He said he knows it's something. He said she wasn't a normal three-year-old." I bite back a sob as I think about that. What an absolute motherfucker that man is.

"What the fuck!" Jasper bellows in my ear so explosively I have to pull it back and glance at Adalyn to make sure she didn't get that. She didn't. She's still in her own world. "Where are you now? Where was Thomas?"

"We're in the car on the way back to the hotel. It wasn't Thomas's fault, Jasper. It's mine. The guy must have been following us and waited for the couple of minutes when Thomas went in to use the restroom." I stare into the back of Thomas's head, feeling bad for throwing him under the bus. His shoulders are stiff.

"I saw him," Thomas says, his voice steady, but contrite. "I did. I watched him move around you and Ady, but he didn't linger. In fact, he disappeared for the last half an hour. It's not an excuse. I should have been more aware of the people around you, and I wasn't. We haven't had a problem until now, so I didn't think about it. I'm so very sorry."

Jasper must have heard all that because he blows out a hot, heavy breath into the phone.

"I'm sorry too." My face falls into my hand, my chest so tight I can barely breathe. I wipe away at my forehead and the useless moisture pooling beneath my eyes.

"I have to do this interview, but then I'm coming back to the hotel."

"Okay. It's going to be fine," I say, because I feel like I need to say something reassuring, but I think I chose the wrong thing to say because Jasper roars in my ear.

"It's not fine, Viola. Get her back to the hotel and do not leave that suite until I return." Then he hangs up on me. *Crap.* But I can't even hold his ire against him. I would be just as furious as he is.

The world he's in is ugly. It exploits. It thrives on differences.

And if Adalyn were mine, I'd do everything in my power to protect her from it.

The way he has.

Until now.

We make it to the hotel in record time, going up the private elevator until we reach our floor that the band has rented out in its entirety. On one side, it's Jasper and Adalyn's two-bedroom suite. Next to it is my room, and then each guy has his own room as do all of the security people.

I enter Jasper and Adalyn's suite, carrying her over to the dining room table and setting her up with a snack just as my phone rings.

It's Sophia Bloom.

She might be the last person I want to speak to right now besides Jasper.

"Hello?" I answer cautiously.

"I just got a call from Intertainment," she says coolly. "They're telling me that they have a story they're about to run. That this story comes with video of Adalyn and you in the aquarium not even twenty minutes ago. Is this true?"

"Adalyn and I were approached by a man who seemed to be press of some kind, yes."

"I knew this would happen," she snarls under her breath. "You have one job to do, Viola. Keep. Adalyn. Safe. Keep her away from the media. We discussed this on the plane before we even left Alabama. Is it that difficult for you to do your job?"

I swallow hard, my hackles raising. "There was nothing I could do, and the moment I realized what the guy was after, I left with her. I didn't tell him anything."

"It doesn't matter now, does it?"

Does she have to sound so goddamn smug? I realize I messed up, but I'll be damned if I allow this woman to have the upper hand. As far as I'm concerned, I answer to one person about Adalyn and that's Jasper.

"It's done," she continues. "And now Jasper is going to have to make a statement in the middle of the tour. A statement about his three-year-old daughter. This is only going to push more press and a bigger spotlight on her. How do you think she'll handle *that*?" I glance down at Adalyn, my stomach in knots. "Well done, Miss Starr. I wouldn't be surprised if you were on the next bus back to whatever tin can you crawled out of."

Bitch.

"That's not your call to make, now is it? I didn't mean for this to happen, and I would never do anything to hurt Adalyn intentionally."

Sophia scoffs into the phone. "A bit too late for that now. And don't be so sure that it's not my call, sweetie. Jasper and I are a lot closer than the two of you are. I don't care what your past is with him or the band. I'm the one who's been here with him for the last few years. You're the one who just screwed up your job." And then she hangs up on me, the same way Jasper did.

I don't think I've ever felt so wretched in my life. But really, what was I supposed to do? How could I have prevented this?

And how the hell did this guy know where we were anyway? Who I am? It's not like Jasper, Adalyn, and I have been out together much. Or like we've been photographed when we were. As of two nights ago, I was still an unknown.

Well, they know who you are now.

An hour later, the door to the suite opens, and Jasper and Gus come storming in, Jasper staring me down like I just killed his cat and cooked it up for him for dinner. My hands jut out reflexively, like I'm trying to stop whatever he's about to say or do. "Jasper–"

"Don't," he snaps. "Not in front of Adalyn. Gus will watch her while you and I talk in your room."

With that, he spins around on his heels and marches back toward the door. I glance sheepishly over at Gus, who is now sitting beside Adalyn while she plays with her Mickey and Minnie figurines.

"It's already out there, Vi. That video. It's ugly."

I try to swallow down past the lump clogging my throat, but it's impossible. "I'm sorry," I whisper shakily, unsure of what else to say. Words haven't been invented yet to convey my level of shame and regret.

I'm two seconds from sobbing, and Gus sees this. He shakes his head, reaching out and grasping my hand. He squeezes it before intertwining our fingers, and instead of comforting me, it decimates my last semblance of composure.

I'm sniffling and wiping away at my face. Sucking in ragged breath after ragged breath. I can't get control.

"Babe, it's okay." He stands up and holds me, immersing me in his warmth as his arms slink tightly around me.

His lips press into my temple, and I breathe out, absorbing the feel of him. His familiar scent.

"Stop freaking out over this. You did the best you could with a seriously messed-up situation. It was bound to happen at some point, and Adalyn's diagnosis is nothing to keep secret. He knows this, babe. He does. He's just upset. He'll calm down. Go talk to him. It'll be fine."

But it won't be fine, will it? How can it ever be?

TWENTY-ONE

Viola

I RELUCTANTLY LEAVE Adalyn with Gus, wondering if I'll be seeing them again as I head over to my room. Jasper is already inside; the door propped open with that metal bolt thing.

I push the door, flip back the latch, and then close it behind me.

Jasper is facing the window, his eyes trained on the rain beyond, his back to me.

"I told Sophia I didn't want you," he begins without any preamble. "That there are hundreds of other people who could do this job."

I freeze mid-step, his words stunning me completely. I didn't realize that. That he didn't want me for this job. I also didn't realize it was possible to feel worse than I already do, but I was wrong. This man has the ability to cut me up like a paper snowflake.

"She told me you were it. That if I didn't want her to do it, you were the only one. And now my daughter's face is all over the internet. Her throwing a tantrum, fighting in your arms while you yell at the guy taking the video, is all over social media." His hands go to his hips, his back rising and falling with his heavy breaths.

"I'm so sorry–"

He spins around, his eyes narrowed and dark, enmity dripping from him like blood dripping from a wound. "Do not tell me you're sorry, Viola," he yells. "Do you know what they're saying about her? The insensitive prick who videoed you referred to her as mentally challenged."

I gasp, covering my mouth, sick to my stomach. Bile climbs up the back of my throat, and I swallow it down, hating people and their intrinsic cruelty.

"Well, then he's the asshole. Who the hell uses words like that to describe a little girl? To describe anyone?"

"Uneducated half-wits. That's who. But it doesn't matter now, does it?"

I launch forward, only to stop short when I reach the center of the room. I'm lost in here. I'm so enraged and revolted, and I don't know what to do. It feels like my skin is crawling, agitation boiling up inside of me.

My hands ball into fists; my toes scrape against the insides of my Docs.

"The hell it doesn't, Jasper," I yell back at him. "You can't let someone use words like that. You can't let them get away with doing this to her."

"Me?" he points to his chest. "Do you think I don't have people on this right now? Do you think I haven't just spent the last half hour talking to Sophia and my PR team, demanding that they get this removed?"

He takes a step, staring down at me with fire and a fury I've never seen before.

"One job, Viola. You have one job. You fucked that all up and now look." His hand flies out beside him. "How did they even know where you were? What your name is?" I shake my head, my lips dipping into a frown, because I've been wondering that myself. "Did

J. SAMAN

you tell them? Tip them off? Did they pay you?" His green eyes narrow. "Am I not paying you enough?"

"Screw you," I bellow, reaching out and shoving him with all my might.

He barely moves, doesn't even flinch, and it's so damn unsatisfying. Anger flares within me. My hand flies up, smacking him across the face before I can even stop it. I'm so goddamn angry my body is exploding with it.

Jasper's cheek reddens before my eyes, and I stifle yet another sob.

Oh my god, I just slapped him.

And he looks like he's ready to kill me.

And poor Adalyn, she doesn't even know what's happening.

I spin around, no longer able to face him, my arms wrapping protectively across my chest. I'm puffing hard, tears burning my face that I'm desperate to hold at bay. I close my eyes, breathing in through my nose and out through my mouth. Anything to stop them.

The last thing I want to do is cry in front of him after he accused me of that.

I'd rather die than let him see me break.

"I would never do that," I whisper when I think I have control over myself, only my voice cracks on the last word. I swallow, clear my throat, and try again. "I love that little girl. I would never ever do anything intentionally to hurt her. Ever. I'm so sorry," I sob before I can stop it, sucking in more deep breaths, but nothing is helping. It's too late. "I never meant f-for any of this to h-happen."

Jasper blows out a heavy, frustrated sigh. His hands meet my shoulders, and I begin to tremble, losing my composure completely. His arms snake around me, tugging my back into his chest, holding me so close and so tight.

I can't stop my tears now.

His embrace undoes me.

"I know you wouldn't," he murmurs into my ear. "I'm sorry for saying that, Viola. I didn't mean it. It was cruel and wrong, and I'm

angry and scared. I lost it." He heaves out a hot breath across my
neck, and I shudder, trying so hard to rein myself back in. His forehead drops to the back of my head. "Why did you have to bring her
out? Why have you been dragging her everywhere? I need her to be
safe, and now she's not safe. The whole world is talking about her,
and I don't know how to stop it."

I twist in his arms to face him; his reddish-brown hair is wavy and
all over the place. I stare up into his oh-so-green eyes. Adalyn's eyes.
They look so much alike.

So achingly beautiful.

He takes me in, his gaze dancing across my tear-stained face, his
arms now locked around my lower back.

"She's not a doll, Jasper. You cannot lock her away in an ivory
tower. She's a little girl who deserves to go to the park and run
around. Who loves the fish in the aquarium. Yes, she has some
deficits, but she works at them, and all that guy saw was her signing
with me and then becoming agitated when he got up in her face.
Hell, I was agitated too." I reach up, running the tip of my finger
along the lines of his cheek. "What are you so afraid of? Why are you
so ashamed of her?"

Jasper's eyes widen, stricken, like I just slapped him again. A
scowl crinkles his forehead, his lips tightening as his jaw grows rigid.

"I'm not ashamed of her. How could you even ask that?" He
shakes me slightly, clutching at my hips, desperate for me to see him,
hear him. "I wouldn't change *anything* about her. Not her diagnosis.
Not the way her brain works. Nothing. If possible, I love her more
because of it. There is nothing more special or precious to me in the
world than Adalyn. But this world is cruel. And people in this
industry build you up just to watch you fall, smiling as you go down. I
can't let that happen to her." He searches me, darkness flitting across
his face. "She's so young. So perfect and unspoiled by it. I'm terrified,
Viola. I don't want my profession to be the thing that hurts her most."

My hand drops from his face, falling to his chest, over his
pounding heart. His eyes close for a moment, only to reopen, softer

somehow. Like he's been holding onto that agonizing truth forever, and now that it's out, he can breathe easier.

"Then tell those assholes what you just told me. Tell them that she's as perfect as every other little girl out there. And if they come at her, then you fight them off. But you cannot hide her. She deserves a life. One where she's able to go out and experience the world. There will always be people out there who enjoy hurting others or are too apathetic and self-involved to care if they do. But that's not most people. You cannot protect her from the world forever. Be her daddy. Be her superhero. But teach her how to fly on her own."

Jasper's eyes bounce back and forth between mine, all of his anger shedding into torment.

Pure. Raw. Vulnerable.

"She's all I have, Vi. Her, Gus, and this stupid band. They're all I've got in this world. I am her daddy," he whispers gruffly, and my heart breaks. More of these stupid tears I'm useless to hold back leak over the edges of my eyes and roll down my cheeks. "She has no mother. My dad and stepmother are older and live in Palm Desert and hardly ever see her. It's my job to protect her, and I mess that up constantly. I don't know how to keep her safe."

God, this man.

This perfectly broken man.

He has no idea how lucky Adalyn is to have him.

I stare into him, and wish I could stop this feeling from growing inside me. I wish I could hold it off just a little longer before I fall completely.

But it's too late.

I think about him constantly. At night before bed. In the morning when I wake up. All throughout the day. Visions of his furtive glances when he doesn't know I'm watching him haunt my dreams.

Somewhere along the way, I gave this man my heart.

Only he doesn't know it. Worse yet, he doesn't want it.

And I'm a fool for letting a man who treats me the way he treats me have it. It's everything else about him that owns me.

"Yes, you do," I tell him, cupping his face with my other hand, the one not pressed against his heart. A shuddered breath passes his lips at my touch. "You've done a tremendous job with her. I know you don't want the world to focus on her. But maybe they're so interested because you've been so secretive. Once you say, hey, this is who she is, what else do they have to go after?"

He shakes his head in my hand before releasing me, taking a step away and forcing my hands to fall. I'm cold without him, and that feeling of being lost consumes me once more.

He's still here, standing in front of me, but he's now shut himself off from me.

I can see it.

Like pulling down a shade and blocking out the light.

He gives me a sobering look, so terrifyingly serious that my heart starts to race right before he cripples me with his truth. "They'll find something. They always do."

TWENTY-TWO

Jasper

VIOLA EXPELS ALL the air from her lungs and takes a measured step back, like she needs to place more distance between us. She nods, swallows thickly, and stares me down.

"Am I fired then?" Her cheeks cling to their rosiness, remnants of her tears and anger, and I don't think she's ever looked more beautiful.

It's funny, or not funny, that she asks. Sophia told me I should fire her, and I considered it. I didn't want her for this job and not because I didn't think she was qualified or capable.

Maybe I should fire her.

I'd give anything to miss her again instead of having my heart ripped out day after day.

"No. You're not fired."

Because even though I'd like nothing more than for her to leave this tour so I can fucking breathe again, Adalyn loves her. I'm sorta in a bind with that, considering there is no one else. At least, no one else who would be right for the job.

Plus, I watched the video.

Twice.

Viola was doing everything she could to get Adalyn out of there. It's not her fault, even if it's easy to blame her. Fuck, why didn't Thomas tell her sooner about the guy who was following them? It's his goddamn job!

"It's going to get harder before it gets easier. It's impossible to keep safe what others want to break."

She nods her head slowly as she contemplates what I just said before her gaze shifts away from the window back to mine.

"Tell me what you want me to do, and I'll do it. If you want me to stay in the hotels or buses with her, I will."

"I do, and I don't. I'm not sure what the right answer to this is."

Viola tilts her head, a strand of her wild blonde hair falling across her face. She walks over to the bed and drops exhaustedly onto it. Leaning back on her elbows and crossing her legs, she stares openly up at me.

I shouldn't be in here anymore.

I should be going to the sound check. Or spending time with my little girl. I shouldn't be in here, looking at this woman on her bed.

I'm forever fighting a battle I'll never win.

I've spent these last couple of nights since she was on my lap in that suite, hell, since the tour started, putting up wall after wall, barrier after barrier. Doing everything I can to keep my distance. To keep this professional.

And I fail. Repeatedly.

Like right now.

"Wanna talk it out?"

No. I don't want to.

She pats the space next to her on the bed, and I should walk out of here right now. Because her hazel eyes are darker somehow, and her blouse is clinging to her beautiful breasts that are enticingly pointed in my direction, and the scent of her is like a drug, and...

I step toward the bed and sit beside her, dropping my elbows to my spread thighs, staring down at the gold leaf pattern of the carpet.

Anywhere but at her.

I wonder if she's aware of the burning she ignites inside of me or if she thinks every touch I've given her is based purely on lust. I can't decide which I'd rather she believe.

She stands, sashaying in front of me over to the minibar where she bends forward, opening it up. Dear God, does she not realize she's wearing a skirt? A short skirt? I can see every inch of those long, creamy thighs all the way up to–

"I'm thinking we need a drink." Her head rolls over her shoulder, and my gaze drops back down as quickly as it can, hoping, praying, she didn't catch me eye-fucking her ass.

I'm thinking that's the worst idea I've ever heard.

"Okay."

Shut up. Shut up! Roll your tongue back into your mouth, ignore the hard-on about to escape the waistband of your jeans, and get the hell out of here.

"Johnnie Walker or Maker's Mark?"

"Whatever."

Slipping a few bottles from the fridge, she twists the caps, pouring the contents of the small bottles into two glasses and then handing one to me.

Then she sits beside me again.

Crossing those long, bare legs.

Bouncing one of her Doc Martens up and down.

"Cheers." She holds her glass up to me. "I don't exactly have a toast since this afternoon was probably one of the worst of my life, but fuck it. I need this."

I smile at that and clink her glass against mine, downing the shot in one smooth gulp. She has no idea what a worst day is like if this was one of them.

"Scotch."

She shrugs a shoulder. "I wanted the bourbon."

"I'm sorry I made you cry," I say, staring down at the slow glide of the remaining liquid in my glass. "I'm sorry I accused you of that."

"I know. You already apologized, and I already apologized, so I think we need to move on. The truth is, I'm tired of fighting with you, Jasper."

I turn to look at her. "We don't fight. Anymore."

"You're right," she scoffs with a bitter note. "You'd have to exchange more than one or two-word sentences for that to happen. I try with you, and you push me away. I'm friends with Gus, and that wanker cheated on me. I've known you since we were eight. *Eight*," she emphasizes. "I don't know why you hate me, Jasper—"

"I don't hate you," I bristle, my eyebrows knitting together. "Besides, you're the one who said you hated me."

Her cheeks color, and then she laughs. "Yeah. I guess I did. But only because you were being an asshole." She bounces into me, her shoulder brushing against me, shooting a zing of electricity through my body.

"So you like to tell me."

She smiles brightly at that, showing off all her white teeth. She shrugs with a sorry, not sorry expression before she sobers up once more.

"But frankly, I know you never really liked me all that much in high school. At least...," she trails off, the pink in her cheeks growing to a deep crimson. "At least, it's always seemed that way, and your attitude toward me since I've arrived here hasn't reflected anything different. We've had our...moments," she grins, looking away for a beat. "But those aside, you and I need to be completely on the same page with Adalyn. We have to communicate better, or this is never going to work. I feel like I'm stumbling around blind with her a lot, and I know you have all these rules and ways you want things done for her."

She's right. I have been an asshole.

It's like I'm sixteen all over again, and I don't know how to be around the girl I can't stop thinking about without her knowing I can't stop thinking about her.

"I'll work on it," I promise, the words coming out thick and rough. "But only if you stop aggravating me," I tease.

She puffs out a nervous laugh, like telling me all of that was difficult for her. She does that body leaning thing again, brushing the same spot on my side, and it feels so good having her touch me. It's become my drug. The thing I obsess over and dream about and pine for.

I'll take it any damn way I can get it.

"Only if you stop being an asshole. Otherwise, I make no promises." Her smile grows mischievous. "It's like a challenge. It's oddly fun. How can I get under Jasper's skin today?" I chuckle. If only she knew she was already there. "Wow," she muses, her eyes growing comically wide. "Is that a smile, Jasper Diamond? Like a real, genuine smile? Who knew you had so many teeth?"

"I smile all the time. You've just never given me much to smile at *you* about."

"Ouch," she grabs her chest like I've wounded her. "Forever the asshole." Her elbow glides along my flank, and some more of her warmth seeps into my cold soul. I'm staring at her, and she's staring at me, and I can't make myself stop staring at her.

Not now that I've allowed myself to.

She's so beautiful. Everything about her.

Everything you can never have. I clear my throat and force myself away from her.

"So, now what?"

That's the question, right? Now what?

"Now the world knows Adalyn is autistic. That's the statement my PR people put out in addition to requesting privacy. It was something I was going to make public after the tour anyway. It just happened a little earlier than I had planned. The bastard who called my little girl mentally challenged and asked what was wrong with her will be fired because I've threatened to sue the hell out of Intertain-ment. And now we take her out for ice cream because we're not the only ones who've had a bad day."

"Ice cream, eh?"

I shrug. "We can't very well give her a shot."

Viola rolls her eyes at me. "What happened to your sound check?"

"Gus and the guys can handle that."

"Okay," she hums and then stands up. "Let's go get her ice cream then."

I reach out and take her hand, admiring how small it feels in mine. How warm and soft it is. I stare at my hand holding hers, and I wonder how that happened.

It certainly wasn't a conscious thought.

I feel Viola's eyes on my face, and I know I shouldn't look up. Because if I do, if I look at this woman right now, after all the ways I've bared my soul to her, after all the secret moments we've shared, I'll kiss her, and then everything in my world will crumple around me.

I look anyway. I have to.

And instantly, I feel it.

This perpetual tension and heat that sparks between us.

Her eyes are so bright, so pretty. Her other hand, the one I'm not holding, comes up, running through the side of my hair. She likes that, I realize. Toying with and touching my hair. She's done it every time we've been alone like this.

My eyes close, succumbing to her touch.

I open them again, finding her just a bit closer than she was before. We stare into each other, having a conversation with only our eyes, telling each other things we're incapable of vocalizing.

She wants me to kiss her.

And I want to kiss her back. So goddamn bad.

But I don't. I *can't.*

I can't kiss you, Viola. No matter how much I want to.

No matter all the things Gus does and says, there are certain lines that can never be crossed. If I do this, if I cross it, all this will blow up in my face. My band will be over. My relationship with my brother decimated. My world, annihilated. I can't let that happen.

Not again.

"Jas?" she whispers when I don't so much as move or breathe.

Instead of kissing her, I grin, desperate for some levity. "Have I ever mentioned that I love it when you call me that?"

"Better than asshole?"

My grin slides up into a smile. "Definitely better than asshole."

We continue to gaze into each other's eyes, the pulse on her wrist thrumming beneath my fingers. It takes every last shred of willpower I have, but I release her hand, and I head straight for the door.

Adalyn. Ice cream. My sights are single-minded.

I enter my suite, Viola somewhere behind me. Gus is staring at me from the couch, Ady tucked into his side as she watches Mickey Mouse Club House–of course, she's watching that–on the television. He's nothing but questions I'm not sure I have the answers to until Viola walks into the room, and his face erupts into pure joy.

"Can you handle the sound check?" I ask him. "I want to take Vi and Ady out for an ice cream."

"Aren't you adorable," Gus teases, and I ignore him. Walking over to Ady, I drop down to my knees in front of her. She scoots around, trying to see past me over to the television. "Can't we all go, dad?"

I throw him a sideways glance. "Only if we want to sound like crap tonight, brother."

"Fine. You win this round, Dr. Evil." A zing of pain shoots through the back of my skull. It takes me a second to realize Gus just smacked me. I glance up with a what-the-fuck look. "You made her cry."

Viola comes over and sits beside Gus, reaching out and gently resting her hand on his forearm, her head on his shoulder. He kisses her face, and I hate everything.

"I made myself cry." She glances at me with a tilt of her head and a wink. "Well, sorta," she laughs, leaning into Gus further before just as quickly righting herself. "But, we worked it out, right?"

"Right," I echo, my throat clogged. I turn to Adalyn. "Do you want to go out for ice cream?"

An unstoppable smile erupts across her face, her green eyes sparkling. She stands up on the couch, flipping herself upside down. "Ice cream."

"Can you say, I want ice cream?"

"Ice cream."

"Chocolate or vanilla?"

She doesn't reply.

"Jasper?" Viola starts. "Where are you going to get dairy-free chocolate or vanilla?"

"There's a shop close to here that has a few flavors. I already looked it up. I was going to text it to you in case you wanted to take her after the aquarium, but I never got the chance."

"Would you mind giving me a minute with my brother?" Gus interjects, an unmistakable edge to his voice that I'm in no mood for.

Viola volleys back and forth between the two of us before she stands up, reaching over to take Adalyn's hand. Ady rights her body, and then Viola helps her off the couch.

"Come on, Miss Ady. Let's go use the potty before we go out for ice cream."

"No. No potty, Vi."

"First potty. Then ice cream."

"No potty."

"Come on. First potty, then ice cream. We've got this."

"First potty, then ice cream," Ady parrots, sticking out her tongue and blowing a raspberry that makes her displeasure at going potty known. Viola giggles as the two of them head into Ady's bedroom, shutting the door.

I turn on my brother, my eyebrows knit together.

"I should kick your ass."

"Your girlfriend's fine."

He's undeterred, his gaze as hard as I've ever seen it. "I haven't said much about the way you've been treating her. Mostly because I assumed you'd grow out of it, but you haven't. Not even a little." His eyes narrow, his jaw clenching. "Get over your bullshit with her and man the fuck up now that she's working for you."

"I'm trying," I grit out.

"You've always been a surly bastard," he continues, leaning sideways until he's practically in my face. "The serious one. But what happened with Karina was the final nail in your coffin. It's like you've been dead for the last three years of your life."

His gaze is heavy on mine as he assesses me. I stand up and walk away from him, heading to the door, because I can't stand the pitying look in his eyes.

"It wasn't your fault what happened with mom. Or Karina." I stop short. "None of it was your fault," he continues, speaking to my back with a little more force now that he's garnered my attention. "Sometimes bad things happen, and you can't change them. At some point, you're going to have to stop blaming yourself and move on."

My hands find my hips, my face the floor as I breathe heavy.

Everything hurts.

"If you had married Karina, she still wouldn't have been a mother to Adalyn. Yes, maybe she wouldn't have run off so soon. Maybe she wouldn't have gotten into oxy and fentanyl that quickly. Maybe she would have pretended she gave a shit about you and that little girl just a bit longer. But you and I both know it was where she was headed anyway. Putting a ring on that and locking it down wouldn't have changed the outcome."

"You don't know that."

"Yes, I do, and so do you."

I shake my head. Because I don't know that. No one does.

Not for sure, anyway.

I made zero effort with her. I had Adalyn, and she was all I cared about. Karina hardly even registered with me, which is probably why she left. Maybe if I had put in the effort with her the way she wanted me to, things would have turned out differently. For Karina. For Adalyn.

I don't know. And now I never will.

"You deserve to be happy. I know you've always felt unworthy of that. Maybe that's partially my fault. I don't know. I never told you that I didn't blame you for what happened with mom. I should have, Jasper, and for not doing it sooner, I'm sorry."

Fuck. I can't. I just fucking *can't!*

"But it's time you start living again. Adalyn is not the only good thing in your life."

Shut up, Gus. Just shut the fuck up.

"I know she's not," I bite out, my eyes cinching shut as the familiar cocktail of guilt and remorse course through my veins, as toxic and corrosive as they've always been. I can't do this with him. Not now. Not after everything that happened today with Adalyn.

With Viola just now in her room.

"I thought this tour would help. I honestly believed that performing would do it. Making music has always been the light of your life. And Ady, of course," he adds evenly. "But even they're not enough. I hoped that Viola, with all her energy and spirit, would breathe some life back into you."

"Get to the goddamn point already."

"I've been selfish," he half-pants, and I can't take this. I cannot take this from Gus. Not now. Not ever. "About everything, really. I'm working on that. I told Vi so the other night. I've made that girl a million promises and set fire to them all with my mistakes. I'm going to fix them. She deserves that and more from me. But if you make my beautiful girl cry again, I'll end you, brother. I don't care about the past. I don't care about the bullshit that's been like an albatross around your neck. Figure it out, and stop taking your shit out on her."

I spin around and face him, my green eyes to his gray. "Is that what you think I've been doing with her?"

"Isn't it?"

He's challenging me. Because this is not the first time we've had this conversation. My brother dated Viola for four years. All through high school. And all through high school, I was callously indifferent toward her.

Or so I made it seem.

But I can't tell him the truth.

Not on this one.

I won't have Viola drive a wedge between my brother and me. It's no one's fault. Not Gus's or Viola's or even mine. Feelings are what they are. Love has no boundaries.

But actions do.

Acting on the way I feel is something else entirely, and I won't do that to him. To us. I've already crossed so many lines with her that should never have been crossed.

I stare him down a moment longer, my heart in my throat. *I've made that girl a million promises and set fire to them all with my mistakes. I'm going to fix them.*

I head to the door. "Tell Viola I'll meet her and Ady in the lobby."

"I'm just trying to help you, Jas," he calls out, and I just can't. Not now. Not ever.

The door shuts heavily behind me, and I blow out a breath. I make it all the way to the elevator at the end of the hall before I start to lose it, my body shaking with rage and regret to the point where I can't push it off the way I typically do. I can't go out for a run. I can't go to my gym and punch a bag until I'm too exhausted to feel or care.

Goddammit!

I kick the metal doors of the elevator, beyond frustrated that it's so slow when I need to move.

Screw this.

I plow past it, barreling into the stairwell and sprinting down, not even caring if it's more than a dozen stories.

I need air, and I need it now.

Not my fault, he said. Only, Gus grew up without a mother because of me, and now Adalyn is suffering the same fate. Maybe that's why I didn't fight the way I wanted to over Viola coming on this tour. For Gus. For Adalyn. I owe them a debt I can never pay off, and Viola has always been the closest I could come to that.

She is everything Gus said and more.

It's why I walked away from her all those years ago.

Gus deserves her. I don't.

TWENTY-THREE

Jasper

THE SHOW ENDS, the four of us marching off stage into the blackness as the crowd continues to cheer. Despite the day I've had, the show went extremely well.

Viola and I took Adalyn out for ice cream, and no one bothered us. No one followed us. I'm not sure what I was expecting, but after what happened to Viola at the aquarium, the quiet was surprising. And nice.

The three of us ate our almond milk ice cream, talking and laughing. Ady was talking so much. A million words and short sentences flowed from her lips.

It's the most I've heard her speak at any one time in months.

I can't shut off Gus's words.

That I've been walking around dead for the last three years.

He's not wrong about that, as much as it hurts to hear and admit. Despite my emotional shortcomings, Ady is really beginning to come into her own. That's all I care about.

I know some, if not most of that, is Viola. I know she works with her constantly. In ways I never knew I needed to. Like playing games where they work on Ady deciding between two objects by naming the one she wants instead of just pointing. Like playing games where she takes turns, asks instead of grabs for an object she wants, or says yes or no when answering a question.

Saying no thank you instead of yelling or screaming–even if she says, say no thank you.

Getting Ady to do a thousand things she hates to do simply by saying first, we do this, then we do that.

It only makes me feel like less of a father. Less of a person.

So since we returned from ice cream and all through the show, it's been nearly impossible not to take Gus's words to heart.

Have I been an empty void of a man? Did I let Karina's death be the thing that pushed me over the edge into the abyss?

And then there's what Viola said about Adalyn.

How I can't treat her like a doll and lock her up in an ivory tower.

I want Adalyn to have a full life. But I wasn't lying when I told Viola that I'm scared. Terrified is probably more accurate. It's more than her autism or the press. It's the thought of losing her that paralyzes me.

The two of us have already lost so much.

But maybe it's time I work on that. Work on myself. Accept that there are things I can't change, like Gus said.

Easier said than done.

"Fantastic show," Marco booms excitedly as we approach the dressing room. "I swear you guys get better each night."

"Thanks, man." Henry pats his shoulder as he passes him.

We enter the dressing room, and I drop down onto the couch, my head falling back, and my eyes closing.

I'm exhausted.

"I got passes to that club you requested," Marco continues, but I don't care enough to move. "They've sectioned off an entire area, and

they've agreed to let Marsellus stand guard over the entrance as well as one of their guys."

"Do we need that kind of detail at a club?" Keith asks incredulously.

"You do today. The front of the arena is mobbed with press." Now I do open my eyes. Lowering my chin, I find Marco. He stares at me miserably and shrugs. "I'm sorry, Jas. It's bad."

"Because of Ady?"

"Yes. I've had dozens of calls requesting interviews. Everyone from The Today Show to every entertainment magazine there is to all the late-night shows. You're already booked to play SNL and The Tonight Show when you're in New York, but the calls haven't stopped."

I groan, throwing my head back and closing my eyes once more. "I'm not doing an interview about this. She has autism. Something like one in every fifty kids has it. We're not talking anything rare here. No one would give a shit if she weren't my child. It's a stupid reason to do an interview."

"I don't know what to tell you. We've got a media storm on our hands. It's good PR," he adds enthusiastically, and I pop an eye open to glare at him, ready to snap his scrawny neck. Marco throws his hands up in the air. "I'm sorry, but it is. Your albums are selling like mad. So is all of your band merchandise."

"My daughter is not PR. And I will not make her PR. If people want to ask us about our music or our band, awesome. Adalyn is off-limits."

"Right," Marco replies, but it's not in agreement. "Jana has been trying to push them all off. Sophia said she's all over it. We'll see if it slows down. I'm sure it will. I mean, it all happened today. In the meantime, are you going to the club?"

"No," I state firmly. "I think I've had enough for one day."

Marco frowns but knows enough not to push it. "Don't worry, brother," Gus jumps onto the couch, elbowing me in the side. "We'll take care of all the pretty ladies for you since you're on a celibacy quest."

Tossing his sweaty arm over my shoulder, he shakes me side to side before I push his annoying ass off. He chuckles, wiping himself down with a towel.

"If I wasn't so tired, I'd give you a black eye. Then see how many pretty ladies you get."

"Probably more," Henry snickers. "Girls love that shit. Makes you look tough."

"Then maybe I should fuck up your face. Might help your chances of getting some action," Keith laughs, chucking a full bottle of water at Henry. He ducks to the side, and the bottle goes crashing to the floor, spilling water everywhere.

"Bring it on, bitch," Henry growls out with a playful smirk. Keith flips him off. "You remember the hot chick I got the other night in New Orleans? You know, the one you were all over until she chose me instead." Henry raises his eyebrows, folding his arms across his chest in satisfaction.

Keith and Gus burst out laughing, practically cackling, and I open my eyes to see what I'm missing.

"Dude," Keith manages through his laughter, bending over and holding his side like he has a stitch from laughing so hard. "That chick was a guy."

"Bullshit." Henry turns beat red, his eyes narrowing, but suddenly, he doesn't look like he's so sure."

"Well," Gus says, smiling like the devil as he tries to hold back his amusement. "Not anymore. But she was once." He throws his hands up defensively when Henry twitches as if he's about to charge him. "I'm not judging," he adds quickly. "She was hot. I'm just not sure if she had completed all her surgeries, if you know what I mean."

"Did you fuck her?" Keith asks, picking up a bottle of his signature Jack Daniels and taking a swig.

"No," Henry replies quietly, looking like he's swallowed a bug. "She just sucked me off."

Now we all laugh.

"Relax, dude. What happens in the back room, stays in the back room. And if she was hot...," I trail off.

Henry glances over at me with relief in his eyes, nodding vigorously. "She was definitely hot."

I shrug. "Then it's all good." Only Gus and Keith are still laughing their asses off. And Marco is grinning like the cat who ate the canary. "What?" I ask him.

Marco glances over at Henry and then back to me, his grin growing by the second. "I hooked up with her later." My eyes widen, and my mouth pops open. He laughs, loud and enthusiastically, head thrown back and everything. "She most definitely had *not* finished her surgeries." Gus and Keith lose it, actually falling to their knees as they laugh. I'm right there with them, but Henry does not find this as amusing as the rest of us do. "Sorry, Henry. I'd welcome you to my squad, but getting head from a tranny woman hardly makes you an honorary gay man. It's a shame really; I've always found you kinda cute."

"Fuck," Henry hisses out, snatching the bottle of Jack from Keith and chugging it down. Keith grabs the bottle back as Henry wipes his mouth with the back of his hand. "To the grave boys. This goes with us to the grave." He points to each one of us in turn.

"Stop being such a drama queen," Marco says, and we all burst out laughing again. "You'd think a chick with a dick sucking you off is like the worst thing ever. Grow a pair and man up. Sex is sex, bitch. And you got head out of it."

"Yeah," Gus agrees. "He's right. Sex is most definitely sex. I'm all over double penetration with a hot chick in between. Even if I've never had a man suck my cock."

"You're all assholes. Every one of you."

"Grow up," I grouse. "Who even cares."

"Henry, apparently."

I cock an eyebrow at Marco, and he smirks at me.

"Stop being juveniles. You sure you still want to go to the club tonight?" I tease Henry.

"Hell yeah. Now I have to redeem myself."

"Then you might want to slow down on the booze," Keith suggests. "Otherwise, in addition to hooking up with women who are anatomically still men, you'll have whiskey dick. Stick to your tequila, Hank. Leave the whiskey to the big boys."

"I hate you," Henry declares, pointing at Keith and then the rest of us. "It's official. You all suck."

"Isn't that what she did to you?" I ask.

Everyone cracks up, Gus literally falls completely over, and Marco turns a strange shade of red before he slaps his pink-clad thighs.

I stand up, struggling to move my sluggish, sweaty body. "I'd like to go back to the hotel now. I've had enough of all these gender sexual experiments." They all laugh again, but I cut them off with a glare. "No interviews or comments about Ady to anyone. Especially not with the women," I raise an eyebrow, "or men who are sucking you off." Keith and Gus are dying on the floor, still riding our performance high, while Henry flips me off. I look to Marco, who is having the worst time controlling his amusement. "Is there someone who can take me if Marsellus is going with you all to the club?"

He nods, biting down on his smirk. "Yeah. Thomas can. He's waiting on you."

"Thanks, man. Have a good night. And Marco?" He turns back to me. "Don't let them do anything you wouldn't do." They all laugh harder—well, except for Henry—and Marco treats me to a wink.

I throw everyone a wave and head for the door.

Thankfully, the stadium we played in tonight is in Atlanta. When we play in certain stadiums that are not in a city, we end up having to sleep on the tour bus, because it's nearly impossible to get through the after-show traffic and back to the hotel.

Thomas is waiting for me in a private area, and in under an hour, I'm waltzing into my suite.

My dark and quiet suite.

Usually, Viola's head pops up when I enter, and then she immediately leaves for her room, but tonight, no Viola. I was friendly with her when we went for ice cream. I can do friendly in short bursts. I don't think I have any other choice.

She's right; we need to be allies for this to work.

I peek into Ady's room, and she's there, her small body sleeping on top of Viola, both of them tucked under the covers. I watch them sleep for a moment, that warmth that seems to crash into me when I see the two of them together spreads through me.

They're my elixir. My antidote—didn't I write that for her?

Neither wakes, so I take a quick shower, change into a pair of gym shorts and a white tee, and then I enter Ady's room to wake up Viola so she can return to her room.

Only, now when I enter, she's already awake.

"Hey," she whispers, smiling up at me in the darkness. She peeks down at Ady, whose head is on her chest, breathing slow and even, and back up to me. That same smile still there, and I wonder how I'll ever survive this intact.

My daughter is sleeping on her, head over her heart. Mine most definitely hurts.

"She had a lot of trouble going down. I snuggled with her for a bit, and I guess I fell asleep too."

I smile, edging closer to the bed. "It's fine. You can roll her off you, if you want. She's typically a pretty heavy sleeper."

"She's warm," Viola admits with a small giggle. "How was the show tonight?"

"Good. Really good."

"Since I'm already here, you can join the guys out if you want."

I shake my head slowly, taking in how beautiful she looks with her sleepy eyes and light hair sprawled across the white pillow. With my daughter sleeping peacefully on top of her.

"I'm exhausted."

"You look it."

"Thanks," I deadpan, and she casts up a sorry-but-it's-true smile.

"Come lie down with us," she offers, patting the bed gently beside her.

"I–" I hesitate. I shouldn't. Climbing into bed with Viola is the last thing I should do. Even if my little girl is right there.

Even if I really, really want to.

"At least for a few minutes?" she pushes. "I want to talk to you, and I'm afraid to move her. She already woke up twice when I tried earlier."

Drawing back the sheets, I climb in bed, keeping as much distance between us as I can. But it doesn't matter. I can still feel their body heat under the covers. I can still smell Viola's shampoo on the linens. I take a deep breath, sagging further into the soft bed.

Maybe I should have stayed above the covers. "Rough night?"

"I tried not to watch the news, but Jules kept texting me stuff. And there are reporters outside the hotel."

I nod. "I know. I saw them. They were outside the arena too."

She blows out a breath, her eyes glittering. "Why?"

I shrug a shoulder. "No idea, honestly."

"Those entertainment shows kept talking nonsense. Talking about how Gus and I were a couple again. How I was driving a wedge between the two of you. Going on about my qualifications to care for an Autistic child. It was unbelievable. Where do they get this crap from?"

I stare blankly up at the ceiling.

I guess it's not entirely without merit what they're saying. Viola and Gus may not be officially together, but I know that's ultimately what he wants to happen. His future wife, he called her. Promising to fix all the mistakes he made with her.

So yeah, not so far off base.

Other than the driving a wedge between Gus and me stuff. I won't let that happen, which is why after that night on the couch, I haven't done anything. Haven't tried anything.

But admittedly, her question is a valid one.

Where *do* they get that crap from?

Is it simply speculation or is it from something, someone, else?

"There were a lot of pictures, Jas," she continues in the midst of my contemplative silence. "Of me with her. Pictures of me with Gus. Of me with you. They seem to be from earlier on in the tour. Like around when we hit Dallas, I think."

I didn't realize that. Something feels off about all of this.

When Karina died, the mess I waded through wasn't nearly this bad. Sure, it was on the news and splashed across a few tabloids. There were even some people camped outside my house in California.

But nothing like this.

"Jules mentioned my mother was recently back in town looking for me. She said she wasn't going to tell me about it because she didn't want to upset me, but then this happened. Do you think my mother could somehow be behind this?"

"I don't know," I admit. "I guess it's possible. If she's looking for more money, selling us out is a good way to get it."

"I don't know how they found us all those times without my even being aware of them." She swallows audibly. "Maybe I should leave the tour, Jas. I've been thinking about it. That Sophia woman mentioned that she offered to take care of Ady. And obviously, I'm missing things I shouldn't be missing."

"No," I tell her emphatically. "Ady does not particularly like Sophia, and she has zero experience with kids." I puff out a breath. "To be honest, she drives me nuts."

She laughs lightly. "And I don't?"

"It's different," I concede. "Regardless, you're not leaving the tour, and you're not leaving Adalyn. That would make things a million times worse for her. You'll just have to be more cautious when you two are out."

We fall silent, and this is the moment where I should climb out of bed. But I don't. I don't want to leave in spite of the conversation that crushes my chest like a lead weight.

"Can I ask you something else?"

"Sure," I answer, reaching over and rubbing Ady's back beneath her pajama shirt. She still has that baby soft skin I can't get enough of. Ady lets out a delicate hum and then a loud snore, making both Viola and I laugh.

"I heard you talking with Gus earlier before we went for ice cream."

I freeze for a beat before resuming my rubbing. "Is that your question?"

"No."

I grin to myself in the dark. "Are you afraid to ask it?"

"Yes."

My grin spreads into a smile. I roll over onto my side, propping myself up on my elbow and gazing down at them. I lean in and kiss Ady's head before meeting Viola's eyes.

"You can ask me anything, Viola. I'll either answer or I won't."

Her expression is lined with apprehension. "What happened to your mother?"

That's not what I thought she was going to ask. I assumed she was finally going to challenge me on things between us.

My mother's death is not something I speak about. Not with Gus. Not with my dad. I told the police what happened that morning, and after that, I couldn't relive it. At least not with other people. But the idea of opening up to Viola feels different somehow.

I *want* her to know. To understand me.

Even if it feels like making a deal with the devil.

I reach out and brush some of her hair from her face, curling the silky strands between my fingers.

"When I was six, my mother drowned." Viola gasps, her eyes instantly glazing over like this pains her to hear as much as it pains me to say. "This was before we moved to Alabama, obviously. Before we met you. Gus and my father didn't come with us to the beach for reasons I can't remember. There was a strong riptide warning in the Gulf, but it was still filled with people swimming. I was playing, splashing around while my mother watched me from the beach, and I ended up wading in too deep. I felt the riptide pulling me out, and I didn't know what to do. I panicked, which only made things worse. My mother came rushing in after me. But...," I trail off, swallowing hard as I think back on what happened.

My eyes close, and it's like I'm right there, back to that awful day. Hell, I still remember the way the water smelled. The way the sand felt as I lay in it, screaming. A violent shudder wracks through my body.

"Jasper?" Viola prompts when I stay silent. "If it's too much, you don't have to tell me."

I open my eyes, and I stare into hers. "My mother didn't know how to swim. She ran into the water on instinct, and typically, the Gulf isn't all that deep. She managed to get me inland enough that I could swim myself back to the beach, but the riptide pulled her under, and she couldn't swim enough to fight her way out of it." A tear rolls down Viola's cheek, and I reach out to wipe it away. "Someone found her, pulled her out, and they worked on her for a while. But there wasn't anything they could do. She had been under too long."

Viola glances down at a Ady, like she's desperate to move her and embrace me, and I've never been so grateful for my sleeping daughter in my life. Viola hugging me might just be my total undoing.

"That's why you told me I had to stay by the shoreline with Ady when we were at the beach in California."

I nod.

"I'm so sorry, Jasper. That must have been horrifying to watch. To live through." She takes a deep breath as if she needs it to stop her tears and steel her nerves. "Gus is right, though. It wasn't your fault."

"Except he grew up without a mother because I went in too deep."

"You grew up without a mother too. And I've experienced those riptides. They pull you back before you even know how deep you are. It was just a horrific accident."

That's twice today those words have been said to me. *It wasn't your fault.* The impact no less severe now than it was the first time.

"I'm surprised Gus never told you the story before."

She shakes her head. "I asked him once, and he told me it wasn't his story to tell."

"I guess it wasn't."

"Thank you for telling me."

"You have a habit of breaking down my resistance."

I meant to say that in a light way. In a joking way. But it came out as anything but. It came out serious and needy, and Viola doesn't miss that for a minute. She's staring at me like she wants me to kiss her.

And I want to kiss her.

So goddamn badly, my body hums with the need for it.

So goddamn badly, I can't stand it a minute longer.

I *have* to kiss Viola.

My face inches toward hers, our eyes locked, her warm breath tickling my lips. A couple more inches and my world will forever change. If I do this, there is no going back.

My breath hitches with anticipation. My stomach tightens. My lips crave. Inches. That's all there is until I cross this irreversible line. Just inches before my lips press to hers, and I lose my mind completely. Can I do this? Can I betray Gus like this?

Then the word, "Daddy," stops me dead in my tracks.

Or, better yet, saves me from committing the ultimate mistake.

TWENTY-FOUR

Viola

I HAD the day all planned out. We hit Washington, D.C. early this morning, and on the bus–yes, we're still on the damn bus–ride up from Charlotte, North Carolina, I was informed that today would be my day off, and I could spend it however I wanted. Now, I'm a teacher, right? So the idea of touring our nation's history was like handing a loaded needle to a junkie.

Too good to pass up.

Jasper's father and stepmother were scheduled to land here yesterday and were planning on spending all day today with Ady. As much as I love Adalyn, I won't fight over having a day off. Especially, when the stupid paparazzi have been sticking to us like dog shit on a shoe.

Because as far as I'm concerned, that's what they are.

I have no idea what they're after. Why they freaking care.

But they do.

It's become their life's mission to get to us. They made it so that Ady and I could not leave the event area in North Carolina. I don't know if it's me or Ady or Jasper or the band or what, but our faces are everywhere. Marco went to the pharmacy to grab me some supplies and came back with five different rags, covered with photos of us. It didn't take long for the press to discover who I am, and that I once had a relationship with Gus.

Now it's all they talk about.

All about my 'secret' relationship with Gus. About how the band is on its last legs and Jasper is threatening to walk because he hates me. How I'm only the nanny to Adalyn because Gus demanded it be so.

Essentially, I'm painted as the devil.

The harlot who is breaking up the world's favorite band.

And they all talk about Adalyn's diagnosis.

One referred to their article as an exposé into the epidemic known as Autism. An epidemic by definition is a widespread occurrence of an infectious disease. Ummm...yeah. Last I checked, autism isn't Ebola.

And maybe they should have fact-checked because their shit was so off it was the epitome of bad journalism. If she were any neurotypical child, none of this would be a discussion.

I'm embarrassed and angry and sick and jittery. It feels like I have a constant red spotlight on me. And if it's bad for me and Jasper and Gus, it's a million times worse for Ady.

So yeah, this day off was going to be fan-bloody-tastic.

And then Jasper and Gus's parents' flight was canceled for no real reason we could discern, and they decided to wait until we return from overseas to meet up. Marco said he'd step in and hang out with Ady while I took a few hours to explore.

But then Ady got sick.

And not just any old sick.

I'm talking stomach bug or food poisoning sick.

Marco calls as I'm exploring the Smithsonian Art Museum, gagging into the phone. "I can't do it, Vi. I'm trying. I swear." Gag. Dry heave. "But the smell. It's killing me. And Ady may like me, but she doesn't *love* me, ya know? I don't think she's enjoying me holding her hair back either, and wow, her hair, girl. The baby needs a bath or a shower or whatever you give kids her age."

It's been like what, six weeks? Something like that, and I've had so very little time off.

"Tell her I'm on my way." Sigh. Groan. Fake cry. I'm doing all of those.

"You're an angel."

"So they tell me."

I huff and puff all the way back to the bus. Because that's where we're sleeping tonight. Where poor Ady is sick.

Seriously.

All I can say is, it's a wonderful thing that she's not old enough to be embarrassed by bodily functions because those buses are tight, and those bathrooms are tiny, and she's got it coming from both ends, according to Marco.

I pull into FedExField, and all around the gate that separates the private area from the rest of the place is lined with press. What they're expecting to see, I don't know, but I'm tempted to give them access to Ady right now if that would get them all off our asses.

The door to the bus is already open, and Marco is standing there, waiting for me. His dark skin has a green hue to it, his hair is a mess, and he most definitely has something on his shirt that I don't want to think about what it is. If he saw himself, he'd cry.

He holds his hands up in supplication when he catches me approaching. "Do you hate me? Don't hate me."

"I don't hate you."

"I've been giving her Coke and those awful crackers she likes with almond butter," he starts, and I sigh aggressively. "What?"

"She's three, Marco. Don't you have Google? She should be drinking Pedialyte or something like it. And no food-especially not something like almond butter. At least until she's twenty-four hours without vomiting or diarrhea. Plain crackers maybe would have been okay."

"Fuck," he hisses, running a hand across his stomach, because he'd rather die than muss up his perfectly coiffed hair or bronzer. Too late for that I'm afraid. "I'm a much better manager than I am babysitter." I step onto the bus and frown before glancing back over my shoulder at him. "I know. I tried to clean it up, but I ended up almost throwing up on top of it. Why do you think the bus doors are open?"

"Okay." Because *wow.* "Marco, love kitten who owes me his life, I'm texting you a list of everything we need because if we can't keep up with her hydration, we'll have to take her to the hospital for an IV."

His black eyes widen. "Okay. Shopping I can do."

"Thank you."

"I'm really sorry. I know this sucks the big suck, and your suck has already been sucky."

I shrug. "I'll live. Let's just take care of her."

"I'm on it." He leaves, and I text him everything, and then I go back into the bedroom to find poor Adalyn, lying on the bed with her eyes open, staring off into space. I check her out, making sure her mouth isn't too dry, and her pulse isn't too fast.

She's hanging in there.

Miserable, but hanging in.

Then, I set to work on cleaning up the bus, and since there is no bathtub on here, I strip us both down, and we climb into the tiny shower together.

Adalyn does not like the shower. She typically screams and fights whenever Jasper or I try to give her one. And she *really* doesn't like water being splashed on her head.

But right now, this little baby has no fight in her.

She lets me wash her hair and her body, and I clean myself up, and when we step out, wrapped in towels, things feel better.

At least for me, because Ady proceeds to vomit all over the freshly cleaned bathroom. And it's only pale-yellow bile.

"Boogers!" I yelp.

The boys are nuts today. They have meetings and interviews and press conferences and sound checks. I haven't even texted Jasper yet because I don't want to worry him, but I'm thinking if she continues like this, I might not have a choice.

After cleaning up, again, I sit with Ady in only a pull-up diaper on my lap, rubbing her back in slow, gentle circles.

She's been having some potty regression since we started this trip, and with her stomach being a mess, I am taking zero chances. Marco enters the bus like a triumphant gladiator returning from battle with the kill on his back.

"I texted Jasper so he's UTD."

I glance up, staring dumbly at him. "UTD?"

He rolls his eyes. "Up-to-date. I felt like that was an obvious."

"It probably was, but I'm not 'UTD' on anything other than my gossip rags, and that's only because my face is on them. Is he coming back?"

"No. He was really upset, but he couldn't manage it. He was relieved I called you and that you're here with her."

That shouldn't make me smile. But it does.

Jasper and I have not had another close call like the one we had in the bed that night, but that doesn't mean things haven't shifted between us. He's...nicer. I'm no longer the bane of his existence. I wouldn't say we're close or even friends necessarily, but he's definitely easier on me than he was.

"Do me a favor and pour some of the Pedialyte into a cup with a lid and a straw. They're in the cabinet above the fridge."

"Great. I'm on it. And thank you for cleaning up. I'm sorry about leaving that for you."

I wave him off, and for the next two hours, we work on nursing Miss Adalyn back to a healthy state of hydration.

Marco ends up leaving me because he has to go into the stadium to ensure everything is the way it should be for the show, and I'm left alone with Adalyn on a bus in a deserted part of the stadium. And I'll be honest with you, it's creepy over here. And dark.

Ady is wiped. So am I, truth be told. Being sick and taking care of the sick is no joke.

My phone pings with a text from Sophia. *You should take her to the hospital. How irresponsible can you be? You're not a doctor, and you have no idea what you're doing.*

I legit hate this woman. Like from the depths of my soul, hate her. *She has been taking and keeping down fluids. No vomiting or diarrhea for the last hour and a half. Her color is improving, and her mucous membranes are moist. I don't think taking her to the hospital and shoving a needle in her arm is in her best interest and will likely cause more emotional trauma than is necessary, considering she's improving.* And I don't remember asking for your input, I don't add.

She doesn't reply, because what the hell can she say?

Jasper texts me shortly after for an update, and I send him a picture of me with Adalyn lying in bed watching Peppa Pig on her tablet. I get a thumbs-up emoji for that, so I'm assuming he's good with me not taking her to the hospital.

This girl has trouble in the pharmacy and the grocery store–she likes to face-plant herself on the floor in stores. No idea why. I imagine an emergency department would be like dragging her into the pits of hell. For everyone involved.

I apply online for a few dozen teaching positions while Adalyn watches her device, and when I check on her again, she's asleep, the tablet precariously hanging off the bed.

Placing the tablet on the small built-in nightstand hanging out of the wall, I tuck Adalyn in, kissing her head. No fever. Thank goodness for that. I text Jasper to let him know that Adalyn is sleeping and hasn't been sick in a few hours.

And I text him letting him know he can go out with the boys if he wants, as much as I hate myself for it. It's easier for me if he's not around on this tiny bus.

I'm the nanny and nothing more. He's my boss, and that's all he'll ever be.

The more I force that on myself, the better off I'll be when this is all done.

On the ride up, the boys were heckling Jasper about how long it's been since he's gotten laid. I tried not to listen. Well, I tried not to listen for a couple of minutes, and then when I realized the attempt was futile, I tried to make it *appear* like I wasn't listening.

Marco offered to stay the night and watch Adalyn–this was before she got sick–Gus offered as well. I didn't have the stomach to see what Jasper's expression was over this conversation. To see if he snuck a peek at me at all during it.

We've had so many moments.

All that touching and tasting and teasing and coming. I actually had an orgasm on him! And yet, nothing has progressed. I told him I wanted his heart, and he's given me nothing in return.

Message received. Loud and clear.

Still, I couldn't help the way my stomach flipped over on itself when they were talking about finding him a girl for the night. I couldn't stop the prickles of jealousy as they climbed up my spine and colored my cheeks. I haven't had sex in a hundred years. Or at least it feels like that. A teacher I worked with and I had hit it off briefly.

Until I found out he was married.

That was an all-time awesome moment.

That was close to a year ago now, and I can't even say the sex was all that great. Mediocre at best.

Before him, I dated Spencer for about six months. Nothing spectacular there either. Listening to the guys talk about their various conquests is depressing. But listening to them try and find Jasper some wild hot sex makes me want to throw up the way Adalyn has been all day.

So when I get a text from Gus informing me that he's staying in with me tonight so Jasper can go out, I can't stop my growl of frustration and irrational jealousy and stupid, purposeless heartache. Then I laugh at myself for being so ridiculous. I essentially gave him the green light to go, and he took it.

He hasn't gone out once this entire tour.

The guy has needs too.

Pulling myself away from Adalyn's room in the back of the bus, I head toward the open space at the front with the television and eating area. Maybe Gus and I will stream a movie tonight. I'd make popcorn, but that would stink up the whole bus and might make Ady sick again. I'll let Gus pick the flick, but I'm in charge of snacks.

I need dairy. And chocolate. And gluten.

The sound of the doors to the bus opening startles me while I'm face-deep in the back of the pantry–which is really just a small cabinet where they keep the food. "Hey," I call out. "I thought we could watch a movie tonight. And eat something non-Adalyn-approved since she's asleep."

"Sounds good." Jasper's voice startles me so bad I jump, smacking the top of my head on one of the shelves.

I slide out of the cabinet, my eyes wide. "You're not Gus. I got a text saying Gus was playing babysitter with me tonight so you could go out."

Jasper's eyes narrow, his expression hardening. "Sorry to disappoint you, but I didn't feel right about leaving Ady while she's sick. I guess you'll have to deal with me tonight." He tilts his head, taking me in. "Unless you want to change and go meet up with them. You haven't had a night out either, and today was technically supposed to be a day off for you."

I shake my head before I can formulate words. I don't want to go out. I want to stay here and watch a movie on this bus with Jasper while I eat my weight in chocolate and carbs.

"It's fine. I can hang out."

"You don't have to," he presses, and there is something in his voice that I can't quite figure out. "I know Gus would love for you to join them. He's been talking about nothing but you tonight."

My cheeks color at that. "I'm sure he was just messing with you. Gus and I are only friends."

Jasper takes a small step in my direction, crowding me back until I hit the counter behind me. "You and Gus have been a lot of things over the years. But I don't think you've ever *just* been friends. I'm going to check on Adalyn and give you some privacy to change for your night of fun with Gus."

And then he marches off, heading for the bedroom with determined steps.

Why the hell is he pissed at me? Maybe they had a bad show? I don't know, but there is a definite and distinct edge to him.

Fuck that and fuck him. I'm so sick of his hot and cold routine with me.

I follow him back to the bedroom, "What's your problem tonight?" I whisper, watching as he bends down to kiss Ady's forehead like he's checking for a fever. "Maybe you should go out and get laid. Maybe then you'd stop being such a prickish bastard to me."

"Shhh," he hisses and not at a quiet decibel either. "You're going to wake her up."

"Me?" I point to my chest, incredulous. "You're the one whisper-shouting."

"I am not whisper-shouting," he whisper-shouts, and I roll my eyes before cocking a brow.

My phone buzzes in my back pocket, and I slide it out to see who's calling, but Jasper grabs my wrist, turning my phone so he can see, and I can't. "Hey," I protest, trying to yank my wrist free of his grasp and move my phone out of his sightline. "That's my phone. You have no right."

"The fuck I don't," he barks. "You work for me." He catches the name on the screen, his eyes growing dark and narrowed. "It's Thomas. Why is Thomas calling you?"

"None of your business," I snap defiantly, raising my chin to him. Honestly, I have no idea why my security guy is calling me at this hour. He's probably just checking up on Adalyn to see if there is anything she needs since he's also assigned to her and is a super big sweetheart.

"It is my business. He works for me. You work for me. You watch my daughter. I think I'm entitled to know why my daughter's nanny is whoring herself out with her security guy."

He did *not* just go there.

"You're such a goddamn asshole. I cannot believe you just said that to me. First, you give me crap about Gus, and now Thomas?"

"Shhhh," he hisses again. "You're going to wake her up! And we don't say asshole around my daughter. We say a-hole or hole-in-one."

Oh, but we say whoring and fuck?

I snort, crossing my arms over my chest, because really? Is he kidding me with those? Not only do they sound insanely stupid, but the boys are far worse with language around Adalyn than I ever am. I'm seriously like two seconds away from smacking him again.

"That is absolutely ridiculous." His glare is menacing. "Fine. Then you're a hole," I make a loop with my thumb and pointer finger, "in one." I take my middle finger on my opposite hand and slip it through the hole I just made with my other fingers. Let him feast on that.

I spin on my heels and storm off, out of Adalyn's bedroom. I'm done with Jasper Diamond. He's officially crossed the line, and I'm done. I'll give him a week, maybe two, to find a new nanny to take care of Adalyn, and then I'm gone.

Adalyn.

Dammit. The thought of leaving that little girl hurts like hell.

"Why is Thomas calling you at midnight, Viola?"

I growl, thrashing over to my stupid, uncomfortable bunk.

Yanking the curtain aside, I try to draw it closed around me, essentially blocking him out. He grabs it, tugging it back.

"Hey!" I protest. "This is my space. Get out." I snap my head over my shoulder. "And I'm not whoring myself out, you *asshole*," I emphasize now that we're out of Adalyn's bedroom. "He's our security detail. Maybe he was just checking up on Adalyn. Seeing if I needed something." I glare harder if that's even possible. "You know, being fucking considerate!"

Jasper chuckles, lacing his fingers together and dropping his hands behind his head. I can't help but stare at his biceps as they bulge in this position, at the colorful tattoos that draw my eyes like a magnet. A smug, satisfied–*asshole!*–smirk spreads across his too-handsome face.

"Or maybe he's calling for a different reason at this hour. Gus. Thomas. How many men are you stringing along exactly?"

I smile deviously. "Who says I'm stringing anyone along?"

His eyes return to their previously narrowed state, his arms dropping back heavily to his sides. I close the curtain in his face again, spinning around, so I don't have to look at him. Or acknowledge him. Or breathe the same air as him. Especially since I want to strangle him. Maybe kick him in the shins.

God, I don't think a man has ever infuriated me more.

He rips the curtain back open, practically tearing the thing down. "You better not be screwing around with him."

"I am not screwing around with him! And just because I work for you doesn't mean you have the right to dictate who I fuck and who I don't."

"Oh, but it does, sweetheart. I already told you, I own your ass. And right now, I have half a mind to fuck that smart mouth of yours to prove that point."

The bastard just seriously–

I pivot back to him, my eyes blazing, my fists balled up so tight I can feel the blood draining from them. "And I have half a mind to shove my foot up your hole-in-one until you learn some manners. I quit. I'm done with you and your bullshit. You've got a week to find a new nanny for Adalyn."

He blinks at me, floored by my declaration. "You're quitting?"

Tears burn the backs of my eyes and the tip of my nose as I say, "Yes."

TWENTY-FIVE

Viola

"YOU CAN'T QUIT."

"I just did." I push him away with my fists, spinning back around while closing the curtain once and for all. I'm wrecked. This man wrecks me. He owns my heart, and he uses it like a punching bag.

God, I really just quit. I can't believe I did that.

How will I tell Adalyn? How will she ever understand? I can't abandon her. The thought is pure agony.

He hasn't moved. Why hasn't he moved?

Just leave me alone to wallow in peace.

"Go away," I bark, my voice catching. "I'm going to bed."

He doesn't say or do anything for a moment, and I take that as my win and his loss, and I start to pull my shirt over my head.

"No," he clips out, tugging that damn curtain back again and finding my back to him in just my bra and jeans. "You're not quitting. You can't just walk away from Adalyn like that." He pauses. Clears his throat. "What the hell are you doing?"

"I told you," I snap, trying to unhook my bra, but it's so damn old that the hook is all warped and is, naturally, picking this moment to not come undone. "I'm getting. Ready. For. Bed." I punctuate my words as I struggle against the stupid clasp.

Jasper's hands glide up my back, and I freeze, my eyes widening, knowing he can't see them. My teeth slam into my bottom lip, and it takes every ounce of power in my body not to move or shudder or even fucking moan.

His touch is so freaking light, like a butterfly flapping its wings against my skin.

Only, he's not usually the gentle butterfly. Not with me. He's the tsunami at the end of the chaos.

He manages to unhook it, and I mumble out a, "Thank you." Sliding my threadbare tee on with my back still to him, I manage to rein myself in. And when I think I have some semblance of control over myself, I say, "I don't want to leave Adalyn. She's the reason I'd stay. I believe I already made that clear to you."

He's right behind me.

Closer.

So close, I can feel his body heat pressing into me. The scent of his cologne and anger permeating the air.

I undo the button on my jeans, sliding the zipper down. The metal hooks falling apart is the only sound, shooting sparks into the thick, statically charged atmosphere.

"Is she the only reason?" he asks, his voice husky and deep. His hand runs along my hair, sweeping it over one shoulder, and exposing my neck to him. The tips of his fingers skirt along the column of my neck, and I erupt in delicious tingling chills.

"No," I push out and refuse to elaborate further, because if I don't hold on to my last shred of pride, then he'll unquestionably have all of me, and I'll be left with nothing.

I get my jeans undone, slip them down a little, and bend forward to take them off, smiling to myself as I do.

That is, until my ass presses against the huge, *hard* bulge in his pants.

Oh. My. God. He's got a freaking steel pipe in there. I don't think my eyes have ever bugged out of my head quite like this before.

So much for me winning that round.

Jasper groans, reaching out and clasping my hips like he doesn't know whether to push me away or pull me harder against him. I somehow locate my shorts, dragging them on, and Jasper releases me, taking a small step back.

It doesn't help. I can still smell him. Feel where his large, warm hands were on my skin.

How can I still yearn for this man, even after everything he's put me through?

Love is a determined, resilient beast. It won't be destroyed without a fight. It won't give up, even when you beg it to. Even when you sincerely hate the one you love. No, love likes to hang on and beat you down until you're unrecognizable, despising everything, especially it.

I hate that I love him.

"Are you intentionally trying to be a tease?"

Yes. Obviously. Duh.

I turn around to face him, and it's quite possibly the biggest mistake of my life. Even more so than never removing my mother's name from my bank account. Because Jasper Diamond is staring at me with dark, hooded, lust-filled eyes. His large, muscular chest is rising and falling heavily, straining against the cotton of his white tee. He looks so goddamn sexy like this I can hardly stand it.

"Me?" I snap, losing the last shred of my composure. "You're the one who's hard."

A slow, sly grin crawls up his lips as his eyes eat me up inch by inch. He pauses briefly on my hard nipples that are practically saluting him through the thin fabric of my shirt and then dips lower to the exposed flesh of my stomach, on down to my shorts.

"And I bet if I slipped my hand into those tiny shorts, *nanny*, I'd find you wet for me. Again."

I shake my head. "You called me a whore."

He shakes his head back and forth, encroaching on me. His eyes blaze into mine. "I didn't mean it. You drive me up a motherfucking wall, Viola Starr. I can't think straight with you. I say shit, and then I regret it. I never had this problem before. But then again...," he trails off, his gaze slowly trickling along every inch of me once more. "I was very much a boy back then, and you definitely remind me that I'm very much a man now."

My throat bobs on an audible swallow. "How hard are you for me, Jasper?"

His eyes snap back up to mine. He licks his lips, almost reflexively, and any last shred of his restraint evaporates. "Rock hard. How wet are you for me, Viola?"

"Soaked."

His lips crash into mine, the force of his kiss slamming me against the top bunk before we tumble into the lower one. His body presses into mine, covering me in his incredible heat. For a second, I'm too stunned to move.

Jasper Diamond doesn't give in.

He doesn't relent.

I've wanted this man's mouth back on mine since that first kiss when we were fourteen, and twelve years later, I'm finally getting it.

That stunned second passes quickly as his hand roughly cups my jaw, angling me to him, so his mouth can devour mine. His tongue forces its way into my mouth, battling with my own. A slow sexy growl rips from the back of his throat the moment our tongues meet.

I've never felt such out of control need in a kiss before. Such ferocity. Weeks and weeks of fighting and dancing around each other, and now we're ravenous.

I don't care about tomorrow.

I don't care how ugly this will all end.

I want this man, and I'm going to put everything I've got into this moment. Even if it's fleeting. Even if it rips out my heart, I know I won't regret it.

I grip the back of his shirt, balling up the soft cotton in my fists as I let him take the lead. As I let him own me.

His mouth moves to my chin, nipping and licking as he glides down the length of my neck with harsh hot kisses. The coarseness of his stubbled jawline shoots sparks of painful pleasure straight to my core. My neck arches to give him better access, my eyes closing as I lick my lips, tasting him.

My fingers dive to the back of his head, running through his thick wavy auburn hair, still slightly damp from the shower he took after the show. His mouth captures mine once more, and I groan, clutching him as if I'm afraid he'll disappear if I relent even an inch.

He smells of masculine body wash and lust. He tastes like Jack Daniels and mint toothpaste and raw burning desire.

For me.

This man wants me like I'm his next breath and taste better than the most decadent dessert.

His hands clutch my hips, his forehead pressing into mine as he pants, smiling down at me. "You're driving me crazy, dream girl."

I grin against him. "I thought I was nanny?"

Reaching out, his teeth capture my lip, nibbling gently on it. He squeezes my hips and stares into my eyes. "No, baby, you've always been my dream girl."

Christ. I tug him back down to me, claiming his mouth before I find his neck, sucking hard, memorizing everything about this moment. The way he feels. The sounds of his heavy breaths.

He moans, dragging my mouth back up to his. Our tongues dance, sliding across each other's, our lips fused. The pressure of them is so much and yet not enough. It's the type that curls your toes and rolls your eyes back. The one you don't want to ever end, because it's just. That. Good.

It's everything and simultaneously not enough.

I yank hard on his hair. I want to hurt him. I want to mark him.

Force him to think of me every goddamn time he looks in the mirror. Forget him owning me; I fully intend to own him right back. First. Foremost. Wholly.

There is no one else but him, and it's time he realized that.

He breaks the kiss, breathing hard, his heart pounding against mine. Our eyes lock from inches apart, and he stares into me as if he's never seen me before.

"Viola," he whispers, but then stops, and I know he's waging a war within himself. "Is this what you really want?" He pauses, searching me before taking in each one of my features. "Because it's what I want. What I've always wanted."

I open my mouth to tell him that I've wanted this for so long that I can't remember a time when I haven't wanted him. But I can't make the words come out. I'm too stubborn. Too proud.

And part of me still doesn't believe this is real.

My life is not a bed of roses. I've slept on thorns for so long now that I don't know what it feels like not to be pricked with the sharp edge. I'm the one no one loves enough. The one who's cheated on and betrayed and used. And when that happens with Jasper, I won't survive it.

"Don't stop," is all I can come up with.

His mouth slams back into mine, and instead of giving him my truths, I give him my pleasure. I groan into his mouth, and he swallows it down, taking it for himself.

His fists grip angrily at my shirt, and before I know what's happening, he rips the fabric from my body in one effortless motion. His hands come up, cupping my bare breasts, squeezing them together as his mouth slides down to meet them.

"Oh God," I moan and then squeak as he bites hard on the top of my breast, running his tongue over the sting to soothe it.

He sucks a nipple into his mouth, my tits still squeezed and pressed together, trussed up in his strong hands as he applies just the right amount of pressure. My eyes roll to the back of my head, my back bowing as I tug on his hair, forcing him in deeper. He alternates between biting and licking, sucking and kissing. It's driving me wild. I can't stop squirming, rocking forward, desperate for friction.

Needy and hot and wholly crazed.

His hand slides down my stomach, dipping into my cotton shorts and beneath my thin panties, rubbing up and down over my pussy. "I've had so many fantasies about this," he says, his voice hoarse, his breathing harsh. His fingers continue to slide up and down, spreading my moisture across my clit without applying any pressure, without sinking inside. It's so much and not nearly enough. "So many dreams of what I'd do if I ever got my shot. How many different ways I'd make you beg me for it."

"Please," I hum, giving him exactly what he's asking for and not feeling any shame about it. If begging gives me what I want, what I need, I'll fall to my knees and beg. I want him to fuck me crazy. Make me come like I've never come before.

If begging gets me that, I'm all for begging.

He grins over me, his cheeks flushed, and his hair tousled. I love him like this. Off-kilter, riled up, and utterly depraved with lust.

He's going to ruin me, and I will relish every damn second of it.

"Mmmm, Viola." His fingers continue their maddening pace, and I whimper, grinding up against his hand, urging him on. "Not yet, greedy girl." I groan, my head flopping back, and he laughs, kissing along my arched neck. "I want to take my time with you. We raced through those other times. Not tonight."

Screw that. "Tell me, Jasper," I breathe out, frustrated with pleasure. "Tell me all about how you jerked off to me. Tell me what I did in your fantasies that made you explode your hot cum in your hand. Tell me how good it was, because I can promise you, this will be better."

I've officially lost my flipping mind.

"Fuck," he hisses, his hand sliding out of my shorts and sucking his fingers into his mouth. His cheeks are red, his chest rising and falling rapidly with his harsh breaths as his eyes consume every inch of me, lingering on my breasts, my lips, the marks on my skin he's left.

"Flip over. Ass in the air. Cheek on your pillow with your hair back so I can see your face."

Christ. I do as he commands. I'm his instrument. So turned on, I can hardly breathe.

He slides my shorts down to my knees, slipping them off and over my feet. My panties follow, and now, I'm open, exposed completely. His hands glide along the cheeks of my ass, massaging them before I feel cool air followed by the stinging *smack* of his palm.

It jerks me forward and stuns my eyes open, a gasp escaping my lips.

"You're not quitting, Viola. Get that illusion out of your head now." He smacks me again, switching to my other cheek. A rush of heat explodes through me, my empty core clenching. I moan, rocking back, wanting more. Two more smacks, and then his mouth is there, kissing me gently. "Your ass is so pretty like this, red with my hand-prints." He strokes me again. "You want to know how I got myself off to images of you, dream girl? You want to know all the dirty, sinful things I did to you in my fantasies?"

"No," I whisper, so wound up, I feel my wetness leaking down onto my upper thighs. "I want you to *show* me."

He growls, burying his face in me from behind, licking from the bundle of nerves in the back all the way to the top of my mound. I cry out, the assault of his mouth welcome and electrifying. One of his hands snakes up, twisting my nipple hard in warning, the other covering my mouth.

"If you wake up Adalyn, this is over. I'll gag you if I have to."

I never thought the idea of a gag would sound hot to me, but right now, everything is turning me on.

"Can you be quiet?"

"No."

"Then open your mouth."

I do, and he shoves one of the pieces of my torn t-shirt into my mouth. Holy Christ, I cannot believe this is happening. But in the next second, I no longer care as I bite down into the soft cotton, anything to smother this moan as it escapes past my vocal cords.

Jasper sucks on my clit as two fingers slide deep inside me, pumping in and out. His tongue flicks back and forth, his fingers curling, rubbing that magical place inside me. Moan after moan pours from my mouth. He grins against me. I feel it. Hot and primal as he delights in my response.

I can't even stop it.

I don't even want to try.

He fingers me at a torturous pace, with slow licks and deep thrusts. "More. Please more," I garble through my gag.

"Show me what you want, baby. How you need it." I grind back against him, my body taking over as he licks me, sucking and pumping his fingers until I come apart. Screaming and crying out into the cotton stuffed in my mouth, I claw at my pillow and sheets, pushing myself back harder into his face as I ride out this wave that never seems to end.

In a flash, I find myself on my back, the gag stripped from my mouth, staring up into Jasper's dark, hungry eyes. His lips are moist, slick with my arousal. His shirt is gone, the hard contours of his muscled chest and abs drawing my gaze.

I sit up, desperate to touch him, to explore him, but I'm just as quickly pushed back down.

"Are you on the pill?" I swallow, jerking my head up and down in what I think is a nod. "Good. Because I really don't want to use a condom with you. I cannot handle any more barriers between us. I'm clean. I swear it to you."

"I'm clean too."

He smiles, his fingers reaching out to caress my cheek. "Look at you," he whispers reverently. "You're so goddamn beautiful, Viola. The girl I could never get out of my head no matter how hard I tried."

Jasper stands up slowly, his eyes never wavering from mine as he undoes his jeans, dropping them to the floor along with his boxer briefs. His thick, hard cock springs free, and my eyes widen. He gives it a few lazy strokes, watching me as I watch it.

"Your body was made for mine, Viola. I'll fit."

I sure as hell hope so.

He climbs back on this bullshit bunk, the wood planks creaking beneath his weight. He raises one of my legs up to his shoulder and slides into me without any warning, his lips fusing to mine to stifle my cries.

My back bows off the bed, my eyes cinching shut, a shuddered breath passing from my lips and into his. He holds himself still, settled inside me to the hilt.

"Too much?" I roll my head back and forth against the pillow. "Breathe, baby. You're squeezing my cock like a vice. Your pussy is so damn tight I'm about to explode." His hand cups my cheek, his thumb gliding along my lips. "Open your eyes, Vi. Look at me."

I do, and I find him smiling down at me. A warm, tender, affectionate smile. It's so rare. So unexpectedly wonderful that I smile back at him.

Has a girl ever been so crazy for the wrong guy before? For the bad boy who takes what he wants and offers so little back?

But I'm here, opening myself up to him, giving him my body, which was the last thing I had yet to fully give him. The last thing for him to own. Even with that thought, there is nowhere else I'd rather be right now.

I stare back at him, and I let out the breath I've been holding.

"You're so beautiful to me. So perfect. My crazy sexy dream girl. Can I move?"

"Yes," I whisper, and then he does. He slides back and forth, achingly slow at first, pulling nearly all the way out before sinking back in.

He does this repeatedly, staring down at where our bodies are connected, alternating between that and my eyes. It's maddening and delicious and so good and yet not enough.

And only when he knows I'm ready, when I'm clawing at his

skin, scraping my nails impatiently down his back, begging him for more, does he pick up speed. My knees bend up, one pressed against his chest, the other above his shoulder as he pounds into me with a relentless rhythm.

"Yes," I say again, only this time, it's a moan, an expletive, an echo of something I've never experienced before.

His teeth sink into my breast, branding me to him. A flash of pain shoots through me, and I cry out, the sensation raising this to a whole new level. His mouth finds mine, his tongue takes over, swallowing down my cries.

"I can't slow down," he rasps into me, breathing hard, sweat coating his forehead. "I can't stop. It's too good. You feel too good."

"I'm close," I manage. "So close, Jasper."

"Yes, baby." He picks up the pace, pounding into me, skin slapping against skin. Both my legs are over his shoulders now as he bends me in half, his mouth all over mine. His fingers dip between us, finding my clit and stars dance behind my eyes.

My orgasm begins low, slow, slinking up my spine and tingling my toes, before it grows, multiplies in intensity, skyrocketing through me like a bolt of lightning.

"Fuck," Jasper hisses as my body convulses around him. "Yes. Just like that. You're so hot. So tight. Fuck. Nothing has ever felt this good."

My thoughts exactly. My kinky imagination has nothing on Jasper Diamond in the flesh.

He shakes, shuddering and biting out a slew of curses as his face drops into my neck, riding out the last of his orgasm. He's panting for his life, his heart slamming against his chest, against my chest. Mine matching his, bleeding into him.

"You're so much better than the fantasy," he whispers, and I repeat, *my thoughts exactly.* He chuckles against my skin, pulling back and meeting my eyes with a lazy, sated grin. "Hi."

"Hi." I return his grin. Mine equally as lazy and sated, I'm sure.

"I bit you."

"I know."

"I think I left a mark."

"My clothes will cover it."

He peeks down at his handiwork, tracing what I assume are his teeth marks with the tip of his finger. "Does it hurt?" I shake my head no, and he looks relieved, that small grin pulling up the corner of his mouth. "Good. Because I have to admit, it's pretty damn sexy." He leans in, slowly, eyes locked on mine before he kisses my lips. "You're a kinky little slut, aren't you?" he asks playfully.

"Me?" I snap, smacking at his arm, trying for indignant and coming up way short. He's laughing at me now. "You're the one who gagged me. And spanked me. And bit me."

"You loved it." *Can't deny that.* "I'm sure I'll come up with more for next time."

Next time. *Don't do it. Don't smile at that. Don't allow that giddy, excited anticipation to take over.* "Now who's the kinky little slut?"

"I never said I wasn't." His expression sobers, and I feel my heart picking up a few extra beats. "You're not really quitting, are you?" His eyes search mine, suddenly cautious.

"Was this your way of getting me to stay?"

He frowns, and I wish I hadn't said that. His eyes tell a completely different story about what just happened between us.

"Unfortunately, I don't think I can leave Adalyn. You, on the other hand...," I trail off, and he drops his forehead to mine, closing his eyes and releasing a slow even breath.

He whispers something so faintly I can't make out any of it, and then his lips meet mine. Relief coursing through them and into me.

His kisses shouldn't feel so right. Being with him shouldn't feel like everything I've been missing and searching for all at once. And it definitely shouldn't terrify me for what I fear is next to come.

I feel him growing hard in me. "More?" I ask, desperate for this never to end.

"More," he agrees. "More."

TWENTY-SIX

Viola

I WAKE UP ALONE. I fell asleep with Jasper's body covering mine in a tailspin of bliss. I fell asleep to soft words and gentle kisses that contradicted everything he had just done to my body.

We fucked like animals only to be wrapped up in each other like lovers after. Two more times, and then I was done. Utterly spent. I don't even have to open my eyes to know he's gone. His warmth, the scent of his skin, his touch, none of it is left.

I roll onto my side, sore and tired and hurting.

What did you expect?

Honestly, I'm not sure.

He looks at me with love, touches me with fire, and speaks to me with hate. We fought, and we screwed and exploded with the raging inferno that had been burning between us.

Maybe that's all he needed. To fuck me out of his system. To eradicate me from his dreams, his fantasies.

I have no idea what time it is, and I'm not sure I care all that much. My day off was taken from me, and the band doesn't have anywhere they have to be until the show tonight. That should give me all day, if I take it, which I frequently don't.

I like spending time with Adalyn. I like being around the boys I grew up with. It makes me feel connected instead of suspended, alone in midair.

I have no idea what today will bring, but I'm not going to dwell on it.

I went in with my eyes open.

My mind replays our dirty night. Every touch. Every word. The images swirl, my cheeks blushing, and my overworked lips spreading into a smile of giddy delight. He cannot take away this feeling, and nothing else registers as I comb through detail after detail, my body reigniting into a heat only he's given me.

Except, I'm the nanny for his daughter. And his brother is my ex-boyfriend.

And he left me alone with no trace of him to be found.

And he can be such a mean bastard that it makes me question my basic sanity for loving a man like that.

You said you weren't going to let it get to you.

I did.

But insecurity is a nefarious bitch, pledging her devotion to the dark side of the force as she gleefully takes over your common sense and rationality. Because waking up alone after a night like that, sucks.

Any way you slice it or figure it.

I catch the faint sounds of Adalyn fussing, so I draw myself up and out of bed, pulling on the first outfit I come upon, which mercifully consists of yoga pants and a vintage Guns N' Roses tee. I pad barefoot, ignoring my screaming bladder, until I reach the back room. Opening the door, I find Adalyn tucked into Jasper, her small body naked except for a pull-up covering her adorable bum.

He's rubbing her back in gentle circles as his eyes meet mine. "She woke up early," he explains, like it's the reason I woke up alone.

"I didn't want to wake you. You looked so peaceful sleeping." *I hate that I love you so much.*

He's the definition of conflicted heartache.

I walk into the room, crawling onto the bed and running my hand through Adalyn's hair. "Thank you," I whisper, my stupid cheeks heating like I've never had sex with a boy I like before. Or a morning after with one. Maybe I haven't, not on this level at least, and that's the difference in my butterfly-filled gut. "How's she feeling?"

"Better, I think. I have the pull-ups going as a precaution, but so far, she's kept down some of that Pedialyte stuff you got her."

"That's great," I smile, leaning in to kiss the back of her head. "Morning, Miss Adalyn. Did you sleep well?" She doesn't answer this question. She never does when I ask it, but she does turn her head to peek over at me, and her green eyes are much clearer today. "Did you have good dreams?" She drops a kiss onto Jasper's shoulder, much the way I did on the back of her head.

"Good dreams," she parrots. "Silly daddy," she tells me softly, scrunching up her nose with a happy smile on her soft lips.

"Me?" he says with mock indignation, but the smile on his face isn't exactly selling it. "You're the one who's been giggling all morning." He tickles under her chin, and she shrieks shrilly, laughing and squirming around on his lap. I plug my ears, wincing at the sound. "I think you just woke up everyone within a ten-mile radius with that, bug."

I lie back on the bed, still so tired. "Speaking of, I wonder what time the boys got back last night?" I muse, and then freeze, peeking over at Jasper to catch his expression. He looks...guilty. And maybe a little sick. And slightly happy, but I'm thinking that's last, and the other two outweigh that happiness.

It's the same expression he had after our encounter in the bathroom.

Only this time, I'm done running and hiding.

"Are we going to talk about this?"

"I don't know what to say," he starts, his eyes bouncing between me and Adalyn, who he's still tickling and roughhousing with. Darkness creeps across his features, and I know this is going to hurt. "You're Adalyn's nanny, which means I'm technically your boss. But more than that, you're Gus's." I shake my head no, but he cuts me off with, "Yes. You are. It doesn't matter if you don't think of yourself that way. *He* thinks of you that way. He's my brother, and you're his ex. The woman he still admittedly loves. That's an automatic off-limits if ever there was one. He's loved you since we met you. So yeah, I don't know what to say."

My heart sinks. My lips tighten as disappointment, thick and heavy, coats my stomach, and I have to swallow to hold back my emotions. I want to ask if he regrets it, but I don't think I can handle his answer. Even if he says no, I know a part of him does, and anything else he tells me would be a lie. I'm certainly not about to say something stupid like, *it's okay,* or *we can just forget about it.* Because I can't just forget about it, and it's not okay to pretend like it didn't happen.

My pride won't allow me to be swept under the rug as a mistake. If that's what he wants to do, then he has to be the one to do it. To say it. I've put myself out there with him so many times only to be pushed back and brushed aside.

With jerky movements, I try to get up and off the bed.

I can't be near him right now.

He didn't just fuck my brains out. That was only the first course. That man dug inside me and greedily tore out every single resistant piece of me I had been clinging to. I'm open now. Exposed.

And I don't like it.

Especially when he says things like, I don't know what to say, and that's an automatic off-limits.

He reaches out before I can make my escape, grasping my hand and giving me a firm squeeze. "I'm not sorry for it, Viola." He waits me out until I'm able to meet his eyes, and then he smiles at me. A type of smile that warms my iced-over blood. A type of smile I'm not sure he's ever given me before. "I meant everything I said to you last night. All of it. Last night was..." His grin grows boyishly. Mischievously satisfied. Impish. Goddamn adorable. His thumb brushes over my knuckles, and I hate my reaction to him. "Christ, Vi. Last night with you was my dream come true. I just don't know where we go from here, and if I told you anything else, it would be a lie."

Damn him and his stupid honesty. I think I would have healed faster if he said he just got carried away and lost his mind, and oops, he screwed me three times like a man on a mission.

I'm not even making sense anymore.

"Me either," I admit. Because it appears Gus, his twin, his best friend, his bandmate, is always going to be the divide that keeps us apart. I suppose in some way, I understand it. I even respect it. It's like a guy code or something. But upped a level since it's his brother. A brother who sleeps around with groupies and girls from clubs. A brother who cheated on me before we broke up all those years ago.

Whatever. It just sucks. A lot.

I numbly shrug, because I offer no real answers.

"How about we start with coffee?" he asks gently, his tone laced with sweet hope. "Let's all go out for coffee. I haven't slept in a hundred years, and I could use some caffeine. Then, maybe later, Ady will take a nap with me. And maybe Marco will watch Ady tonight if she's better, and all of us will go out after the show. Together," he adds, like it's not a date or a one-on-one thing. Thanks, I get the message without the elaboration. "We leave for London tomorrow, and Europe is going to be insane with very few days off."

"Sure," I say, because I have no idea what else I'm supposed to say. "That all sounds great."

It doesn't.

Not even a little.

It sounds like a consolation prize. Like a brush-off and a blow-off and a will-never-happen.

Dragging myself up and off the bed, I locate an outfit for Ady that consists of a Minnie Mouse shirt, black leggings, and the sneakers she wears, because shoes are a battle with this one, and she'll only wear these shoes. Then I leave them to use the bathroom and pull myself together.

I just don't know where we go from here. Nowhere together, it seems. At least not as an *us*, that's for sure.

We do go out for coffee, and since it's early, there are no razzi to follow us. Ady can't eat much here because most everything has dairy and gluten, and she was already sick yesterday. Jasper asks the googly-eyed barista if she would mind toasting up a piece of gluten-free bread, and she readily agrees. But once we return from our breakfast, I tell Jasper I'm going to take a few hours for myself. He doesn't fight me. After all, I gave up my day off yesterday.

Honestly, I think he's relieved to have the space from me.

I end up taking an Uber into Georgetown and just walking the streets until my feet ache, and my head hurts, and it's getting late. I sit down in a restaurant, sipping a Diet Coke and staring down at my phone. I debate texting Jules but decide a phone call is better.

She picks up quickly, and it's a relief until I blurt out, "I slept with him."

"Who? Gus? The world already knows that."

I glance around, making sure I'm alone here. I wasn't followed, and truthfully, no one gives a shit about me without Adalyn or one of the boys with me, so I don't know why I'm bothering.

"No. The other one."

Jules sucks in a rush of air. "You're kidding me. When?"

"Last night." I slurp down more of my soda, feeling miserable again. It's been a day of emotional ups and downs, and I really wish I were stronger than I feel in this moment.

"Was he good? Oh my god, I bet he was amazing."

I smile softly around my straw. "Yep. Pretty damn amazing."

"Wow. I'm like...*wow*. Are we happy or sad, Miss Starr?"

"I honestly don't know."

She sighs deeply, her voice dropping two notches. "So, what happens now? Does Gus know? Is the band breaking up? What does that mean for your job with Adalyn? And where the hell are you now? Are they with you?"

"Slow down, Rita Skeeter. One question at a time."

"I wish you would stop calling me that. That chick was a psycho bitch in Harry Potter."

She has a point. "Fine, but stop with the barrage of questions. Gus does not know. At least not yet, and I have no idea what Jasper will tell him and what he won't. It was probably just one night anyway. That's what he implied this morning. I mean, we were fighting. Surprise, surprise, right? But things got a bit heated, and then they got extremely heated, and it just sort of happened. This morning he basically hit the retreat button. And no, the band isn't breaking up over me. That's ridiculous. I have no idea where the tabloids get this crap from, but it's all crap. Every bit of it."

She's silent for a beat, and I lean back in my seat, staring out the window at the street, watching people dressed for a warm spring day walking about. I realize I don't even know what day of the week it is. It's like I have no concept of reality anymore.

I'm a teacher without a job.

I'm a girl traveling the world without a home to return to.

My mother stole everything I had, and yeah, I'm earning good money with this job, but it won't last forever, and I really need to get myself together.

"If I had to guess, I'd say the band's PR people are where they're getting this from. I mean, think about what all this press is doing for their careers. It's driving their sales way up, no doubt. I bet you it's them. It's not like anyone is getting hurt with this so...," she trails off, and I immediately frown, thinking back to Atlanta.

"Except, Adalyn."

"She's three, Vi. She'll live. I doubt she even knows what's going on, and her rich daddy can make it all better for her. Don't stress out about that."

I scrunch my nose up at that. I hate the way she's speaking about them. That's not who Jasper is and certainly not what Adalyn's world is.

In any given situation, our perceptions are often wrong. Reality is typically so much uglier than we imagine. Perfections, the grass is always greener, are illusions we manufacture. Jasper's life and the way he leads it with Adalyn is certainly no exception to that.

"That's not how her world works. That's not how any of this works. Who cares what they do for a living or how much money they have? These are people's lives. A little girl's life."

She hums. "I know, and you're right. I'm sorry. I didn't really mean that. But this is what PR people do. Whatever you do, do not tell them you screwed their front man while the world thinks you're in love with the band's second."

"I suppose," I mumble, my body slinking down further into my seat.

She's probably right. I feel like someone has to be feeding the gossip mill to keep it churning like this, and there is no one else it could be other than those awful PR people I spoke to on the phone that first day on the plane.

"I'm gonna be honest with you, Vi. I sorta hate you," she snickers. "Hot rock stars throw themselves at you, and you're traveling the world, earning serious scratch for it. I'm insanely jealous. Any woman would be. So why the hell do you sound like Adalyn peed in your Cheerios? You should be so happy right now, babe."

"Because it's not the pretty package the illusion comes in," I retort defensively. "They're not rock stars to me. They're Gus and Jasper and Keith and Henry. This traveling stuff is miserable, uncomfortable, and exhausting. The press follow us all over the damn place now. I am playing with fire with Jasper, and I'm already feeling the burn." I sigh out, rubbing my hand across my weary forehead. Am I sweating or just losing the last of my coping strategies? "I'm a mess, Jules. All of this is getting to be too much. And I know I have no right to complain about any of this, right? Boo-freaking-hoo. But I have no idea how Gus will react to it. He's so hard to gauge with this stuff, and I don't want to cause a fight between Gus and Jasper."

"Oh, Vi. It's going to be okay. Really. You won't cause any issues between Gus and Jasper. You already said that Jasper hit the retreat button, so take a breath and relax. You did nothing wrong with Jasper."

"Then why does it suddenly feel like I did."

"Because you're you and he's him, and you're both a mess. Think of the bright side, if he tries to fire you, you can sue his ass for sexual harassment," she laughs loudly.

I roll my eyes at her mocking tone. "That's not what I meant. I'm not quitting, and Jasper is not firing me." *Yet.*

I hear her blow out a breath into the phone. "*I was kidding!* Yikes. You need to stop worrying so much. My advice is to go for it with Jasper. And Gus. Try with both of them. Have fun. Enjoy this unique situation for what it is. You really have nothing to lose at this point." *Except the job and the little girl and my lifelong best friends and their relationship with each other.* "Hang in there. It'll all work out! I gotta run, babe. Class is about to start, but text me when you get to London, so I know where you're staying and what you're up to there. Talk soon. Love you."

Then she hangs up.

But instead of feeling better the way Jules intended, I feel worse. Her words unsettle me in the worst of ways. Gus. Jasper. Adalyn.

There is no telling how any of this mess will turn out.

TWENTY-SEVEN

Viola

BY THE TIME I RETURN, the boys are getting ready for the show, and Marco is playing with Adalyn in the dressing room of the stadium. "Vi," she exclaims, her face lighting up. "Hi, Vi. Hi, Vi. Hi, Vi."

"Hi, sweet girl," I interrupt, picking her up and giving her a kiss. I feel terrible that I was gone so long. "How are you feeling? All better?"

She doesn't answer. Just squirms out of my arms and onto the floor.

"What's that noise?" I tilt my head and then glance over to Marco, who shrugs helplessly. "What's that noise? What's that noise?"

"You hear daddy playing?" I ask, but she just falls quiet, not responding.

"She's been doing that. Repeating words and actions a lot. Like, running and jumping from the coffee table to the couch, flipping over, and then doing it again and again. What's that called? She's counted to sixteen like a million times over. I can't stop her. She's like the Energizer Bunny."

"Perseveration. And you realize you just totally dated yourself there?"

"Perseveration," he repeats. "Right. That. And I'm not old, just gorgeously mature." I snicker. "Age aside, I'm not sure how to stop her, so I just try to shift her onto something else."

"That's perfect. I take it she's feeling better?"

"Yes. Jasper said she hasn't been sick once today."

"Awesome. And I'm sorry I'm so late."

Marco brushes me off. "You deserve the time off. Jasper, God of all things, has commanded that you go out with them tonight." He waves a hand up and down my body, scrunching his nose and shaking his head in dismay. "Get changed into something...else."

I glance down at my outfit and back up to him. "What's wrong with what I'm wearing?"

"Other than everything?" I cock an eyebrow before my gaze drops again, and I stare down at myself. He might actually have a point. "Just put on something hot, okay, because I'm playing babysitter tonight."

"I have nothing to wear," I admit, giving Ady a good squeeze and then setting her back down to play with the Shopkins set Gus got her. They're choking hazards if you ask me, but she loves them, and thus far, hasn't tried to put them in her mouth.

"Yes, you do," Marco says in an admonishing tone. "I've seen you in those leather pants of yours or that hot little flared skirt. Pair either with some sort of sexy top." He searches around the dressing room and then spots a rack off to the corner. Getting up off the couch, and going through the rack, he tosses me a short, black sequin tube top. I eye it like it's Satan, but he gives me a look that says, don't try him. "That will make your tits look fab. You have to wear it. It's not a choice. I don't suppose you have anything other than your beat-up old Chucks and those goth-girl Docs?"

"I have a pair of yellow ballet flats," I offer meekly.

"No." He covers his eyes, extending his other hand like he's warding me off. "I can't even hear that. My ears are burning at the idea of those. Go with the Docs. You'll rock the slutty bad girl emo-Barbie thing. Just straighten your hair and do up your eyes by making them smoky. Better yet," he smiles devilishly, his dark eyebrows bouncing up and down, "I'll do your hair and makeup."

"No," I shake my head.

"Yes," he nods emphatically. "Ady and I will play dress-up with you. We'll make you look hot, not skanky or cracked out. Promise. Now go. I need you back here in ten because I have to put my best little lady to bed soon."

"You're adorable when you're maternal."

"I know. I'm multitalented. I like it much more than being a bi–" he glances down at Ady, "booger," he corrects, "to venue owners. But you're wasting time." Marco points to the door. "Run and get those pants, Viola, and come back to us. We'll be waiting."

I roll my eyes, but I leave them to fetch my faux leather pants because I'm actually a bit giddy at the prospect of going out. I cannot remember the last time I had a night out. Back in Alabama, after a day of teaching kids, I would go to work at Spencer's bar for extra cash. Any free time I had, I spent sleeping or relaxing, and I wasn't exactly rolling in boyfriends or friends, so I stayed in most nights.

I show my fancy backstage VIP badge to a few of the security people, but the sound of the show, of the guys playing, draws me over to the stage instead of the exit. I stand in the shadows; security and roadies and even a few groupies line the area, but they don't pay me much attention.

Even if they did, I wouldn't notice because I can't peel my eyes from the stage.

From Jasper.

His black t-shirt is soaked in sweat, clinging enticingly to his chest and abs, giving every girl in here a peek at the perfection beneath. His reddish-brown hair is mussed, damp, wavy, and sexy as hell.

He's every woman's dream come to life.

Mine included.

Purple lights flash around the stage in time to the drumbeat. Jasper is in the center, near the edge, singing his heart out to a song I haven't heard before. I'm assuming it's from their new album, and before I realize what I'm doing, I'm rocking slowly along.

It's a ballad.

Deep and soulful. Heart-wrenchingly beautiful.

The other guys are in the background, giving Jasper the spotlight, and I listen, trying to take in the words as he sings them. It's about mistakes. How some mistakes are too big to come back from. That they're life-changing in the worst of ways.

Call it what you want.

No lessons learned after it falls apart.

It's the inescapable.

The rush of water. Prick of a needle.

And you die. You die. You die too.

Because what else can you do?

He blames himself for his mother's and Karina's deaths.

God, this man is all regret and guilt.

He's not even singing about me, but I know those two emotions rule everything about him. Make every decision for him.

And I know instinctively he won't allow me to become another mistake. Another regret. I'm the one he may want; I believe that, I see it, I felt it last night in his arms. But not enough.

He doesn't want me enough.

It's the needed slap to the face. The bitter sting of realization. The agony of losing something you never possessed.

I take a deep breath and wipe away my useless tears. I leave the stage and Jasper behind. Because what else can you do?

TWENTY-EIGHT

Jasper

I SPENT all day thinking about her. Not even about last night necessarily. Just her. The way she blew back into my life, painting color on my gray canvas. The way her smile lights up her face and makes those hazel eyes a shade lighter. The way Adalyn gravitated toward her from the first moment they met. The way I found everything I never realized I was missing when I was buried inside her. When I was kissing her sweet, soft lips.

She's my homecoming. My reckoning. My salvation.

And I love her.

There is no denying it.

I'm forever torn in two when it comes to this woman. I cannot keep her. I cannot let her go.

But I don't realize how well and truly screwed I am until I walk into the dressing room, Gus behind me, and stop short, forcing him to plow into my back. "What the fuck, dude?" But then he spots what I can't look away from, and all his ire slips into awed appreciation. "Christ, she's a goddess," he whispers, and I can't help but agree with his sentiment and despise him for it at the same time.

Because Viola is a goddess. A sexy siren who calls to me, hardening my cock and making all that brilliant resistance I built up today evaporate.

She's wearing a tiny black, sequin top that shows off the smooth, toned expanse of her lower abdomen while hugging her perfect full tits, revealing a crest of cleavage above. Her pants are skin-tight, black leather, and her long, normally wild waves are pin-straight and so glossy, they reflect the overhead lights. Her eyes are lined in black liner with smoky deep purple shadow on her upper lid, and her lips are their natural deep rose, but shiny.

She's facing the mirror, staring at herself as if she's unsure if she likes what she sees, but when she catches the four men dumbly standing frozen in the doorway, she smiles, and my chest clenches.

"Too much?" she asks, peeking down at her outfit and then turning around to face us.

"No," Henry replies quickly, walking past Gus and me, who still haven't learned how to walk again. "You look beautiful, Vi. I hardly recognized you."

"Gee, thanks," she laughs, and Henry's head drops back as he lets out a self-deprecating groan.

"That's not what I meant. You're always beautiful, I just meant–"

"I know what you meant," she interrupts, cupping his jaw. "I'm just messing with you."

"Thank God. I was terrified you'd smack me."

She laughs, leaning up to kiss his cheek, wiping away the smear of gloss after.

Her eyes meet mine, and I can see all her pain and reluctance in them. All her restraint and uncertainty. I can't claim her as mine, and that's killing me in ways I will never rebuild from.

"Marco is on the bus with Adalyn, and I was told to wait here for you boys. But...," she wrinkles her nose, turning back to Henry and away from me as if I no longer exist. "You're going to shower before we go out, right?"

Everyone laughs.

Everyone except me.

She meets my gaze once more and smiles. I smile in return, giving her everything, so she knows. The effort behind it somehow unknotting my limbs as Gus and I finally manage to drag ourselves into the room.

Pushing past me, he saunters over, throwing his arms around her. Pressing himself as close as he can get. "You saying I smell, babe?"

"Ah!" she cries, shoving him away and laughing as he attempts to drag her back in. "You're sweaty. Gross." He tugs her against his chest. "Gus, you're going to ruin my pretty. Marco will cut off your balls if you muss me up."

"It's impossible to ruin your pretty, darlin'. You're a work of art." His eyes rove over her slowly, making a fucking show out of it, and my jaw tics. "You wanna go dancing with me? Make out like teenagers on the dance floor the way we used to?"

Viola smacks his chest, prying herself free of his clutches. My chest is so tight. My stomach in a million knots. Fuck all to sin...this *hurts*.

Her eyes meet mine, a visible question in them that I cannot answer. She stares me down, and I still can't come up with anything. My lips tighten, and my body tenses.

Her expression calcifies over, and I can't stand it. Can't stand the casual indifference.

Both from her and from myself.

You did this. It's your fault. I know, but that doesn't make it any easier to handle.

"What time is our flight to London tomorrow?" Keith asks, grabbing his requisite bottle of Jack and opening it up.

Everyone is totally oblivious. I can't go out with them tonight. I can't watch her with Gus. Christ, if he kisses her in front of me, I'll lose my mind. I'm liable to kill him with my bare hands.

That's how strong this jealousy is. It's eating me alive. This was my idea, my plan, and it's completely backfired on me.

"Eight tomorrow evening," I tell him, my voice smooth and even despite the war raging within me.

Walking over to the bar, I grab the first bottle I see. Viola's eye catches mine again, and this time I'm rewarded with a small, polite smile, but that's it.

That's it?

She's goddamn beaming at my brother.

I can't do this. I thought I could, I thought I could push it all down and act like nothing has changed, but everything has changed.

Or maybe that's just me.

Last night obviously didn't mean a tenth to her what it means to me. She was gone all day. Didn't even try to find me before I went on stage. No calls or texts either.

I told her I didn't regret it. That I meant everything I said to her last night, and she hasn't said one thing in return that indicates she's there with me. Apparently, I was just a way of firing off our excessive heat and energy.

Goddammit!

I take a swig, swallowing down vodka. I don't even like vodka, and everyone here knows it. Why did I think all of us going out tonight would be a good idea?

You know why.

Yes. Because I'm a masochist. Because I was hoping that if I saw Viola and Gus out like that, it would serve as the reminder I need.

"I think I'm gonna bail on tonight," I grit out, setting down the bottle and trying to find something else. I snatch the Jack from Keith and take a hearty swig.

"Whoa, brother. What's gotten into you?" That's Keith, and I wish he would shut up.

"You're coming," Gus demands, marching over and standing directly in front of me, his gray eyes all over my face, trying to read everything I don't want him to see. "It's our last night in the States for like two months. And you haven't come out once. I want to go out with my band, my brother, and my girl."

His girl. I am the ultimate traitor. I didn't think I could hate myself more than I already do, but evidently, I was wrong.

"I want to celebrate, because this tour deserves a little celebration. But most importantly, I want you to start living a little again."

It's funny–or tragically ironic–last night, I felt like I had.

The eyes of everyone in the room are on me, but I don't look away from my brother. How hurt would he be if he knew the truth? Could he ever forgive me? Would we ever recover?

"Okay. I'm in."

I take another swig of the Jack because, at this point, I might as well go down with the ship.

I plow past him, heading for the showers located in the locker rooms since this is where the Redskins play. I need to be alone, and there just aren't enough showers on the tour buses. By the time I'm dressed and ready, I'm feeling more in control. And by the time we reach the club Henry has chosen for tonight, I'm impervious.

We're led through a back entrance, to an elevator that shoots us up to the third floor, and directly into a private, roped-off area. Marsellus is with us, and he leans into me, asking if I want the usual number of girls to be allowed in or more since I'm here.

I tell him whatever.

I could give a fuck about other girls tonight.

Marching over to the bar, I order myself a double whiskey neat. There are already three bottles of whatever bullshit Keith and Henry ordered on the table, but I want to have a drink without curious eyes watching me have it.

Without noticeably staring at the woman who is now dancing with my brother.

His arms are wrapped around her body, holding her close as he stares adoringly into her eyes. I can't see her face, but his is enough to get where this night is headed for them.

Just. Fucking. Perfect.

"I need another," I tell the bartender before the last drop is even across my lips. She's young. Pretty. Has a nice set of perky tits, and my brother isn't in love with her.

But I don't see her. Not even when she smiles seductively. Not even when she tells me that whatever I need tonight, she can give me.

I doubt that, I want to say.

There is only one person who can give me what I need, and it's not her.

TWENTY-NINE

Jasper

I TAKE my newly refilled glass and find my way over to join the other guys at the table. But now there's a group of scantily dressed women all over them. The music in here is loud and heavy, the beat matching the pulse pumping through my ears.

I sit down dejectedly onto the unforgiving bench seat, and instantly, there is a brunette beside me, so damn close all I can smell is her aggressive floral perfume.

"Hey," she yells over the music, leaning into me further and pressing her large fake breasts up against my arm. It does absolutely nothing for me, and I happen to be a guy who typically doesn't mind fake breasts. "You're Jasper Diamond."

"You're kidding me," I come back with. "And all this time, I was hoping I was Gus."

She laughs. I don't.

"I really love your music. I'm a huge fan. Do you want to dance?"

I stare into my drink. She hasn't even offered me her name. What does that tell me about what she's after? How much she cares about anything other than my wallet and my profession.

"How many musicians have you fucked?" I ask, still staring down into the amber liquid swirling around my glass.

To her credit, she doesn't even seem affronted. "None," she admits, and everything about her is wrong.

Her voice is too high, too sharp. Her fragrance is too floral, too strong. Her hair is brown, not blonde. I can't even speak to the rest of her because I haven't cared enough to look.

"But, I'm hoping to change that with you," she presses when I don't even acknowledge her words or presence.

At least she's honest. She's honest, and I'm...drunk?

"No, thanks."

"For real?" She's incredulous, which probably means she's beautiful, and men never turn her down.

"You're not her."

"Who? Your nanny?" I finally manage to glance up, if only to glare. She is pretty. But nothing all that special. "What? I saw you watching your brother with her before. She's his girlfriend, right? I read all about them in *E-Buzz* Magazine. Word has it that you guys are splitting up because you hate her, and he loves her. Or are you referring to the mother of your daughter? Do you still love her?"

The fuck?

"Have a good night." She's a reporter or way too into her tabloids and is hoping to be on the cover of one.

I stand up and catch Marsellus's eye. I point to the brunette, who is still sitting down, and shake my head no.

She needs to leave now. We've had enough problems with our lives being splashed across magazines. We don't need any more. Marsellus nods, and I amble back over to the bar.

Anything to get away from this bullshit.

Scrubbing my hand down my face, I blink, my eyes having difficulty adjusting between the blinding multicolored lights and the

LOVE TO HATE HER   295

darkness of the room. I order myself an ice water this time, taking a slow sip as I lean back against the bar, desperate to clear my head.

My resistance slips, teasing and taunting me.

I refuse to look, and yet, my mind can't focus on anything other than the dance floor not even ten feet from me. I take another sip, and with my next breath, I pathetically falter, excuses for my weakness shooting through my head, hitting their target one after the other.

Restlessly, I scan the crowd of gyrating bodies, searching for her.

I don't see Viola, but I do spot Gus. It takes me a minute to realize it's him, because instead of Viola, there are two random women wrapped around him, one kissing his neck, the other rubbing his dick over his jeans. I continue to stare at him, mystified.

He's utterly blissed-out, and all I can think is how stupid my brother is.

Has Viola seen this? Did it hurt her, and she ran off?

Christ, I want to kill him.

My mouth flattens as my fists and jaw clench. How could he do that to her? *His* girl, he called her. Motherfucker. That bastard does not deserve her.

I push off the bar, ready to march over there and finally kick his ass, but then I catch sight of Viola's smile and freeze. She's dancing with Keith. His hands on her lower back, hers up in the air as she swivels her hips back and forth to the beat.

As Gus and his women get it on not even five feet away.

What the hell?

If he actually loved her, cared about her the way he claims to, he wouldn't be doing that with those girls while she is right here.

And if she loved him back, she'd care that he is.

What the hell have I been doing?

Moping like a petulant little boy who lost his prized possession? Only, I didn't lose her. I've been pushing her away, believing she belonged to Gus. That he was trying to win her back.

That he was the better man.

For the first time in I don't know how long, I feel deserving.

I deserve Viola Starr. Because if she were mine, I would never cast her aside the way Gus has, time and time again. I would never cheat on her. I'd kill myself just to make her happy. To make her smile. To light up every star in her sky.

I'd treat her like the fucking queen she is.

I march across the dance floor, halting my steps once I'm directly beside her and Keith. "Sup, brother?" He grins at me, his eyes glittering with amusement. "You finally deciding to have a little fun?"

"Something like that," I reply, staring at Viola, who's smiling. It's one of her full smiles. One of her uninhibited ones.

It's her happy smile, and it's aimed at me.

"Dance with us," she offers, and I step in, yanking her into my arms. Some of her smile slips, and she stumbles a step. Keith's hand is thankfully still on her back, and he rights her, pulling her back up.

"Hey now," Keith says. "I've got you." I can feel his eyes on me, but I don't care enough to acknowledge him or his questions.

"I've got her now," I tell him, staring deeply into her eyes.

I hear Keith whistle between his teeth, but he doesn't say anything else. I don't even know if he's still there, or if he's gone off in search of another woman to grind against.

And I don't care.

Viola snakes her arms around my neck, and mine encircle her waist, gliding along the exposed skin of her back. I pull her into me, and the knot inside my chest begins to unfurl. Her body against mine is what home feels like.

"You okay?" she asks when I don't speak.

"No. I'm not."

Her fingers twirl up the ends of my hair above my neck as a soft frown gently touches her lips. Her hazel eyes slay through mine as she says, "I don't want to be a problem for you. And I can't have you be one for me."

"What does that even mean?"

"It means I can't keep playing this game with you. The hot and cold. The fuck me and hate me." *The fuck me and break me.* "There's too much at stake for me."

"Are you walking away from me?"

Her teeth bite into her lip, and she stares out into the crowd. I squeeze her tight, holding her closer against me, terrified that she'll slip away any second. My palms rest fully on her back, partially beneath her shirt.

I can't lose her. Last night...

"I can't let you go." Her eyes flash back to mine, a tense silence building between us as more of my control slips. "Did you hear me?"

Her mouth tightens, but her eyes show so much vulnerability it knocks the breath from my lungs. I don't know how I'm still on my feet.

"I won't be used, Jasper. I won't be the one you fuck because I'm here until someone else comes along."

Stepping in, I press our bodies together until we're flush, my forehead all but touching hers. Our eyes lock and I let go. I hold nothing of myself back. It's all hers anyway, she might as well know it once and for all.

"Viola Starr, there is no one else. There has never been anyone else. There has only ever been you. There will always only be you. *Always.*"

Her breath hitches, her eyes bouncing back and forth between mine as if she's trying to determine if I mean it or not. I do, and the moment she realizes that, she swallows hard, something resembling hope sparkling in her hazel depths.

I don't want to be here in this club dancing to this music. I want to be somewhere alone with her. Somewhere I can touch her and talk to her.

"Come with me," I demand, but she hesitates. Her eyes cast about the room, and if she's looking for Gus, I swear I'm going to lose it. She quickly finds me again, her expression guarded, nervous. "Please. I want you and no one else."

I don't give her the chance to second-guess. Reaching out for her hand, she takes mine. And this time, she doesn't let go.

I drag her away, out of the VIP area of the club, toward a back stairwell.

We burst through the door, still holding hands as we fly down the heavy cement steps that thunder beneath our feet.

"What are we doing?" she shrieks, her voice slightly alarmed as I make for the door that will lead us outside. "Jasper?" I still don't answer. "Are you drunk? Where are you taking me?"

I am drunk. On my need for her. I'm high. On the knowledge that she wants me and not him. I'm utterly intoxicated on this feeling. On the sweet, criminal bliss that courses through my veins.

The stale warm air of the back alley hits us as the heavy metal door slams shut behind us. It's quiet back here as the crowds and the long line to enter the club are all the way in the front.

"Come here." Snaking my arm around her waist, I lift her off her feet.

She yelps in surprise, and I inhale the sound, my lips crashing into hers. Walking us further into the darkness of the alley, I press her into the bricks and lose my mind.

Her mouth opens for me on a moan, her fingers raking through my hair, yanking hard on the strands. That's right, Viola. Give me all your anger. Give me all that stubborn fucking pride I love so much. I want it all. Everything. I want this kiss, this passionate fight between our tongues and lips, this vicious spell she's put me under, to be my death. To be the last thing I ever feel.

Because now I know.

I fucking *know* it will never be this good with anyone else. She's it.

And I refuse to waste another second without her.

I wrench down her top, exposing her tits to the air. A startled cry explodes from her as my mouth covers one of her pink peaked buds.

"Jas," she groans, pushing my face further into the soft swell. She rocks into me, begging, searching, a pleading whimper escapes the back of her throat. "More. I need so much more."

God...this girl. This insanely sexy girl.

"I'm keeping you, Viola," I breathe against her, biting her nipple before I pull back to meet her eyes. She opens hers cautiously, her chin dropping to meet my steady gaze. "Tell me I can keep you."

Her hand cups my jaw, and I lean into her touch.

"Now that I finally have you, I can't give you back. I can't let you go. You're everything to me, and I need to keep you."

Her face brightens with a smile as we stare into each other. I just opened my heart to this woman, and though I'm terrified this will all fall apart on us, I meant what I said. She's my world, and I can't let her go. My hand slides into the front of her leather pants and panties, my fingers finding her slick clit.

She lets out a breathy gasp as I glide up and down, my eyes never leaving hers. "You're so wet for me."

"Only for you."

A feral growl climbs up the back of my throat. Setting her on her feet, I tug down her pants enough to give me access before I undo mine, freeing my cock, jerking it slowly.

"This is not the best place for this, but I can't wait. Is this alright?"

"Yes," she whimpers, her movements growing more frantic as I continue to rub her clit before pushing two fingers into her. Damn, she's soaked. "Fuck me," she begs, and I just about lose it.

I pull out my fingers, slipping them into my mouth so I can taste her, and then I spin her around to face the wall. I want to look into her eyes as I slide inside of her. As I make her come. The way I did last night with her. But this really isn't the situation for that, so it will have to wait until later.

Her hands brace against the rough bricks, small pants breaking through the night air as I run my cock up and down in her slickness, pressing the head into her clit and then back down to her opening.

She hums, bowing her head, sinking into the sensation of what I'm doing to her.

I slide into her, slowly, savoring every inch as she expands to my size, squeezing my cock with her tight heat. I can't get enough of her moans, of the sounds she makes, as she comes undone around me.

I pump into her, continuing my languid pace. I want this to last forever, but the risk of us getting caught out here is real, so I drive into her deeper, thrusting my hips harder.

"Yes," she groans. "Like that. Please. Harder."

God yes.

One hand on her hip, the other on her breast, pinching and rolling her nipple as I piston my hips in and out at a punishing rhythm. The sounds of sex echoing off the hard surfaces we're surrounded by only spur me on to take her harder. Deeper.

"I'm close... God, Jasper, I'm so close."

I growl, bending her forward further and sliding in even deeper, all the way to the hilt.

Her moans turn into cries, her body beginning to shudder.

My fingers slide down, rubbing her clit, and she erupts around me, milking my cock and pushing me over the edge with her. Stars explode behind my eyes, my forehead falling to her back as I continue to fuck her through both our orgasms.

I slide out of her slowly, loving how my cum leaks down her leg like a brand. *Mine. Only mine.*

Kissing her spine, I flip her around to face me. I'm breathing hard and covered with sweat, but I don't think I've ever felt this light before.

I capture her mouth in a fevered kiss, pressing her body against mine.

"Let's get you dressed and get out of here," I murmur against her. "I want to do that again at least a few more times before dawn."

THIRTY

Viola

"I DON'T THINK that's a good idea," I say, staring into Marco's dark eyes.

"Honey, it's not like she'll know if you're not here. You'll go down after she's asleep, and I'll hang out here with my boyfriend, Netflix. You'll actually be doing me a favor. I'm behind on my binge-watching."

It's tempting. So very tempting.

I haven't seen the guys play, not a full live show anyway, in forever.

We've been in the United Kingdom and Ireland now for a little more than a week, traveling our way around. First, London for three nights. Then, Manchester for two. Up through Scotland, and now we're in Dublin, Ireland.

It's been a whirlwind.

A treasure trove of once-in-a-lifetime experiences and sites I'll cherish forever.

But the greatest part so far...Jasper Diamond.

I feel like that's sort of the wrong way to be doing this, but it's true.

That man. I swear, I could live in this suspended reality with him forever and never grow tired of it.

By day, I'm the nanny. The one making sure Adalyn is learning and growing and kicking ass all around. By night, I'm in his bed. Always his bed as he shares a suite with Ady, and then I do the walk of shame in the wee hours, so she doesn't see me in her daddy's bed when she wakes up.

I should care about that. But I don't.

It's too new. Too beautiful to disrupt by allowing external forces to have a say.

Like Gus.

Jasper has yet to tell his brother, and it eats at him. I see it on his face every time he's with him. He can hardly look him in the eye, and I know I should feel bad about that. I know I could be the catalyst of dividing these twins, these best friends, and their band.

But I just don't see it coming to that. I can't even pinpoint why exactly, but I feel like Gus will understand.

That man is a walking, talking erection for other women.

Yes, he's touchy-feely. He's flirty. He's occasionally downright adoring.

But it has a different texture to it than when we were together.

His words echo a knee-jerk reaction. I am Viola, and he is Gus, and once upon a time in the land of mismatched fairytales, I was his Viola, and he was my Gus. We just weren't meant to have a happily ever after together. But I know it eats at Jasper all the same, and I wonder if that's been the guiding force behind him holding our secret tight.

"You realize if you do this, you could be missing out on hot Irishmen with sexy brogues backstage?"

"I've considered that," Marco concedes, flopping down on the couch in Jasper's suite. His arms spread across the top of the cushions, his head dropping back as he stares up at the ceiling. "Did you know that HIV is on the rise again?" I choke on the water I was just taking a sip of, coughing and sputtering, wiping the spittle from my chin with the back of my hand. "It's true," he continues, ignoring my near-death experience. "It's like now that you just have to take a pill a day people don't see it as a problem and think they can fuck like rabbits without a condom."

I glance over toward Ady, but she's deep into her signing videos, singing and signing along. Damn, I love that girl. She's so freaking smart it takes my breath away.

"I remember when HIV turned into AIDS, which turned into death. It still does, people just gloss over those facts with their own crap notions that sexually transmitted diseases are no big deal. 'Chronic disease not fatal.'" He puts air quotes around the words. "Total bullshit."

"Okay," I draw out the word, because I'm seriously at a loss.

"Maybe I should have been a public health nurse instead of a manager. Those bitches are rad."

"I have no words for you, Marco Morales. Like none. What the hell are we talking about here?"

His chin drops, and he meets my eyes. "I know," he says, and I can't even play dumb on this one and ask, you know what? He knows. It's that simple. "I saw him steal a kiss when he thought no one was watching. I've seen him stare at you like the lost puppy who's found his way home again. He's also been...nicer. Less Jasper." I can't help but grin at that one. It's true. "So while part of me wants to tell you that you're playing with a bunch of live grenades or a fire launcher or whatever the right metaphor is for fucking the brother of your ex, I can't tell you to stop. So instead, I'm telling you to go to the show tonight and watch your boyfriend and your ex-boyfriend play."

"God," I whisper, shaking my head. "You totally suck. You know that?"

He pats the space next to him on the couch, and I run over, crawling in beside him.

"Yes. But I'm not the one playing Russian roulette with the hottest twins in the world."

"I think I'm done with your deadly metaphors."

"I hope you know what you're doing because we have a little more than three months left on this gig, and Gus may act all lack-adaisical and shit, but I think he might still love you too. Even if his dick suggests otherwise."

"Is this your way of saying I'm going to get HIV?"

He laughs, kissing the top of my head. "That was my way of saying, don't be reckless with people's emotions because things appear different than they once were."

"Do you honestly believe Gus still has feelings? I mean, some days I do, but most I really don't. And I've told him that we're just friends. Nothing more, so it's not like he doesn't know that."

"I think he considers letting you go the mistake of his life. He's said so a time or two."

Christ, that hurts. What the hell do I do now?

I love Gus, and I'd rather die than hurt him. I know Jasper feels the same way, but I think I'd also rather die than give Jasper up. It's a pickle wrapped in a hard spot wrapped in a conundrum.

"I don't know how to stop. I'm totally crazy about him."

"I know." He blows out a heavy breath. "And he's even crazier for you. So go to the show. Take the night off and watch your rock gods do their thing."

"Okay. But only because you compared my screwed-up love life to getting HIV and playing with deadly weapons."

He laughs, kissing the side of my face. "Is he good? I mean, he looks like he'd be good."

"Incredible."

Marco sighs. "Damn. This is going to end so badly, Yoko."

"Hey," I smack his chest. "I am not Yoko."

I'm not. I won't be.

If it's a choice between his brother and his band or me, he'll choose them. I know he will. They're his life, and I'm the girl he's always wanted. The one he's scratching the itch with. The one he enjoys in his bed at night only to push away in the light of day.

The one he doesn't love enough.

Because if he did, he'd have told Gus by now. And I wouldn't have to sneak out and hide.

But like I told Marco, I don't know how to stop.

Even with that lovely piece of knowledge added to my pie. And even when I know that pie is going to dry out and crumble since we're all about the metaphors tonight.

"You're right. You're way prettier than Yoko. Now go and get changed into something not so boyishly depressing. You've got a concert to attend."

TWO HOURS LATER, I'm on the side of the stage, watching the opening act finish up. There are like a zillion people here tonight. Backstage as well. I clearly don't know enough to understand if this is standard practice, but I swear, I've never seen so many beautiful girls in one small space in my life.

Ten minutes later, just when I'm starting to grow antsy and impatient, the building goes completely dark, and the crowd screams in delight. I can't help but mirror their enthusiasm, a joyful smile spreading across my face.

Keith drags past me, walking into the blinding darkness, his body climbing onto his stool, behind his drums.

And then I hear it.

That *bump. Bump. Bump.*

It beats like a heart, something that causes your blood to rush with gusto through your veins. That beat continues, and the crowd somehow manages to boost their screaming to an entirely new decibel.

I turn around, desperate to watch the rest of the guys walking onto the stage, just as Henry passes me. "Hey," he says, catching sight of me at the last second and smiling like

I've just made his night. "Our girl. Now we're going to rock this shit."

"Play me something special," I tease, and he leans in to kiss my cheek.

"For you? Absolutely."

His eyes gleam in the darkness, and then he's gone, on stage. Swinging his bass over his shoulder, he strums a few chords as he and Keith synchronize.

And I feel it.

That magical thing that only music can give you. Only live music at that. It's a flutter. A palpitation. A tingly jolt across the skin.

Gus comes next, Jasper right on his heels, just as a hand snags around my wrist. "Hell yeah," Gus booms, tugging me into his large warm body, enfolding me in his embrace. "I'm so happy you're here," he whispers into me, and I hurt. I'm an awful, ugly person. "You'll watch all night?"

"Yes," I promise, pulling back and cupping his handsome face. A face I still love, albeit differently. Marco's words echo in my head. *I think he considers letting you go the mistake of his life.*

Emotion clogs my throat. I never imagined it possible to feel so much hurt for one person and so much happiness with another.

"Perfect." Gus pecks my lips, and then he's gone, onto the stage, leaving me in the crowded, women-filled space with Jasper. And these women? They're exceedingly interested and not to be ignored, though he's doing a pretty damn good job.

Wow. Just the sight of this man makes my stomach flutter with dopey restless butterflies.

"Why are you here?" Jasper asks, the crowd in the stands growing more impatient, more demanding.

"Nice to see you too." I do everything in my power to hold back my disappointed frown.

He stares into me, and even in the blackness, covered in shadows, I feel his eyes on mine. He steps closer, his hand reaching out, intertwining our pinkies.

"I didn't mean it like that, baby. I just didn't expect to see you, and it worried me. Ady's okay?"

"Ady's great. Fast asleep. Marco is with her. I wanted to watch you play a show."

He glances to his right, toward the stage, and then back to me.

"I have to get out there." I nod, and he shifts into me, his other hand grazing my lower back, pressing me against him. He leans into my neck, whispering into the shell of my ear, his hot breath against my skin, "I love that you're here. My girl. My muse."

He drops a small kiss below my ear, and then he's gone, running out onto the stage as the crowd explodes just for him. My heart along with them.

THIRTY-ONE

Viola

DEEP BLUE LIGHTS fly across the stage in strategically prepared patterns. Jasper glances surreptitiously at me, throwing me a wink before he returns to his fans, and the band launches into a song. The girls surrounding me scream, matching the decibel the fans in the seats are giving off, and I can't help but join them. I can't help but join them as the guys hypnotize us all.

Their sound is infectious.

They play through three songs straight, and since I still haven't listened to their newer albums, I'm not familiar with them the way everyone else is. After the third song ends, Jasper approaches the front of the stage, sweat dripping down his temple.

"Hey," he says, and the crowd goes absolutely batshit crazy. "How are you doing, Dublin?" Deafening screams fill the air, thousands of flickering flashes of light pop off, one after the other, like lightning bugs in the summer sky. "I asked, how the fuck are you, Dublin?!" He cups his hand to his ear, like he's straining to hear them as they go nuts before him. "Alright!" He grins widely. "Let's get this going. This song is called Wildfire, and it's my brother Gus's favorite."

He throws Gus a wink, and then it's like the night really begins.

They rock this place; not a single person is sitting in their seat. I take a video of Jules's favorite song and text it to her.

I can't stop dancing, even as I listen to the girls around me, placing bets on who's going to sleep with Jasper Diamond first. I can't help the swell of jealousy I feel, even when I know nothing will come of their posturing.

It's a difficult pill to swallow, knowing so many beautiful women want the man you've given your heart to. Especially after you've already experienced the same situation once before. And were cheated on.

But they don't know him.

They don't know the quiet behind the headlines. The calm after the show. The reticent, lonely heart of the man who does little more than write, play music, and love his daughter.

What would I give to fill that heart? To complete it? What would that feel like?

To be a family with him and Adalyn. A real family.

Toward the end of the night, Jasper rips his soaking wet shirt over his head, and the women in the crowd scream ballistically. I do too; his muscular chest and cut abs all the way down to his glorious V are dripping wet and shiny and sexier than anything I've ever seen before. His tattoos on full display.

Bad boy rock god.

My sexy god.

That's what he is, and I'm all over it.

He laughs, running his hand back through his wet hair, brushing the long reddish-brown strands from his face.

"Don't get too excited," he teases. "I'm going to grab another shirt." The women boo in protest, and he laughs even harder. "I bet if you cheer loud enough, the rest of these guys will go shirtless for you."

He runs in my direction, while the crowd demands their favorite men strip down. "Oh my God," one girl near me screeches, practically vibrating in her heels. "He's coming this way."

Jasper snatches the towel handed to him by one of the stage crew, whipping down his body and tossing a clean, dry, black tee over his head. But then his eyes lock with mine, and he smiles so brightly my insides quake. He jogs over with purpose, his arms capturing me, melding his body into mine. The scent of his musky body wash, sweat, and infectious wonder, bleed into my every pore.

Jasper shifts as if he's going to whisper in my ear when his lips catch the corner of mine, sneaking a small kiss. I feel his smile glide along my cheek as he whispers seductively, "Pay attention, dream girl. This next song is all about you."

And then he's gone.

Leaving me bereft and turned on and freaking blissed-out. His eyes meet mine briefly from the stage before he launches into a song from their first album, and my heart soars.

He wrote this for me.

And he's singing it to me in front of everyone.

Thousands of people.

I had no idea I could feel like this. That love was capable of these heights.

I'm home. With this man, I'm home. My heart has a place. My soul, a partner. My body, a warmth unlike any other.

I sing along, jumping about and rocking my hips and bopping my head. I can't stop moving. Can't stop singing.

It's all about wanting the girl of your dreams. That's what I was to him. What I still am.

"Oh my God," a girl next to me squeals, springing up and down, clutching onto my arm and shaking it so hard I'm surprised she doesn't dislocate it from my shoulder. "What did he say to you?" She pivots to me, and a flash of recognition lights up her face. "Wait. You're Viola Starr. The nanny, right? Gus's girlfriend?"

"Right," I half-whisper, my throat suddenly thick. "The nanny." *But not Gus's girlfriend.*

She doesn't say anything else to me, but I catch her returning to her friends and talking to them. The number of new eyes I feel boring into the back of my neck is aggravating, but I push it away. Who cares what those girls think? They know nothing of the truth.

No one does.

The show finishes up with a stellar encore, the guys playing their hearts out.

A swell of pride rushes through me. They've done it. I mean, I knew they were big. We wouldn't be here if they weren't. I've seen the girls rush the bus. I've seen our faces all over tabloids.

But I hadn't witnessed it in terms of their music, not like this anyway, and it's so beautifully overwhelming, I'm choked up over it.

After the last chord is played and the last note sung, they run off stage, and before I can congratulate them or tell them how amazing they were, Keith lifts me up and tosses me over his large shoulder.

I yelp, bouncing up and down against his unforgiving body as he jogs me backstage while laughing his sweaty ass off. I'm launched onto the couch with a startled giggle, and after a round of traditional 'shots'–they're basically several bottles of alcohol passed around–I find myself naked in Jasper's bed. It's close to one in the morning, and sleep has continued to elude us as endless nights have turned into more than a week.

I don't care, and I don't think he does either. Most days, we can sleep in a little.

Most days.

"Are you going to tell me what you thought of the show?" he asks, resting on his side, his face tilted toward mine in the darkness.

"It was okay, I guess." Throwing in a shrug of the shoulder for good measure.

"Okay?" he barks incredulously. "*Okay?*" This time with more emphasis. "Are you kidding me? I sang my heart out to you."

I try to hide my smile. I know he did. And it makes me love him so much I can hardly see past my love-tinted glasses.

"I don't know what to tell you, Jas. It was just okay."

He rolls until he's on top of me, his hands pressed into the mattress, his head bowed, inches above mine as he holds his weight off me and stares deeply into my eyes. A soft smile spreads across his face. "You're so pretty."

"And you're too pretty." His nose pinches up at that. "Handsome? Gorgeous? God-like?"

"Now you're getting it." He bends his elbows like he's doing a pushup and kisses my lips.

"There was a line of girls backstage, taking bets on who would get to spend the night with you. It was like you were that five hundred million dollar winning lottery ticket, and they were about to fight to the death to win you."

He chuckles, but I don't. It's impossible not to be jealous of that. Not to be bitten with the bug of insecurity. Especially when you've been cheated on before by a man who you never thought would betray you.

I look away, but he adjusts himself, cupping my jaw and forcing me back to him. His eyes gaze down at me.

"Viola, baby," he grins. I kinda want to smack it off his face, but he's so sexy when he grins, it's impossible. "There are always girls who hang out backstage. There are always girls who offer me their bodies for the night. Karina was the same way. But that's all it is, their body. It's not their heart. It's not their soul. They don't care about me beyond my name and that I'm the lead singer of Wild Minds." I stare up into him, hating my vulnerability as my teeth gnaw at my bottom lip. "Do *you* care about any of that?"

I shake my head no, because his job might be one of my least favorite things about him—at least the fame behind it.

"Thought so. Can you guess how into the meaningless women and sex I am? Into people who know nothing of the real me?"

"Very?"

He laughs, dipping down again to kiss me. "Do you love my daughter?"

"With all my heart," I reply automatically, and he kisses me again for that.

"Other than tonight, have you listened to our last three albums?"

"No. It hurt too much."

Another kiss. This one followed up with his nose gently brushing against mine.

"Have you been posting selfies of us on Instagram, boasting about what we do in this bed?"

I scrunch my nose. "I don't even have Instagram."

"What's my favorite ice cream?"

"Chocolate chip on a sugar cone with chocolate sprinkles," I laugh, smiling so goddamn big. "Like a little kid."

"Yours is mint cookie in a cup with hot fudge. What's my favorite color?"

"It was always red. And I liked to pretend that came from the red dress I wore to our freshman formal."

"It is, and it was. Yours are black and purple. Deep purple, like eggplant. Favorite book?"

"Harry Potter. I might like that best about you. Because you actually read, Jasper Diamond. But if we're talking little kid books, you love Elephant and Piggie because they're Adalyn's favorites, and they always make her giggle."

"We won't even get into your favorite books." He rolls his eyes dramatically, and I nip his jaw. "I can't stand the classics."

"That's because you have no idea what's good." He pinches my nipple, and I yelp, smacking his hand away. "Bastard." He laughs, ghosting his lips over mine. Once. Twice. And then again, before his smile slips, and he turns oh-so-serious once more.

"What did I call my truck in high school?"

"Deathtrap," I smirk. "Oh no wait, that's what everyone else called it." He drops his weight fully onto me, and I laugh out, trying to push him off as he smothers me. "You called it Big Red because you liked the gum, and the stupid truck was red. Not all that creative if you ask me."

"I didn't, but thank you for proving my point."

I reach up to cup his cheek, gliding my fingers through his rough stubble, his light eyes glittering down at me. He props himself up so he can see me better.

"I could keep throwing out question after question, and you'd be able to answer them all about me, and I'd be able to answer them all about you. Because you know me, Vi. And I know you." His nose meets mine on the word you. "Very few people in my life actually know me. Truly understand me. I know you feel the same way. That no one really gets you. Sees you for who you actually are. The world views us as they want to. But that's not how it is with us. We get each other. We *see* each other. And that's how it's supposed to be. So I don't care how many of those girls line up. They're just girls. But they're not *my* girl."

His body drops down onto mine again, his hard cock slipping into me on my next breath.

My legs wrap around his waist, and I take him in deeper. There is no deep enough with this man. Our eyes hold each other steady as he pumps in and out of me. Our noses touch, sliding back and forth with each push and pull.

"My girl," he pants against my lips.

"Yours," I breathe against his.

There is no end to this. No limit.

Like I said before, I could live in this suspended reality.

Who needs gravity when they have Jasper Diamond? If I had a choice, I'd never touch earth again. Unfortunately, life doesn't always grant us our wishes.

THIRTY-TWO

Jasper

TECHNICALLY, this is our second world tour. We toured the United States after our first album—we were an opening act for Cyber's Law, a huge British indie rock band. After our second album, we did our first world tour as a headlining act.

That was four years ago.

Our third album released when Adalyn was six months old. Two weeks later, her mother was out of the picture, and shortly after that, she overdosed and died.

Our last album released about a year ago, and it's our biggest success to date.

I knew going into this how important this tour would be for our band.

What I didn't expect was that I would get to see the world with Viola. That I could *show* her the world.

We spent a week touring through the United Kingdom and Ireland, and now we're in Paris. The city of love.

And loving Viola is all that occupies my thoughts.

That and Adalyn.

And fucking Gus, because I still haven't manned up and told him.

The only excuse I can come up with is, even though I know I love Viola, I don't know if she feels the same. I should be jumping into this with both feet, but I can't seem to make myself launch. I'm terrified of wading in too deep again. Of drowning. Terrified that I'm going to make the wrong decision and then she'll leave me. Leave Adalyn.

So I don't tell her the words that burn my lips every time she enters the room. I keep it all locked away, restricting myself to loving her at night when we're the only ones awake or around.

But hell, it feels so wrong on so many levels that I'm succumbing to a different form of guilt. And what happens if Gus can't accept it? Or forgive me?

Add to that, the foreign press.

They might actually be worse than the American press. I thought that once we hit European soil, everything would fade into background noise, but they're everywhere. Most keep their distance because somehow my PR people managed something, but they're still there. They just photograph us with a better lens.

Viola, being the stubborn, tenacious woman that she is, insists on taking Adalyn out. She refuses to restrict her life because people are 'crazy over nothing' to use her words.

And part of me, begrudgingly, agrees with that.

So today, we're walking along the various bridges, or ponts as they're called. Adalyn is on my shoulders since she won't go in a stroller, and Gus is jabbering away while he steals licks from Viola's ice cream cone. It's driving me insane, and I can't say anything to him about it. She pushes him off and smacks at him when he tries to reach for it, but he doesn't stop. He even lands kisses on her cheeks and lips, earning himself more smacks and a kick or two.

I spent every day for four years being jealous of my brother and his relationship with this woman, and now I'm with this woman, and I'm still jealous.

I know Viola senses this because she keeps throwing me furtive glances, offering me weak smiles that are meant to be reassuring. They're not.

"Who's up for something other than ice cream?" Gus asks as we approach a café with outdoor seating overlooking the Seine. "Ady, baby doll, you want some french fries?"

"French fries," she repeats gleefully, and he reaches up for her, taking her off my shoulders and holding her against his chest. She gives his cheek a kiss, and he returns one on hers.

"Then let's get my best girl some fries. I'd love a glass of wine and some french fries."

Gus carries Ady toward the café, and before I can follow, Viola grabs my hand, forcing me to turn and look back at her. I release her hand instantly as I can see people with cameras across the pont.

She frowns. "You're quiet," she comments. "You haven't said three words all afternoon."

"I'm fine."

"You're not. Talk to me. Tell me what you're thinking."

I bluster out a sigh, sneaking a peek over at the stupid fucking cameras again and then back to her. Fuck it.

"I wanted to take you around Paris. Just you, me, and Ady. I wanted to kiss you on the observation deck of the Eiffel Tower with all of Paris spread out before us. Meander our way through the Musée d'Orsay so you can see the art and I can watch your face while you take it in. Sit on the Île de la Cité overlooking Notre-Dame and the river and have a picnic while Ady runs around in the grass. I wanted to hold your fucking hand as we goddamn strolled." A soft smile pulls up the corner of her lips. "What? Why are you looking at me like that?"

"You're romantic."

"Don't look so shocked."

She shrugs. "I am a bit. I mean, I know you write poetry, and still waters run deep and all that, but you're also a surly bastard."

"Thanks," I mutter dryly, feeling just a bit more miserable. She giggles. The woman is laughing at me. Fantastic.

"*My* surly bastard. I would love to do all that with you," she says warmly, that smile still on her lips. "It sounds incredible. And romantic. Like something out of a fairytale." She glances over toward the restaurant Gus and Ady went into. "We could have done all those things, Jasper. You mentioned going out in front of Gus. What did you think would happen?"

I blow out a breath, staring down at the bateaux mouches as they glide along the dark waters of the river. "I don't want to share you."

She takes a small, careful step, narrowing the large gap between us. To anyone watching—and they are watching—it appears like we're just having a regular conversation. It's killing me that I can't take her hand. That I can't press my lips to hers in the middle of the street. That I can't walk this city with my arms wrapped around her. We're in Paris together, and I wanted this day to be so different.

"You don't share me, Jasper. I'm yours. But it's not so simple in the light of day." She gestures across the bridge where people are literally leaning against the opposite wall, clicking pictures of us. I sigh, so desperate to flip them off. Fucking intrusive assholes.

"I want to tell him."

"Then tell him."

"It's not so simple, and you know that."

"And it might not be as bad as you imagine." *Or maybe it will be worse.* "I know you're stressed with everything, but it's just a few more months, and then this madness will be over."

My eyes narrow. "What does that mean? Over?" I snap.

"Christ, Jas, that's not how I meant it." She groans out in frustration, shifting her weight and twirling the end of her thin tee between her fingers. "I can't have this conversation with you now while Ady and Gus are being seated twenty feet from us, and the whole of Paris media are snapping our picture."

She's right. I know she's right. I'm being pushy and petulant and going a million miles faster than I should.

But I don't know how to slow down with her.

It's like any second something will come out of nowhere, something unforeseen will take her from me, and she'll be gone. I've wanted her since I was a goddamn child, and now I have her. But I also don't. This feels fleeting, and it twists my stomach up in knots.

"You're right. Let's go join them."

I wave for her to walk ahead of me. Why can't I be more like Gus sometimes? Go with the flow and not take the hard stuff so hard?

We reach the table, and Gus is throwing me a funny look. A look I know I should answer, but I don't. It's not the time or place for that, and all of this might be moot. Ady is sitting on the small round stool-like chair made out of black and white wicker, her eyes on everything and everyone, with a furrow to her brow.

"She doesn't like this. I think there are too many people. Maybe this was a mistake. She's not talking or looking at me when I say her name. She won't let me hold her either."

Was that the funny look Gus was throwing me? Shit. I really need to get control of myself.

"Ady," I start, crouching down, so I'm practically in her face. "Do you want to go back to the hotel?"

She doesn't answer, she just blinks, looking at me but also not.

Some days, I fully accept that I can't have a conversation with my daughter. That when I ask her what would be construed as a simple, easy question, she can't answer. Some days, I understand that the world can be too much for her to handle. That the people in it overwhelm her. That she doesn't know how to process them, and this will often lead to her acting out or going inside her head and closing off completely.

But sometimes, it breaks me into a thousand jagged pieces, cutting up my insides until I'm bleeding out. I don't want her to be scared or overwhelmed. I just want her happy and carefree.

"Are you hungry, bug? Do you still want french fries?"

"French fries," she repeats again, her voice distant.

"Okay," I cup her small cherubic cheek in my large hand and kiss her nose. "We'll get you french fries." They're probably the only thing that is gluten and dairy-free on the menu. And if you try to explain that's what you need, they look at you like you have two heads. This diet is a tricky business overseas. Especially here in France. Everything is bread, cheese, and butter.

We order beaucoup de pomme frites and a bottle of vin, and Ady ends up crawling herself into Viola's lap, snuggling into her. She hardly moves. Her eyes staring out at nothing, and what would I give to know, to understand, what goes through her mind.

"Are we going to discuss this?" Gus asks after the wine has been poured, and the french fries are in front of us. He sets his phone down on the small round table, and both Viola and I lean in to see it while Ady absently chews on a fry she doesn't seem all that interested in.

"What is that?" I ask, my eyes darting from the phone up to Gus's.

"I thought you knew about this?" I shake my head no. "Well, poop on a stick." He winks at Ady. "Someone is aiming for us, brother. Someone is playing games." The headline is in French, but it says something along the lines of, Wild Minds tour too much for Autistic child? It's a question and not a statement, at least. In truth, we've been getting some bad press about that. About Viola. But considering none of them have spoken with me directly or seen Ady other than in random photographs or on that fucking video, they have no idea how well she's doing.

And she is doing well.

Viola's face has gone completely ashen; all the blood drained from it. "That picture is from my phone," she whispers, horrified.

"What?" Gus and I question in unison.

"I took that picture of Ady when we were in Atlanta at the aquarium. Or at least one very similar."

She slides her phone out of her back pocket, unlocks it, and frantically scrolls through it until she locates what she's searching for. Then she sets it down next to Gus's phone. Gus and I study the pictures side by side, and shit, they're so similar. Nearly identical.

"How?" she asks, staring down at my daughter in her arms. Her eyes are welling up, and I don't know what to do. "Could someone have hacked my phone?"

I reach out and take her hand before I can stop myself, giving it a firm squeeze. "That was the day that guy from Intertainment came after you, right?" She nods. Swallows hard. "He was likely next to you while you took it and captured the same image. You probably didn't even realize he was there."

Gus rocks back in his seat, throwing his arm around Viola, tugging her body close. He's comforting her, and I can't. I release her hand, and that's just another thing to make this moment so much better.

"Jas, maybe we should think about taking Adalyn home." That's Gus, and his concern has me leaning back in my seat, scrubbing my hands up and down my face.

I've thought of that.

I've thought of all the angles. But at the end of the day, she's my daughter. My priority. I love my music, and I love my band, but not as much as I love her.

"If she goes, I go with her. I can't spend the next few months away from her, Gus. It's not even possible. I have no idea what will happen in the future with the band. With touring. When she's older, maybe touring won't be such a big deal. But she's young, and I can't leave her."

Gus nods, taking a long pull of his wine. "I know. I'm not even really asking that. I just don't get the hard-on over this BS with her. She's been doing so well overall. And now that they've moved past us breaking up as a band and Viola driving a wedge between us, her well-being is the tabloids' new obsession. That and when Viola and I are going to announce our engagement."

Gus rolls his eyes, trying for levity in a moment that's weighing all of us down.

The picture on Gus's phone is from the cover of a French tabloid. Viola looks sick as she holds onto Ady like she's afraid to let her go. I glance back and forth between the three of them.

"Let them take pictures. Her face is already out there. Her diagnosis too. Eventually, this has to die down." *Right?* I think, but don't ask.

"So you're not...," Viola trails off. "Regretting this? You're okay with me not sequestering us to a hotel?"

I stare at Ady in her lap. Truth is, I'm not good with that. What do you do when your daughter's face is spanning the globe, and you're powerless to stop it?

"If you can handle it, I can."

It's all I've got.

Because I know Viola loves Adalyn with a protective fierceness. Ady's mother never even cared a tenth of the way Viola does. Karina left her when she was a baby. She was more interested in money and partying and drugs than Adalyn. But Viola's heart is pure light. So goddamn beautiful. She loves Adalyn like she's her own.

And I know she'd do anything to keep my daughter safe.

She's the perfect mother for my special daughter, and I don't even know if I can keep her.

We finish at the restaurant, and by that point, Ady has had it. She's fried and overwrought and needs a rest. The hotel we're staying at is along the Champs-Élyseés, which is typically a busy place to be. But as I carry her into the hotel, I feel like we're finally alone for the first time all day.

No one dares follow us in. Our security detail is positioned outside the front doors as well as inside the lobby, and I'm starting to rethink what I said to Viola in the restaurant.

"I need a nap," Gus moans through a yawn, rubbing his eyes. "I think I'm getting too old for the late-night partying."

Viola laughs, leaning against his arm before righting herself just as quickly. "Or maybe you just need to sleep in past seven. There really is no need to knock on my door that early."

I pivot to face them, because this is news to me. Gus went to her room early this morning? Why?

"I had to if I wanted to have breakfast alone with you," he replies, yawning again. "Ady gets up at like seven-thirty. It was my only chance for time with you."

Ugly, green jealousy claws at my skin. I can't take this anymore. I need to talk to Viola and find out where we stand, and then I need to speak to my brother.

Consequences be damned.

We step off the elevator onto our floor, and Gus immediately turns to me and says, "I'll catch you at sound check." And then he walks off, half-asleep already. He doesn't even spare Viola a backward glance, and before she can disappear into her room, I tug her into mine and Adalyn's.

My room is gold. Everything in it from the draperies to the carpet and furnishings to the bed frame. It's like Louis XIV and Versailles threw up in here. I think if we ever do this again, I'm going to make all the hotel reservations instead of letting Sophia and her team do it.

I set Ady down, and she scampers off for her bedroom.

"Good night," she says, and I chuckle, following after her because this is one of her favorite games. But Adalyn, for once, is serious. She climbs into her bed, tucks herself under the covers, and within minutes, she falls asleep.

"Wow," Viola muses. "That has to be some kind of record. All that Parisian air."

"Come with me," I growl softly, intertwining our fingers and leading her across the suite down to my room. I shut the door behind us, and by the time I turn around to Viola, she's at the balcony, staring out at the Arc de Triomphe through the closed French doors.

"It's so beautiful here, Jas. Like a dream."

"I'll bring you back someday. Just us."

"I'd like that."

I can hear the smile in her voice, and it spurs me forward.

My arms snake around her waist from behind, my face drops down into the crook of her neck. "Why did my brother come to your room early this morning?"

She blows out a silent breath, but I feel it all the same. "Because he wanted to have breakfast with me."

"In your room? Alone?"

"Yes. Alone. The room part was just how it was." She twists in my arms to face me. "Nothing happened, Jasper. He showed up with croissants and coffee, and we sat at the small dining table in my room and talked while we ate. That was it."

"If that was it, then why didn't you tell me?"

Her fingers brush my chin, gliding up along my cheek, past my eyes up to my forehead, where she flattens out my pinched brow.

"Because I honestly didn't think much about it after he left, and Adalyn woke up."

"Did he try to kiss you?"

"No. He didn't. We talked. We caught up. Filled each other in on the last seven years. Laughed at stupid stuff."

"You mean the last seven years apart." She puffs out an exasperated breath, rolling her eyes at me. "Don't roll your eyes at me, Viola. I'm fucking serious."

"I can see that. And I'm sorry I didn't mention it. He's my friend, Jas. And yes, he was my boyfriend when we were teenagers. And yes, I still care about him. A lot. But not in that way. Not anymore. I swear, it was nothing. Really."

"It's not nothing. I can't take this anymore. You're mine, but you're not. And now my brother is coming to your room early in the morning, waking you up, seeing you in that ridiculously sexy outfit you call pajamas. It's not nothing, and it's driving me insane."

"I was wearing a robe."

"That's not much better." Cupping her face in my hands, I search her eyes, unable to contain the storm raging within me. "I love you, Viola. I'm in love with you, and I don't want to lose you. Not to Gus.

Not to some job somewhere else in the country. Not to anything. I love you, and I cannot stand the sick fear of losing you anymore. It's everywhere. It's constant." My hands press harder into her face, her eyes wide, lips parted. And silent.

She's silent as she stares at me.

Shit. Maybe I did this too soon.

"You love me?" she finally asks, her voice catching on the last word.

I want to laugh at that. How could she not have known?

"Viola Starr, I've loved you since we were eight, and I first laid eyes on you. I loved you as I kissed you that day under the tree, and I've never stopped loving you all the years in between. There is no way to stop it, no way to hold it at bay." I stare into her beautiful hazel eyes. "You're the other half of my whole. I love you, and I need you."

"You have me. I am no one else's. I swear it to you." She reaches up on her toes and presses her lips to mine. "I love you," she whispers against me. "Asshole and all."

"Say it again."

She smiles into me. "Asshole?" I smack her ass, and she laughs. "I love you. I love you. I love you. Is that enough?"

"For now," I chuckle, picking her up off her feet, holding her closer against me, our hearts pounding against each other as one beat. I kiss her eyes, her nose, her cheeks, her lips. "I love you. My muse. My heart. My soul."

"And I love you. Forever."

Dear God, please let that be true.

Now I just have to tell Gus.

THIRTY-THREE

Jasper

KNOCK, knock, knock. My knuckles rap against the door to Gus's room before I remember he's napping. Crap. Waking up Gus to tell him that I'm in love with Viola might not be the wisest choice.

I was riding the high of my conversation with her all the way down here without thinking this through. Maybe I should wait until later. Or until after the show.

Except, then the door opens, and my brother is standing there with his sandy hair a mess and his gray eyes the color of sleep-induced slate. He doesn't say a word. Not, this better be good, or did I sleep through sound check?

Nothing.

He just steps back and waves me into his room.

"Have a seat." I do, and the second my ass hits the edge of his bed, he says, "I was wondering if this was going to happen today. What with my being all over her during our walk and then dropping the bait of breakfast this morning."

I glance up at him, staring into his dark eyes and clenched jaw. He knew. Goddammit, he knew.

Thunder rumbles through my chest, as waves of nausea cripple my gut, sending a sheen of sweat to my forehead. I hate myself. It's not the first time. Not by a long shot. It's a sensation I'm all too familiar with, actually.

Doesn't make it any easier to take.

I continue to stare at my brother, wanting to offer a hundred explanations.

Things like I'm sorry. Things like I fucked up–I don't believe that. Things like it was a mistake–that's a bold-faced lie. Things like I tried to stay away, and I'm sorry because I never wanted to hurt you, but I know now it's too late–those are the truths I suddenly can't utter.

Instead, I stay silent, allowing the self-loathing to consume me.

I've earned it.

Gus takes his sweet time moseying across the room to me, sitting beside me, and tossing his large arm over my shoulder. A swoosh of air collapses my lungs. He shakes me back and forth the way he did when we were kids, and I smile miserably before I can stop it, the pain in my chest multiplying.

He's known all this time, and I'm the bastard who tried to hide it from him.

"How long have you known?"

He's silent for so long. Minutes ticking by that I don't have the courage to fill. I wait him out. I owe him at least that.

Finally, "That you love her, or that you're fucking her?"

Christ. My eyes plummet to the floor. "Both, I guess."

Gus lets out a loud heavy sigh. The kind that tells me that he really is tired and that this tour and the late nights and the lying prick of a brother are getting to him. He releases me, his elbows dropping to his parted thighs as he stares off, seemingly at nothing.

"Since it began."

I nod. I figured that. Gus is smart, and I'm so very stupid.

More silence as the tension between us builds. I don't know how to fix this. I almost wish he'd just kick my ass and get it over with. That sort of pain would be a relief.

"I don't like that you tried to hide it from me for so long." I open my mouth to say...something, when he follows that up with, "But I'd be lying if I said I didn't deserve that and worse."

I draw back, my eyebrows bunched, though he can't see my expression.

"I knew you kissed Viola when we were kids, even though you never told me." He falls quiet again, letting his words marinate in my beleaguered mind, and I'm not sure how much more of this I can take. "I saw you do it. I was coming over to see her and caught it from across the field." He chuckles mirthlessly, scrubbing a hand over his face. "It made me nuts. Like actually drove me insane with jealousy. In my mind, in my heart, Viola had always been mine. It was like a slap to the face, and I was so goddamn angry with you for stealing her first kiss from me."

And if I didn't think I could feel worse than I did a few moments ago, I was wrong.

I blow out a silent breath through my nose, squeezing the back of my neck.

Gus and I are twins, but something inside of me has felt protective—the way a big brother is protective. Maybe it's because I've always been the serious one while he's always been the jokester. Maybe it was the way we lost our mother, I don't know, but I never wanted Gus to feel any pain. I relentlessly tried to shelter him from that.

So to hear that he witnessed my not-so-secret kiss and that it hurt him...

"When you didn't mention anything about it or tell me that you two were together, I confessed to you how much I liked her. Day after day, I preached it to you like a sermon that she was the girl for me. And because you're you, you stepped back and watched as I made my move."

His chin drops to his chest, his back rising and falling with his steady breaths, and I'm too stunned to do much of anything other than listen.

"I knew you were crazy about her, too. I knew all those songs you wrote, all that poetry, was about her. Our entire first album." He does that twisted chuckle thing again, and my stomach lurches. "All through high school, I knew how you felt." He angles over his shoulder to find me, our eyes locking. "I didn't care, Jas. I was beyond selfish, and I didn't care. I told myself that if you loved her as much as I did, you'd fight me for her. That I was the guy she deserved, because you were too serious, and she was too quirky, and you'd never work the way she and I did. I figured you could never make her smile, and her smiles are the best thing in the world. I believed only I could make her happy. That was my mantra. For four years. I made her happy, and you couldn't. Except, I didn't do that. Not in the end anyway. Not when it really mattered. Our band hit it big quick, and with that came the willing girls, and Vi was thousands of miles away, and I got swept up."

Gus sits up straight, pivoting his body fully to face mine, his expression crumpling with a pain I've only seen on him once.

"I regret it. All of it. I regret the way I took her from you when I knew how you felt. I regret not talking it out with you the way I should have. I regret cheating on her because all those girls had no face, and hers was the only one I saw when I closed my eyes. That's why she's here," he says, his steely gaze spearing me through the heart. "I mean, she's perfect for the job, right? That's just a craziness that worked in my favor. But I had always planned on fixing my mistakes. Being with her again."

His admission—even though I pretty much knew that's what he was doing with her—steals the breath from my lungs and replaces it with acid. Something corrosive. It's eating me alive from the inside out.

"Except, this time, I stole her from you and not the other way around. And I didn't talk to you about it beforehand. I know how you feel about her. How you've always felt. You told me so the day she arrived in California. I did that to you this time. *Fuck.*"

My face drops into my hands.

I knew he was trying to win her back. From the first moment her name was mentioned, I knew that's why he put her up for the job. I know he considers her the love of his life. Everyone knows because he's not shy about telling us.

And look at what I did.

Gus may have been selfish in the past, but he was also a teenager. I'm a grown man. A father. I should know better.

I did know better.

So, where does this go from here? There is no joining of two opposing forces.

"You were screwing all those other women, Gus. In front of Viola. I just–"

"Like I said," he murmurs, interrupting me. "I'm a selfish fool. But it's something I'm working on. And Viola is still the only girl I see when I close my eyes."

I shoot off the bed, marching over to the window and staring out at Paris. My hands drop to my hips as the sun shines down on me, but I feel no warmth from it.

I should have talked to Gus before I went anywhere near Viola. I should have told him about my feelings from the start. Should have demanded someone else to watch Adalyn from the get-go.

But then you wouldn't have had this time with Viola.

I sigh. Everything inside of me hurts.

"I tried to stay away from her," I breathe out. "I honestly did. I tried hating her. Ignoring her. Being fucking mean as hell. Everything I could think of, but she was there. Back under my skin before I could find a way to stop it. You're my brother and my best friend, and there is no limit to my love for you or the lengths I would go to for you." I pause, turning back around and meeting his eyes head-on. "But I love her, man. I fucking love that woman so goddamn much, and I can't choose. I seriously have no clue what to do."

Gus stares me down, the smallest of perceptible smirks tugging up the corner of his mouth. He shakes his head and then chuckles like I'm the biggest of idiots on the planet.

"You totally misunderstood me, dude." He laughs harder at my baffled expression. "I didn't bring Viola along on this tour for *me*. I brought her here for *you*." He points at me, punctuating his words, and I don't think I've ever been this confused in my life.

"Huh?"

He chuckles some more, smiling like the goofy, crafty bastard I love.

"Well, that's sort of a lie. I brought Viola here for me initially. I figured if she was at all receptive to getting back together, I would move heaven and hell to make it happen. But when I saw you with her that first day, it crossed my mind that you might still have feelings locked away in that bag of ice you call a heart." I scowl, and he grins cheekily at me. "After that, it was a matter of watching Vi to see where her heart was in all of this, and it was pretty obvious from the start, it wasn't with me."

"But...," I trail off, thinking this through and rejoining him on the edge of the bed. "You called her your girl. Your future wife. You've been all over her all the time. Which now that I think about it makes me feel a zillion times worse for going behind your back with her."

"Yeah. That was kinda dick of you." I let out a slew of curses that make Gus laugh. "I was hopeful I could fix things with Vi. But then, once I saw the two of you together, I knew I wasn't the guy for her, and you were." He smirks. "And no, I didn't tell you, because there is no telling you something like that. You loved her and hated yourself for it, so I couldn't tell you to go for it when I still loved her. If that makes any sense at all."

I punch his shoulder. Not hard. But enough. "You were fucking every girl that came along. Every one that looked in your direction." I narrow my eyes. "You don't deserve her."

He throws his hands up, still laughing at me. I must look like I'm ready to kill him, which I kind of am, I guess.

"And you do. I know. Why do you think I was doing all that in front of both of you once I figured all this out?"

I still don't understand. It's like I'm staring at all the clues, and the answer to solving the case is right in front of me, but it's completely eluding me.

"Were you serious about all that stuff you said about her? About her face being the only one you see when you close your eyes? About still loving her?"

He shrugs a shoulder, staring up at the ceiling. "Yes. She'll always be the one I let get away. The one I regret letting get away. I don't know. I did a million things wrong by that girl, and I hate myself for each and every one of them. I think part of what I feel for her is wrapped up in that. I don't know anymore."

"Why the fuck then?"

"I told you before; I'm working on being less selfish. And...," he trails off, blowing out a breath, "I don't deserve her, like you said. I'd like to think that maybe I do, but I don't. I screw around, and I drink a lot, and I wouldn't make her happy. In fact, I think I'd make her miserable, and she'd grow to hate me." He chuckles again, rubbing his hand over the top of his head. "Bottom line, she doesn't want me. I blew my shot with her years ago. So I said things to her. Touched her in ways I knew would drive you up the wall. Push you just a little harder. And when you saw me screw around with a bunch of girls under her nose, you'd finally come to your senses and go after her. She lights you up, and I wanted you to come back to life."

"This again." I roll my eyes, and I feel like Viola when I do it.

"I love Viola, Jas. I always will. But it's not the way you love her. I see that. I know it in my gut. If I did, I would never have looked twice at another woman. You love her the way she should be loved. I tried, but I never quite got there. I was with her for four years, and she was my world. But then I found that I enjoyed my freedom too, and that hasn't changed. I can't give Viola what she needs. You can. It's really that simple. I want you to be happy. I want her to be happy. And you seem to be very happy together."

"Gus...," I trail off, at a complete loss for words.

"It's cool, man." He smacks my back hard. "I'm fine with it. Promise. We're good. Same as we've always been. This was my plan, which makes me the motherfucking brilliant Wizard of Oz that it all worked so well." He winks at me, still with that cocky grin on his face. "And those things I said about her, well, old habits die hard and shit like that. I'll try to stop. She's yours. Not mine."

It feels like that acid-coated weight I've been carrying around in my gut for the last twelve years–hell, longer than that–is finally gone. I don't know how to describe the sensation, but taking a deep breath just became a whole lot easier.

Viola is mine.

Not Gus's.

Hell yeah! "I feel like I should say thank you."

"Don't. I didn't do this for that. I did this to make it right. And now it is."

"No more secrets."

"No more secrets. Incidentally, the other guys already know about you two. So does Marco."

"I knew about Marco. Vi told me. I wasn't sure about the others."

"We like you better this way. You're more diamond and less coal now."

I snort out a laugh. "Fuck, that was terrible."

He laughs, rocking into me and throwing his arm back around my shoulder. "I know. But it made you laugh, and this was starting to get too intense, considering I'm only on about three hours of sleep."

"You've got five more hours before the show."

He shakes his head. "We've got sound check soon."

"Skip it. We'll handle it."

"I would argue, but I just gave you Viola without breaking your nose, so I'll take you up on that offer." I laugh, leaning back into him. "How many more months of this?"

"Three."

"Right. Piece of cake," he deadpans. "Take Vi out tonight. After the show, take her somewhere. Just the two of you. I'll crash with Ady. Lord knows I could use a break from the action. My liver and even my cock might thank me for it."

"Christ," I stand up, rubbing a hand across my jaw. "I really hope you're using condoms. I'm too young to be an uncle."

He pushes me away, forcing me to take a step back toward the door. "Fucker."

"Sleep tight, princess. And I think I will take you up on your offer of a night out with Viola." I bounce my eyebrows up at him, and he flips me off. "Love you, brother."

"Awesome. Now get lost. I'm done bonding."

The door shuts behind me, and I can't help my incredulous headshake.

The bastard knew.

Not only that, he planned the whole goddamn thing.

Couldn't he have just told me that? How long have I spent pushing off and fighting with Viola? Hard to be pissed, though. About anything.

The door to the suite shuts with a quiet click, and I pause, listening for my two girls who make me feel at home, even here in this hotel.

Silence.

I slip off my shoes and pad down the hall toward Ady's room. She's in the center of the bed, tucked under the blankets, one arm above her head, the other clutching a stuffed Mickey Mouse to her chest. Her eyes flutter like she's deep in a dream.

I'd give anything to know what she's dreaming about. And that familiar, joyful ache hits me square in the chest. I'm a lucky bastard. I want a dozen more, just like her. She's my perfect girl, and I wouldn't trade her or change her for anything.

"I love you, bug."

She doesn't even stir at the sound of my voice, and I turn around in search of my other girl. I ran out on Viola, practically sprinting down the hall to talk to Gus. I wonder if saying I love you and then leaving is considered worse than fucking and leaving right after.

I did both with Viola.

She woke up alone after our first night together.

Having her was all that mattered to me that night.

Being with her is every dream I've ever had come true.

I've been alone for so long. Never truly felt what it meant to be connected, intimate, with another person in that way.

That dream come true quickly morphed into hope of more. The next morning, when I opened my eyes, and her small, sexy, naked body was snuggled firmly in my arms, that hope began dripping panic into my blood like an IV.

My desire for her set fire to every inch of my skin, and all I could think about was how badly I was going to get burned. How badly I could burn her. I needed to think, to figure things out, and lucky for me, Adalyn was making noises in the back room.

But now, everything is different.

Viola is supine on the bed, her forearm over her eyes like she needs to be shielded from the mid-afternoon sun. She's above the blankets, her blonde hair fanning out across the white of the pillows. Her black skirt hoisted so high I catch the hint of her pink panties. Pink panties I want in my pocket when I play my show tonight, the taste of her sweet pussy on my lips as I sing the songs I wrote for her all those years ago.

Climbing on the bed, I crawl on all fours toward her.

The arm covering her eyes slips across her face, resting beside her as the bed shifts with my weight.

Her eyes lock on mine as a slow, easy smile slides effortlessly up her beautiful face. "Good talk?"

"Great talk. I'll tell you all about it after I eat your pussy."

Her cheeks warm at my words, her lips parting on a breathy gasp as my fingertips reach her calves, sliding tantalizingly slowly upward. Her focus shifts between my eyes and my fingers like she can't tell where she wants to look more. Those pretty, bright eyes of hers smolder, heat caressing every inch of her skin.

I skate up the inside of her thighs, goosebumps rising in the wake of my hands until I slide up the fabric of her skirt, revealing those pink panties I was admiring only seconds ago.

"Do you like these?" I ask, floating the tip of my finger along her slit over the satiny fabric.

"Yes, actually," she laughs, the sound half-hearted as a small whimper follows it.

"I'll buy you new ones." She opens her mouth to protest, but in the next second, I loop my fingers through the thin strings on the sides and rip. The fabric shreds apart, and my face drops, my upper lip on her clit, my tongue teasing her opening.

The sexiest sound I've ever heard in my life crawls its way out of the back of her throat, her hands diving into my hair, her legs wrapping themselves around my shoulders.

Her pussy rocks against my face, chasing her pleasure on my tongue.

I lick her, sucking on her clit as I slide two fingers inside her, angling them so I find that sweet spot that always makes her hips buck harder. I pump in and out, alternating between flicking and sucking on her slick clit.

I could do this forever.

There is nothing better than being buried in this woman.

"That's right, baby," I hum against her, making her back arch off the bed. "Fuck my face. Show me what you want. My dirty little dream girl."

"Yes," she gasps, grinding harder. "Like that, Jas. Just. Like. That." She groans and then, "Oh!" She explodes, shattering against my mouth as I continue to lick her, loving the hell out of how lost she gets in this. In us.

Viola does not half-ass anything. When she commits, she commits. With her heart. Her soul. Her mind. Even her body. Not one inch of her is spared, and it makes me even crazier for her.

I give her pussy one last kiss before I climb up her body, hovering over her slacken form. She's so goddamn pretty. "Hi."

"Hi."

"You are, you know." Her eyebrows pinch together, and I smile at her. I still can't believe she's mine. "Pretty. Beautiful. Stunning. Whatever adjective you like. They all fit you. You take my breath away, baby. Drop me to my knees. And I don't just mean with your looks."

Her eyes sparkle as she shines up at me. "You certainly do have a way with the words, Mister Diamond."

"Good thing. It's how I make my living."

She laughs, shaking her head back and forth against the pillow. "I want you inside of me."

"There is no sweeter place in the world."

Jumping up to stand on the bed, my feet straddling her legs, I tug off my shirt, tossing it to the floor. Viola scoots back, sitting up and going for the button on my jeans, but quickly decides she doesn't like the angle and climbs up onto her knees. She slides the denim down my thighs, my boxer briefs with them, and then she takes my dick into her eager mouth as far as she can. She gags, her throat rolling as she swallows, and holy shit that's so good.

I groan, my head dropping back, my eyes closing, because there is no way I can keep them open.

My fingers dive into her hair, gripping her by the roots, but not clutching hard. I want to shove my cock further down her throat, and it takes every ounce of restraint to stop myself.

But then she does the wildest thing.

She reaches behind her, squeezing the hand I have in her hair and pushing in, letting me know I don't have to be gentle. That she wants everything I can give her.

Fucking hell.

I pump forward, and she moans in pleasure, the sound shooting bolts of electricity straight to my balls, tightening them up. My stomach coils with anticipation. I let go, enjoying the feeling of her mouth on me as I take what I want. Her eyes water, but she doesn't shy away. I'm so goddamn close, but this is not how I want to come.

I slide out of her mouth as she releases me with a wet pop. "I need to be inside you."

She falls back onto her haunches, her head tilting. "Then get inside me. I'm more than ready."

I smirk. Damn. How the hell did I get this lucky?

Lowering her body down, I slide inside her, all the way to the hilt, her back arching, her legs widening to accommodate me. My eyes train down on where my body enters hers, and I pump in harder, loving the way she looks swallowing me up.

My fingers hit her pink nub, my hips pistoning in and out as she grips onto me, holding on tight as our bodies meet over and over. We find our rhythm quickly, it never takes us long, and within minutes, she's clawing at my back and crying out in pleasure.

"Never enough," I groan as I come inside her.

"Hmmmm...," she hums against my mouth as I devour her.

"Never enough," I repeat, pulling back so I can stare into her glazed, contented eyes. "I love you, and I'll never get enough. This thing with us is forever."

"I'd like that."

I bend down, fusing our lips together, my body covering hers.

If only I could keep her here. If only I could keep her and Ady here. Safe. Tucked away from the expectant world.

Except, we all know the world doesn't stop moving. Even when we want it to, it keeps going, dragging us reluctantly along for the ride.

And the vultures?

Yeah, they never stop either. Especially when their prey is within their grasp.

THIRTY-FOUR

Viola

JASPER EXPLAINED all that he and Gus had spoken about. It took everything in my power not to laugh. Fucking Gus. Only he'd come up with a plan that elaborate and not clue anyone in about it until we're all at our tortured end. I should have figured in a way. I knew he wasn't after me again. I knew his comments were from a different place than they had been when we were young.

Adalyn woke up shortly after Jasper and I finished making love, crawling into bed with us. The three of us snuggled until her boundless energy rebooted, and then we spent the rest of the afternoon before sound check playing. It was blissfully unexpected.

And it felt like...like we were a family.

I know I'm not her mother. I know I could never fully enter into that role, even if her birth mother was never around, and Adalyn never knew her.

But I'd like to.

And with that hope comes an awareness that is as beautiful as it is tenuous. Jasper may throw around words like 'never enough' and 'forever,' but what do they actually mean to him?

Are they just flowery prose he lays down when he's in the heat and swell of the moment? Will he still want me around when this tour is over, and my nannying services are no longer required?

Here comes that hope again.

That exquisite climb that can lead to the hardest of falls.

I want to have more faith in this fledgling relationship. In the limitless possibilities it holds for us. In the love he claims to have for me.

But I've been burned. I've been burned bad. By people who claimed to love me most of all.

And those scars run deep.

I'm hoping–there's that word again–that those days are behind me.

Jasper left with kisses and promises of a night out, just the two of us. So when it's nearing very late, and Ady is sleeping sweetly in her room, I'm surprised to find Gus–alone–entering the suite. He's freshly showered, his sandy hair sticking up in all directions, his gray eyes bright, but with noticeable purple stains beneath them.

"Sup, babe? You're looking deliciously sexy."

He crosses the room and envelops me in a hug for the ages. "Gus Daniel Diamond," I laugh his name, leaning back to slap his chest. "I have no words for you. Like none. Or maybe I have too many, and I don't know where to start."

He laughs, squeezing me back to his chest, but his whispered words in my ear are so very serious. "I'm sorry, Vi. For everything. For the cheating. For the lying about the cheating. For letting you go in the first place. For hurting you. That one most of all. But I think this is the way it was always meant to go."

Ah, Gus.

"I love you, you bastard. I've missed you. Missed my best friend. I'm so thankful you brought me here."

He steps back to meet my eyes, cupping my face in his large

warm hands. "You love him? Like love him, love him?" I nod without hesitation, and he nods in return. "Okay. Can't ask for more than that. Go get him."

"Where is he?"

"Waiting in the hall. I told him I needed a minute alone with *my* girl."

"God," I laugh, rolling my eyes. "You really are a bastard."

"The best sort."

"Yes," I breathe softly, reaching up to gently press my lips to his. "The very best sort."

He leans in and kisses me back, a bit deeper than the peck I gave him. It's sad and sweet, and it's a goodbye. It's a letting me go, and part of me can't help but twinge a little at that. My Gus.

I leave him in the suite, heading for the door with excited butter-flies fluttering wildly in my belly. Opening the door, I find Jasper there, standing across the narrow hall, his back pressed against the wall, looking so unbelievably hot I can hardly stand it.

"You two work everything out?"

"Yep."

His eyes do a slow sweep of my body, burning with barely contained fire as he goes. And when those fiery emeralds find my hazels, deliciously decadent zaps of electricity jolt through me. I could spend my life here in this hallway with this man staring at me and never grow bored or tired of the way he makes me feel.

I'm beautiful. I'm smart. I'm gorgeous and sexy.

I'm fucking perfect to this man.

That's what this look says. He can't get enough of me, and even if this all falls apart tomorrow, I'm going to hold onto everything he's offering me tonight.

"Do you know what I'm thinking?" he asks softly, hoarsely, like just getting the words out is a challenge. It very well might be. The man did just perform on stage for nearly three hours, but I don't think that's what this is all about.

"Tell me," I reply, equally as soft, but instead of heavy, my voice floats above us like vapor. That's how light it is. That's how high he makes me.

"I'm thinking today might just be one of the best days of my life. The day Adalyn was born and today. Those are it."

I smile, not even trying to curb it. "Why's that?" I tilt my head, propping my hands on my hips, turning my smile into a tough-girl grin. I'm not fooling him for a second.

He smirks, completely onto my game. "Because I'm mother-fucking Prince Charming, Viola. Haven't you figured that out yet?"

"What?" a bemused laugh escapes me.

"You heard me. Motherfucking. Prince. Charming." He points to his chest. "That's me. Because I slid that glass slipper on your foot, and it fits you just right. The ball is over, and there is no more midnight for us. No magical time when our fairytale turns back into a pumpkin, and we have to pretend. You're finally, officially mine. This is our happily ever after, princess."

My teeth sink into my lower lip, and I shake my head back and forth. "I've always fancied myself as Rapunzel. You know, long blonde hair and greenish eyes." I lift a lock of my long hair to empha-size my point while cocking an eyebrow. "Falls for the sexy criminal."

Jasper laughs. "As long as you fall for me, I'll be the criminal. Stealing you was the best thing I've ever done."

Damn...this man.

"I'm thinking a romantic late dinner at a pretty café. I'm thinking a nice bottle of wine and then you for dessert."

I shake my head, and he tilts his in question.

"I'm in Paris. I'm going to need a French pastry for dessert. Whatever you choose is up to you."

Pushing off the wall, he stalks toward me with achingly slow steps. Wow, this man really knows how to get my heart racing. His arms wrap around my waist, and he drags me against the length of his body.

"Whatever you want, baby. It's just us tonight."

And, with that promise, he kisses my mouth, stealing a small taste, and then intertwining our fingers, leads me to the elevator.

Moments later, we step out of the revolving door of the hotel and onto the busy street, and all I can say is, Paris. It's just...Paris. C'est magnifique.

We walk in the opposite direction from the Arc de Triomphe, no fancy cars tonight. We're any old couple, taking in the city, heading out for a late dinner.

No one notices us. No one cares, and I wonder if that thought is always going to be in my mind. Being with Jasper Diamond, lead singer of Wild Minds, is not going to be easy. It will be rife with challenges. Fans. Women. Press. Tours. It's not for the faint of heart or the weak-minded.

But tonight, I push all that away.

Tonight, we're just Jasper and Viola.

"Where do we go after Paris?"

"Brussels, Frankfurt, Berlin, Copenhagen, Stockholm, Moscow, Prague, Budapest, Vienna, Munich, Zurich, Milan, Rome, Marseille, Barcelona, Madrid, Lisbon, and then to New York to begin the rest of the US tour."

"That's it?" I laugh the words, slightly stunned. "All that in three months."

"Goes by quickly. It'll be over before you know it."

Over before I know it.

"What are your plans for after?"

He asks that with no emotion. His tone as blank as his expression, and it's making this moment impossible. I realize what a contradiction this man is. He's all this emotion. Poetry and lyrics and deep-seated feelings that rip you apart from the inside out, piece by piece, only to rebuild you until you're whole in a way you never imagined you could be.

He offers so much of himself.

Everything really.

And if you're lucky enough to be on the receiving end of that love, it's endless. So encompassing, it's impossible not to return it with equal ardor.

But Jasper Diamond is also cautious with that love.

So reserved, it can make your head and heart spin from the whiplash.

This is one of those moments. Because I want him to tell me he wants me, this, for the long-haul. He's briefly touched on it, but right now, he's not doing that.

Not at all.

And even though I consider myself a pretty strong woman, I'm afraid. I'm stupidly insecure. It's lame, and I hate it, but it's there.

I've been let down one too many times to be cavalier with my heart. Fear makes mortal fools of us all.

But at the same time...

I take a step forward, opening my mouth to bear my soul, ready to go for broke, when I'm pushed back. The movement happens so quickly I hardly register what's happening until I'm practically forced into the street—into oncoming traffic.

Jasper reaches out, grasping my hand and yanking me back onto the sidewalk, his eyes wide with fear. I trip, stumbling forward, my hands planting onto a lamppost to right myself.

Shifting to the right, I skirt a couple, my head whipping wildly around, only to realize how I got here.

There are three girls aggressively surrounding Jasper, asking for autographs and selfies.

Those crazy bitches pushed me!

He blows out a loud breath, relief etched in his features that I'm not about to be smashed by a car. His hand slips from mine as the girls push him back further from me, speaking loudly, and with so much animation, they take over everything. His eyes meet mine, and once he finds me smiling, shaking my head incredulously, he grins and morphs into Jasper Diamond lead singer mode.

Probably because these girls are determined as they drag him back against the building wall.

He's smiling, indulging them completely with their every request–including kisses on the cheek. But it's the attention he's drawing with them that has other people stopping to snap pics and get close and ask for autographs.

Within minutes, he's surrounded by adoring fans.

I step back, leaning against the lamppost that helped save me from eating shit on the Parisian streets, coming to grips with this reality.

This is Jasper's life.

Why he doesn't go out a lot without a bodyguard or a hat and crazy sunglasses.

Jasper is a first-rate celebrity, and even though I don't think of him that way, it's a truth I'm forced to accept. He glances up, in between fans, scanning the sidewalk, and when his eyes meet mine, he gives me a 'sorry' shrug and a 'what can you do' smile, and I return it with an 'I'll wait all night for you' wink.

I love that people love him. That they're so eager and excited to meet him. To get his autograph and take a picture with him.

Jasper doesn't rush anyone.

He smiles and laughs and is gracious with each fan. And every few seconds, he seeks me out, ensuring I'm still here. That I'm okay. That I'm not pissed off at him taking forever with his devoted fans. I'm not. I think it's sexy as fuck that people love him like this. I could watch this all night. It's an incredible thing. Probably because I adore him too, but I'm the one who spends the night in his bed. Not them. Never them.

It's a truth I didn't consider with Gus. With Gus, I knew he fooled around. I ended it because of that. Well...it was one of the reasons I ended it.

But Jasper won't do that to me.

I know it in my blood.

Finally, after he's done with the last fan, he excuses himself and moves toward me with purposeful steps. His eyes alight, sparkling hellfire as his hand extends for me to take.

"Sorry about that," he whispers, but there is no missing the joy and lack of remorse in his tone. It has me smiling up at him, my insides quickening.

"Is this what it's like to be the Great Jasper Diamond? Sexy man. Rock god," I snark playfully.

He chuckles, trying to play it cool when he's anything but. "Evidently so. Too much for you, dream girl?" Lord help me; he looks nervous. How can something so stupidly simple make me love him so much more?

He's staring into me like he'd give it all up if I said yes.

I want to kiss him. I want to eat him up with a spoon for being so goddamn sexy and devoted. For looking at me like I'm all he sees. For checking on me while attending to his fans. For showing me what I've been missing out on my entire life.

For never forgetting me.

"No. It's not too much. It fills me with fangirl-level giddiness. I think I might need your autograph, Mister Diamond. Right. Here." I point to my chest, my fingers gliding up along the cleavage I have peeking out of the top of my blouse.

His face erupts into an all-encompassing boyish grin, stretching from ear to ear.

And that desire to kiss him grows stronger.

But his beloved audience is lingering, watching us. Some are even snapping some pics, and I don't feel like making any more headlines than I already have. So I bob my head to the right, and he nods his up and down, and we head to our unknown romantic café.

We leave the lights, camera, action behind us, our shoulders rubbing, our fingers still touching, and I don't think I've ever been this happy. This excited for a first date.

Because that's what this is, our first date as a couple.

But it's so much more than that. It's the start of us.

And nothing will tear us apart. Nothing.

THIRTY-FIVE

Jasper

"VIOLA, TRUTH OR DARE?" Viola bursts out laughing, nearly into a cackle. We're all a bit sleep-deprived, punch-drunk, and straddling the line between sober and buzzed.

"Adalyn?" Viola asks, staring down at my daughter, who is wrapped around her like a vine, contentedly getting her back rubbed. Me? I'm sitting across the way, on a lounger, enjoying the cool night air and watching them.

And writing.

Fuck, I've been writing like a demon on speed.

"What do you think we should do?" Adalyn reluctantly pries her head away from Viola's chest–it would take more than a simple question to get me to do that. Her large, round eyes guilelessly blink up at her. "Should we go with truth or dare?" Adalyn, of course, does not answer. "Are you thinking truth? Because knowing Keith the way we do, a dare is dangerous territory."

"Truth," Adalyn repeats.

"Completely agree. You're a very wise woman not to trust that man."

"Hey," Keith protests only to shrug a shoulder once Viola tosses him a challenging brow. "But I'm trustworthy for my girl, Ady. Right, sweetie?" Adalyn glances over her shoulder at Keith, who gives her a wink.

"Hi, Keith." He blows her a kiss. "Mickey Mouse?"

"Tomorrow, sweetie. We'll watch Mickey tomorrow."

Adalyn turns back into Viola, jutting her back out as a reminder for Viola to resume rubbing.

It's late. Like somewhere close to nine pm.

And while that's not late for most of the world, it's late for a three-year-old. We spent a much-needed day off in the lakes region of Italy, and now we're hanging out in a rental house on Lake Como. Our next show is not until tomorrow night, but this is the point of the tour that hits you the hardest, which is why Sophia set us up with this house instead of a hotel.

We're now three months in with another two to go. Instead of feeling like we're more than halfway there, we feel beaten down and wrung out by the animal that is perpetually sucking at our teat.

That animal is the show.

That animal is the music and the night after night of playing and singing your heart out. It's the travel schedule and the interviews and the groupies and the autographs and the record company telling you to change this or that. Henry calls it the beast, but I don't think it matters which euphemism you use.

Like I said, we're all a bit punch-drunk at this point.

Maybe burnt-out is a better description.

It's the time when I grow to hate—just a little—the demands.

Most of that fades back into the abyss when I step on stage. When the fans scream our names and the jolt of adrenaline slides through my veins like a perfectly choreographed cocktail. I swear, that rush never gets old. It's everything else that wears you down to your last drop of sanity and patience.

Adalyn stares exhaustedly up at Viola. "Bedtime?" Viola whispers to her.

"After my question," Keith demands. "Then you can put her to bed."

Viola dramatically rolls her eyes. "Then ask already. What inappropriate sexual question do I have to entertain you with tonight?"

Keith finds me. Then looks to Gus, who is quietly wrapped around his acoustic like it's his lover, and then back to her. "Who's better in bed? Gus or Jas?"

I cough out a laugh. Gus glances up for a quick moment, scowls at Keith, and then returns to his strings. Henry practically falls off his chair, half his beer splashing onto the stone patio we're all sitting on. The flickering glow of torches light up the dark sky, and the mild scent of the lake permeates the air.

Henry rights himself quickly, flicking his hand out to remove the excess drops of spilled beer before smacking Keith's large shoulder.

"Fire," Henry points at Keith. "That's exactly what you're playing with, man."

Keith shrugs, still staring intently at Viola, who is a lovely shade of red at the moment, her eyes anywhere but on Gus or me. A month ago, this question would have bothered the hell out of me. It's still not my favorite. I mean, no one wants a reminder that your girlfriend used to belong to your brother. But nothing over these weeks has been awkward between any of us. It just continued to flow as if nothing out of the ordinary occurred.

Viola and I are together.

Gus claims—and acts—as if he's happy for us.

The other guys never even batted an eye.

The world? Well, they're not exactly clued in yet, and who cares anyway.

"Are we taking bets?" I ask.

"Maybe we should have a showdown," Keith suggests, smiling impishly at Gus, who is still frowning into his guitar. "Winner takes all."

Viola hisses something unintelligible under her breath, but I believe it's along the lines of, "Don't ever get involved with pig men."

"Is this a spectator competition?" Henry asks mischievously. "Because I'd be in for that. Especially if we could do more than just watch." Henry sits up straighter like he's just had the most perfect idea in the history of perfect ideas. "How about some crazy band love action with our favorite adult girl?"

"What say you, Gus?" Keith poses like this is a serious discussion that requires serious answers.

"How about what say you, Viola?" she interjects sharply. "I don't remember offering myself up on a block for your reverse harem."

"Reverse harem?" the four of us question in unison.

"Never mind," she grumbles. "But I'm not answering your question or playing your stupid game or having sex for sport and betting. And thanks, Jas. Very noble and manly to stand up for me."

"You're right." I glance over at Keith and Henry, unable to hold in my smile. I'm in too good of a mood tonight. "Stop talking about Viola like that, or I'll have to kick your butts and stuff." She growls. "Better, baby?" Now she flips me off, and the guys laugh.

"That's a bullshit question, dude," Gus states oh-so-dramatically, going back five minutes in the conversation as he strums a few chords that sound like the beginning of something new. "You don't even need to watch a throwdown to know the answer. Everyone here knows I'm a God in the sack and hung like the David we're going to see in a couple of days. You're all players, but fucking is my stage or however that quote goes. It's why the lovely and virtuous Viola wouldn't answer. She doesn't want to hurt her new boy's gentle feelings."

"Aaand, that's my cue." Viola stands up with Adalyn still in her arms. "Jas, do you wanna help me put her down, or are you too busy entertaining weird sexual experiments for me and your friends?"

"I would love to help. Especially if it gets me out of this insanity. I think we've officially been on the road too long, boys." I stand up, tossing back the end of my beer and setting the glass down. I smack Keith, followed by Henry, upside their heads.

"Hey!" Keith protests. "You're just pissed she didn't answer from the start and say it's you."

I shrug, walking past him and patting my brother on the shoulder. "Real men who are gods in the sack and hung like the David we're going to see in a couple of days never have to brag."

"Fucker," Gus hisses under his breath, swatting me away like he would a fly.

"I plan on it."

Everyone, including Gus this time, laughs, and all Viola can do is shake her head, her lips pursed.

How she's lasted with a group of guys like us for so long is a wonder. It's not even like we're different than we were in high school. If anything, Keith and Henry used to be worse. But, I didn't exactly indulge much with teasing Viola back then.

I reach Viola and lift Adalyn out of her hands, cradling her in my arms and pressing her sleepy, warm body against mine. I kiss the top of her head, breathing in her scent. "I've got her," I whisper. "I want to put her down myself tonight." Viola leans in and kisses Adalyn on the cheek. She doesn't fight me on that. She's as beat up as the rest of us.

"Okay. Night, Miss Adalyn. I'll see you in the morning light. Sweet dreams."

"Goodnight, Vi," Adalyn slurs, her eyes barely open.

Adalyn rests her head on my shoulder and looks to Gus. "Goodnight, Gus."

Gus glances up, smiling at her like she's the moon and the stars and the sun all rolled up into one. "Goodnight, baby girl. I love you so much."

"Love you too."

Keith and Henry say goodnight to Adalyn, though she doesn't

return the sentiment the same way as she does for Gus, and then I carry her off to bed. Adalyn is already in her pajamas, her teeth brushed, and two bedtime stories deep. But she likes to hang on, play the elusive sleep game kids like so much. I think she's just a junkie for physical contact, and I feel like any chance I get to spend more time with her during the tour is a bonus.

"You tired, bug?" I whisper into her ear. She doesn't respond, just squeezes around me tighter like a monkey.

This house is old and very Italian, so it takes me a bit to meander my way through the first floor and up to the second. Ady's room is directly beside mine and Viola's, and I set her down in the small twin-sized bed, nearly tripping over the stack of pillows I have piled up on the floor in case she falls out. She never has, but she's also never slept in a twin before.

Adalyn rolls onto her back, staring up at me as she grasps onto the Mickey stuffed animal that was patiently awaiting her arrival. I climb in bed beside her, tucking her small body snugly into my large arms. Immediately, she curls into my chest, and God, this feeling.

There is nothing like it.

Warmth spreads through my veins as my chest tightens in the best possible way.

"I'm so happy you're mine," I whisper, kissing the crown of her head. Her soft breathing is the only acknowledgment of my words. "All I want to do in this world is make you as happy as you make me. I want to give you everything, and so far, I've failed you." I close my eyes at that admission. It's a truth that only hurts more by setting it free. "I want Viola to be your mommy. I think she'd be so good at it, but I wanted to talk to you about it first. Because mommy is not a word you've ever said. It's not a concept you've ever known, and that...," I pause, swallowing past the thick lump in my throat. *Is my fault*, I don't finish.

I never tried very hard with Karina.

And when she left, I let her go. I didn't chase after her. I didn't hunt her down. I didn't beg her to stay or be part of Adalyn's life. She left, and I let her because I was pissed she'd do that to Adalyn in the first place, and then she died.

I wish I had made more of an effort to get her to stay or at least be a mother to Adalyn.

"I want you to have a mommy, Ady. I want that so badly for you. I had a mommy, and she was the best. The absolute best. I took both my mommy and your mommy from you, and I know that's something I have to live with, but hopefully, we can convince Viola to be ours forever. What do you think?"

Adalyn doesn't move, and I know by the way her breathing has gone from shallow and choppy to smooth and deep that she's asleep.

"What about you, Mickey?"

And now I think I've officially lost it.

I blow out a breath, lying here for another few minutes, savoring my baby in my arms. When she rolls away from me, further into her true love, Mickey Mouse, I slide out of bed to return to the fray outside.

Only, when I reach the precipice of the patio, blinking out into the dark night, I find a vision that momentarily stops my heart.

Viola is alone, standing stock-still, one hand pressed against an ancient stone pillar as she stares out at the water only illuminated by the ethereal glow of the full moon.

I take a silent step forward and ask, "Ever dance with the devil in the pale moonlight?"

Her back is to me, but I can feel the warmth of her smile from here.

I move further out onto the patio, searching around but finding it completely empty. It's only then that I catch the sound of the guys from somewhere inside.

She waited for me.

"Does that make me Vicki Vale or Batman?"

Fuck, I love this woman.

"Vicki Vale," I reply softly, now standing behind her. "I can't dance with Batman if I'm the Joker."

"True," she muses, turning to face me. My arms snake around her waist, hers sliding up until they're around my neck.

"Dance with me."

"There's no music."

"I'll sing to you."

Staring deeply into her eyes, turned onyx by the darkness, I lean in and press my lips to hers. Then I sing the very first song on our very first album that I wrote for her.

Her face lights up in recognition as we slowly sway back and forth with only the moonlight and the faint flickering of gas lanterns to see by.

And when I'm out of words, my forehead drops to hers, our noses kissing as I say the words that have been on the tip of my tongue since she became mine. "When the tour is over, I want you to stay with me and Adalyn in Los Angeles."

Her breath stutters; her steps falter.

"That bad of an idea?" I ask when she doesn't respond or even move or breathe. *Dammit, Viola, don't say no.*

"I don't have a job there." Okay. I can work with that. I open my mouth to tell her she doesn't need one, but she reads me quickly and interrupts before I can get a word out. "And don't tell me that I don't need to work. I don't care about your money, Jasper, and I will not live off you like that."

"What if I promise to find you something? A teaching position?"

She blows out a breath, the warm sweetness fanning across my lips.

"I love you, Viola, and now that I've got you, I'm not letting you get away. You're talking about a job, and I'm talking about our future together. Don't connect the two. Do you want to live with us after the tour is over?"

Her response is immediate. "Yes. More than anything."

An unstoppable smile erupts across my face. "Then we'll figure out the rest. I promise you we will. I love you, and I'll do anything to make you happy. To make this work."

"I love you too. Without limits. Always."

There is nothing better than that. Everything else we can take as it comes. Together. Nothing and no one can ever tear us apart again. No matter what.

THIRTY-SIX

Viola

"TELL me what New York is like," Jules asks through the phone as I watch Adalyn slide down the metal slide with a loud 'Wee.' I tuck the phone between my shoulder and ear and clap my hands for her. It's the fifth time in a row she's gone down, but this time, she waited while another child went. She didn't even get freaked out when he got close to her. She didn't look at him, or even acknowledge him really, but she didn't push him off either, so an improvement is an improvement.

"Nicely done, Ady. Good waiting for your turn. Awesome job." I grasp the phone with my hand before I answer Jules. "New York is nuts. Miss Adalyn and I are at a playground made out of cement. I have no idea how children don't kill themselves on it constantly, but it seems like the most normal thing in the world to everyone here. Also, the congestion is unreal. Like walking here was nearly impossible. People are everywhere. It's also dirty and smells, and sometimes we have to step over puddles of emerald-green-tinted water."

"Emerald-green-tinted water?"

"Yeah. I'm afraid to ask what makes it that color. I'm going with the crazy stuff that turned the Joker into the Joker in the comics." I grin at that, thinking back to when Jasper and I danced under the moon in Italy. "But other than that stuff, it's pretty cool. Tall buildings and amazing stores and restaurants and Central Park is pretty awesome. I want to walk Ady through it after we're done here, but I don't know how much she'll be up for."

"That's where you are now, right? That's what your text earlier said."

"That's where we are."

"Then why are you calling me if you're at the park with Adalyn? Shouldn't you be watching your charge? Or is it now that you're Jasper's girlfriend you have a different title when caring for his daughter?"

I pull back and actually stare at the phone. Is she kidding me with that? "What's your problem, Jules?"

"No problem. Just curious is all. And maybe a little pissed that it took more than a month for you to tell me you and Jasper were a thing. I mean, you told me you slept with him and then nothing more about him. I figured you and Gus were back on, and you were hiding your one-nighter from him. The tabloids agreed with me, by the way. They were all over that one here in the States after a few of those pictures hit the net."

"Is there a reason you're being a bitch?"

"Not being a bitch. Just honest."

I sigh. "We're doing honesty? Okay, Jules, I never heard from you unless I called you. And then, you were only after pictures and gossip on the guys. You had also just broken up with that new guy you were seeing, were pissed off that nothing went down between you and Keith when we saw you at the tour stop, and I didn't feel like shoving my new relationship down your throat. But I still sent some texts and pics to let you know I was thinking about you even while I was far away."

The phone beeps in my ear, indicating another call, and when I check it, I see it's Jasper. "Hold on, Jules. Jasper is calling on the other line." Jules makes some kind of sarcastic sour sound but doesn't comment. I click over. "Hey," I say, smiling stupidly before the man even speaks to me, even though I'm still annoyed with my best friend, who hasn't been all that friendly lately.

"Where are you?"

Oh. Okay. Not his typical greeting. "At a playground in Central Park. Why? What's up?" Flipping my wrist over, I check my watch. "Aren't you supposed to be in an interview or something?"

"Yes. That's exactly where we are. I need you to take Adalyn back to the hotel. Now," he demands with the type of force I haven't heard from him since the beginning of the tour.

"What's wrong? You're scaring me." I scan the playground, but nothing appears out of sorts. Adalyn is at the top of the structure again, waiting to go down the slide, and I walk toward her, waving for her to hurry up instead of lingering up there. "Come on, sweetie. Time to go."

"No. Bye, bye, Vi." She gives me the sign for all done, waving her hands back and forth at me. "Say, no thank you."

Shit. Not now. "Come on, Ady. Let's go, please. Slide down for me."

"Get her out of there, Vi. I don't care if you have to drag her."

"What the hell is going on?" I half-yell, before I check my voice.

"I'll tell you about it when I see you. We'll be back at the hotel in about half an hour."

He disconnects the call, and now my heart rate is rapidly starting to jack up. "Hey," Jules says, and I completely forgot she was on the other line.

"I can't talk, Jules. I gotta get Ady out of the park. Something is wrong."

"Oh. What is it?"

"I don't know. I'll call you later."

"You really don't have to. I get that your life is busy now." And then she hangs up, but I don't have time to wade through Jules's crap at the moment.

I slip my phone into my purse just as something flashes straight ahead of us, catching my eye.

Paparazzi.

They're lining the edge of the playground and park. Dozens of them. All with cameras trained on us.

How the hell did they know where to find us?

I swear, it's like they have the inside track.

After Paris, it was as if the world lost interest. We spent the last month in Europe without any issues. I mean, sure, there were still some press and still tons of fans, but nothing beyond the ordinary. Mostly some of the US gossip Jules was speaking about, but it wasn't much at all.

So this?

Something happened.

And whatever it is, has Jasper freaked.

We landed in Boston five nights ago from Spain. The guys played two nights there and are doing three nights here, including playing SNL and The Tonight Show. We're in the homestretch–if you can call six more weeks of this, the homestretch. It feels like years since we started the tour, not just a few months.

But right now, I wish I were back in our European bubble.

Adalyn finally slides down, and I lift her up and into my arms with little protest. Walking at a fast clip through the playground, we reach the street in no time. Thomas is next to us, keeping pace, but it doesn't do much good. Adalyn is starting to squirm in my arms.

"Down," she says, and I shake my head.

It would be so much easier if she'd sit in a stroller, but she won't. We've tried it a few times, and she freaks. Adalyn likes, *needs*, to be able to move. So I typically let her walk as much as I can because, well, she's heavy when you carry her for long periods of time. And walking is good for her, I figure. Tuckers her out.

But this is not the moment for walking at a toddler's pace.

"Not now, sweet girl. I'm going to carry you, okay?"

"Vi squeezes?" she asks, because the perceptive little bug, as Jasper calls her, has already picked up on my uneasiness.

I squeeze her body against mine. "How much does Vi love you?"

"Vi loves you *so* much," she half-sings, back to our game.

The moment we hit the sidewalk, the paparazzi call out our names. I don't have any other option but to continue toward them unless I want to cross the street, running against New York City traffic with a toddler in my arms. They come at us, shouting a million different questions that all get rolled up into one loud noise.

I try to maneuver around them, but three of them block us in.

"Please let us through," I request as calmly as I can.

But they're not letting us through.

They're getting up in my face, trying to take pictures, and generally set me–and Adalyn–off. Thomas shifts in front of us, blocking us as best he can with his size and strength, ordering them to push back, but naturally, they don't listen. They never do, and Adalyn is becoming more and more upset as the minutes pass.

I've learned the more I engage the paparazzi, the more they come after us. I mean, that's their game, right?

But when one of them asks, "Is it true you're having an affair with Jasper behind Gus's back?" And then another calls out, "Did Jasper know you had worked as an escort when he hired you to take care of his daughter?"

What the fuck? I glance up, only to have a camera click directly in my face.

"Is that why you were fired from your teaching job in Alabama?" "How long have you been cheating on Gus with Jasper?" "Is that why Gus is leaving the band?" "How do you feel about breaking up one of the biggest rock bands?" "How does it feel being one of the most hated women in the country?"

Question after question is fired at me like bullets out of a gun.

And just as deadly.

I swallow hard past the lump in my throat, willing my tears to stay hidden. I won't give these bastards the satisfaction. Adalyn, for once, is clinging to me instead of squirming. She's also quiet, which is a blessing.

That is until one of them says, "Adalyn. Look at me."

She shakes her head in my chest. "No. No. No. No."

I pin him with my most malevolent stare, not even caring how it looks, and tell him, "She's a little girl. Have some decency and give her privacy and space."

Finally, Thomas is able to push them back, and we break through.

I take off, practically at a sprint with Adalyn tucked into my chest, toward the hotel's private entrance. Their questions, one after the other, continuing to assault my back. Apprehension swims laps in my gut, sloshing my insides about. I'm woozy and sick and scared.

We're staying in a two-bedroom suite at The Plaza. Jasper thought it was too flashy, but it's where Sophia booked us, so that's where we are. In this moment, I'm grateful the hotel is so close to the park.

We reach the entrance, and the three of us pack into the private elevator. Adalyn is stone silent, hardly moving as her face presses into my neck. I kiss her head, rubbing gentle circles along her back, hoping I can reassure her that everything is okay when it absolutely is not.

"Thomas," I speak softly, glancing in his direction as we ascend. "Talk to me. What the heck is going on? How did they know where we were?"

Thomas shakes his head, just as baffled as I am, throwing me a sideways glance and looking miserable.

And what the hell was with that escort crap? Or the being fired from my teaching job? Or the cheating on Gus with Jasper? Or being the most hated woman in the country? Jesus, those bastards really know how to cut you up so they can capture you bleeding.

The doors to the suite open, and I practically roll my eyes at the opulence of it. Gold. There is so much gold plating on everything. Jasper is nowhere to be found, but as I turn the corner, heading toward the master bedroom to see if he's miraculously back before he said he'd be, I'm greeted with none other than Sophia Bloom.

What was she doing in mine and Jasper's bedroom?

"Hello," I say a bit stunned, taking a step back and searching around for signs of Jasper. "Jasper didn't mention you were coming, is he back?"

She gives me one of those Hollywood fake grins that I bet she practices in front of the mirror. "Not yet, sweets. I'm here to try and handle the press situation you seem to have gotten yourself into. *Again.*"

I ignore her jab because fuck this cunt. I hate her where she stands and don't care even the slightest if she knows it.

"Where is Jasper?"

"I'm expecting him to return any minute." *I'm* expecting him, she says. There is no missing that emphasis. Her brown eyes zero in on Adalyn, who is still tucked into my arms. "Hello, Adalyn. How are you, dear?" she coos at her, reaching out to touch her hand only to have Adalyn jerk away, cowering in closer to me. Sophia frowns.

I swear, I take no personal enjoyment in that. None whatsoever.

"When he returns, would you please let him know Adalyn and I are in her room?"

I turn to leave, unable to stand this woman another second, when her words stop me in my tracks. "I won't be doing that, Viola. Because by the time he returns, you'll already be gone."

I narrow my eyes at her. "What exactly does that mean?"

"It means I never took you for the sort of person who would sleep with men for money. Or cheat. Or lie. But the pictures are rather compelling." *What pictures?* She tilts her head, her black bob hardly moving as she does. "Imagine what this will do to the rest of the tour. To the band. To Jasper's credibility as a parent." My eyes pop out of my head before they narrow into twin slits of anger. She grins, enjoying the hell out of my reaction to her. "Still haven't figured it out yet? You're fired!" she shrieks, her voice rising an octave, her cheeks reddening, losing some of that polished cool. "Jasper directed me to get rid of you the moment you returned from the park. I am to have you escorted to the airport. Don't worry, cupcake, your things have already been packed for you."

"You're a liar," I spit.

A smug grin curls evilly up the corner of her face. "Am I?"

She pulls out her phone, presses a button, and then Jasper's voice rings through the air. "I want her gone before I get home, Sophia. I don't ever want to see her face again."

What the hell is happening?

Everything was perfect this morning. We woke up, made love, played with Adalyn. How could things have derailed so quickly? Something isn't right. Jasper wouldn't do this. He wouldn't say that.

But he did. That's his voice.

"I'm not going anywhere until I speak to him face-to-face."

"He doesn't want you anymore, Viola. Get the message. You're done here. A washed-up escort. A teacher with no job. Do the right thing and leave before you ruin all their lives." She looks to Adalyn with raised eyebrows, stressing her point. I flip her off. If only I could say the words, but Adalyn is in my arms. "I'm calling security to throw you out."

I turn on my heels and leave her behind, marching down the hall to Adalyn's bedroom. My mind is reeling, my stomach rioting, and my broken heart is somewhere I can't even locate.

I'm not about to get into something with this woman while I'm holding onto Adalyn. Jasper loves me. He told me so this morning, dammit.

But that message?

How could he say those things about me? He can't possibly believe whatever bullshit tabloid crap they're spewing. I mean, it's all lies. Stacked, ugly lies.

Where are you, Jasper?

I carry Adalyn across the suite and into her room. Setting her down, she immediately climbs onto the bed, does a somersault, picks up a stuffed Mickey Mouse, and then jumps up and down.

"More Sleep," she requests, dropping down and closing her eyes as she pretends to snore.

"Good night, Ady. Sleep tight."

"Sleep tight," she repeats.

"I love you."

"I love you."

Her eyes pop open. "More sleep."

That means it's my turn. Lying down on the bed beside her, I pretend to snore. A tear leaks out of the corner of my eye before I can wipe it away. She nudges me, wondering why I'm not continuing the game, and I smile despite my aching heart. I tickle her under the covers. "Wake up, wake up, wake up."

She giggles like mad, rolling around and peeking her face out from under the blanket. "More sleep."

I nod, and then she covers up her face again, starting all over with, "Good night."

While she pretends to sleep, I grab my phone and immediately Google my name.

And what I find has my hands trembling with anger.

Pictures of me standing in the corner of the bar I used to work in, Spencer Johnson slipping money into my pocket as he leans in and kisses me. Another with me wrapping my arms around him, smiling up at him as he returns his wallet to his back pocket.

It's really not all that compelling.

At least not the way Sophia said it was.

I remember that night. It was when Spencer and I were dating. He was giving me my half of the shift tips. I was on break, and we were having a private moment in the corner.

But it's a wad of cash he's handing me. And his smile is nothing if not seductive.

But that's not even what's giving me pause.

It's the pictures themselves.

I read through the small story beneath them. It refers to a credible source, someone close to me. They claim I accepted money in return for sexual favors. That I was fired from my position as a special education teacher due to parental complaints, not laid off due to budget cuts.

It says that Jasper and I have been dating in secret behind Gus's back. That Gus is furious, and the band is breaking up as a result.

More pictures.

This time of me with Jasper in Rome, staring into each other's eyes in front of the Trevi Fountain. Another picture with Gus scowling at us, looking like the devil bit him.

Only, I remember that moment.

We were in Barcelona, having a debate over the merits of tapas. Gus was adamantly opposed to shared food. Said it was an excuse to spend more money for less and that he liked his own meals without someone else nabbing them.

Seriously. That's what that conversation was about. Us razzing Gus and him pouting like a petulant little boy.

A picture with Gus's arms around me, us smiling at each other. His lips pressed into my cheek.

The power these pictures wield.

A thousand words, indeed.

They're just the wrong words. Soaked in innuendo and lies. It's too late, isn't it? It's already out there. What does it matter now to the world if they're lies?

Tears burn my eyes, blurring my vision.

I don't think I've ever been this hurt and angry and confused in my life.

I can't believe this is happening to me. I can't believe it's come to this.

Why?

It's the one question that continues to repeat over and over in my head. Scanning the deepest, darkest recesses of my mind, I come up empty. I can't think of anything that would lead to this level of betrayal. From both of them.

How could they hate me so much that they would willingly, knowingly, ruin my life?

The knife pushes in deeper, twisting around and around as I continue to scroll. God, this hurts. It hurts so damn much. Tears stream down my face, one after the other, as I wipe furiously at my face.

I don't want to cry. I want to be strong. Impervious.

But I'm not.

I'm human and sad.

This totally and completely wrecks me.

I try calling Jasper's phone, but it immediately goes to voicemail.

Adalyn crawls over to me, directly onto my lap and holds me tight. Like she knows I need her comfort. God, this girl. I can't leave this girl. She owns my heart, same as her father. I'm trying so hard to be brave for her. I don't want her to see me break. But I can't stop myself from taking solace in her small body.

"I love you," I whisper.

"Love you too," she whispers back automatically.

I can't let go. I can't give in.

I love them too much to let them go without a fight.

THIRTY-SEVEN

Jasper

THE ELEVATOR RIDE UP is deadly quiet. We're all feeling the heat of this betrayal. The sting of it. It's so much more than Viola. This impacts all of us, and there will be hell to pay.

By the time I'm done with her, there won't be a hole big enough for her to hide in.

How could she do this to me? After all our time together?

The doors slide open, and the four of us file out. I had called Sophia from the car on the way back here, so it's not surprising that she's standing in the foyer of this ridiculous suite waiting on us. Her smile is big and bright, her brown eyes clear as they zone in on me.

"You shouldn't have come back," are the first words out of her mouth. "The situation is being handled, and you have obligations. Band obligations."

"Marco is still there. They don't need us. Where is she?" I demand, and the color rises in Sophia's cheeks.

"Jasper," she starts calmly. "I already told you, I've taken care of it. There is nothing more to do. Go back to the radio station. Finish your interviews."

I roll my head over my shoulder and find my brother. "Do you think we should do that? Go finish those interviews?"

He shakes his head. "Nope." He pops the p.

I turn to the other guys who both have murder blazing in their eyes. "Do you think we should let this go? Let Sophia handle it?"

"Definitely not," Keith replies.

"Screw that," Henry spits.

Sophia steps forward, her eyes scanning each one of us in turn before they finish on mine. She gives me that smile. The one she uses on me when she's trying to keep me calm.

Not working this time, sweetheart.

"She's bad news, Jasper. Did you see those pictures? Did you read the headlines? She's bringing you and the band down with her. Child Protective Services in California has already reached out to me about Adalyn and your ability to care for her."

The fuck?

I narrow my eyes at her, my fists balling up. She's a goddamn liar. "They would call me directly if that were true. Not you."

Sophia huffs out a breath, her eloquence slipping along with the seconds. "She quit," she rushes out. "When she came back with Adalyn, she quit. Packed up all her belongings and told me she never wants to see you again."

That's it. I'm done with this.

"Where is she now?"

Sophia scans around the small space quickly, her eyes jetting this way and that as if the answer will somehow magically present itself. I have to admit, I'm only playing along because I'm stalling for time.

"She left. She took a cab to the airport. It's too late, Jasper. Just go back to the radio station. This is done." I narrow my eyes. "I'm just trying to protect you." She stomps her expensive heel on the floor, and it would be amusing if it wasn't so screwed up. "Don't do this. Don't throw everything away over some stupid girl."

Now I'm starting to lose the last shred of my patience. I'm about to unleash holy hell, but then I hear Adalyn giggling and decide I'm done with pretenses. I push past Sophia, following the sound of my daughter's laughter.

"Jasper, wait!" Sophia cries out behind me, but I don't stop.

I want her to follow me. I want her there when this all goes down.

I reach the door to Adalyn's bedroom; Sophia and the guys hot on my heels. Twisting the knob, I open it up to find a tear-stained Viola and a happy, smiling Adalyn playing on the bed. Viola's head whips over, her eyes welling up once more the moment they meet mine.

I'm going to destroy them for this.

"Jasper," Viola starts like she's gearing up for a battle. Righting her body, she moves to stand up. I shake my head at her, and her bottom lip trembles. "There's something you—"

I close the gap between us in three strides, cup her face in my hands, and fuse my lips with hers, cutting off any excuse she was about to give me.

I can't hear it.

I can't hear her sweet mouth tell me she's sorry when she has done nothing wrong.

Viola clings to me, her hands covering mine, her body shaking. I pull back, breathing hard, partially from her, partially from everything that's transpired in the last few hours.

"You okay?" She shakes her head, her teeth sinking into her bottom lip to hold back her emotion. "Henry? Keith?" I glance back over my shoulder at my friends. My brothers. "Would you guys mind taking Adalyn out into the living room? She can watch Mickey Mouse."

"Mickey Mouse," Adalyn squeals in delight, jumping up and down on the bed as she starts to sing the theme song to Mickey Mouse Club House in broken words.

"Come on, little darling. Let's go watch Mickey." Adalyn jumps across the bed and then launches herself into Henry's outstretched arms. "Do you want a snack? I'm so hungry I could eat a bear." He winks at me as he carries her past. "Or maybe I am a bear," Henry growls, grabbing at Adalyn and pretending to eat her neck. She yelps out a peal of laughter, loving any game these guys play with her.

The door clicks shut, and then it's just the four of us as silence ensues.

"Did you mean what you said?" Viola asks, her voice catching on the last word. "Did you really want me gone before you got back?" She swallows hard, shaking her head.

"What are you talking about? I never said that."

"Sophia played me a voice message from you."

"Soph?" Gus questions with a sharp edge to his tone.

Sophia puffs out an exasperated breath from behind me. "It was an old message. One from when you wanted me to fire one of Adalyn's therapists because she yelled at Ady. I was just trying to help. You can't trust this woman, Jasper. This is all her fault."

Gus's eyes meet mine, and I nod at the silent message in them. Time to end all this bullshit.

"I think we all know the truth, Sophia? You're the one who's been feeding the media this bullshit about Viola. About our band falling apart," I snap, my voice gruff like I've been using it to shout for the last two days.

It doesn't feel that far off. I turn around and face Sophia. Her complexion has gone completely ashen, void of any blood or color or life.

"No," Viola says, standing up next to me. "She's not."

"What?" Gus and I say in unison. Sophia's eyes widen, likely just as stunned by Viola's denial of her as we are.

"I have no idea what Sophia's game is. I know she doesn't like me, and I know she's trying to get rid of me, but she's not the one responsible for the pictures or the bogus stories." A tear falls, and I reach out, wiping it away, only to have two more chase it. "Jules is. And my mother."

Gus steps forward, grasping her hand and urging her to sit back down on the bed. She does, sinking her head onto his shoulder, his arm clutching around her. I sit down too, holding her other hand, feeling helpless.

"How do you know?" Gus asks softly, brushing her hair aside so he can see her face. His eyes meet mine, emitting anger and sympathy.

Sophia shifts her weight, like she's desperate to flee, but I hold up a finger, telling her to wait. That woman is not innocent, despite what Viola says, and she's not going anywhere until she tells me everything.

"Those pictures. The ones of me with Spencer?" I nod. "My mother took those. I know she did. I remember her teasing me about them at the time, saying it looked like he was paying me off for a night of fun. And that selfie of us in Rome? Of Gus in that restaurant in Barcelona? I took all those pictures. They're some of the many I sent to Jules. Same with those pictures of Adalyn that were in that French magazine. Every time the paparazzi found us, I had texted with Jules before it, telling her what we were up to that day. That's why the end of Europe was fairly quiet, I hadn't been texting with Jules much at that point. Just sending a quick text or pic here and there. I went back through all the pictures I sent her. All our conversations. She knew everything, and she used it against me. I shared my life with my best friend, and she used it against us." Tears leak from Viola's eyes, one after the other. Fuck. I can't stand watching my girl hurt like this. She wipes them away, laughing mirthlessly. "Bitch even enlisted my mother's help. Some of the comments in those articles are straight from her. I know it."

"Why would Jules do it? Your mother, unfortunately, is not a stretch, but Jules?"

She shakes her head, sinking further against Gus. He holds her tighter, his face etched in stone, and I know it's taking something very powerful for Gus to sit here calmly when what he really wants to do is rage.

"I don't know. She's jealous. Jealous of me being with you. Of my former relationship with Gus. Jealous that I'm here, and she's not."

Viola throws her hand up in the air, shaking her head ever so slightly. "I tried calling her, and she didn't pick up. But I just spoke to her before we came back to the hotel, and she was nasty. Snarky and short and accusatory." She blusters out a loud, shaky breath. "I don't get it. Why would she betray me like that? She had to assume I'd know it was her. Especially with those pictures of me with you in Europe and from the bar with Spencer."

"Money," Sophia chimes in, and the three of us look over to her, her lips thin and tight, her eyes stricken. "After the first incident with Intertainment, where the paparazzi started following you, I did my research. So did Jana, but I called the right person first, and because they owed me a favor, they told me who had given them the tip. I told Jana I would handle it, and she let me because she was backlogged with other things."

Sophia blows out a weighted breath, her head dropping back to stare up at the ceiling, her hands fisting her hips.

"Why, Sophia?" I bark at her when she doesn't continue. "Tell me why you'd do that? To me? To Adalyn?"

"I've loved you for a very long time, Jasper."

Her chin drops, and our eyes meet, and my breath has been stolen from my lungs.

Jesus, that was not what I was expecting.

There were times when I knew she wanted more with me. But I always assumed it was just sex. Never in my wildest dreams did I ever anticipate it was based on genuine affection.

"Sophia–" I stand, but she shakes her head, pushing a hand out toward me like she's trying to ward me off.

"At first, when Gus told me he wanted Viola for the position, I assumed it was so he could win her back. I thought it was sweet and romantic and was all for it. Plus," she shrugs, "she was qualified. But then, I noticed the way you looked at her, the way you looked at each other, and...," she shifts her attention to Viola. "I wanted to get rid of you. The press pictures seemed like the perfect way to do that. Especially given the stipulations we had placed on you regarding your employment. But Jasper held on so tight to you. It drove me crazy." She smiles miserably, her eyes glistening with emotion. "So, when I found out who was behind the press following you, I contacted Jules directly. I figured you must have done something wrong for your best friend and your mother to hate you enough to turn you over to the press, and that meant you didn't deserve him. I offered Jules more money, and she said she was splitting it with your mother. All of that was in exchange for anything they had, and Jules was only too happy to oblige me."

"Did she tell you why?" Viola asks, her voice light, cracking on the end. Damn, how much betrayal can one woman take?

"I think her reasons were similar to mine. She was jealous that Jasper and Gus wanted you and not her. That you were getting all this money to travel the world with them. Your mother, on the other hand, was only interested in the financial gain. My understanding is she had threatened Jules in some way or another, which is why she was involved at all."

Vi hums out something. Her sadness is gut-wrenching. "I've known Jules my entire life. Been best friends with her since we were babies. I just can't imagine she'd do all that simply because she was jealous."

Sophia clucks her tongue, offering Viola an embarrassed half-grin.

"Never underestimate the power of the green-eyed monster, Viola. Because I can tell you, I never imagined I'd ever do anything like this." Her gaze drops to the floor, and she releases a silent breath. "But it's too late now. I know that. All I can do is try to make it right. I understand you'll never love me back." Her eyes bleed into mine, and I can't help but hurt for her, even just a little. "I'm so sorry, Jasper. I truly am. I was jealous and angry, and it all flew out of control. I wasn't trying to hurt you. Or Adalyn." She shrugs helplessly, her hands going back to her hips. "I just wanted you to fire Viola. That was it. And then, once I discovered you two were together, I pulled back, because I knew I had lost you for good. I stopped paying Jules after Paris." Her voice trails off as she swallows hard. "I really am sorry."

Sophia takes a step toward us, bypassing me and heading straight for Viola. Viola's face tilts up. Neither appears angry anymore. Just heartbroken.

"I'm not the only one who was paying her. I had nothing to do with what happened today. Jules was furious with me when I stopped, and furious you hadn't been texting or talking as much as you had been. She was enraged when I mentioned you and Jasper were together, and you didn't tell her first. Today is the result. She must have sold you to someone else. Sold you off to the tabloids directly. I only took advantage of the original opportunity, and I'm so very sorry for any harm I've caused you, Viola." Sophia turns to me. "You have my resignation. I wish you nothing but the best with everything. I'll speak with Jana."

"I already have," I tell her. "It's how I knew you were involved. She figured something was off and assumed you were the one behind the situation today. She called me right before we made it to the radio station. Good thing too," I tell her, raising an eyebrow. Jealous or not, there is no excuse for this level of betrayal. She should have spoken to me directly, and she didn't. She hurt Viola, and she hurt Adalyn, and she hurt our band. "Otherwise, we would have been blindsided by the questions they flung at us. I'm sorry if I ever did anything to mislead you, and I'm sorry if I ever hurt you. But what you've done is unforgivable. You intentionally hurt my family. My girlfriend. My daughter. My band. I accept your resignation, and I hope you end up in a better place than where you are now."

With that, Sophia turns and walks out of the room, shutting the door softly behind her and leaving the three of us stunned speechless.

"Damn, Vi," Gus says, breaking the tense silence, dropping his lips onto the top of her head and giving her a kiss. "I'm so fucking sorry, sweetheart. If I could do anything, I'd make this better for you."

Viola's head is tucked into the crook of Gus' shoulder as he runs his hand down her long hair. I look at my girlfriend in my brother's arms, and I find I'm okay with it.

I love that they're still close. That love is not lost between them, even if it's shifted to another form of it. I watch them, and I feel...good.

I feel fucking right.

But if this were a few months ago, I'd be the green-eyed monster. I'd be the one insane with jealousy. So on some level, I understand Sophia's reasoning. Maybe not everything. Not her methodology, but her reasoning.

Now Jules, on the other hand... And Vi's mother?

Fuck that, and fuck them.

"I thought I understood betrayal when my mother stole my money," Viola speaks softly, her voice so dejected it makes my heart ache, and I squeeze her hand, inching closer.

The damage is already done. It's the sort of bullshit that will follow her. More lawsuits. More denials.

But will it be enough to save Viola's reputation?

That's the thing with this business. With this world we live in. Shit doesn't even have to be true. It doesn't even have to be plausible for it to be a scandal. For it to have air beneath its soaring wings.

There is no innocent until proven guilty.

Accusation has become enough to prove guilt. Or, at the very least, destroy.

I need to hold my girl.

I give her a tug, and she willingly leans forward, her face dropping effortlessly into my chest, where she inhales a deep, resonating breath. Gus offers me a smile, but his eyes are still hard, and I know that look. It's a look that says something has to be done.

It's a look that says we cannot ignore this.

I give him the slimmest of nods, my eyes flickering down to Viola and then back up to him. He returns my nod, knowing exactly what I have in mind.

We've talked about it before. All through southern France and

Spain, he and I had these conversations. No more secrets between us. Ever.

It's time to finish this. Once and for all.

Gus stands up, running his hand down Viola's head again before leaning down to plant a kiss onto the back of it. "I'm going to go check on Ady. Get some stuff ready for the show tonight. I'll catch you two later. But Vi?"

She pivots to face him.

"You're our world. Our light. And as long as someone shines as brightly as you do, someone will always be there trying to dim it. Please, don't let that happen. This was a reflection of their ugliness. Their darkness. Don't see it any other way."

"Thank you," Viola whispers, her voice hoarse. "I really needed to hear that. I love you."

"I love you. Forever."

He throws me a wink, and then he too leaves us.

The moment the door clicks shut, I lay Viola onto her back, hovering over her, propped up by my elbow. She blinks rapidly, staring sightlessly up at the ceiling, her hand on her forehead as she tries to work through everything in her mind.

"She told me for months how jealous she was. Made nasty comments about you and Gus and even Spencer when we were in Alabama."

She falls silent, and I stare down at her.

I never told her about Jules coming on to me in the hotel room. Never told her what she said, because I honestly didn't think twice about it after she walked out. My mind was too wrapped up in Viola. But that night, I knew Jules was spiteful. That she had a belligerent, mean streak to her, and I said and did nothing.

It just never occurred to me she would be capable of doing something like this.

"I knew she was resentful, but I didn't consider it was to this extreme. I thought it was the sort of happy jealousy you feel for a friend who's experiencing something you wish you could. I had no idea it was saturated in spite and vengeance. She hid it so well from me, and I kept feeding her. Pictures and texts and gossip."

I run my hand through her hair, twirling it around my finger. "Are you going to call her again? Try to get some answers?"

She contemplates this for a moment and then shakes her head no and then shrugs like she's not sure.

"By now, she has to know that I know it's her. And truthfully, what explanation could she give me that would make me understand? Or forgive her, though I doubt that's what she's after. She sold me out, used me, intentionally hurt me, could have ruined my future with you and my career as a teacher. I don't need or want people like that in my life. I think I'd like to hear it from her, but I don't know." She looks at me. "I have to think about that."

I lean down and press my lips to hers.

"I love you. I love you so much that I let my brother hold you, comfort you, and kiss your head when I wanted it to be me who did all that. I love you so much that I'm hoping you'll become Adalyn's mother."

A shaky, shuddered breath exhales from her chest, her eyes welling up instantly, one tear leaking out, sliding down her temple. I bend down, licking it from her skin.

"I'm hoping you'll help me give her brothers and sisters. Dozens of them, Vi. I want a fucking army of kids with you."

She belts out a small laugh, rolling her eyes skyward. But I'm not done.

"I love you so much that the thought of hurting you, in any way, is abhorrent." I kiss her again, cupping her face in my hand before I release her and point to the door. "And those guys out there? They love you too. Gus, most of all. But Henry and Keith were out for blood when they saw that bullshit that was printed about you. My little girl loved you instantly, and as you know, she is not one to warm up easily. You've become part of her world, her heart. I have no idea how to make you feel better about what Jules or even your mother did to you. We generally like to believe people are inherently good and have our best interests at heart. Especially the people we love. Unfortunately, that's not always the case. Sometimes, a person's own selfish agenda wins out. But you're not alone, baby." I dip down and kiss her once more. "And you never will be again. You're home with me. Your heart is safe with mine. And I will never hurt or betray you."

Viola leans up and kisses me, her tongue begging entrance into my mouth.

I willingly, eagerly, give it. Fuck, I'd give this woman anything– she already possesses the best parts of me. Everything else is hers.

Her kisses are like nothing else. They're soul-quenching. My fingers lace with hers, raising them above her head as I deepen it, my body rolling until it's completely on top of hers, pushing us further into the mattress.

"Tell me, dream girl. Tell me it's forever."

"Yes," she pants as I grind myself against her pussy, hitting her in just the right way. "I love you with all of me."

My body takes over, stripping our clothing in seconds, my fingers pressing into her soaking wet heat. "You're always so wet for me. Always ready."

"I should leave, Jasper," she whispers against me, my heart shattering with hers. "I've brought you and Adalyn nothing but trouble. The world is clamoring for our destruction, your band's destruction, and it doesn't seem like it'll stop until they get it."

The walls of my chest collapse around me, caging me in, filling me with lead.

I don't give up, and I don't give in. Ever.

She knows this about me. So, she's got to be kidding me with that.

"I'm not letting you get away." I press my cock against her opening. "Fuck them. I'm not letting you walk out of my life just because I don't like what the tabloids are saying." I push inside of her slick, warm pussy. Her eyes close before they reopen, liquid fire. "For so long, Viola Starr, I felt undeserving. For so long, I let myself be consumed by guilt. But with you..." I pump into her, holding her gaze tight with mine, "With you, I'm deserving. With you, the world makes sense again. The rest of it doesn't matter as long as I have you."

Her breaths falter, more tears spill from her eyes.

"Do I have you, Viola?"

"Yes," she whimpers as I begin to pump into her harder, my hand cradling her face, our eyes locked.

My love. My life. My heart. My soul. My fucking essence.

She's here in my arms, and I'll fight the world for her if I have to. I'll fight off our shared darkness.

Her legs wrap around my waist, holding me to her.

Our sweaty chests pressed together, our hearts pounding as one. She's close. I can see it. The way her cheeks flush, and her breaths become erratic, and her nipples harden even more.

God, she's so sexy. A siren. My vixen. The temptress of my life.

"That's it. Feel me. Feel us together." She moans, her neck arching. "Yes, baby. Like that. You're so beautiful. Come with me, Viola." Her body spasms around mine, as we both tumble over the edge, freefalling into absolute bliss.

"You have me, Jasper," she promises once our breathing has slowed, and our bodies are still fused as one. "I'm yours. You're mine. And you're right. Nothing else matters but that."

"That's all I needed to hear."

Time to go slay some dragons. And I know just how to do it.

THIRTY-EIGHT

Viola

I FELL ASLEEP, wrapped up in Jasper. After we made love, we dressed, talked, kissed a ton, and then I passed out. My brain was just too heavy. My soul too wrecked.

I want everything Jasper is offering.

All those pieces he set before me will forever be mine. Jasper. Adalyn. Gus. Keith and Henry. This life. This band. These people.

But when I wake up alone, knowing that Jasper has a million fires to put out, I succumb to my inner demons. The ones telling me that I need answers. The ones telling me that I must have done something wrong for my lifelong bestie to do this to me. For my mother to continually choose herself and her drugs over me.

And part of me is scared.

So much of my life has been fleeting. So little of me connected, and the people I have been connected with, up until now, have used me like fucking Kleenex.

Climbing out of bed, I contemplate heading back out into the suite, but the large window steals me before I can find my footing and courage. I stare out the window at the sun setting over Central Park, marveling at the dusting of pink and purple as they dance across the sky.

It's beautiful in a very tragic way.

Or maybe that's just me.

Because I don't know how to step outside and hold my head high when people are saying the most awful things about me.

Part of me wants to go out there and tell them all the truth. But that's not what those tabloids are after, and they'll spin that as they've spun everything else. I've only been at this a few months, and already I know that.

With my eyes on the park and my hand on my hip, I use my other hand to call my former best friend.

This time, she picks up.

"I'm shocked you called."

"Are you really?"

Jules releases a breath into the phone. "What do you want me to say?"

That's a good question. She's obviously not sorry. She clearly doesn't give a shit about me. So why did I call? For closure? For answers? For something that will make this moment easier for me?

I don't know.

"I guess I just wanted to hear you admit that you're a two-timing cunt-rag."

She laughs. Actually fucking laughs.

"If that's what helps you sleep at night next to your Rockstar, then fine. I'm the bitch. You're the princess. Feel better now, pumpkin?"

I grin. And then I frown.

"You sold me out for money? You teamed up with my mother, who stole from me and admittedly never gave a shit about me. We've been best friends since we were kids, Jules."

"It's not like you were coming back here, Viola. You were already gone. I had nothing to lose and everything to gain. Besides, if you really want honesty, I was so fucking tired of everyone always wanting you. Those guys, every fucking guy, orbits around you like you're the sun and the moon and the stars. All I did was earn a little money off your drama. You're the one who fucked the brother of your ex. That shit is on you. Not me. Now you have to live with the repercussions. Next week, they'll be onto something new and forget all about you."

What a sad world Jules lives in. My mother's might be worse.

I can't even contact my mother. After she stole my savings, she changed her number. Message received. In multiple ways. I guess Jules just delivered the same crushing blow.

"Part of me wants to laugh, tell you I'm unfazed by your crap. Remind you that at the end of this, you're still there, and I'm here. That you can't take away my happiness no matter how hard you and my mother try. But then I'd be as bitter and shitty as you are. And fuck that, right? Why should I be you when I can be better? Bye, Jules. Hope you and my mother got what you wanted out of all this. I certainly did."

Then I hit end.

Then I let my phone slip from my fingers.

Then I ignore it as it tumbles to the carpet, and I'm forced to try and accept this.

People will try to tell me that I'm better off without them in my life. That it's their loss, not mine.

And I know that's true. I know it.

But I'm still so hurt. Why is it we can hear countless positive things about ourselves, see so much love reflected at us, and yet we only seem to be able to focus on the negative?

Human nature sucks.

I take in a deep breath, square my shoulders back, and pivot away from the window. Scarlett O'Hara said it best, 'Tomorrow is another day.' I'll get through this. I'll bounce back. Not much else matters to me right now other than Jasper and Adalyn.

I don't hear much as I open the door, entering the hallway that will lead me into the common areas of the suite. Not a whole lot of noise other than Adalyn screeching when I enter the living room of the suite. Marco is there, his expression one of delight as he watches Adalyn jump from one couch to the other, her long reddish hair flying all over the place.

"Jump. Jump. Jump. Jump," Adalyn squeals in pure delight.

"It takes a very special kind of lady to figuratively piss all over thousands of dollars' worth of furniture and not care."

I laugh lightly, watching her smash the expensive cushions with her feet as she goes. "You could try and stop her."

"I could. But I'm angry tonight, Viola. I'm angry, and I don't feel the need to restrict a small girl who deserves nothing more than a little fun after she was accosted on the streets."

He has a point.

"Vi!" Adalyn screams, jumping on and then rolling her body along the plush fabric.

"Hi, sweet girl. Having fun?"

She doesn't respond, but her beaming smile is enough to tell me she is.

"I even let her have an extra scoop of that soy milk ice cream crap Jasper forces her to eat. Have you tried that? It has the consistency of paste."

"They were out of the almond milk one. That's much better than the soy."

"I believe you. The soy tastes like camel dung."

I snort out a laugh now, and he pivots to grin at me. "That took five whole minutes. Five whole minutes longer than it should have." He crosses the room, dropping his hands to my shoulders and slaying me with a gaze not to be ignored. "Fuck those skanky bitches. Legit, you're my girl, and I'm telling you, they're stupid for doing that to you."

"Thank you." Because Marco is nothing if not honest, and I think

I needed that from him most of all. "I also appreciate you not drop-ping deadly metaphors."

"Honey, if Liz Taylor can live through the worst of it, you can too. This business is serious, and the boys you roll with are the cream to the milk, if you know what I mean by that. There will always be succubi out for a good time, coming in their cheap shorts while those who are better than them are the ones who fall."

I nod numbly. I can't even chuckle at his comments. He's not joking or trying to be light. He's dead fucking serious.

"I know. I know it's them and not me. I know all of that. It's just..."

"Nobody expects the Spanish Inquisition."

I giggle, shaking my head. "Monty Python?"

He winks at me. "See. This is why I like you. You get my weird, and I get yours. That's how this works. The people out there who don't get your weird or don't know how to accept it, and instead try to destroy it, are the sad, tragic ones. They're the ones who have to wake up and face themselves in the mirror. We will never be happy to hurt others. That's not our boys."

"I know it's not."

"Or you." He raises an assertive dark eyebrow, ensuring I get his full meaning.

"Or me. Never for money and always for love."

"Good. Because tonight, honey, you're going downtown to MSG to watch the show."

I shake my head furiously. "No. I want to stay here tonight."

"Sorry," he shrugs with a sorry-not-sorry jump to his shoulders. "Boss's orders. End of. Dress pretty and get going. Thomas is waiting, and no one and nothing will see you leave this building other than your driver and security."

"I hate you."

"I know. I totally love you too."

I throw my arms around him, tugging him into me. "Thank you. I really needed that."

"That's not why I said it."

I grin, getting choked up. "I know. That's why I meant it."

He kisses my cheek, shoving me in the direction of my bedroom. "Get going. I need to put this little lady down. It's going to take a bottle of vodka and some Xanax to accomplish that the way this night is going." My eyes widen, and he laughs, shaking his head. "I meant for me. And I was only kidding."

"Right. I get your weird."

"Now you're catching on."

I lift Adalyn into my arms and give her a kiss. She wants nothing to do with it, far more content with jumping around, so I release her, heading in to get dressed.

"Night, sweet girl. I love you."

"Love you, too," she and Marco sing together.

A laugh bursts from me, a smile splitting my lips, and I'm starting to feel a little better. A little lighter. The people I have are the people who matter.

The others are wasted time.

I have no idea why Jasper wants me to come down to Madison Square Garden tonight of all nights. As much as I love watching the band play, all I want to do right now is crawl into bed, maybe shed a few pathetic tears, and fall asleep. Especially if Marco is putting Adalyn down for me. But I won't disappoint him by not showing up.

It's nearing eight-thirty, and the show has already begun, the boys set to start in about half an hour. I take my time, slipping into a skirt I know Jasper can't help but stare at and a simple white tee that I slide over my purple bra.

I apply a smattering of makeup and make sure my hair is flawless and walk out the door, smiling as I hear Marco reading to Adalyn from her bedroom. It's well past her bedtime by this point, I'm shocked she's not already passed out.

Thomas meets me in the hall, and thirty minutes later, I'm led through a private back entrance in Madison Square Garden. But instead of being directed to the side of the stage where I watched the guys from last time, I'm brought into an empty room that looks like the room they typically get ready for the show in. There are a few untouched bottles of alcohol–probably for after the show–a tray of cheese and fruit that's also untouched and a wall of mirrors set above a dressing area.

"What's going on?" I ask Thomas, who gives me nothing in return, his expression completely blank.

"Sorry, Vi. I was told to bring you here and have you wait."

The door shuts behind him, and I spin around, taking in each item in the empty room. "Wait for what?" I question aloud to no one.

I pick up a piece of cheese from the tray and pop it into my mouth. I haven't had dinner, but I'm not all that hungry.

The sounds of the band playing fill the air, and I sit down on the couch in a huff, crossing my legs at the knee and folding my arms over my chest. Why the hell would Jasper drag me down here just to sit in this stupid room alone?

Not even ten minutes later, I get my answer.

Gus walks in wearing a dark gray shirt that matches his eyes, worn jeans, and a devilish smile aimed in my direction that suddenly has my heart ricocheting around my chest.

He's also holding a blindfold.

"Evening, darlin'. Glad you could make it to the show."

THIRTY-NINE

Jasper

MY FINGERS CARESS the black and white keys of the piano as I sit down on the hard bench. The crowd always grows quiet at this juncture in the show. I'm not sure if it's the fact that I'm sitting, or if it's because they cannot anticipate my next move and are curious to watch it play out.

When people pay a minimum of a hundred and fifty dollars to come and see your show, you don't shirk them out of a good night. We play hard every single night, and we do it for hours.

Two and a half plus an encore, to be exact.

I think this is why the guys haven't pushed me harder to tour before now. It's grueling. And the blood, sweat, and tears of the show are the pinnacle of it all.

That said, with the show comes the high. I think I've already mentioned that a time or two. The high is like nothing else.

Except for tonight.

The high tonight is dulled. Lost in the amorphous senselessness of lies.

Lies that hurt people. Lies that ruin lives. That tear people apart.

Maybe it's why I've stayed to myself for so long. Why I've kept Adalyn in her ivory tower, as Viola once put it. I would love to play a song and tell the world that we've risen above the chaos. But I'm not completely sold on that. Because lies don't just evaporate with the truth. Their poison is insidious.

They won't die without a fight.

So, as I sit here, staring down at the keys, I contemplate what I'm about to do.

It's drastic.

It's going to be all over those tabloids I've been avoiding.

But I have to fix this. I have to make it better for her, and really, it's time. It's been time since my lips first pressed to hers. Since the first moment she truly became mine and no one else's.

The crowd rustles, their impatience at my quiet making them restless.

To my left, Keith starts to pound out a slow, even beat with the bass drum. It's a diversionary tactic. One I'm grateful for because it causes the crowd to grow from fidgety to captivated. Drowning in anticipation as their hearts begin to pound in line with the drum. *Bump. Bump. Bump.*

It's the encore, and typically, we finish the show with our biggest hit from our third album. It's an anthem. A call to live in the moment because you never know which moment could be your last. It's the one song positively everyone sings along to, and when the show is over, it's the one that's still humming from their lips.

But tonight, everything is different.

Tonight is about fixing Viola's heartbreak.

Her reputation as a person, a caretaker, and a teacher is tarnished, and I cannot abide by that.

Henry strokes his bass with a G-flat major scale in time with the drums, and now the crowd starts to cheer.

"They're ready, man," Keith hollers over to me. "Showtime."

Adjusting my position, I address the mic attached to the piano.

"How are we doing so far?"

The roar that fills the room has me chuckling, waving my hand in the air for them to quiet down. I angle my head, facing them while making sure they can still hear me.

"Let me tell you, you guys are awesome. I mean, fucking incredible. We love playing New York." More deafening screams. "So, I wanted to tell you all a story. Do you think you can humor me for a few minutes?" A lot of whistles and clapping this time. "But I have a favor to ask. Everyone who has a cell phone at the ready, turn it to video and start recording. Because when this is done, I want you to post the video on whatever social media you prefer."

And now they're silent. I swear, a pin could drop, and I'd know where it hit the ground. It makes me grin. My fans know me, and that hits my heart in such a special way.

"Not our usual style, right? But everything is different tonight. Because today, well, for months really, a woman I care about, a woman we all care about," I wave my hand around the stage at my bandmates, "was wrongfully accused of doing things she absolutely did not do, by the ugly jealousy of others. And I cannot let that go. I cannot let her name be slandered, and her integrity questioned. So let's address the charges, shall we?"

A thunder of cheers fills Madison Square Garden, and I patiently wait until they quiet once more. I grip the microphone with one hand, twisting a little more to them.

"You see, we grew up with this girl. All of us. And I'm here tonight to set the record straight. Are you all recording?"

Several flashes go off, flickering around the arena, but the fans are quiet, and what little I can see of the first few rows, their phones are raised high. My fingers press into the keys, playing out the first few notes of the tune I wrote only a few weeks ago.

"Let me start by saying, I've loved Viola Starr since I first saw her." I wink at the audience shrouded in shadows. "I was eight." I laugh, and the crowd rumbles with an indiscernible sound. "But you see, my brother also loved her, and for reasons I won't get into, I stepped back and let him have her. They dated for years until their worlds went in separate directions. While our band was touring the world and creating music, Viola dedicated her life to helping children who needed her warmth, determination, sunshine, and heart the most. Let me tell you, Viola Starr has a heart unlike any other I've encountered. She loves selflessly. She endures hardship with a smile and the sort of infectious optimism we'd all do well to emulate.

"The first lie I'm going to address is with regard to her previous job as a teacher. She was laid off from it due to budget cuts. Not fired for any impropriety. She left that position with high recommendations from the principal, fellow teachers, and the parents of her students. If you're looking for proof of it, you can find that posted on our website."

I begin to play through the melody as Keith grows more urgent on the drums.

"The second lie is that Viola accepted money in exchange for sex." I shake my head, my anger dripping past my lips. "All I can say is give me a fucking break. Did you see those pictures? Bullshit, right?" The audience goes nuts, screaming and cheering. "The guy in the picture is a friend of all of ours, and a man she dated for a brief time a couple of years back. The cash he handed her was her share of tips from working in the bar that night. End. Of. Story. If you need more than that, our friend offered to speak on her behalf."

I catch movement from the side of the stage, and my smile grows so wide I can barely contain it.

"As for Viola and I dating behind Gus's back and our band breaking up, well, I don't think I'm the man to answer that question for you."

I sit back, straightening my spine and pivoting on the bench to watch Gus push a blindfolded Viola toward the stage as she fights against him, yelling something I can't hear, but can guess at. She spins in his arms, smacking at his chest. He shakes his head, clutching her biceps, dragging her reluctant body toward the lights of the stage.

Finally, he manages to tug her out, holding onto her waist firmly as he guides her blindly toward the piano I'm sitting at. The arena erupts, the pounding so loud I feel it vibrate through my body, the stage, and every hard surface around us.

My fingers fly across the keys, and as they get closer, I hear her cries of protest. "Come on, Vi. Grow some balls."

"Screw you, Gus. You're not the one blindfolded, walking on stage in front of thousands of people."

Gus laughs, shoving her a little harder in my direction. "They can all hear you, babe."

"Fantastic. Remind me to poison all you bastards for doing this to me."

I chuckle, rubbing my hand along my jaw as cheers and whistles reach us from the crowd. Twin spots of rose stain Viola's cheeks, her head whipping in that direction, though I doubt she can see much of anything through the blindfold.

"Hey, Gus?" I ask, standing up and ambling toward them, taking the microphone with me. "Are we breaking up? Is our lovefest over?"

Gus spins a blind Viola around in his arms and plants a kiss on her cheek before turning her back to me and stepping away. "If anything, we're just getting started, brother."

And shit, I didn't think this place could get louder than it already was.

And fuck, I didn't think I could love my brother more than I already do.

"Jasper?" Viola calls out shakily, her head twisting toward the audience once more as she slips the black silk from her eyes. She blinks several times, taking in what she can. The rose on her cheeks turns bright red.

Her hands sag at her sides, her jaw slightly agape. The blindfold begins to slip through her fingers, destined for the stage, so I snatch it up, tucking it into my pocket for later.

A blindfolded Viola is too good of an opportunity to pass up.

Viola's eyes are comically wide as she seeks me out, and once she finds me, they narrow into tiny slits of venom.

"I'm going to kill you for this," she hisses. I watch as she visibly swallows, insanely nervous, and then I step forward, taking her hand and intertwining our fingers. She shakes her head at me, begging me, but instead, I guide her over to the piano I just vacated.

No more hiding.

"Say hi to all our friends, Vi."

She gives a half-wave. "Um. Hi?"

I give her a self-satisfied grin as she sits beside me, staring daggers into me with an expression that promises retribution. *Bring it on, Viola, bring it on.*

This is not something I wanted to do publicly.

I wanted to play this song for her for the first time in private. But I need the world to vindicate her. I need her to be able to hold her head up high. I need this to not follow her around every time she applies for a job or goes to the store or to the park with Adalyn.

I could tell the tabloids myself.

I could do interviews, but screw it and screw them.

This is far more persuasive, and with the crowd posting it on social media, it removes any power the tabloids have because they've been beaten to the story by the masses.

I set the microphone back in its holder, adjusting it, so it's mouth level.

My fingers begin to fly across the keys as Gus picks up his discarded guitar, tossing it over his shoulder and playing along. The four of us start, but there is something I have to do first.

I catch Viola's eye. "Viola, I know you're mad at me for this. You don't like being the center of attention. You don't like the world I've dragged you into, but you've stuck it out. You've endured the madness, the lies, and the hurt for me and for Adalyn and for the guys. And hell, that only makes me love you so much more. I was just telling our friends here," I pan my arms out toward the audience, "that I've loved you from the moment I first saw you. And it hasn't stopped." Our eyes lock. "Not for one minute, regardless of years of absence. The first second I saw you again, it was as if no time had passed. But what I haven't told them, or more importantly you, is how much I want to marry you."

The barrage of sound is unlike any I've ever experienced before.

Viola gasps, her beautiful hazel eyes glossy with emotion, her lips parted as she reaches up to cover them. "Viola, for the first time in my life, I don't have a lot of words. You've stolen them all from me, so I wrote them down into a song. If you'll bear with me, I'd like to play it for you and this amazing audience we have with us tonight."

We let loose, the words flowing from my lips in a love song unlike any I've written before. My gaze holds hers as the room beyond us slowly dissipates into the sounds I sinuously extort from my piano. From Keith's drums and Henry's bass and Gus's acoustic guitar.

It all pours out, compiles into one synergy of sound and light, the force so powerful it makes my chest clench and my voice thick.

But at the epicenter of it all is her.

Viola. My dream girl.

Tears stream effortlessly down her face, and she does nothing to wipe them away. She's as raw with this moment as I am.

And when I'm finished playing my heart out to her, bearing my soul to the world, I rise up off the bench, walk around it, and lower myself onto one knee.

"I love you, Vi. With you by my side, I'm complete. The two of us with Adalyn are a family. And together, we can get through anything. Viola Starr, will you marry me?"

"Yes," she cries, half-laughing, half-weeping.

I slide my mother's engagement ring onto her finger, because Viola is the type of woman who would rather have this meaningful ring than the biggest most expensive one money could buy. She dives down onto me, kissing me crazy, and the world explodes into a clamorous cacophony.

"I love you," she whispers into my mouth. "Sexy god. Rock man."

I grin into her mouth. "I love you. Dream girl."

"Thank you for always having the perfect words. For never giving up on us. For being my hero. But most of all, for making me believe in love again."

"Baby, you haven't seen anything yet."

EPILOGUE 1

Jasper
6 months later

"ONE OF THESE DAYS, we're going to have to go in search of a white Christmas," Viola muses as she stares out at the sun setting along the angry Pacific, watching the waves rush in with a vengeance. Today is Christmas Day, and Viola, Ady, and I have been walking along the beach for over an hour. We're expected for Christmas dinner soon at my friend Lyric Rose's place out here in Malibu, but we decided to have a quiet walk first.

Just the three of us.

"Since when do you like snow?"

Viola shrugs, staring out into the milieu of endless wonders before us.

"I don't know if I do. That's the point. But I'd like to experience snow once in my life, at least."

Since we returned from the tour four months ago, we've been going nonstop. Viola moved in with Ady and me immediately and set to work on finding a teaching position. Not so easily done, believe it or not. So she's been substituting as often as she can, which has come out to at least three days a week.

We enrolled Adalyn in a preschool program that has a special needs component to it. She's in an integrated class with neurotypical children as well as children with both physical and developmental delays and disabilities.

Some days are better than others with that.

She has bonded well with her primary case manager as well as her paraprofessional, but being around the other students in the class and adjusting to a classroom setting has been a steep learning curve for her.

Viola insists it's good for her to be challenged like this.

I agree, but it's still gut-wrenching when she clings to me at drop-off in the morning. A father can only handle so much.

That said, since she began the program, she's been stringing more words together into short sentences, and they work with her on strategies she can implement to meet her own sensory needs.

Gus, Keith, Henry, and I have been working tirelessly in the studio.

You'd think after touring for five months, we'd want a break from the music, but considering I wrote a total of eighteen songs on the tour–including the one I sang to Viola the night I proposed–it was just too much to sit on hold with. Lyric, who is also our producer, claims this is our best album yet.

We'll see how the finished product comes out in the end.

The media storm slowly died down as we neared the end of the tour.

It followed us around for a bit, especially after the videos of me proposing to Viola went viral. But now, it's all but quieted down. And life is…normal. Fucking awesome, if I'm being honest. I haven't married Viola yet, but we plan to do that soon.

Something small. Just us. Just our family.

"How about next year we all go skiing?"

Viola turns away from the ocean and orange fire of the sunset to pin me with an 'are you crazy' expression. "*Skiing?*" She shakes her head. "Are you trying to kill me, Jasper Diamond? I may not be as clumsy as I was in high school, but some people are not meant to hurtle themselves down a mountain while standing on two sticks of wood."

I can't help it. I crack up, and when I start to laugh, Adalyn does too.

She's been kinda quiet today.

We did a whole Christmas morning thing with the guys, and I think it was a lot for her. She got so many presents it overwhelmed me. Ady and I got Viola a few presents, but I've been working on the main one with Adalyn, and thus far, she's not delivering on her side of things.

"Fine then. No skiing. How about some outdoor hot tubbing and hot chocolate by the fire while we watch the snow fall?"

"Yes. Now you're starting to get it."

Viola turns back to the water, a small hidden smile on the edge of her lips. "What?"

"Nothing," she says, but she's lying. I know Viola's every expression.

"You're hiding something from me."

"Maybe," she laughs, but doesn't immediately follow that up with anything. I nudge her with my shoulder, and she rolls her eyes. "Ady and I have a present for you, but I don't want to give it to you until later. Until we're home, just the three of us."

"Can I have a hint?"

"Nope. Right, Ady?"

Adalyn takes this moment to want us to swing her between us. "One. Two. *Three!*" she yells up at us, tugging on our respective arms until we give in and repeat the count before we launch her forward. Adalyn squeals with delight before requesting, "More," but time is dwindling, and soon we'll have to head up the beach to Lyric's, and I really, really want Adalyn to help me give Viola this present.

Mine, whatever it is, can wait.

So I motion for us to sit down in the cool sand under the pretenses of watching the final rays of the sun as they glow against the sky. It's breezy out here today, only in the low sixties, but it feels crisp instead of cold as the wind brushes against our skin.

Adalyn immediately starts to dig in the sand, asking for a star, even though we don't have our sand toys with us.

Viola sits beside me, her head resting on my shoulder. "I like California," she declares like she's just making that decision now. "I wasn't sure I would. Los Angeles is so not my scene. The school system is a total mess. The traffic and congestion are something else. But all that aside, I'm pretty damn happy."

"Yeah?" I ask, angling my head to catch her expression.

She's smiling. "Yeah. You can stop worrying now," she laughs. "I know you've been trying extra hard to make me feel like the house is mine too, and doing everything you can think of to make me feel at home here."

I'm smiling like a damn fool.

"Hey, Ady?" I ask, hoping this works out the way I've planned. Adalyn tilts her head in my direction like she's listening to me, but doesn't want to pull her focus away from the sand. Maybe I should have done this earlier at the house with her. "Come here, bug." I drag her onto my lap, and though she squirms and fights for a second, wanting to go back to the sand, she ultimately gives in when I squeeze her close to me. "Did you have a good Christmas?"

"Christmas," she repeats in a sort of broken way that sounds more like chriscux.

"Are you ready to play our little game now? Show Viola the new thing we worked on?"

Viola twists herself away from the water, over to us, curiosity perking up her brows. Adalyn is silent, but I'm going to take that as a yes.

"What do we want to say for Christmas?" I ply, whispering in

Adalyn's ear. She spins in my arms to peek up at me, searching for the answer. "Adalyn, who's this?" I point to Viola.

My heart starts to jackhammer in my chest. I've been trying so damn hard to get Adalyn to do this, and some attempts are better than others.

Adalyn glances over to Viola and then back to me, her eyebrows knit together. "Who's that?"

Adalyn swallows and then murmurs, "Mommy."

An unstoppable smile breaks across my face as I hear Viola gasp.

I nod my head, kissing Adalyn's nose. "That's right. Good job. That's mommy. Do you want to wish mommy a Merry Christmas?" Viola reaches out, clutching my hand so tight my fingers start to go numb as they lose their blood supply. I hear her sniffling and can feel her beaming smile, but I'm dying for Adalyn to finish this off with a masterstroke. "What do we want to say to mommy about Christmas?" I prompt when Adalyn doesn't reply.

"Merry Christmas, mommy." Adalyn breathes the words. That's how soft they are. And Christmas is still difficult for her to say, but she did it. My fucking brilliant, sweet girl did it.

I squeeze Adalyn so tight, peppering her face with kisses.

"Jas," Viola's voice cracks on my name. "Oh my—" she swallows. Then she steals Adalyn from my arms, enveloping her in a hug for the ages. Adalyn's long hair flies all around her, covering Viola with a blanket of auburn. "Yes, sweet girl. I'm your mommy."

And now she's sobbing. Like a full-on hiccupping mess of a woman.

"Mommy, what's wrong?" Adalyn asks, bewildered, not under-standing why Viola is crying.

That's a new one. Her asking what's wrong.

She asks Mickey Mouse that question all the time. I think it's probably one of the most adorable things ever, but her using it on a real person like this is a first.

Viola pulls back, wiping at her face as she beams down at her daughter. "Nothing. I'm just so happy right now." She turns to me as more of those happy tears drip down her rosy cheeks, her hazel eyes bright with wonder. "Thank you. This is the best present ever. But–"

"I'm positive," I interrupt, wrapping my arms around the two of them. "You're her mother. No one else." I kiss the side of her face. Her lips. "You're stuck with us now."

"This is the best Christmas present anyone has ever given me. Thank you. I guess that means Ady and I should give you your present now too then."

I chuckle, kissing more of her tears away. "What's that?"

Viola shifts her position, careful not to jar Adalyn off her lap, and reaches into her pocket, pulling out what looks like paper. "Ady?" Viola leans in, kissing her nose. "What's in mommy's belly?"

Now it's my turn to gasp, my heart rate jacking up a notch. My gaze darts from Adalyn to Viola to the piece of paper in her hand and then back over to Adalyn.

"Baby," she says, clear as day.

"Yes. Mommy has a baby in her belly." Viola kisses Adalyn's cheeks. "You're going to be a big sister, sweet girl." She turns to me. "And daddy is going to be a daddy times two."

"For real?" I stare at her, at them, the loves of my life, smiling in a way I'm positive I never have before.

"Yup. My doctor told me when I was there for my regular check-up." She hands me the slip of paper, and I read it over. Sure enough. Pregnant. "I'm not very far along. That's why I wanted to wait until later when we were home alone, but this was too perfect of a moment–"

Capturing Viola's face in my hand, I fuse my lips to hers, cutting off anything else she was about to say. Reaching out, I wrap my other arm around Adalyn, tucking her into us.

"I love you," I tell them both. "So much. I didn't think I could be any happier than I was a few moments ago, but I was wrong. So very wrong. Somehow, every moment with you is better than the last. It only gets better from here."

EPILOGUE 2

Gus

I SHOULD HAVE EXPECTED THIS.

And maybe part of me did. There was an element of dread locked low in my gut. But not to this extent. I didn't anticipate standing up there, beside my brother, feeling like my heart was being ripped out of my chest.

I let him have her. I gave him the girl who has owned my heart since we were kids. My first girlfriend. My first everything.

The only one who has ever given me life and love and hope. Who broke through a darkness most know nothing of and few suspect.

It's rough. Feeling like you're split in two and the only one who has ever made you feel whole is no longer yours.

Viola looks beautiful.

Exactly the way I used to picture her looking on this day. Only, instead of me being the groom, the man by her side, kissing her lips and saying 'I do,' it's my brother.

Jasper, being the intuitive bastard that he is was onto me from the first moment.

He offered to have Henry or Keith take over for me. To make the speech. To walk her down the aisle, since there was no one else who could do it, and then stand beside him as best man.

But there was no one else I wanted to have do it. Any of it. It's why I volunteered in the first place.

So, I told him no.

He's my brother, and they love each other, and she's carrying his baby, and it's all as it should be. It's. All. As. It. Should. Be.

I know this. But still...

The heartbreak was on his face. The worry for me on a day when he shouldn't have any. The man deserves some peace and happiness, and I'm sucking it from him because I'm nothing if not a selfish prick.

A man who should not be picturing himself with the bride, but is and has been all day.

Slender arms wrap around my waist, a warm, soft body hugging me from behind draws me momentarily out of my dark thoughts. My eyes close, and I blow out a slow, even breath.

"You've been quiet all day," Vi says, face pressing into my back the way it used to when we were teenagers. I set down my drink on the nearest table and take hers, the ones pressed into the center of my chest, in mine, intertwining our fingers.

"I know."

"You want to tell me about it?"

"Nothing left to say that hasn't already been said."

She makes a humming noise, and I'm just fucking up this wedding all around.

"I'm so happy for you..."

My words trail off only for her to pick up where I left off with, "But this hurts." I swallow hard and silently nod. I wish it didn't. It honestly shouldn't at this point. I was the mastermind of Viola and Jasper becoming Viola and Jasper. I set it all into motion.

I *wanted* this for them, dammit.

I still do. I wouldn't change the way it all turned out. The only thing I'd change is myself. Something I should have done so long ago. And maybe that's it.

The wonder: If she knows I only slept with those women to make the loneliness without her a little more tolerable?

The lingering question: If I hadn't cheated and broken her heart and trust, would it have been me today instead of my brother?

I hear her sniffle, her body starting to tremble against mine, and Jesus, how many different ways can I fuck up one woman?

"Aww, Vi. Shit. Don't cry, babe. I didn't mean to upset you, sweetheart." I spin her around in my arms and she shakes her head furiously, sucking in ragged breaths and forcing out a watery smile.

"No. It's fine. It's just hormones, right?"

Except a tear falls, and I didn't think I could feel worse. Hurting this woman, again, after all I've done to her, is like the ultimate knife to the gut.

She lets out a self-deprecating laugh and asks, "Dance with me?"

"I would love nothing more."

I take her into my arms, tucking her in against me, my hands on her lower back, hers around my neck. "Just like when we were kids," she laughs as I start to sway her a bit on the outskirts of the dance floor.

"I remember a lot more grinding, actually."

She laughs some more, smacking the back of my head. "Always with the dirty mind."

She has no idea.

I open my eyes and immediately lock on my brother, who is standing by the bar talking to Lyric Rose, but his eyes are on me. And in them, I see so much. So much love for me. For the woman in my arms. So much hope that one day I'll have this too.

Just not with her.

And that's what I have to tell myself. Because it's one thing to know it, another to see it, but finally accepting that the one you love is lost to you forever is a brutal, crushing reality that defies logic and rationalizations.

"I love you, Gus."

I smile, turning away from my brother so I can kiss his bride on the cheek. "I love you, Vi. Always."

She pulls back and meets my eyes, her hand sliding along my head until she's cupping my jaw. "No, Gus. You won't," she states simply, but the conviction in her voice pulls me up short. "Not the way you think you will. You don't love me that way now. The woman who will truly own your heart will tie you up in knots." She rolls her eyes. "Knowing you, probably both literally and figuratively." I smirk, despite the serious mood and tone she's pushing on me. "This woman will consume you. She'll be the one you fight everything and everyone for. That's not me, babe. It never was."

Something in her words, in her quiet truth, hits me hard. Steals the breath from my lungs. Forces a shudder from somewhere deep within.

No one has ever consumed me like that. Not even the woman in my arms.

She smiles brightly up at me, almost as if she's reading my thoughts. Leaning up on her toes, she plants a small kiss on my lips. "Go find her, Gus. You're ready."

*** The End

Want to see Gus get his HEA plus get more of Jasper and Viola? I promise, you'll fall so hard for Gus in this forbidden, rock star, friends to lovers, emotional romance! Get his book, CRAZY TO LOVE YOU and continue getting lost in the Wild Love series.

If you enjoyed reading about Jasper and Viola please consider leaving a review. Sign up for my newsletter to get all my latest updates plus a free book!

ALSO BY J. SAMAN

Wild Love Series:

Reckless to Love You

Love to Hate Her

Crazy to Love You

Love to Tempt You

Promise to Love You

The Edge Series:

The Edge of Temptation

The Edge of Forever

The Edge of Reason

Start Again Series:

Start Again

Start Over

Start With Me

Las Vegas Sin Series:

Touching Sin

Catching Sin

Darkest Sin

Standalones:

Just One Kiss

Love Rewritten

Beautiful Potential

Forward - FREE

THE EDGE OF TEMPTATION

Chapter 1
Halle

"No," I reply emphatically, hoping my tone is stronger than my disposition. "I'm not doing it. Absolutely not. Just no." I point my finger for emphasis, but I don't think the gesture is getting me anywhere. Rina just stares at me, the tip of her finger gliding along the lip of her martini glass.

"You're smiling. If you don't want to do this, then why are you smiling?"

I sigh. She's right. I am smiling. But only because it's so ridiculous. In all the years she's known me, I've never hit on a total stranger. I don't think I'd have any idea how to even do that. And honestly, I'm just not in the right frame of mind to put in the effort. "It's funny, that's all." I shrug, playing it off. It's really not funny. The word terrifying comes closer. "But my answer is still no."

"It's been, what?" Margot chimes in, her gaze flicking between Rina, Aria, and me like she's actually trying to figure this out. She's not. I know where she's going with this and it's fucking rhetorical. "A month?"

See? I told you.

"You broke up with Matt a month ago. And you can't play it off like you're all upset over it, because we know you're not."

"Who says I'm not upset?" I furrow my eyebrows, feigning incredulous, but I can't quite meet their eyes. "I was with him for two years."

But she's right. I'm not upset about Matt. I just don't have the desire to hit on some random dude at some random bar in the South End of Boston.

"Two *useless* years," Rina persists with a roll of her blue eyes before taking a sip of her appletini. She sets her glass down, leaning her small frame back in her chair as she crosses her arms over her chest and purses her lips like she's pissed off on my behalf. "The guy was a freaking asshole."

"And a criminal," Aria adds, tipping back her fancy glass and finishing off the last of her dirty martini, complete with olive. She chews on it slowly, quirking a pointed eyebrow at me. "The cock-sucker repeatedly ignored you so he could defraud people."

"All true." I can't even deny it. My ex was a black-hat hacker. And while that might sound all hot and sexy in a mysterious, dangerous way, it isn't. The piece of shit stole credit card numbers, and not only used them for himself but sold them on the dark web. He was also one of those hacktivists who got his rocks off by working with other degenerate assholes to try and bring down various companies and websites.

In my defense, I didn't know what he was up to until the FBI came into my place of work, hauled me downtown, and interviewed me for hours. I was so embarrassed, I could hardly show my face at work again. Not only that, but everyone was talking about me. Either with pity or suspicion in their eyes, like I was a criminal right along with him.

Matt had a regular job as a red-team specialist—legit hackers who are paid by companies to go in and try to penetrate their systems. I assumed all that time he spent on his computer at night was him working hard to get ahead. At least that was his perpetual excuse when challenged.

Nothing makes you feel more naïve than discovering the man you had been engaged to is actually a criminal who was stealing from people. And committing said thefts while living with you.

I looked up one of the people the FBI had mentioned in relation to Matt's criminal activities. The woman had a weird name that stuck out to me for me some reason, and when I found her, I learned she was a widow with three grandchildren, a son in the military, and was a recently retired nurse. It made me sick to my stomach. Still does when I think about it.

I told the FBI everything I knew, which was nothing. I explained that I had ended things with Matt three days prior to them arresting him. Pure coincidence. I was fed up with the monotony of our relationship. Of being engaged and never discussing or planning our wedding. Of living with someone I never saw because he was always locked away in his office, too preoccupied with his computer to pay me even an ounce of attention. But really, deep down, I knew I wasn't in love with him anymore.

I didn't even shed a tear over our breakup. In fact, I was more relieved than anything. I knew I had dodged a bullet getting out when I did.

And then the FBI showed up.

"I ended it with him. *Before* I knew he was a total and complete loser," I tack on, feeling more defensive about the situation than I care to admit. Shifting my weight on my uncomfortable wooden chair, I cross my legs at the knee and stare sightlessly out into the bar.

"And we applaud you for that," Rina says, nudging Margot and then Aria in the shoulders, forcing them to concur. "It was the absolute right thing to do. But you've been miserable and mopey and very . . ."

"Anti-men," Margot finishes for her, tossing back her lemon drop shot with disturbing exuberance. I think that's number three for her already, which means it could be a long night. Margot has yet to learn the art of moderation.

"Right." Aria nods exaggeratedly at Margot like she just hit the nail on the head, tossing her messy dark curls over her shoulders before twisting them up into something that resembles a bun. "Antimen. I'm not saying you need to date anyone here. You don't even have to go home with them. Just let them buy you a drink. Have a normal conversation with a normal guy."

I scoff. "And you think I'll find one of those in here?" I splay my arms out wide, waving them around. All these men look like players. They're in groups with other men, smacking at each other and pointing at the various women who walk in. They're clearly rating them. And if a woman just so happens to pass by, they blatantly turn and stare at her ass.

This is a hookup bar. All dark mood lighting, annoying, trendy house music in the background and uncomfortable seating. The kind designed to have you standing all night before you take someone home. And now I understand why my very attentive friends brought me here. It's not our usual go-to place.

"It's like high school or a frat house in here. And definitely not in a good way. I bet all these guys bathed in Axe body spray, gelled up their hair and left their mother's basement to come here and find a 'chick to bang.'" I put air quotes around those words. I have zero interest in being part of that scheme.

"Well . . ." Rina's voice drifts off, scanning the room desperately. "I know I can find you someone worthy."

"Don't waste your brain function. I'm still not interested." I roll my eyes dramatically and finish off my drink, slamming the glass down on the table with a bit more force than I intend. *Oops.* Whatever. I'm extremely satisfied with my anti-men status. Because that's exactly what I am—anti-men—and I'm discovering I'm unrepentant about it. In fact, I think it's a fantastic way to be when you rack up one loser after another the way I have. Like a form of self-preservation.

I've never had a good track record. Even before Matt, I had a knack for picking the wrong guys. My high school boyfriend ended up being gay. I handed him my V-card shortly before he dropped that bomb on me, though he swore I didn't turn him gay. He promised he was like that prior to the sex. In college, I dated two guys somewhat seriously. The first one cheated on me for months before I found out, and the second one was way more into his video games than he was me. I think he also had a secret cocaine problem because he'd stay up all night gaming like a fiend. I had given up on men for a while—are you seeing a trend here?—and then in my final year of graduate school, Matt came along. Need I say more? So as far as I'm concerned, men can all go screw themselves. Because they sure as hell aren't gonna screw me!

"You can stop searching now, Rina." This is getting pathetic. "I have a vibrator. What else does a girl need?" All three pause their search to examine me and I realize I said that out loud. I blush at that, but it's true, so I just shrug a shoulder and fold my arms defiantly across my chest. "I don't need a sextervention. If anything, I need to avoid the male species like the plague they are."

They dismiss me immediately, their cause to find me a "normal" male to talk to outweighing my antagonism. And really, if it's taking this long to find someone then the pickings must really be slim here. I move to flag down the waitress to order another round when Margot points to the far corner.

"There." The tenacious little bug is gleaming like she just struck oil in her backyard. "That guy. He's freaking hot as holy sin and he's alone. He even looks sad, which means he needs a friend."

"Or he wants to be left alone to his drinking," I mumble, wishing I had another drink in my hand so I could focus on something other than my friends obsessively staring at some random creep. *Where the hell is that waitress?*

"Maybe," Aria muses thoughtfully as she observes the man across the bar, tapping her bottom lip with her finger. Her hands are covered in splotches of multicolored paint. As is her black shirt, now that I look closer. "Or maybe he's just had a crappy day. He looks so sad, Halle." She nods like it's all coming together for her as she makes frowny puppy dog eyes at me. "So very sad. Go over and see if he wants company. Cheer him up."

"You'd be doing a public service," Rina agrees. "Men that good-looking should never be sad."

I roll my eyes at that. "You think a blowjob would do it, or should I offer him crazy, kinky sex to cheer him up? I still have that domination-for-beginners playset I picked up at Angela's bachelorette party. Hasn't even been cracked open."

Aria tilts her head like she's actually considering this. "That level of kink might scare him off for the first time. And I wouldn't give him head unless he goes down on you first."

Jesus, I'm not drunk enough for this. "Or he's a total asshole who just fucked his girlfriend's best friend," I protest, my voice rising an octave with my objection. I sit up straight, desperate to make my point clear. "Or he's about to go to prison because he hacks women into tiny bits with a machete before he eats them. Either way, I'm. Not. Interested."

"God," Margot snorts, twirling her chestnut hair as she leans back in her chair and levels me with an unimpressed gaze. "Dramatic much? He wouldn't be out on bail if that were the case. But seriously, that's like crazy psycho shit, and that guy does not say crazy psycho. He says crave-worthy and yummy and 'I hand out orgasms like candy on Halloween.'"

"Methinks the lady doth protest too much," Aria says with a knowing smile and a wink.

She swivels her head to check him out again and licks her lips reflexively. I haven't bothered to peek yet because my back is to him and I hate that I'm curious. All three ladies are eyeing him with unfettered appreciation and obvious lust. Their tastes in men differ tremendously, which indicates this guy probably is hot. I shouldn't be tempted. I really shouldn't be. I'm asking for a world of trouble or hurt or legal fees. So why am I finding the idea of a one-nighter with a total stranger growing on me?

I've never been that girl before. But maybe they're right? Maybe a one-nighter with a random guy is just the ticket to wipe out my past of bad choices in men and make a fresh start? I don't even know if that makes sense since a one-nighter is the antithesis of a smart choice. But my libido is taking over for my brain and now I'm starting to rationalize, possibly even encourage. I need to stop this now.

"He's gay. Hot men are always gay. Or assholes. Or criminals. Or cheaters. Or just generally suck at life."

"You've had some bad luck, is all. Look at Oliver. He's good-looking, sweet, loving, and not an asshole. Or a criminal. And he likes you. You could date him."

Reaching over, I steal Rina's cocktail. She doesn't stop me or even seem to register the action. I stare at her with narrowed eyes over the rim of her glass as I slurp down about half of it in one gulp. "I'm not dating your brother, Rina. That's weird and begging for drama. You and I are best friends."

She sighs and then I sigh because I'm being a bitch and I don't mean to be. I like her brother. He is all of those things she just mentioned, minus the liking me part. But if things went bad between us, which they inherently would, it would cost me one of my most important friendships. And that's not a risk I'm willing to take. Plus, unbeknownst to Rina, Oliver is one of the biggest players in the greater Boston area.

"I'm just saying not all men are bad," Rina continues, and I shake my head. "We'll buy your drinks for a month if you go talk to this guy," she offers hastily, trying to close the deal.

Margot glances over at her with furrowed eyebrows, a bit surprised by that declaration, but she quickly comes around with an indifferent shrug. Aria smiles, liking that idea. Then again, money is not Aria's problem. "Most definitely," she agrees. "Go. Let a stranger touch your lady parts. You're waxed and shaved and looking hot. Let someone take advantage of that."

"And if he shoots me down?"

"You don't have to sleep with him," Rina reminds me. "Or even give him your real name. In fact, tell him nothing real about yourself. It could be like a sexual experiment." I shake my head in exasperation. "We won't bother you about it again," she promises solemnly. "But he won't shoot you down. You look movie star hot tonight."

I can only roll my eyes at that. While I appreciate the sentiment from my loving and supportive friends, being shot down by a total stranger when I'm already feeling emotionally strung out might just do me in. Even if I have no interest in him. But free drinks . . .

Twisting around in my chair, I stare across the crowded bar, probing for a few seconds until I spot the man in the corner. Holy Christmas in Florida, he *is* hot. There is no mistaking that. His hair is light blond, short along the sides and just a bit longer on top. Just long enough that you could grab it and hold on tight while he kisses you. His profile speaks to his straight nose and strong, chiseled, cleanly shaven jaw. I must admit, I do enjoy a bit of stubble on my men, but he makes the lack of beard look so enticing that I don't miss the roughness. He's wearing a suit. A dark suit. More than likely expensive judging by the way it contours to his broad shoulders and the flash of gold on his wrist that I catch in the form of cufflinks.

But the thing that's giving me pause is his anguish. It's radiating off him. His beautiful face is downcast, staring sightlessly into his full glass of something amber. Maybe scotch. Maybe bourbon. It doesn't matter. That expression has purpose. Those eyes have meaning behind them and I doubt he's seeking any sort of company. In fact, I'm positive he'd have no trouble finding any if he were so inclined.

That thought alone makes me stand up without further comment. He's the perfect man to get my friends off my back. He's going to shoot me down in an instant and I won't even take it personally. Well, not too much. I can feel the girls exchanging gleeful smiles, but I figure I'll be back with them in under five minutes, so their misguided enthusiasm is inconsequential. I watch him the entire way across the bar. He doesn't sip at his drink. He just stares blankly into it. That sort of heartbreak makes my stomach churn. This miserable stranger isn't just your typical Saturday night bar dweller looking for a quick hookup.

He's drowning his sorrows.

Miserable Stranger doesn't notice my approach. He doesn't even notice me as I wedge myself in between him and the person seated beside him. And he definitely doesn't notice me as I order myself a dirty martini. I'm close enough to smell him. And damn, it's so freaking good I catch myself wanting to close my eyes and breathe in deeper. Sandalwood? Citrus? Freaking godly man? Who knows. I have no idea what to say to him. In fact, I'm half-tempted to grab my drink and scurry off, but I catch Rina, Margot, and Aria watching vigilantly from across the bar with excited, encouraging smiles. There's no way I can get out of this without at least saying hello.

Especially if I want those bitches to buy me drinks for the next month.

But damn, I'm so stupidly nervous. "Hello," I start, but my voice is weak and shaky, and I have to clear it to get rid of the nervous lilt. Shit. My hands are trembling. Pathetic.

He doesn't look up. Awesome start.

I play it off, staring around the dimly lit bar and taking in all the people enjoying their Saturday night cocktails. It's busy here. Filled with the heat of the city in the summer and lust-infused air. I open my mouth to speak again, when the person seated next to my Miserable Stranger and directly behind me, gets up, shoving their chair inadvertently into my back and launching me forward. Straight into him.

I fly without restraint, practically knocking him over. Not enough to fully push him off his chair—he's too big and strong for that—but it's enough to catch his attention. I see him blink like he's coming back from some distant place. His head tilts up to mine as I right myself, just as my attention is diverted by the man who hit me with his chair.

"I'm so sorry," the man says with a note of panic in his voice, reaching out and grasping my upper arm as if to steady me. "I didn't see you there. Are you okay?"

"Yes, I'm fine." I'm beet red, I know it.

"Did I hurt you?"

Just my pride. "No. Really. I'm good. It was my fault for wedging myself in like this." The stranger who bumped me smiles warmly, before turning back to his girlfriend and leaving the scene of the crime as quickly as possible.

Adjusting my dress and schooling my features, I turn back to my Miserable Stranger, clearing my throat once more as my eyes meet his. "I'm sorry I banged into you . . ." My freaking breath catches in my lungs, making my voice trail off at the end.

Goddamn.

If I thought his profile was something, it's nothing compared to the rest of him. He blinks at me, his eyes widening fractionally as he sits back, crossing his arms over his suit-clad chest and taking me in from head to toe. He hasn't even removed his dark jacket, which seems odd. It's more than warm in here and summer outside.

He sucks in a deep breath as his eyes reach mine again. They're green. But not just any green. Full-on megawatt green. Like thick summer grass green. I can tell that even in the dim lighting of the bar, that's how vivid they are. They're without a doubt the most beautiful eyes I've ever seen.

"That's all right," he says and his thick baritone, with a hint of some sort of accent, is just as impressive as the rest of him. It wraps its way around me like a warm blanket on a cold night. Jesus, has a voice ever affected me like this? Maybe I do need to get out more if I'm reacting to a total stranger like this. "I love it when beautiful women fall all over me."

I like him instantly. Cheesy line and all.

"That happen to you a lot?"

He smirks and the way that crooked grin looks on his face has my heart rate jacking up yet another degree. "Not really. Are you okay? That was quite the tumble."

I nod. I don't want to talk about my less than graceful entrance anymore. "Would you mind if I sit down?" And he thinks about it. Actually freaking hesitates. Just perfect. This is not helping my already frail ego.

I stare at him for a beat, and just as I'm about to raise the white flag and retreat with my dignity in my feet, he swallows hard and shakes his head slowly. Is he saying no I shouldn't sit, or no he doesn't mind? Crap, I can't tell, because his expression is . . . a mess. Like a bizarre concoction of indecision and curiosity and temptation and disgust.

He must note my confusion because in a slow measured tone he clarifies with, "I guess you should probably sit so you don't fall on me again." He blinks, something catching his attention. Glancing past me for the briefest of moments, that smirk returning to his full lips. "I think your friends love the idea."

"Huh?" I sputter before my head whips over my shoulder and I catch Rina, Aria, and Margot standing, watching us with equally exuberant smiles. Margot even freaking waves. Well, that's embarrassing. Now what do I say? "Yeah . . . um." Words fail me, and I sink back into myself. "I'm sorry. I just . . . well, I recently broke up with someone, and my friends won't let me return to the table until I've re-entered the human female race and had a real conversation with a man."

God, this sounds so stupidly pathetic. Even to my own ears. And why did I just admit all of that to him? My face is easily the shade of the dress I'm wearing—and it's bright motherfucking red. He's smirking at me again, which only proves my point. I hate feeling like this. Insecure and inadequate. At least it's better than stupid and clueless. Yeah, that's what I had going on with Matt and this is not who I am. I'm typically far more self-assured.

"I'll just grab my drink and return to my friends."

I pull some cash out of my purse and drop it on the wooden bar. I pause, and he doesn't stop me. My fingers slip around the smooth, long stem of my glass. I want to get the hell out of here, but before I can slide my drink safely toward me and make my hasty, not so glamorous escape, he covers my hand with his and whispers, "No. Stay."

Want to know what happens next with Halle and Jonah? Grab your copy of The Edge of Temptation today, free with Kindle Unlimited.

END OF BOOK NOTE

For those of you who have read me before, you know this is the part of the book where I try (and usually fail) to break it all down.

First, I need to thank my amazing beta readers and my incredible editor who is so much more than that! Thank you Gina for always dealing with my insanity with love and support!

Second, I need to thank my family big time on this one. I mentioned in the dedication that Adalyn is a fictional representation of a real person. In case you haven't figure it out, the real person is my little girl. So yeah, this story, these characters, bled me dry.

I'd be lying if I said that many of Jasper's thoughts with regards to Adalyn weren't my own or my husband's. It's not easy being a parent. EVER. But it's even harder being the parent of a child with special needs.

It's a daily struggle. A ton of joy and tears.

And I needed an outlet. A way to readjust my preconceived desires for her and us as a family. I started this book (which was one turned into two) as a sort of reflection. A way to process E's diagnosis. The challenges she was facing. The challenges we all were facing.

She's a little older now. Not so much like Adalyn anymore, but in processing who she was then, it made me fall even more in love with who she is now. If that even makes sense. But damn... I am the luckiest mommy ever! And there is not a day that goes by that I do not have that thought and that smile on my lips. My girls are my gold. My platinum and my diamonds. If you have babies, I know you feel the same!

So enough about me as a parent as I'm sure you're all bored to tears.

When I started writing Jasper, I viewed him in terms of color. A spectrum (see what I did there?) of shades. Some so light and beautiful they take your breath away. Some so dark and angry you can't help but want to smack him. Viola, to me, was his antidote. I really loved her character. Her optimism and strength. Her resiliency. Her fucking unconditional love even when others tried to beat it out of her.

Writing their love story (especially in the second book) became something of an honor. I love that I was able to untangle their web, their craziness, and turn it into something beautiful. At least that's my take on it.

Because love is never easy. And that's what makes writing it such a privilege.

Now on to Gus! I wasn't initially planning on writing his story, but one of my betas was up my ass about it and she was right. He needs a story. I'm working on plotting it out and hoping to release it this year if I can do it. Fingers crossed!

Thank you again for your continued love and support! As Drew from The Edge of Reason said, there is no me without you.

XO ~ J. Saman

Made in the USA
Monee, IL
19 March 2025

14242808R00246